Carter-Krall Publishing

Printed in the United States of America
Published by Carter-Krall Publishers First Edition

Book cover, headers and footers within the text uses the Bookworm Font by AJ Palmer
Edited by Marian Bickenbach

Whippins, Switches & Peach Cobbler/ Brian Egeston
ISBN 0-9675505-21

Library Of Congress Catalog Number
99-091216

Second Edition January 2001

WHIPPINS, SWITCHES & PEACH COBBLER

For Kim

Live The Words!

Brian Egeston

www.brianwrites.com

3/9/02

DEDICATION

For John & Delores Egeston. Thanks for all you've done.
A special thanks for not sparing the rod.

ACKNOWLEDGEMENTS

First of all—Thaaank ya God! One day, I hope I'll fill twenty-five percent of a book with the people to whom I am so grateful. Until then, these few pages will suffice.

FAMILY: There is a person that has been a member of my family for a few short years, but my love for her is so strong we must have known each other in another time and place. Latise, my beautiful wife, thank you for all you are and all you do. I could write a book about the way that I love you. My brother and sister Johnathan & Christie, the Phillips, Egestons, Nashes, and Searles all over the world. Had it not been for the memories and lessons of my own family's reunions, I'd have no story to tell.

CO-WORKERS: From Thomson Consumer Electronics to Motorola, every person I come in contact with becomes a part of my life and a part of me. My golf buddies—never lay up, always go for the green! Two of the best managers I've ever had or known, Bob Gorgol and Tom Kirby. You guys are awesome; From the security guards to the VP's up front, Motorola gives you wings baby! ESG rules! Here's an awesome acknowledgement for the ultimate manager, team leader, motivator, and co-worker a person could have, Mrs. Kristen Shappert—there are no words. She's written a touching tale entitled "Defining Moments." Now hurry and finish it! Special thanks to all the Motorola employees that supported my work.

CHURCH MEMBERS: The Jesus in me, loves the Jesus in Y'all! A shoo bee, doo bee, doo doo doo! Special recognition to Pastor Hale and Pastor Felder, the most dynamic diva and dude of Dekalb County that dared to defeat the devil! To the brothers of the Tribe of Judah and CMF, keep on keepin' on. Everyone in all of the wonderful ministries and ministerial staffs. From the people that sweep the floor to the people that control the traffic in the parking lot, you all have been a part of my growth and I love you all for any and everything that you do.

DA BRUZ: My beloved brothers of the soul, what more can I say other than the men of Omega Psi Phi have had such an influence on my life. From the brothers that uplifted me and showed me the way, to the brothers I've had the "opportunity" to go to the greens with for whatever reason. I'm a sponge for knowledge and every time I meet, greet, and disagree with a brother, I learn something. This is the creed I believe all Omega Men should strive towards. One man, one vote-let's talk about it. Mighty Rho Psi, it's a long road to become Mighty once again, follow the stars and you'll get there.

TENNESSEE STATE: I'll forever be indebted to TSU, because it's there that I became a man and there that I learned about people and about life. Every student and alumnus should embrace the school on the Cumberland's fertile shore as their own child and ensure that it flourishes forever. Thanks to the TSU bookstore for hosting my very first book signing. Thanks to Alku-Bulan Images for being the cornerstone of African Culture in Nashville as well as being there for Black authors.

Much respect to John and Kimee and all of the creators and presenters of the spoken word at the Patti Hut Café. If you're reading this and you've never consumed a small whiff of the positive energy on Thursday nights...you'd better.

Thanks to my faithful test readers, Kris W. Hinz (The Man!) keep on strummin'. Cheryl Mckinney who keeps it real up in the NYC. Portia Lewis, the mightiest Motorola manager from MIT! Dejuan Knighton, there's such a bright effervescent light burning inside of you. I see it and so do other people. My hope is that you will find it and it keeps you warm and comforted all of your days. Phyllis Brown, my SUPER proofer! Thanks for taking the manuscript and making it bleed with your red pen of correction. The Village Writer's Group, thanks for the encouragement. Aileen, thanks for the late night phone tutorial on Microsoft Word. You saved my computer's life!

A great big couldn't-do-it-without-ya thanks goes to the best investment a writer could make, the professional editing services of Marian Bickenbach. I appreciate your candid and insightful comments more than you'll ever know. Your candor was the validation I sought to press on and make this project work. Thanks also for completing the job on budget and ahead of schedule.

Thanks to the BMAR book club(Black Men Advocating Reading). Keep it up, you'll run this place one-day.

And I simply could not forget a special group, the brother's of the world's smallest fraternity, black male fiction writers. Eric Jerome Dickey, Omar Tyree, Franklin White, Michael Baidsen, Van Whitfield, R.M. Johnson, E. Lynn Harris, Walter Mosley and the other members who are slowly but assuredly taking the publishing industry by storm. We won't miss the manna much more, just wait and see. Thanks to my main man, the iconoclast of this fraternity, Brandon Massey. Everyone put Thunderland in your hands.

Thanks to the readers of Crossing Bridges, perhaps one day you'll see that book reprinted in the bookstore. Thanks to book clubs across the world that keep authors like myself busy and challenged. Without reading, there is no writing. Thanks to the second grade class of Ms. Delzotto, Mrs. Schimb, and Mrs. Oliveira of Centennial Place Elementary in Atlanta, what an awesome group of kids!

To all the parents and guardians who wrestle everyday with disciplining and nurturing children. Raising children is perhaps the most significant contribution to the human race but seldom recognized. It is my contention that leaders, professionals, and creative people are the result of long and concentrated parenting processes. Without your efforts as parents, this world would stop functioning.

To the protectors of children. Protectors from those persons who don't realize the importance of a child's life or upbringing. You are members of that extended village that is required to raise children.

And to the restorers of children. The counselors, therapists, and other professionals, who are charged with re-building those children that have been destroyed by the roots of evil. You are the chiefs of the extended village that is required to raise children. With little pay and even less recognition, you passionately take the children others turn their backs on, and you rebuild their lives—or risk your own trying.

To those people who changed my life during my year 2000 birthday party. I'll never forget you or that moment.

Last but not least—Thaaank ya God.

CONTENTS

1 Captain D's or Black-Eyed Peas
2 Other Side Of The Fence
3 Please Don't Call My Mama!
4 Before And After The Storm
5 Cousin Consequences
6 Explanations
7 Insightful Instigation
8 Be Thankful, Be Very Thankful
9 Teenager's Transitions
10 Deeply Devoted
11 Conviction
12 What Just Happened Here?
13 Influence
14 Unproven Theories
15 Talking
16 New Interests
17 Man Talk
18 New Branches, New Generations
19 Ryan's Revenge
20 Differences
21 Reasons And Excuses
22 Leaving The Nest
23 What Happens Now?
24 Discoveries
25 Comparisons
26 Here And There
27 Life, In High Gear
28 Appreciation
29 Confessions
30 Futile Changes–Fatal Choices
31 Results And Reflections
32 Balm From The Beam

33 Welcome To The World
34 Rejuvenation At The Reunion

1978–1979

Chapter 1
Captain D's or Black-Eyed Peas

"Mama, I ain't eatin' none of Granny Osee's food today. I want some Captain D's. Okay?"

"Okay. You can have Captain D's, Benny," Sheila Dempkins replied to her son.

The stern mother cloaked her real thoughts and comments with cynicism. Sheila was actually thinking to herself—*You must be outta yo' mind.* As often as she could, Sheila avoided embarrassing her little Benny in front of others. Now that he was becoming more active in his early years, her patience was often tested. Benny, more often than not, failed her test.

"Mama, when you gon' get my Captain D's? I'm hungry now!" Benny yelled with as much authority as his skinny body and nappy head was capable of asserting.

Now the entire family's attention was diverted from their Sunday afternoon activities. Some were watching the basketball game. Others were watching Granny Osee skillfully produce one of her beautiful afghans. They were all bewildered by the demand the smallest person in the house was making.

Sheila, still exercising her sarcastic craft, turned away from her sister Margie and slowly walked over to Benny while calmly grabbing his hand.

"Come on, baby, let's get your Captain D's."

Everyone in the house was shocked at the action taking place. Surely, they all thought, Sheila hadn't lost her knack for discipline. Did a pair of sad little beady eyes and a small tantrum dumbfound a mother's command of discipline? Sheila led Benny into the kitchen where Granny Osee had prepared her usual spread of turkey and dressing, chicken and dumplings, yams, greens, homemade rolls, black-eyed peas, creamed corn, macaroni and cheese, and various desserts. Included with the delectable dandies was her signature homemade peach cobbler.

Little Benny seemed confused by the actions of his mother, but as he would soon find out, Sheila's act was approaching its final performance.

"Here's some Captain D's black-eyed peas, some Captain D's chicken and dumplings, some Captain D's creamed corn and…." Just as Sheila was making her way to the next menu item, Benny snatched his hand away from his mother's clutches and yanked his body away from her turning his back on her unappreciated antics

"I don't want none of that mess! I said I want some Captain D's!" Benny exclaimed.

The entire house was blanketed in silence with the exception of the basketball game on television. *Dr. J drives the lane and scores!* That was the only sound heard in the house after Benny's bold proclamation. Sheila was boiling hotter than the delicious dishes in front of her on the stove. In one fell swoop, she grabbed Benny's arm, picked him up off of his feet, and ran to the back room with her son tucked under her arm like an oversized football.

Once in the back room, Benny's mannerism changed from an aggressive underdeveloped little man to a humble boy who was quickly realizing his wrongs. He was frightfully frozen as he watched his mother rummage through items in the back-storage room. Sheila searched frantically for an object that she could use to discipline her son. The angered woman was desperately looking for something, but only found items that were either too severe or not effective enough. There was nothing in between. First, she picked up a bed rail, but quickly dropped it, realizing the insanity behind the thought. Then she picked up the branch of a fern plant, thinking that it might serve as a switch. The weak branch wilted in her hand as she tried to swing it. She settled for the electrical cord on a Weed-Eater. Swiftly and quickly the mother administered the boy's much deserved punishment. WHACK, WHACK, and WHACK.

Benny immediately broke out into his whipping dance. High knees and running in circles was an art form that he and his cousins had all mastered, perhaps handed down from many generations. As quickly as it had all begun, it ceased. Sheila immediately dropped the cord and ran out of the room, unable to witness the sight of her son's crying. Benny sobbed uncontrollably for a few more moments then walked out of the room holding his bottom. His cousins, peering around the corner of the hallway, were snickering at the embarrassed boy.

Benny was no stranger to discipline. His mother and father were believers in the rod of correction, although it was self-torture for Sheila to punish her precious son. Like any other child, Benny didn't look forward to the punishments his parents delivered. But even more so than the discipline itself, Benny absolutely hated to be laughed at after a whippin'.

"What y'all laughin' at, you old African booty scratchers?" Benny asked, yelling at his cousins.

"Ooh! I'm gon' tell Ant Sheila, and she gon' come back here and beat you wit' a lamp this time," Benny's cousin Cynthia replied. "Ant Sheila! Benny back here callin' people names!"

Benny once again found the fear he had at the beginning of the painful ordeal. He thought surely this meant the commencement of a sequel. Standing perfectly still listening for footsteps or perhaps a stampede of high heels, he heard his mother yell,

"Benny, do you want me to come back there again?"

With fear in his heart and tears dangling in the bottom of his eyes, Benny answered, "She back here laughin' at me, mama!" He was hoping that his rebuttal would be enough justification for his actions. The cautious boy would monitor his every move now. The children stood in the back room awaiting the results. Their curiosity was satisfied when the distinct voice of Granny Osee rang out.

"Cynthia, leave that boy be. You could be next wit' yo' fassy tail self."

This round had come to a close. Cynthia admitted defeat but tried to have the last say by sticking her tongue out at Benny. She quickly turned away in an attempt to whirl her shoulder length braids in Benny's face. The pink and yellow barrettes on her braids collided with each other and the hair decorations clapped together as she shook her head and rolled her eyes. Benny and his other cousin Clem, sat and watched the pretty yet prissy little girl who was always clean, neat, and sassy. They wanted so much to push her in the mud, or perhaps run the dirty wheels of an Evil Knivel motorcycle over her dress. It would have taken both of them to complete the task because Cynthia was tall for a seven-year-old girl, taller than Benny and Clem who had both just turned seven themselves. In reality, the mischievous thoughts were far in the back of their minds. They dared not disobey the forbidden family rule; boys don't hit girls. The rule applied to all boys and Cynthia had no brothers, therefore she had open season on teasing her male cousins.

Cynthia's father, Paul, wanted desperately for her to be around her cousins and other family members even if he wasn't. Paul was always busy trying to please his second wife, Kristine so there wasn't always time for Cynthia, Kristine, and the extended family at the same time. After his divorce, Paul was intently focused on making this marriage work at all cost, even if it meant less time with his daughter. As a result, Cynthia spent much of her time with other family members like she did during today's visit.

"You think you so pretty," Clem said. Well, you ain't gon' be so pretty when I throw this rat on you."

"I am pretty. And you ain't got no rat, boy. If you did throw it on me, my daddy'll run you over in his El Camino. I'm prettier than yo' old ugly mama!" Cynthia said in her rebuttal.

"Shut up, girl! My mama pretty!" Clem was angered now.

Cynthia put her hands on her small hips and began her barrette clacking head shake again.

"Ain't yo' mama pretty. She got meatballs in her titties. She got scrambled eggs between her legs going beep beep beep down Sesame Street." Cynthia was taunting her cousin something awful. She was about to start another verse of the Mama-Titty song when Clem blurted out to the ruler of the house.

"Granny Oseeee!" Clem screamed.

"What is it, chile? What y'all back there doin' now?" That was all Cynthia needed. She ran into the living room with all of the grown-ups. Clem and Benny could hear her weaseling her way out of the trouble she'd stirred up.

"Granny Osee, did I tell you yo' peach cobbler is the best in the world?" Cynthia said in an effort to connive her grandmother.

"Mm-hmm. Every time somebody about to lay into yo' behind you tell me. Move out the way, girl. You in my light."

The boys were relieved to have the troublesome terror out of their sight.

"Dag, Benny. Yo' mama strict. She be tearin' you up," Clem said to his favorite cousin trying to heal his wounds.

"I don't know what you talkin' about. Ant Margie be whippin' you and snot be comin' out yo' nose." The two boys laughed, and all was well.

"You don't like Granny Osee's food either, huh?" Clem asked.

"I do sometime, but sometime I just want somethin' else."

"Me, too. I want some Mr. Dan's right now."

"I'll be glad when I get big and I can drive to the Mr. Dan's hamburger stand and eat what I want to. Hey, let's go get us some cars on the front porch?"

"Okay, I'm first," Benny stated.

"Nawh, you got to call it when you see it." The boys paraded through the living room as if nothing had ever happened and no one was there. Benny's father Ronald stopped them.

"Where y'all goin'?" Ronald asked.

"We goin' to sit on the front porch," Benny humbly answered. He was still walking on eggshells.

"Don't go far, 'cause yo' mama want to talk to you." Sheila raised her head from the magazine she was reading surprised by the statement her husband made. She had administered the punishment and believed that Ronald should come and complete the nurturing with some type of consultation.

The boys ran out of the front door, sat at the bottom of the steps, and proceeded with their game.

"That's my hot rod!" Clem yelled out, as an antique blue '57 Chevy sped down the street.

"That's my Volkswagen beetle!" Benny yelled out.

"Ugh, you can have that thing," Clem said in disgust for his cousin's taste in cars. "But that's my Trans Am!"

"That's my Pinto, and I'm gon' have mo' money than you because I ain't got to buy a whole lotta gas."

"That's my Corvette!"

"That's my moped!" Benny blurted out.

"That's my Winnebago!" Both of the boys claimed at the same time.

"You can have it on the weekends," Benny relented.

"Okay, I get the bed by the window up near the top." The whippin' wounds were slowly healing, as they always did with time.

"Sheila, I don't know why you whip that boy like that. He's just a little baby," Sheila's father Macon, said.

"He need his butt to' up, 'cause he always be…," Cynthia started.

"Girl, if you don't stay out of grown folks business. Get yo'self back there and play with that Easy-Bake oven you wanted so bad," Cynthia's Aunt Margie snapped at the soon-to-be-grown little girl.

The usual crowd had gathered at 1605 Wolfe Street on the East Side of Indianapolis, Indiana that Sunday. Osceola Jackson, known to all as Granny Osee, began cooking on Saturday to accommodate her guests, although they were hardly guests. Osceola's daughters and their families always stopped by her house after church and golf on Sundays. Sheila and her younger sister Margie would rise bright and early headed for Sunday School with their boys.

Cynthia tagged along, when her father dropped her off early enough. If Cynthia arrived after 8:30, she stayed with her grandfather, Macon, and he would proceed to talk about everything except Cynthia's absent father.

Sheila's husband Ronald and Margie's husband William never missed their Sunday 8:00 a.m. tee time at the Douglass golf course. Their husbands, who seemed to be natural born buddies, left before the women got out of the house. The two golfing buddies did occasionally attend church. In the tragic event that it rained on a Sunday or the brutal winters closed all of the golf courses in the city, the two chums could be found fighting sleep while the service carried on without their attention.

Osceola's home was a small meeting place. Though it had seen many days and many faces, nothing much had changed within the welcoming walls of the brick structure. Her husband, Macon, insisted that too much clutter confused the heart and the mind, although he was not usually home long enough to be around any type of clutter. An uneducated man, he provided for his family with various odd jobs that people felt obliged to give the honest, hard-working soul. He and numerous other Blacks migrated from the South to the North toward Detroit and Chicago in the early 1900's in search of work at the automotive plants and other industrial revolutionized facilities. Those like Macon, that ran out of money or got lost and tired, settled in Indianapolis. He and Osceola managed to save enough money to buy their humble abode, which was actually a duplex. Considering the time period in which they purchased the home, the two were living in high cotton.

After acquiring the home, Macon tore down the doors that separated the two sides of the house. *This home is gon' be 'bout tearing down barriers. We don't need all of these doors. Doors keep people out and people bring life into a room and love into a home.* Macon would say.

Going from room to room was like entering several new dimensions. The first living room was the so-called entertainment hall if one could call a room with a black and white floor model television and a long plastic covered couch a place of entertainment. Pictures of grandchildren, nieces, nephews, and co-workers adorned the walls. Some of the portraits and snapshots had no picture frames and most were surviving on the wall with the support of rusted thumb-tacks or some kind of tape.

The other living room however, was more of a museum. The tacky green shag carpet of the entertainment hall died at the entrance of this shrine. No children were allowed to play in this space because they might knock over one of the many ferns that seemed to grow out of the wall. Osceola had a green arm. Not a green thumb, but a green arm. The sofa was a plush floral pattern that needed no plastic because no more than ten people ever had the opportunity to sit on this throne. The pictures in this room, which all possessed frames, were fortunate enough to have their own table and well they should, because they were mostly priceless older pictures of the family's ancestors. Perhaps the only contrast to the immaculately decorated room were the decorations on the wall. Osceola had many sisters, brothers, and friends throughout the country and she loved to visit all of them. When Osceola visited a city, she made a ritual out of purchasing a small ceramic plate from that state. The trails of her journeys lined the walls. Fifty-two plates all together. She hadn't been to every state in the nation, but simply insisted that a plate be purchased every time she entered a state. Therefore, many of the plates were duplicates. The back rooms, backyards, and front porch were reserved for the children and their antics.

Although Macon worked most of the time, he definitely reigned when he was present. His grandchildren especially liked his presence because he didn't stand much for whippin' his grandchildren or babies as he liked to call them. His babies simply called him Pap-Paw, and when he was near, they were usually safe.

"Daddy, Benny is not just a little boy. He's growing too fast and sometimes he needs to be slowed down," Sheila said. "Why didn't you stop Mama from tearin' my butt up when I was his age?"

"You was just wor'some and you needed yo' hind-end strapped everyday. I swear yo' mama musta used up all the switches from that old tree out there in the front yard," Macon said pointing to the dilapidated excuse for a tree surviving amongst the grass. So many limbs had been torn from the tree, it was sagging over in its old age. The once stout symbol of discipline now looked like a small dying weeping willow.

"That's why that old tree sickly now, because you was so mannish and we used up all the branches on yo' tail end," Margie said, confirming for her father.

"Oh, wait a minute girl! That tree used to sing yo' name for quite sometime too, Ms. Oochie Coochie in the bushes with Tomm...," Sheila began before she was quickly interrupted.

"Eghh emm!" Margie cleared her throat to abruptly end the embarrassing childhood story Sheila was about to unveil.

"That's what I thought," Sheila said smiling with satisfaction. The room exploded with laughter—except for Margie's husband. He was still interested in the story.

"Mama, you want some help in the kitchen?" Margie said in an effort to change the subject. "Mama...Mama," Margie repeated trying to get her mother's attention.

Granny Osee's attention was focused on the behavior of the little boys outside. Granny Osee was very much aware of the fine line that was an intricate part of disciplining children. In her time, she had seen many adults cross the line and destroy a child's inner spirit.

"Chile' what chu' want? I'm tryin' to see 'bout my grandbabies."

"I said do you need any help in the kitchen?"

"Yeah, girl. Gon' in there and clean my kitchen. While you at it, start cleanin' my chitlins for next Sunday." Margie began regretting her escape route from the conversation Sheila started. Granny Osee heaved herself off the vinyl couch. Her legs, like everyone else's that had even a brief relationship with the couch, had the rough plastic wrinkles imprinted on the back of her thighs. Slowly and cautiously she made her way to the screen door that led to the front porch. Not thinking about what she was doing, Granny Osee made the mistake most of her guests made when trying to exit the house. She accidentally pressed her hand against the fragile hole in the screen door, which was now a vacancy sign for insects in search of shelter and food.

"Lord a'mighty. I done made this old do' worser than it already was," she tried to quietly confess to herself. However, the two boys lost in their own auto show, shifted their attention to their favorite type of mama.

"You cut yo' hand, Granny Osee?" Clem inquired, genuinely concerned for his grandmother. "I'll go get you some Witch Hazel if you want me to. It's gon' burn like it be burnin' me when I get a splinter in my hand, but I'll blow on it for you."

"Nawh, baby, I don't need no Witch Hazel. Granny Osee didn't hurt herself. I just came to see 'bout my babies out here. What y'all playin', that old make believe car game?" Benny, who was trying to pretend he wasn't listening to the conversation, quickly turned to his grandmother only to make an abrupt about-face when he made eye contact with the warm spirited woman. Benny had temporarily forgotten that he was protesting against grown-ups, even sweet, elderly grown-ups.

"You wanna play, Granny Osee?" Clem asked politely.

"Nawh. How would I look riding down the street in a convertible Cadillac? My hat gon' blow off, then I'm gon' lose my scarf trying to catch it befoe' it blow out da car. Y'all gon' have me pullin' up to da church lookin' like a fool. People gon' be sayin' who dat old nappy-headed woman talkin' 'bout at least I didn't lose my Bible!"

Both of the boys began laughing, even the protester. Benny, fighting all the rebellion he had left in his small body, walked over to his grandmother and leaned against her gentle loving body.

"Granny Osee, I'm sorry I didn't want none of yo' food. I like the way you cook. You mad at me? I'll go eat some if you want me to, just not no black-eyed peas," Benny pleaded.

"Baby, don't eat because I want you to. Eat 'cause you hungry. All I want you to do is go in there and apologize to yo' mama for showin' out like you did."

"I ain't. 'Cause she shouldn'tna whipped me."

"You shouldn't have been actin' like you did," Granny Osee responded sharply. "You think she would have whipped you if you didn't act up?"

The protesting reconvened, only this time it was a silent protest accompanied by a poked out lip. "You hear me talkin' to you, Benny? Now I know you a good little boy and I don't know who this little monster is you lookin' like. You think yo' mama would have whipped you if you didn't act up?"

"No," he replied softly enough for only he and his poked out lip to hear.

"What did you say, Benny?"

"No," this time in a more distinctive tone.

"Well then, you know what you need to do, don't you?" Benny didn't answer. He just tried to ease his way back into the house so that no one would notice his attempt to make amends, especially Cynthia. Benny would have preferred to slip through the small hole in the screen door with the insects.

Once inside, the spectacle began. The screen door closed behind him and in came Clem and Granny Osee, careful not to push through the hole in the screen when she opened it this time. Granny Osee walked over to the TV and lowered the volume.

"Everybody, Benny has something to say," she proclaimed.

Just as Benny was fighting back more tears of embarrassment and glancing up at his mother, he saw his devilish cousin Cynthia with one finger in her nose and the other one in her ear mocking him. He also saw his aunt walk over to Cynthia. She snatched the little girl by her arm pulling her ear, which made Cynthia regret she even had an ear to shove her finger in. Now Benny could proceed.

"Mama, I'm sorry I acted up and didn't want no food." Each word was a battle between pride and sincerity— sincerity won.

"That's okay, baby. I'm sorry I had to punish you." Sheila held her arms open for her son to fill. As quickly as the apology came, the house went back to its normal Sunday evening routine. The temporary wounds were beginning to heal, this time.

Chapter 2
Other Side Of The Fence

When one of the rare opportunities presented itself, Ronald and Benny did father and son activities in the tiny backyard of their home. Ronald used the time to practice his golf game and Benny used the time to disrupt his father's practice time.

"Daddy, why you always play golf? I thought black folks didn't play golf and that was only for white folks and black people, who want to be white," Benny inquired of his father who towered over him. Ronald, although a dominant skyscraper of a man to Benny, was actually more of a gentle sleeping giant. If awakened by annoyance or a situation he disapproved of, the giant in him was capable of wreaking havoc. He was a midnight dark skinned man with wide flaring nostrils that looked as though they could breathe fire. Beady black eyes guarded the windows to his soul. On his best attempt to strike a buckwheat, wide-eyed face, the whites of his eyes were barely visible.

"Who told you that nonsense, boy?" Ronald snapped back.

"Ryan did. He said if you look at golf on TV you don't never see no black folks unless they carrying a white man's bag."

"Ryan don't bit mo' know what he talkin' about than the man on the moon. Black folks been playin' golf since the 1920's. If nappy-headed niggas like Ryan had more accessibility to golf, then you'd see more of 'em on TV instead of playing in the NBA."

"Daddy, what is accessibility?" Benny asked.

"It means you can do something whenever you want to do it. You know how easy it is to go and play basketball or kickball?"

"Yeah."

"It's easy because it's access-ible," Ronald explained, as he slowly enunciated the word his son misunderstood. Benny and his father had rare moments of conversation. Typically they talked while doing chores in the backyard or while

Benny was serving as his father's automatic golf ball retriever.

Ronald used a small piece of shag carpet for his makeshift golf course and could only practice his short game in the backyard. Each time he practiced, it reminded him of how much he wanted to move his family into a bigger house up near the affluent north side or even Carmel, Indiana if he really wanted to reach for the stars. Ronald always thought about how Benny would get bigger and need more room in which to play, or he might eventually make the streets his backyard. If Benny got into the streets, Ronald knew there was no way he would get into college.

Like so many parents, Ronald wanted Benny to do better than his own job of driving dump trucks for the city. However, at seven years old Benny couldn't tell if he was rich or poor. Every now and then Ronald would drive his dump truck through the alley and up to the back gate of his house. If Benny was home from school, he would run outdoors like a thoroughbred out of the gates yelling for his father to put him in the truck. Benny was on top of the world in his father's work truck. To Benny, it wasn't a yellow and brown rusted city vehicle at all. Instead, it was a finely polished limousine. Ronald would leave his son in the truck while he entered the back gate of the small yard. He'd look at the door of the one car garage, which hung on a few hinges and was only one nail away from falling off. Ronald would walk over to the small garden Sheila tried to keep alive. There were a few tomatoes, cucumbers, and things that resembled bell peppers. Mostly the garden was a breeding ground for whatever type of weed needed a home. As Ronald made his way up the back steps, which had more paint shavings than paint left on the rotted wood, he would take one last look at the dilapidated backyard and think to himself—*We got to do better than this.*

Ronald's only solitude was on the Douglass golf course in the city. All of his spare time was spent in the yard doing what little golf practice drills he could. Ronald tried to capitalize on the moments and attempted to have some quality time with his son. Most of the quality was spent disproving whatever seven-year-old-boy theories Benny dragged through the front door.

"Daddy, golf is boring and it's too easy. That's why Dr. J and the Ice Man don't play golf."

"Easy! Who told you it was easy? Ryan? That boy ain't got the sense the Lord gave a penny." Benny laughed at yet another of his father's coined phrases, and Ronald had a book full of them, many of which he learned from his own father. "If it's so easy I'll give you a hundred dollars if you can take this nine-iron and hit this golf ball at..." Ronald looked around for a target about twenty yards away, "...at that Bubble Bee toy you shoulda' put in your room when I told you to."

"But I was playin' with it," Benny said, trying desperately to keep his father in a good mood.

"Um-huh. I wasn't playin' wit' you when I asked you to put it up, though.

Don't think I ain't watchin' you. Now try to hit it with the golf ball."

"Daddy, you ain't gon' give me no hundred dollars."

"That's what I know! You know why I ain't gon' give it to you? 'Cause you ain't gon' hit the toy. You know why you ain't gon' hit the toy? 'Cause golf ain't easy."

"Yes it is. Watch this." Benny focused all of his attention on the black and yellow target, which he hoped would be his jackpot. He made the closest thing to what he thought was a golf backswing—and even that was a bad imitation of a homerun baseball swing. Now honing in on the ball, Benny started down toward the innocent little white dimpled object in the middle of the carpet piece. He somehow managed to hit the back of the carpet so hard, it went flying towards the back fence. Although the ball was not moving, Benny was. The momentum of the golf club possessed the little boy's body and he was spinning out of control towards the vegetable-weed garden. Benny landed in the middle of the crops and burst what was left of the tomatoes with his bottom. Either fear of falling on a tomato stake or the embarrassment of his father's hysterical laughter, opened the dam in his eyes and the boastful little boy became a sobbing oversized plant.

"It ain't funny!" He lashed out at his father careful not to cross the line that separated disgust and disrespect. His father walked slowly over to him and helped the humbled boy out of the garden.

"See, golf ain't so easy now, is it?"

"Nawh it ain't easy, it's stupid. I don't ever want to play it again!"

"Now, if you're not gon' play, it's gon' be 'cause you mastered it and you ain't got no interest. You ain't gon' quit something because you don't think you can do it. Now bring your little vegetable butt over here and let me show you something."

Ronald stood behind his son and helped him properly setup to the golf ball. Realizing that this was probably the closest thing to physical affection he had ever shown his son—Ronald was overcome with guilt. He couldn't help it, nor did he feel he was to blame. The way he was brought up, men just didn't hug and kiss each other. That's sissified Ronald's father always told him. Despite his homophobia, Ronald was touching his son now and he felt bonded to the small boy.

"Now, you too little to have a interlock grip so we gon' start you off with a baseball grip, alright?"

"I don't want no kinda grip. This is stupid and I don't want to do it!" Benny was pushing his father's tolerance to the limit. If Benny had already crossed the line, he didn't know it.

"You gon' do it and you gon' like it! Now hold still and concentrate on yo' target!"

Benny retreated from his rebellious battle strategy and did as his father demanded. The father and son were both eyeing the ball and the target. Ronald lowered his voice and gave his son one last bit of instruction.

"Keep yo' head down until you see a divot and follow through." Benny broke concentration to get the clarity that he regularly sought.

"Daddy, what's a divot?" Benny asked.

"It's the piece of grass you plug up when you hit a golf ball. Now come on and concentrate."

"But it ain't no grass. The ball is on that piece of purple and green carpet you got from Granny Osee's closet."

"Just pretend that it's grass and concentrate, boy!" Ronald snapped. Benny began mumbling under his little inquisitive breath.

"I 'on't know how um gon' pretend, I ain't never hit no carpet or no grass. Told you dis game stupid."

"Benny."

"Yes," he said, articulating this time instead of mumbling.

"I'm not playin' wit' you boy." Ronald, frustrated now, regained his concentrated golf composure and focused his energy on the golf shot, and his son. Benny became focused as well. The two started the back swing and transitioned to the downswing. An explosion of racket from across the fence interrupted them just before the impact of the golf ball and golf club. The ball went flying out of control and far from the intended direction. Ronald was about to damn the golf ball, the golf club, and the backyard all to hell, until he and Benny both turned to witness the spectacle in their neighbor's yard.

Ryan, Benny's friend and next door neighbor, was running out of the back door trying desperately to escape his father's pursuit. Ryan's father, Joseph, was closing in on Ryan. It wasn't necessary for him to catch his son because he was doing Ryan enough damage by beating him with the long fishing cane he held like a death stick. The piercing object was breaking into pieces, the boy was being tortured so badly. Darting out of the house, the two whisked down the back steps of their house. Ryan, with a look of unimaginable fright, dashed towards the rear gate of the back yard, which now seemed to be the boys chamber of fate. Once at the back gate, Ryan tried to lengthen his escape by opening the lock only to be captured by his father's angered grasp.

"Dammit, when I tell you to sweep under the bed, I mean all of the beds in the house, you little knuckled-headed fool!" The boy fell to the ground in the corner of the yard. He curled himself into a ball in an effort to protect whatever part of him that he could. His father, still dispersing the brutal lashes, had now completely destroyed the fishing pole. However, the violent man could not distinguish between the pole and his hand, which he was now using to further demolish the young defenseless boy.

"Aggh Daddy, I ain't gon' do it no more! Please stop beatin' me, Daddy! Pleeeasee! Daadyy!" the destroyed child cried out. "Daddy you hurtin' me! Pleeaasse!"

The boy's begging was futile as the demon of a man relentlessly kept striking the boy. He kept beating him as if he was not cognizant of the screams and pleas his son made. The grown man was clearly thinking of incidents and places that had no bearing on the current situation. Any normal man would have stopped beating the child by now out of sheer fatigue. Suddenly the boy stopped crying and pleading. Ryan was slowly blacking out. Joseph was oblivious to the situation until he could make out faint sounds of his name, followed by commands.

"Joseph! Hey, Joseph! What the hell you doin' man? You tryin' to kill the boy?" Ronald shouted at his neighbor. "Take it easy man. Be cool. Benny, go in the house and watch TV."

"But ain't nothin' on T..."

"Get in the house, boy!" he forcefully demanded. Ronald turned back to monitor his neighbor's. "Joseph, you crazy or something? You can't beat that boy like that, especially outside yo' house." As the crazed man halted his actions, Ryan gathered all of his energy and darted from beneath his father's reach and escaped back into the house.

"Oh my God! What did I do?" Joseph said, either in denial of the incident or as his only escape from the trouble his neighbor had just witnessed. The malicious deliverer of punishment stood squarely looking at his neighbor through the small, poorly kept shrubs that once served as a barrier between the yards, perhaps a chore Joseph gave to his son but was never completed. Joseph looked at Ronald and waited for him to either walk away, or leap over the fence and administer the same beating he had given to his son. Joseph would have been no match for Ronald. All 5'2" of Joseph was struggling to be 150 pounds, and that was only if he was fully clothed and drenched wet with cement. Although naturals were fully fashionable now, the nappy one that Joseph sported was not, but it was right in order with his kinky beard and mustache. If his skin were not so light bright and just right, his poorly groomed facial hairs would not have been such an inconvenience to his appearance. The excuse for a father was surely the same pitiful excuse for a man.

"What the hell wrong with you, man?" Ronald pressed.

"Hey, you worry about yo' little punk boy and I'll raise what's on this side of the fence, you jive turkey!" Joseph realized that Ronald was not falling for his act so arrogance was his next plan of attack.

"Let me tell you something! I ain't that little boy you just beat to a pulp and I ain't gon' be nobody's Thanksgiving Dinner, so you can take that jive turkey talk on back where you came from. However, I will fly across this fence and whip yo' little nappy-headed tail if you talk about my son like that again, you hear me?" Ronald's anger was running over after having seen the man beat the child and then turn to disrespect him and his son.

"Man, you bedda tell dat to one of them peckawoods 'dat be drivin' dem dump trucks wit' you, because I ain't listenin' to yo' jive talkin'," Joseph said nonchalantly as he turned his back on the now distant neighbor. Just when the disrespectful man thought he was out of harms way, Ronald jumped on the fence and stopped just before he could leap over into the neighbor's yard. Joseph started running towards his house before he looked back at the commotion he assumed was coming his way. When he turned around, Joseph was surprised at the devilish look that rested on Ronald's satisfied face. Ronald had no intentions of attacking the man or even jumping into his yard. He was merely proving to himself, and to Joseph, that the man so skilled at harming a child was indeed a coward. Point proven. Ronald climbed back off the wire-fence and laughed all the way back into the house. Ronald thought to himself that Joseph's victim would eventually be bigger and stronger than the perpetrator. If and when that happened, the victim might not show even a hint of mercy.

Chapter 3
Please Don't Call My Mama!

"Man you crazy! Shogun Warriors two times bad as Evil Kineval!" Benny declared.

"They are not! Evil Kineval can go farther than Shogun Warriors without anything or anybody holding them up. Shogun Warriors always have to have someone holding them up or you have to tie them to a string. Besides, with Shogun Warriors, some assembly is required," Benny's friend Steven replied.

"What does that mean?"

"It means that your dad has to fix it before you can play with it."

"So, my Daddy can fix anything," Benny said, trying to defend what was left of his argument. Although there was never really a winner, Benny and his classmate Steven held daily intellectual battles during class, even though they had been instructed several times to refrain from doing so.

Aside from his cousin Clem, Steven was Benny's favorite playmate. Their mothers once met at a PTA meeting and the two became instant friends, so it was very convenient for Benny and Steven to interact and become chums—sometimes too chummy. Steven was a chubby pale-faced seven-year-old with freckles and sandy blond hair. Benny was always attracted to odd things or underdogs. He often picked the kid on the playground that no one wanted on their team. Other times, Benny walked away from teasing the homeliest girl on the playground, although he happily picked on the more popular and prettier girls in school. It seemed only fitting that his class pal was Steven, the shortest and least athletic kid in school. The only saving grace Steven had was his nice clothes and new tennis shoes. His parents obviously kept him up-to-date and in style—at least as in style as a seven-year-old could be.

"Benjamin Dempkins and Steven Wilburg, are you done writing your sentences or are you fooling around again?" their teacher Mrs. Rose inquired.

"They fooling around, Mrs. Rose," a pretty little girl sitting near them volunteered.

"You bedda shut up you old nappy-headed kuckle bug." Benny snapped at the tattletale. The class erupted with snickering.

"At least I'm finished with my sentences, you booger bear!" The girl replied back sharply. Just as Benny fixed his mouth to lash out again at his opponent of insults, Mrs. Rose interrupted the impromptu battle.

"That's enough out of both of you! And Benny, I would expect much better behavior from you, young man."

"Miz Rose, she always talkin' 'bout people when ain't nobody even talkin' to huh," Benny replied, trying to plea his case.

"Benjamin, what language are you speaking, because I don't understand any of that gibberish you're mumbling? Perhaps if you and your partner in crime concentrated on writing your sentences and stopped talking about toys, you would form your language better, which I know you're fully capable of doing. You're too smart to behave that way, and that goes for you as well, Steven. Now get back to your lessons, and I don't want to hear a peep from either of you, is that understood?"

"Yes Mrs. Rose," the boys responded in unison. The gentle yet demanding teacher skillfully stared at the two culprits until they were forced to lower their heads. Humbled, they began their assignments.

Mrs. Rose very seldom administered severe punishments to her class. She was skilled in the art of careful tongue-lashings. Her approach was to tear a student apart and rebuild them all in one fell verbal swoop. The young boys respected the tall slim teacher. Although Mrs. Rose was an accomplished instructor, she reminded the small boys of a young woman who was barely old enough to be a mother but just young enough to trust her with their first boyhood crush. They loved to smell the light scent of her perfume. Mrs. Rose didn't believe in routine, so there was a different scent for each day of the week. Her smell always complemented her stylish wardrobe. Mrs. Rose shied away from the typical clog styled shoes and homemade Hancock Fabrics pattern dresses. She didn't look like the stereotypical hideous teacher children envisioned in their childhood nightmares. Instead, she looked more like the dream girl that a young boy would hope to marry—when they eventually started to like girls. Mrs. Rose had a soothing gentle and articulate voice that attracted all ears to absorb every word. This was probably her most effective teaching tool, when the students weren't distracted by some other activity. Very similar to the type of activity Steven was now pursuing.

"Hey, Benny," Steven whispered, now being careful to disobey with a little more skill than before. Benny hesitated before he raised his eyes to check the whereabouts of Mrs. Rose.

"Benny," Steven whispered again. Benny took one more look around and double-checked the activity of the little girl who had earlier uncovered their crime. She was face-first into her sentences, just as the boys should have been.

"What is it?" Benny asked cautiously.

"Don't talk too loud, that little stinky booty girl will tell on us."

"What chu' mean? She already did. It's too late."

"I know, but that doesn't mean we can't get her back so that she'll know people can't mess with these two bad dudes."

"What chu' gon' do?"

"She's almost finished with her sentences and I'll bet she's gonna take her paper up to Mrs. Rose like she always does. Then we'll put this glue in her seat and then she'll be stuck to the chair."

"Man, you crazy. You gon' get in trooouuuble," Benny said, raising his voice and stretching out his last word for emphasis. Once again he caught the attention of Mrs. Rose.

"Benjamin, Steven. Are the two of you on a mission to get into some serious trouble today?" Agitated, Mrs. Rose's usually soothing voice grew aggressively louder. The two boys didn't respond, but simply plunged their heads back into their schoolwork.

A few minutes later, just as Steven predicted, the little girl sitting near the boys finished her work and excitedly jumped up to show off her accomplishment.

"Mrs. Rose, I finished all of my work. May I get a book to read?" she asked proudly, then giving the boys a look of superiority. As she walked over to the bookshelf, Steven looked over at Benny to give him the go ahead to begin his guard duty for their revengeful act. Benny was very apprehensive at first, but as soon as the girl shot the boys her silly little look, he had no reservations. He nodded at Steven and gave him the go ahead. Steven twisted the orange cap on his Elmer's glue and began fiercely squirting the white substance in the little girl's seat. After he applied a flood of glue, Steven quickly stashed the evidence in his desk and hurriedly tried to finish his lesson but was distracted by his own giggles. Benny couldn't concentrate either. He was red in the face trying to contain his own laughter. Just then, the little girl was making her way towards the chair, which would be her throne of catastrophe by the hands of a cruel deed. With her book in hand, she strolled through the desks making sure that everyone in the class noticed her new dark blue velvet dress with ruffles. Her grandmother had given it to her as a birthday gift. The little girl had been careful all day to keep the dress clean and neat, because she and her grandmother were going to take pictures after school.

The instant the little girl sat in her chair, a feeling of fear and regret possessed the two culprits. As never before, the boys were instantly consumed with their once disregarded lessons. Assuming that Mrs. Rose would be quick to seek out offenders of the classroom law, they were making an adamant attempt to be inconspicuous. Benny and Steven raised their heads only to catch a glimpse of the developing actions next to them.

The once well-mannered little girl was now a jittering bundle of discomfort.

No matter how hard she tried she could not seem to sit still. Finally, she managed to settle down only to produce a puzzled look on her face. At first it seemed as if she were disappointed in something and might cry. For an instant, she thought she'd accidentally wet herself, and it was slowly seeping through her new dress. Then her face transformed to a look of suspicion as if something was not quite right. No, she hadn't wet herself at all and something was definitely wrong. Looking over at the two suddenly studious boys, she had a sense of where the wrong had started. The little girl stood up and reached down to her bottom side and felt her dress. When she looked at her hand it was covered with the white gooey trouble the boys had dispersed in her seat. Benny and Steven looked up at her. They were puzzled about her next move, then overcome with pitiful looks of sorrow. No face the boys could make, draw, or imagine could save them from the events to come.

The little girl took one more glance at her white sticky hand and began filling the small classroom with tears and screams. Suddenly everyone's attention turned to the three desks of the boys, and their victim. Children jumped out of their seats to see what could have possibly caused the outburst by the little girl. When everyone ran over to the screaming child, all they could see was the sticky mess in her hand. One little girl walked behind her and saw the awful sight on her backside and in her chair. She announced the mayhem as if she were the first reporter on the scene of a breaking story.

"Oooh look at yo' dress! Oooh look at yo' seat," the future media mogul yelled out. The rest of the children followed her lead and witnessed the behavioral tragedy. The quiet classroom was now possessed with the sound of children making the common sound when one of their peers was in trouble.

"Oooooooh! Oooooooooh! Somebody gon' get it!" Mrs. Rose who was putting away some learning materials, began making her way towards the small energetic crowd.

"All right children, go back to your seats and continue working on your sentences. There will be no recess unless you all are finished with your lessons. Young lady, why are you over here crying like someone… chile, what you done did to yo' clothes? Where did all this mess come from? " Mrs. Rose was so stunned by the sight of the sticky goo on the little girl, she temporarily lost her professional prim and proper mannerism and reverted back to her country upbringing in Albany, Georgia. "Girl, did you put all dis glue on yo' dress?"

"No… no… some…somebody put, it, in, my, seat and I, I sat down, down in it and now I can't take no picture wit' my grandmama," The little girl tried to respond while crying, sniffing, stuttering, wiping tears, and wiping her nose all at the same time.

"What? Who did this? Who put the glue in the seat? I want to know right now!"

The class once filled with oooh's was now a fearful hush. The entire class was staring at Mrs. Rose hoping that they would not be falsely accused. Everyone was staring at her, except for Benny and Steven who were writing so diligently that they were actually cutting through the paper with their pencils. If the two boys were trying to be inconspicuous, they may as well have been holding signs that read We don't look like we did it, do we?

"Benjamin Dempkins and Steven Wilburg, do you know how this glue got in the chair?" The boys looked up from the ragged pieces of paper pretending to be oblivious to the actions transpiring in the class. Each of them had a dumbfounded look on his face trying desperately to visually proclaim his innocence. "Answer me young men." Mrs. Rose regained her composure of professionalism and she now displayed a little tenacity.

"I finished my sentences, Mrs. Rose. Would you like me to place my work on your desk?" Steven said in attempt to change the subject and test the waters, which seemed to be brewing a storm in the classroom. His attempt was futile. Mrs. Rose only grew angrier at the lack of respect for her wisdom, thinking that she might be hoodwinked by a facade of good behavior.

"Do you think that this is a joke, young man? You two have been goofing off for the past hour," Mrs. Rose said, as she made her way over to the culprits' desks. She began a one-woman search party for evidence she was determined to find. Stashed on top of a pencil box, she found a half empty bottle of Elmer's glue. The cap was twisted into the open position, and there was a long stream of wet glue seeping from the end of the cap. Once again the rest of the class began its ritual.

"Oooooh! Y'all gon' get it," the children said taunting the boys.

Mrs. Rose took a deep breath and realized that she could not let her anger cloud her judgment for the boys' discipline. Benny and Steven would have started crying, but their fear transformed them both into statues. They couldn't move, talk, or think. Neither of them had the slightest idea what to expect. Suddenly Mrs. Rose walked over to her cabinet. The boys thought for sure she was going to pull out her yardstick and administer three wacks to each of the boys in front of the entire class. Instead, she pulled a brown folder from her file cabinet, calmly closed the cabinet, and walked over to the door. Mrs. Rose then instructed the class leader to escort the sticky little girl to the restroom and help her get cleaned up. She then looked Steven and Benny squarely in the face and spoke.

"Class, settle down and stop talking. I want all of you to stay in your seats until I return. Benjamin and Steven come with me to the office so we can call your mothers."

Benny was no longer a statue, he was now a miniature waterfall as the tears flowed freely down his frightened cheeks. As they began walking down the hallway, the crying and sniffing Benny, turned to his once compassionate teacher and articulately pleaded with her.

"Mrs. Rose, I'm sorry for what we did. Can you please just spank us with your yardstick. Mrs. Rose, please don't call my mama at work. Anything but that! Please Mrs. Rose?" For about the length of time it took for her to blink her eyes, Mrs. Rose considered the boy's heartfelt plea. Then, in the length of another blink, she pictured the little girl's dress and decided she was sticking with her decision. She walked the reluctant boys into the office and greeted the secretary.

"Hi Winnifred. How are you doing?" Mrs. Rose asked the school receptionist.

"Just fine, Carolyn. What do we have here?" the inquisitive woman replied.

"I'd like to use a phone, I have some mothers to call."

"Uh-oh girl, not a code red. Go on back to the teacher's lounge and punch the light on the phone." The short trip to the back room seemed like a long walk into a dark doom for Benny. The waterfall on his face was now a flood.

Once in the back room of the smoky teacher's lounge, Benny's demeanor grew more like that of an infant rather than a mischievous little boy. He began whimpering and sniffing trying to prevent his nose from running, while at the same time attempting to draw sympathy from his teacher.

"Young man, you can cry and whimper all you want, but I am going to call your mother whether you like it or not," Mrs. Rose said. "Steven, I don't know why you're sitting their like a snug bug because your mother is going to get a phone call as soon as I'm finished speaking with Mrs. Dempkins." The small blond-headed little boy stood next to Benjamin with a self-assured look on his face. Steven looked as if he knew the jury was bought and he already knew his own verdict. To Steven, the easiest punishment he could get was a call to his parents. He was not doing a very good job of concealing his comfort. "You just keep smiling Steven, we'll see who's smiling when your mother hears about your antics. In fact, why don't I call your mother first."

Steven's expression did not change one bit. Mrs. Rose walked away from the boys to begin turning the rotary dial on the green phone. She dialed the seven numbers then looked back down at the contact number of the student card she pulled from the boys' files. Looking at the guilty boys, she waited for someone to answer. Her attention was focused on the two until her thoughts were interrupted by a voice on the other end.

"Devon and Monroe Marketing, hold please."

"Hi I'm Mrs. Rou...," she attempted. Suddenly the sight of a career woman too busy to discipline her child blurred Mrs. Rose's vision. Let alone teach him manners and proper classroom behavior. Mrs. Rose always imagined that her students went home to caring concerned parents. She had thoughts of parents welcoming their children home with open arms. Then they'd sit down with the children to read stories and watch educational programs until they were allowed to go outside and play. Frequently, she was doused with reality during a parent conference or a PTA meeting. There she would meet parents who were in a hurry to get home instead of seeing their children's work. Some parents never even came to a PTA meeting and some canceled parent-teacher conferences. Mrs. Rose was trying to recall which type Steven's parents were when the voice returned.

"Devon and Monroe marketing thank your for holding. How may I direct your call?"

"Yes. Hello. My name is Mrs. Carolyn Rose, Steven Wilburg's teacher, and I'm trying to contact Mrs. Wilburg.

"Is there an emergency?" The voice probed in a very procedural voice.

"Uh, well..." The discipline of children was always an emergency in Mrs. Rose's opinion. However, she realized everyone did not recognize the urgency as she did. "It's not really an emergency. Steven is not hurt or anything, but he has been involved in some mischief. You see...," the voice interrupted Mrs. Rose's explanation.

"Mrs. Wilburg is only to be disturbed by the school district in the case of an emergency. Would you like me to make an attempt to put you through to her secretary?" Methodically, the voice was brushing off Mrs. Rose.

"No, that won't be necessary. If you would please let her know that her son poured glue into a little girl's chair and ruined her dress. Also if she's interested in discussing her son's behavior she can contact me here at the school," said the frustrated Mrs. Rose, professionally articulating her words to the voice. Expecting a much warmer response, Mrs. Rose waited. The voice was either taken aback by Mrs. Rose's statement or she was actually writing down the message as if it were nothing more than words to relay to the next office jockey. Certainly not Mrs. Rose thought.

"I'll deliver the message. Have a nice day." Just like that, the voice was gone and so was Mrs. Rose's sympathy for whatever punishment Steven was in for once at home.

"Well, Steven, your mother has been informed of your actions and I'm sure she'll decide what's best for you." Steven stood there looking like the same bug still snug as he did before Mrs. Rose picked up the phone. "Benjamin, come over her please. Let's call your mother next." Mrs. Rose began to think that the phone call would be another lesson in futility after the impersonal phone call with Steven's mother's secretary's, secretary. For God's sake, she thought, I never even spoke with the boy's mother. It may have been faster just to send a telegram. Her frustration was overpowering her calm personality as she began the rotary dialing of another seemingly useless act. Once she finished dialing the number and heard ringing, Mrs. Rose noticed Benny's face was stained with old dried tears and his top lip was covered by his failure to prevent his nose from running. Clearly Mrs. Rose could tell that, unlike Steven, Benny was terrified of the phone conversation taking place. As her sympathy returned, she was interrupted by a not so professional voice, presumably a receptionist.

"Department of Motor Vehicles."

"Yes. Hello. My name is Mrs. Carolyn Rose, Benjamin Dempkins' teacher and I'm trying to contact Mrs. Dempkins. Is she available?" Mrs. Rose asked nonchalantly. Her concern for the two boys' punishment was diminishing.

"Mrs. Dempkins is with a customer right now. She doesn't usually accept personal phone calls at work. Did you say you are her little boy's teacher or something?"

"Yes I am. How did I know she wasn't going to be able to talk. You think people would be concerned about..." Mrs. Rose was disturbed by the commotion occurring on the other end of the phone. It sounded as if someone in the distance was making their way towards the lady who'd answered the phone. She could barely make out what the people on the other end of the line were saying.

"Did I hear you say someone's teacher is on the phone Janice?" A voice was heard away from the phone receiver.

"Yeah, girl. It's yo' son's teacher," the receptionist replied.

"Why didn't you say so? Is she still on the phone? Hello, hello?" Sheila said as she snatched the phone from the unconcerned receptionist.

"Yes, hello, is this Mrs. Dempkins?"

"Yes, this is she. Is this Benny's teacher? I'm sorry I haven't been up there to talk to your sooner," Sheila said attempting to make up for lost parent-teacher time. It was Sheila's intention to always know and interact with Benny's teachers and the school officials. Since her promotion at work, she had not had the extra time to go and visit as she did with all of Benny's previous teachers. Suddenly her thoughts turned from the fear of not parenting properly to Benny's well-being. If a teacher had called her at work, something must have happened. "What's wrong with my baby? Is he all right? Is he in the hospital? Did somebody take him from the school?" Sheila asked, instantly transforming into a hysterical mess.

"No Mrs. Dempkins, he's perfectly fine." Mrs. Rose now questioned her own decision to call parents at work and thought perhaps that she should have waited until the evening. Nevertheless, she thought to herself, I'm here now and I may as well finish what I started. "He's all right, but there has been a little trouble with his behavior this afternoon."

"What do you mean?" Sheila said attentively.

"Well, it seems that he and another student have been involved in a little mischief." Mrs. Rose glanced down at Benny and he turned on the floodgates in his eyes again. Just the simple thought of what his mother was saying turned him tearful.

"A little mischief? What did that boy do?" Sheila asked in a voice to indicate that this wasn't the first time Benny had done something mischievous. She now believed that he had been guilty of talking in class or some other kind of school yard misdemeanor, although she was still puzzled as to what type of incident prompted a phone call at work.

"You see Mrs. Dempkins..."

"Girl, call me Sheila."

"Why thank you, that's very kind," Mrs. Rose said, allowing some of her professionalism to take a break and allowing a little of her soul to ease its way in. Again she glanced at Benny. This time his pitiful wet face immediately expressed confusion. There was no clue of what the two instant friends were talking about. "Well Sheila, he and another student decided to play a trick on a little girl. They covered her seat with Elmer's Glue and..."

"He did what?" Sheila exploded, and suddenly there was not a friendly, professional, nor calm voice coming through the phone. "I can't believe this! What was that little fool thinking?" Benny could hear his mother clearly through the receiver that Mrs. Rose was now holding away from her ear. Sheila's booming voice was a little too much for her. Benny could only cry and he still couldn't stop the leak from his nose. Sobbing intensely, Benny felt he had nothing to lose, may as well let it all out because he would not be the most well liked person in his house that evening, but he was sure to be the most popular.

"Yes Sheila, and the little girl had on her best dress because she was going to take pictures with her grandmother after school."

"Girl, nawh! Um gon' kill that little napp...." Sheila instantly checked herself. Momentarily she had forgotten her location—the work place. In fact, she plain forgot where she was due to her anger. Taking deep breaths, she looked around the crowded, and now quiet, Motor Vehicle office. Apologizing to everyone in the room, she collected her thoughts and returned to the phone conversation. "Okay. I'll be there to get him right now." Sheila paused for a moment and began to think more rationally. "What am I thinking, I can't leave work now. Mrs. Rose, would you do me a favor?"

"Sure, and please girl, call me Carolyn," Mrs. Rose said satisfied that there was at least one concerned parent in the world.

"Would you have Benny standing outside the school yard at 3:30 so that I can pick his butt up myself?"

"Sure, that's no problem. I'll stand out there with him so we can meet face to face." Mrs. Rose also wanted to ensure that she wasn't sending Benny home to potentially abusive parents.

"That'll be great. Whew, girl, you just don't know. Ooh, wait 'til I get that... What was that boy...? Mmmm, don' put glue.... Chile, I can't even think straight right now. Put him on the phone. Nawh, that's okay. I can't talk to that boy right now. I might jump through the phone wit' a belt and a red cape wit' a S-B-B on my chest and whip that boy until his Daddy starts milking chickens."

Mrs. Rose could understand the mother's anger, but was very confused by her comments.

"Sheila, what's S-B-B and you mean milking cows don't you."

"No, I mean chickens, 'cause you won't ever get milk out of a chicken so if started whippin' him now I wouldn't ever stop. S-B-B is Super Butt Beater. Girl, I'll see the both of you at 3:30," Sheila said as she hung up the phone.

Mrs. Rose chuckled at the comments the strict and obviously caring mother made. One last time she turned her chuckling face to Benny who was definitely not chuckling.

Chapter 4
Before And After The Storm

“Steven Wilburg, what is the meaning of your behavior at school today?” Steven’s mother was very upset with him. He had been in trouble before, but never for a cruel prank such as the one he had committed earlier today.

“Oh, mom, give me a break, will you?” The little boy sharply responded to his mother as if she were an inconvenience to him.

“Young man, don’t you speak to me in that tone of voice,” Mrs. Wilburg said, trying to scold the boy. She couldn’t help but feel uneasy every time there was a conversation and people were raising their voices. Hopefully, she wasn’t being too hard on him she thought to herself.

When the receptionist had given her the message, she thought there had been an accident. But after further investigation, Mrs. Wilburg discovered that Steven was up to his usual silly childhood antics. Immediately she went back to work and decided to defray her son’s punishment until she made her routine seven o’clock departure for home. After work, Mrs. Wilburg always rushed to her Weight Watcher’s class or to the spa. She simply didn’t have time to exercise in the morning because of her early six o’clock start up workdays. It was important that she look good and keep her skin pores tight. Every since Steven was born, Mrs. Wilburg couldn’t seem to shed the extra pounds she’d gained. To Mrs. Wilburg, a female office manager couldn’t afford not to be beautifully sculpted. Besides, gorgeous blondes only came in one size—knockout. One fat joke from her husband was enough to make her think that if she didn’t keep herself up, an affair was inevitable. “Now that was not a nice thing you did to that little girl today. How would you like it if someone put glue in your chair and ruined your nice LeTigre corduroys?”

“I’d just make you go out and buy me another pair.”

“Is that right? Well, it sounds like I’d have to take them to the alterations shop, because someone is getting too big for his britches.”

“Oh, mom. Sit on it.”

"What did you say, young man? That's it! No TV for you tonight and just wait until your father gets home. He's going to have a talk with you and then you'll get more punishment." Mrs. Wilburg said, turning away from her son and walking towards the dinner table. She couldn't bare to look at her son because she was certain that her words had devastated the little boy. Had she kept looking at Steven, she would not have seen a look of devastation. Steven was sticking his tongue out at this mother as she walked away.

❧

"Boy, go upstairs and get me a belt right now!" Sheila said, wasting no time getting to the meat of the matter and cutting right to the chase. Benny slowly and reluctantly walked toward the stairs and awaited his punishment. "If you don't get yo' little self up those stairs quick fast and in a hurry, I'm going to fly up those stairs like an evil witch and pick out the belt I want, so you'd better hop to it." Benny hurried up the stairs with the thought that he might actually have some influence in his punishment. Once upstairs and in his parent's room, he began frantically going though the choices of belts that were piled on his father's belt and tie rack. Every belt seemed like a leather strap of death. Even the belts made of cloth resembled a tightly woven rope that would deliver lashes of terror with each mighty blow. Finally, he saw a likely candidate, a red, white, and blue golf belt decorated with prints of golf balls and golf clubs that Granny Osee bought for Ronald last Christmas. The flimsy novelty would have been even softer if Benny's father had worn it a few times. Ronald always mumbled he wouldn't be caught dead on a golf course with that strap of trash as he called it. What am I doing? Benny thought to himself. I'm about to get my butt to' up and I'm getting happy about what kinda belt my Mama gon' use. His mother had a way of inflicting pain without even laying a hand on him.

"Benny, where is the belt? Don't make me come up there!" Sheila's forceful voice rang out all over the house as a reminder of events yet to come.

"Mama."

"What is it?"

"I didn't try to get in trouble," Benny cried out in a final plea for his hide. There was a long silence lingering through the house. Did it work? Benny wondered to himself.

"Benny…," Sheila spoke out in the calmest tone of the day.

"Huh, I mean, yes ma'am?" Benny answered.

"Why don't I have a belt in my hand like I asked you to bring me?" Benny's floodgates were running full steam ahead again as he walked downstairs with no enthusiasm and no haste. He surrendered the belt over to his mother and noticed a chuckle very similar to the one Mrs. Rouse had while talking earlier to his mother. She was obviously amused at his belt selection.

"Benny, you certainly had to look far and wide for this thing." Sheila said laughing at her son's effort to make this as easy on himself as possible. Benny was not amused at all; he was simply wet faced as he had been for most of the day. "Benny, why did you do what you did to that little girl at school today?"

"I 'on't know," Benny replied as humbly as he knew how.

"You do too know and you're going to tell me why you did that. What would you have done if somebody had put glue in your seat and messed up your Wrangler jeans?"

"I'd kick they butt."

"That's what you think you would have done. Then you would have remembered what happens if you get into a fight at school and changed your mind. But you would have felt real funny if that little girl jumped up and punched both of you flat out, wouldn't you?" Benny nodded. "You'd want them to buy you some new jeans too, wouldn't you?"

"Yes, mam."

"Good, I'm glad you feel that way because that's exactly what you're going to do, buy that little girl a new dress." Benny raised his head in amazement at the impossible task his mother assigned him.

"Mama, I don't have a job. How am I gon' get the money?"

"You had better start collecting cans or something because you're gon' buy that girl a new dress," Sheila demanded of her son. "Now Benny, tell me why you put that glue in that little girl's chair?" The young boy contemplated his answer and the consequences that would follow his response. He visualized the events of the day and tried to think how he had gotten himself into this situation. One vivid recurring thought was his initial reaction to Steven's request. Benny knew that the consequences of their actions might be severe, but he took the risk and he lost.

"Benny, do you hear me talkin' to you?"

"Cause Steven wanted me too."

"What?"

"Steven wanted to get her back 'cause she was tellin' on us. I said we was gon' get in trouble, and he said let's do it anyway and he did it," Benny explained, while opening up a full-blown cry realizing the stupidity and embarrassment of the whole ordeal.

"You mean you have gotten yourself in trouble for something another little boy has done and you were just sitting there waiting to get in trouble with him? What if Steve jumped off a cliff? Are you going to jump off too? Huh?"

"No."

"Then why in hell are you gon..." Sheila backed off. "Benny go up to your room until your Daddy gets back from the store and while you're at it, go upstairs and get me a real belt!"

❧

Mr. Wilburg closed the garage door with the garage door opener, which was attached to the sun-visor of his Mercedes-Benz. Hoping that his wife and son were both asleep, he quietly eased through the kitchen door. No such luck. Mrs. Wilburg and her anxious face greeted him. Only she wasn't anxious to see him, she was anxious for her husband to do something about the continual misbehavior of their son.

"Do you know what Steven did at school today?" Mrs. Wilburg began immediately.

"Oh fine, honey. My day was great, what about yours?" Mr. Wilburg sarcastically replied.

"This is serious, Johnathan. In case you haven't been noticing, your son has been getting into more and more trouble at school. Of course, you're too busy prosecuting the scum of the earth to have any involvement in your own son's life."

"Don't start with me, not tonight. I've spent the last seventeen hours reviewing evidence to lock up some guy that should have confessed and skip right past jail time so that he could be electrocuted and replace the devil himself."

"Johnathan, you're not the only one that has hard days at work."

"Oh, I don't doubt that you have a horrible time making cute little jingles and cartoons for candy bars and soda. But you know what, I never come home and tear you down about working late and working hard, now do I?"

"Don't you dare stand there and demean what I do for a living because I make a substantial contribution to this house. If you think for one minute that I am..." Mrs. Wilburg, in her anger, had almost forgotten about the matter at hand which was Steven's discipline. Her arguments with her husband usually led to something other than the intentions she had prior to his arrival. "Johnathan, I'm not going to argue with you tonight because your son, whom you rarely spend time with, took a bottle of glue and poured it all over a little girl's seat and ruined her dress that her grandmother handmade for her. So Mr. Prosecutor, your son is in there waiting on his punishment. Now I suggest you go in there and handle Steven before he goes to bed." She had gotten all the details confused, but the message was still the same. Mrs. Wilburg stood waiting for her husband to charge through the swinging door that led to the great room where his son was no doubt playing Atari on the projection television. Instead, Mr. Wilburg, while looking in the face of his concerned wife, tried with all of his power to muffle his untimely laughter. It was all in vain. Mr. Wilburg began giggling and eventually produced a roaring laugh while his wife stood staring in amazement at what was taking place in her kitchen.

"Johnathan, I don't find this one bit funny. Your son has disrupted class and possibly scarred a little girl for life. What could possibly be funny about that?"

The insensitive husband tried to gather himself and attempted to subdue his laughter so he could respond. A few seconds later he was finally able to talk.

"Oh I'm sorry, honey, I just...."

"No, you're not sorry," Mrs. Wilburg interrupted. "You're pathetic and if you don't do something about your son, you'll be prosecuting him one day! I don't find this the least bit funny Johnathan. I cannot believe you." The husband now tried desperately to contain himself. Although he may have at times been insensitive about his wife's concerns, he knew that he was bordering on being somewhat obnoxious.

"Okay, okay, I'm sorry dear," he pleaded as he walked over to his wife with open arms. He didn't receive the same offering of affection in return; his wife was not pleased. "Look, honey, I just don't think it's that big of a deal. He's a little boy and little boys get into trouble. I don't think this is anything to be concerned about. Now it'd be different if he stabbed her in the hand with a pencil or something, but it's a harmless prank," he reiterated with inflection in his voice to strongly covey his message. Mr. Wilburg pulled his wife closer and placed his lips on her cheek in attempt to make a truce.

"Johnathan, do you honestly think that the little girl's grandmother thinks it was an innocent prank?" Mrs. Wilburg said allowing her husband to get a little closer. She was satisfied that they were actually communicating about their son in a productive manner. Now if they could just see eye to eye on Steven having to face the consequences of his actions. "You are his father and you seriously need to do something about his behavior at school today. I think it would mean a great deal to his future and it would mean the world to me, so I'm closing my discussion on this issue. I've said what I had to say and you know where I stand on the matter." Mrs. Wilburg realized that she was practically begging her husband to discipline their son, therefore, she relented and decided to leave the rest up to him.

"Okay, if it means that much to you, I'll take care of it. How's that?" Mr. Wilburg said, appeasing his wife as he walked through the swinging door into the great room.

Steven, as expected, was in front of the Atari video game, which illuminated the projection television. It seemed the kitchen argument and discussion lasted so long the tired little boy had fallen fast asleep. The only reminder of his video game experience were the words GAME OVER blinking on the screen. Mr. Wilburg didn't want to wake his son, but realized his wife would blame him for Steven's slumber because he delayed discussing the punishment. Reluctantly he picked his son up, placed him on his lap, and tried to wake the sleeping boy.

"Steven. Steven, wake up son," Mr. Wilburg insisted as he shook the slumbering child in order to begin his lecture. "Steven get up."

"Hi dad," the young boy said with as much energy as his fatigued body could produce.

"How's it going, big guy?"

"I scored 200 points on combat."

"Wow that's great. Is that your new record?"

"Yeah!"

"Hey, your mom says that you had a pretty interesting day at school today. Is that right?"

"I guess so. Everyday is interesting to me."

"Yeah, but today was interesting because of some kind of trouble with glue is the way I heard it."

"You mean the glue I put in that snotty stupid girl's seat that sits next to me?"

"That's exactly what I mean," Mr. Wilburg said, altering his tone to a more serious and demanding one. "Now why would you do something like that? Were you provoked?"

"What does provoked mean dad?"

"It means someone does something that might make you do something in return. Did the little girl do something to you?"

"Yeah, she thinks she's so smart and she's always finishing her work first and taking it to Mrs. Rose."

"Who's Mrs. Rose."

"That's my teacher."

"Oh, I knew that. Well, anyway, Steven, you can't put glue in a person's seat even if you don't like them, so I don't want to hear about you doing that ever again, you hear me?"

"Okay. Dad are you mad at me or something?"

"No, I'm not mad, but you have to realize that people are accountable for their behavior."

"What does that mean?"

"It means that when you do something then something else is going to happen because you did it. Sometimes what happens is good and sometimes it's bad. Like the guys that I put in jail, that's a consequence of their actions. Get it?"

"Yeah, I get it. So what's gonna happen to me."

"Steven, this is no laughing matter, so I'm going to have to insist that tomorrow night there will be no TV after five o'clock."

"Awh, dad, that's no fair!" Steven said as he jumped out of his father's lap in protest.

"Well, that's just too bad. The next time you think about putting glue in someone's chair, you'll think about your TV."

"But dad, S.W.A.T. comes on tomorrow night."

"I'm sorry, son. I'm sure they'll show a re-run eventually. Now get upstairs, brush your teeth, take your bath, and get in bed."

"But dad."

"But nothing Steven. Now do as I say," Mr. Wilburg demanded with authority.

"Stupid old girl in a stupid old dress. I hate her." Steven muttered as he stormed upstairs.

I hope she's happy now, the kid's devastated, Mr. Wilburg said to himself, thinking of his wife's demand for the boy's punishment. He picked up the joystick of the Atari game, hit reset, and tried to break 200 points until he fell asleep on the sofa—one of his many doghouse sleeping areas in their home.

"He did what?" Ronald exclaimed at the announcement that his son was misbehaving at school. "Where is he? I'm gon' tear his little as..."

"Wait a minute, baby," Sheila insisted of her husband, while trying to calm him down. If there was anything Ronald and Sheila despised more than Benny being unruly, it was his being unruly at school or at someone else's house. Sheila knew that Ronald would be furious when he heard about Benny's activities, so she had started early preparing her speech for her husband, so that he would discipline their son reasonably.

"Baby, now you know how much he hates to disappoint you, so he's already been suffering mentally all day long. The boy's probably been thinking about his whippin' every since his teacher called me."

"What? You mean the school called you at work! I'll kill him! Benny!" Ronald screamed out in a frightening tone, which signaled that the doom of discipline was near for the little boy.

"Huh?" Benny replied back as his voice cracked in a pleading manner.

"Ronald," Sheila said, looking deeply into his eyes in an attempt to soothe the monstrous tones the angry man was spouting out all over the house.

"What?" He caught a glimpse of his wife's pleasant face, which threw him into a wall of civility.

"Ronald, he's already suffered enough, so don't discipline your son out of anger. Do it out of love," her resounding gentle voice delivered. Ronald lowered his head and took a deep breath. He looked up the stairs towards Benny's room then back at his wife. The angered father was battling between his temper and the compassion he felt for his son whom he loved dearly.

"Ronald," Sheila repeated, this time in a very concerned and loving tone.

"Alright, alright," Ronald said, frustrated by the emotional fight that had just taken place in the battleground of his mind and his heart. Although he seldom admitted or confessed, Sheila was the balancing act that he so desperately needed. Where he was brash, she was pleasing. Where he was resolute, she was reasonable. Where he was quick tempered, she was as cool as a fan. If ever a man and woman complemented each other and filled each other's gaps, God had certainly guided Sheila and Ronald down the same path. Never was it more apparent than when it came to the nurturing of their precious Benny. Even though the results weren't always desirable, Benny received more than enough effective discipline.

"I ain't gon' hang the boy or throw him through the wall, this time," he said jokingly to assure his wife that his thoughts were rational. "What's wrong wit' dat boy Sheila? Is he crazy? What did you eat while you was pregnant?" Ronald said, joking with his wife. Both of the once furious adults were making light of the situation, although they both realized what had to be done.

"Oooh, Ronald Dempkins, no you are not going to sit there and try to act like something is wrong with Benny. I know for a fact that your mother said you was the worst heathens on the block. She told me how you took that stray cat and threw it on your grandmother, knowin' good and well yo' granny was scared to death of cats. No wonder your son's gettin' in so much trouble. I'm surprised he hasn't been throwin' mud covered rocks at the cars drivin' down the street."

"Yeah, I threw a cat on granny," Ronald boastfully replied. "I bet my mama didn't tell you that she broke about seven switches on my butt after I did it, did she?"

"No, she didn't say all that."

"That's what I thought. Baby, boys are gon' be boys and they gon' get in trouble. But what Benny did can't be excused, because he don' hurt another child, and he can't go on thinking that he can cause harm to other people and not suffer severe consequences."

"I hear ya, baby. I agree," Sheila said admiring her thought-provoking husband. Moments such as this one always made Sheila admire her loving husband. "So what are you gon' do?"

"I'm gon' go upstairs and take care of some business," Ronald said as he finally made his way up the stairs.

"Ronald," Sheila called out to her husband again in a tone to remind him of the conversation that had just taken place. Ronald turned back to her with a facial expression letting her know that he understood, and that she was being a bit of a nag.

Opening the door to his son's room, Ronald could hear Benny sniffling and easing out a hint of a whimper. The young boy obviously was overcome with fear when he heard his father's footsteps tromping up the squeaky stairs. At that moment, Benny regretted his entire day. He regretted the fact that he hadn't simply gotten up out of his chair when Steven suggested the stupid prank. He even regretted knowing Steven. One thing was for certain, Benny would look at glue in a entirely different way from now on.

"What you in here cryin' fo', Benny?" Ronald began his battle of correction.

"Cau...cause, you...you gon' whip me," Benny managed to stutter out between his tears and sniffles. He couldn't bare to look his father in the face.

"Now why you think something like that?" Ronald inquired in a conniving manner. "Have you done something that needs a whippin'?" The father was tearing the young boy's mind apart. Psychologically, Benny had no place to run

"Yeah-sniff-We put glue in this girl's seat and it messed up her dress-sniff." His own confession made him feel even worse. Now that he had said it so many times and admitted to it over and over during the course of the day, Benny realized just how stupid he had behaved. He felt that if he told his father that he didn't deserve a whippin', then he would have to go into a long explanation and it might anger his father if he tried to manipulate or lie his way out his fate. By confessing, he was giving his father a front row ticket to the 'Whip Little Benny Show.' He was trapped in his own doom. Now the boy was thinking he just wanted to get this over so he could start a new day.

"Well, I'm glad that you can admit to that, because you do need a whippin' but it's not that simple this time, because you did harm to somebody else by yo' foolish actions. You can't go around hurting people and not try to make them feel better," Ronald explained. He noticed that Benny immediately looked up at him when he mentioned the word hurt. It was as if his father was confused about the facts of the incident.

"We didn't hurt her, we didn't even touch her," Benny said in his own defense.

"Yeah but you hurt her feelings!" Ronald exclaimed, then paused as Benny lowered his head again retreating back into his emotional shell. "You may not have hurt her physically, but you hurt her mentally and she probably feels real bad. Would you want somebody to do that to ya' mama?"

"No." Sniff

"Then why would you do it to somebody's daughter?" Ronald inquired rhetorically. "So what do you think you should do about hurting that little girl?"

Sniff "I 'on't know. Say I'm sorry?"

"Well, that's a start but that ain't good enough. Saturday we gon' go over her house and you gon' meet her grandmother and apologize to her too. Then you gon' tell her how you plan to make enough money to buy her granddaughter a new dress. And when you get to school tomorrow, you gon' stand in front of the whole class and apologize to Mrs. Rouse then to the rest of the class for being a troublemaker today. You got all that?"

The thought of the humiliation made Benny wallow in his tears. Please, just whip me, he thought. He didn't want to face his peers all humbled and broken down. The class would think of me as a chump, Benny thought. What would his friends say when they found out he had to go over to the little girl's house and talk to her grandmother.

"Yeah," Benny said cowardly. "Am I gon' get my whippin' now?" Benny asked, almost as if he were pleading for this to end.

"You get in the bed and turn these lights out. I want you to think about everything you gon' have to do," Ronald replied as he exited the boy's room.

Just like that, the torture was over. I got away! I can't believe I didn't get a whippin'. Wait until I tell Steven. I bet he got his butt to' up Benny thought. Although there were a few loose ends to tie up, Benny was thinking how lucky he was that he had actually avoided getting a whippin'. That was until his father came back into his room the next morning before he left for work.

After Ronald slept the anger out of his heart, he awoke with a civil mind. The calm father woke his son and administered five sharp and quick whacks on Benny's backside with a seasoned black leather belt and said to him,

"Don't forget what I told you to do at school today, and I expect you to have a better day at school, Benny. I don't want nothing like this to happen again."

Any plans that Benny had of celebrating his narrow escape were wiped away by the painful reminder of his surprising wake-up call that morning. Now Benny had truly and completely realized the error of his ways. Sheila came in after awhile to help Benny get ready.

After minutes of school preparation and what seemed like an eternity of uncomfortable silence, his mother spoke out.

"Benny, I want you to have a good day at school today, and I also want you to know that me and your Daddy love you very much, okay?"

The young boy, still pouting from the wake-up whippin', accepted his mother's heartfelt words and simply nodded to acknowledge that he received the message—all of the message.

198Ø–1982

Chapter 5
Cousin Consequences

"I'm so glad y'all could come to the family reunion. Chile, Benny is getting so big! I ain't seen half of these chilluns since watermelons was water. Seem like y'all city folk don't never want to come down here to Hope unless somebody dying or somebody giving out money. And ain't nobody down here got no money 'cept fo' ya Uncle Toe-Man. Lord knows, he ain't gon' give nobody a half of a nickel."

"Oooh Antee, I don't even believe you," Sheila said, responding to her Aunt Bessie Mae. Indianapolis isn't all that big of a city and we were down here for the last family reunion."

"I ain't talkin' bout you, chile. I'm talkin' about yo' heathen cousins. How old is little Benny now?"

"Well, he's turning nine next week."

"He sho' is turnin' out to be a fine young boy. Look at him, he got his grand-pappy's walk. Come over here and give yo' Antee Bessie Mae some suga, baby," the elderly woman demanded as she lured Benny into her awaiting arms.

Benny attempted to make a quick escape from the traditional display of affection to his family elders. But to his demise, he was trapped in the wrath of the stringy haired beard of his loving aunt. At all cost he avoided lip to lip contact. In fact, the evasive young boy did a masterful job of avoiding the woman's mouth altogether. Benny and all of his cousins knew that once you were within the tobacco lair of Aunt Bessie Mae, you were sure to become a victim of a tobacco juice drowning. The children of the family all had vivid memories of the ugly experience that their older cousin Phillip encountered during a previous family reunion.

Aunt Bessie Mae, during one of her more playful times, tried to show Phillip he wasn't too old nor too big to be handled by an old woman, so she put him in the headlock to initiate a wrestling match of the young and old. Phillip knew better than to even think about wrestling with his Aunt. Instead of retaliating, he simply let the elderly woman have her way. She managed to wrestle him down with both of his arms pinned on the ground above his head. Then as she began to look down at the helpless and submissive boy, Aunt Bessie began to say, *See boy I told you ain't too big!* and whaled out a big laugh. But when she began chuckling, a huge glob of tobacco juice came oozing out of her mouth and directly towards Phillip's forehead. Of course everyone was watching because they loved to watch Aunt Bessie Mae's antics. The children standing around the two, instead of laughing, ran from the grotesque scene yelling, *Ugghhh! Look at Phillip he's a slobber dobber!* Since that time, Phillip was known to all of his cousins as *slobber dobber,* a name he would never live down. Benny was determined not to be the next victim of an Aunt Bessie Mae nickname.

"Antee Bessie Mae," Benny started.

"Yes, baby dumplins?"

"Can you please not put no tobacco juice on me like you did Phillip one time?"

"Benny!" Sheila said to her son, as she tried to hide her embarrassment.

"Chile, that's alright, don't yell at that boy. He's just so cute. Benny, Antee ain't gon' spit on you. I done switched to Beechnut and it ain't as juicy as that corner store tobacco I used to chew," the kind old country woman replied grinning showing all the seventeen dingy off-white teeth that she had left.

Sheila lowered her head and smiled to herself. She was suddenly reminded of the never-ending country comedy of the family reunions here in Hope, Arkansas. She knew this one, would be no different.

"Mama, can I go in the house and play wit' Clem and 'nem?" Benny asked his mother. This would probably be the only opportunity he had to make one last attempt to escape the clutches of the tobacco terrorist.

"Yes, Benny, you know you don't have to ask me to go in the house." Sheila knew her son was running from his aunt. In the back of her mind, she didn't blame him one little bit. After watching Aunt Bessie Mae launch a wad of tobacco spit into her old rusty Folger's coffee can, she wanted to join her son inside with the rest of the family.

Once in the house, Benny was greeted by familiar faces, excited kids, and the ever-present smell of southern cooking. All of the family members attending the periodic reunion, made their traditional first stop at Aunt Flappy's house. Aunt Flappy was the oldest of four sisters in the family and Granny Osee was the youngest.

As a child, Flappy was known as quite the loquacious student in school and in the watermelon fields. Her uncle, while baby-sitting her one day, took her to a not so well known neighbor. The uncle was so frustrated at the little girl's talent for never ending conversations, he ran to the neighbor's house and immediately dropped her off saying, *Will y'all watch dis here chile, I can't take no mo' of her mouf. She just been goin' on all day long just a flappin' at the mouth. Take this chile and when huh mama come back, I tell huh she ova at y'all place. Just Flappy Flappy Flappy all day long.* Having never met the neighbors, they didn't know the little girl's name so they simply called her Flappy. When the mother came to pick up her daughter, she was so afraid that the neighbors might not be friendly, she immediately grabbed her daughter and whisked her off to the house without telling the neighbors the little girl's name. After a while the neighbor's became quite fond of the little girl whom they considered inquisitively cute. When the little girl visited them with her school friends, the neighbor's addressed her as Flappy, and the name stuck. Benny and his younger cousins called her Aunt Flappy because she tried to talk without her dentures and the best she could do was flap her gums together making it difficult for anybody to understand what she was attempting to say.

Now nearing her seventieth birthday, Aunt Flappy hadn't lost her gift of gab, however, she didn't hold many conversations in her old age. Aunt Flappy simply watched people, listened to their conversation, and yelled out bible verses relevant to what people said. The only problem was, Aunt Flappy yelled at the top of her lungs and yelled out regardless of where she was or who was in her company. She was a beautiful and wise elder. Women in her family grayed early, so at seventy years old, Aunt Flappy's hair was snow white. Often wearing her hair in ponytails, she managed to keep the beautiful locks silky and well groomed. Her smooth midnight colored skin complemented the white wooly strands like an anointed combination of ebony and ivory.

"Well, lookie here, it's little Benny!" One of Benny's uncles yelled out, announcing the young boy's arrival.

"Benny, come look at Tadpole's mouth! He got a toof knocked out tryin' to catch a bird in his mouth!" Clem yelled out to his favorite cousin. A gathering of kids was looking into their cousin, Tadpole's mouth.

Clem's family always arrived a day early so that they could get a good room in Aunt Flappy's house. The cozy little home sheltered five bedrooms, although very small. At the very least, fifteen people could sleep in Flappy's house. Everyone else, or those who didn't wish to stay with Aunt Flappy, sought lodging at the motel just up the highway.

Aunt Flappy's house must have definitely become confused about its own identity over time. It was a cross between a yesteryear shotgun shack and an attempt at modern day housing amenities.

Masonry red brick covered the front of the old structure while wooden panels took over near the back end of the house. The bricklayer either ran out of bricks or Aunt Flappy changed her mind before the job was completed. Insects were always welcomed into the house on hot days when the windows were open. Most of the screens on the windows had small holes near the corners where children repeatedly landed their overthrown baseballs or an occasional inside the yard homerun. The headers above the doors were probably a handyman's project that he never finished. Occasionally one of the family members painted over the rectangular cracked pieces of wood that barely hung over the entry to each room.

The kids loved to run through the living room and take off, imitating rockets as they jumped over the bumps in the floor caused by the damp bowing wooden floor joists. The bumps in the floor were very decorative because Aunt Flappy insisted the handyman take his time when he applied the orange and purple rainbow pattern linoleum on the living room floor. Well, it was the closest thing to a living room in the house. It was more along the lines of a covered porch with walls.

All of the bedrooms were proportionally the same size. Each one had its own distinct color scheme. Some of the relatives called it a color *scam.* There was the pink room, really pink. The walls, ceiling and floor were all pink. Another room was not so bold but creative. What looked like striped wallpaper was actually a blue background with brown stripes painted diagonally from the ceiling to the floor. Another reason for the home's confused identity was the wood panel walls of the third room. In fact, this was the only place in the house where the walls were made of wooden panels. The handyman obviously used whatever material he could find on whatever day he came to work on the house.

Flappy's house was not yet quite acclimated to modern plumbing and air-conditioning. As a birthday present for her sixty-fifth birthday, the family had an air conditioning unit and new plumbing professionally installed, but only for a few rooms, which is all they could afford. As a result, the offended handyman refused to attend any more family reunions. Other than the typical tobacco cans in all of the rooms, the remaining two bedrooms were somewhat normal, which was why Clem's family arrived early—to sleep in a normal room

"Clem, how long y'all been here?" Benny inquired of his cousin.

"Man, we been here since yestiddy, Clem replied in a strange dialect that Benny was not accustomed to hearing from his cousin.

"Yestiddy?" Benny answered with a confused look.

"Yeah man, you know, yestiddy." The day befo' today. If we was back home we'd say yesterday but when we in the country we got to say yestiddy."

"Man, you crazy. You bedda not let yo' mama hear you say that. You know how they be making us talk like white people all the time.

"My mama gon' to see huh Uncle Tank and they ain't gon' be back until tonight. I can say whatever I want to," Clem rebutted as he turned back to take another look at his cousin Tadpole's dental damage.

"Honor thy pappy and thy mammy so all yo' days can be long on da land dat da Lord don' gave you boy!" The children in the house turned quickly to verify the loud yet stringy voice. It sounded as if some type of wild bird was just learning how to speak. Their assumption was correct, it was Aunt Flappy.

"You listenin' to me? " As was tradition, everyone in the room still not old enough to pay rent replied slowly in unison.

"Yes Antee Flappy."

All the adults were attentive observers, eyeing all of the children to catch a glimpse of any one that tried anything funny or sarcastic after Aunt Flappy had spoken. All of the children stood respectfully still. If the children wanted to continue enjoying their pain-free backsides they dared not disrespect Aunt Flappy.

Behind her house was a structure, an old decrepit outhouse that she swore would never be destroyed. And sitting right next to it reaching in all directions near and far was the ever-blooming plant known by all family members as was the switch tree. There was a time when Aunt Flappy didn't hesitate to stroll out to the tree with one empty hand and a disobedient child in the other. Upon arrival at the tree, she'd grab a switch and commence whipping all of the disobedience out of anyone that dare challenged her. Aunt Flappy did not play.

"Uncle Rudolph, can we go outside and play? It ain't nuthin' to do in here," Clem asked.

"Nawh, it's too hot to go out there right now. Y'all need to wait 'til a little later. 'Sides we gon' eat in a little while. Go on back there and wash ya' hands so when the food ready, we can go ahead and eat," Uncle Rudolph ordered. Any one of the numerous family members crammed inside of the unique house could have instructed the children on what to do. There were so many aunts, uncles, and cousins that nobody actually knew who was who, nor did they care. The entire family was together, among the others were Uncle Jube, Uncle Dude, Aunt Sho' baby, Aunt Peaches, Aunt Mag, Uncle Suga Main, Aunt Oree, Uncle Hosie, and good old Aunt Doll.

Benny had no thoughts of Captain D's this time. Not because he knew what the consequences would be, but when all of his family members came together, it made the food magical. As the children lined up to wash their hands, the aromas wafting from the kitchen near the back of the house, attracted the miniature army. One of Benny's cousins walked toward the inviting smells coming from the kitchen and the others followed suit. The small hungry kids made a bee-like swarm in the kitchen. Looking on the counter and on the tables, they saw a smorgasbord of soul cooking. There was ham, turkey, chicken, both baked and fried, as well as two or three pot roasts. Another counter was packed with fresh corn, squash, collard greens, cabbage, carrots, green beans, and mashed potatoes. A folding table had been brought in just to hold the baked beans, greens peas, macaroni and cheese, and the slabs of ribs bar-b-qued the night before. Benny was wondering where everyone was going to eat because even the kitchen table was spilling over with pounds of pound cake, red velvet cake, lemon cake, chess pie, and chocolate pie. The rest of the table was consumed with eight different kinds of peach cobbler, the family's traditional favorite.

"Well, well, what do we have here? Looks like some goblins are here trying to start eating before everyone else gon' have a chance to," Aunt Bessie Mae said walking in through the back door. "Y'all come here and give Antee Bessie Mae some suga, y'all just so precious." Again, the woman stood with empty outstretched arms. No longer were the children mesmerized by the scrumptious food. Now their young minds were contemplating how could they make an expedient escape. Each one was waiting on the other to make the first move. Surely no one would give in and actually kiss Aunt Bessie Mae if their parents weren't forcing them to. Suddenly Benny spoke out, taking the lead in the youthful revolution.

"I gotta get my Mama's ear ring out of the sink, Antee," Benny blurted out as he made his quick exit. Aunt Bessie Mae didn't have time to respond before she was bombarded with an outpouring of ridiculous obligations from the children who up until now, had no responsibilities.

"I gotta paint the brick in the grass Antee," another child said running out of the kitchen.

"I gotta go cut the rocks, I mean the grass, Antee."

"I gotta go and see a man about a horse, Antee," one child said as she was already walking out of the back door. The other children scampered away without saying a word.

Now Aunt Bessie Mae was getting suspicious and there was only one child left standing before her. The youngest of all the cousins, Pee Wee, was thinking to himself there were no more good excuses left, so he made this attempt.

"I gotta go too, Antee," PeeWee said, trying to run past his now lonely aunt, but his was caught in her grasp.

"And just where do you have to go with yo' little self?"

"I gotta...go to... um...I gotta go to the store!" Pee Wee said quickly.

"And why do you need to go to the store, sweet baby?" Aunt Bessie Mae said to the little boy still attempting to flee. Then she smiled at Pee Wee with her not so shiny teeth.

"I gotta go and um...and um... buy you some toothpaste 'cause yo' teef look like doo-doo! Bye Antee!" Pee Wee said and darted out of the room. Aunt Bessie Mae just laughed to herself and said aloud, "God bless 'em."

All of the family members gathered at Aunt Flappy's house were finally assembled near the kitchen. Granny Osee had come back from making her rounds visiting her cousins, sisters, brothers, and her only living uncle. Afterwards, she made her way back to her older sister's home and joined the more lively and spirited group of people. Granny Osee loved to be around the younger generation, especially after a visit with the older family members. It was like jumping in her Ford El Dorado time machine and going back and forth in time. She'd see the more seasoned family elders and jump back in the car so that she could go and revisit them again in the images of the young children running around her sister

Flappy's house. Granny Osee always insisted that Ronald and Sheila bring Benny to the family reunions, because Ronald didn't care to visit his family up north in Chicago. Granny Osee saw the importance of a child knowing and being an active part in family history.

Once in the kitchen with all of the other attendees, Granny Osee grabbed her husband Macon's hand and asked him to bless the table as he traditionally did. She wanted him to feel and be recognized as a pertinent member of her family. The next hour was the quietest thirty minutes of the evening with the exception of smacking lips and the sounds of forks being scratched against the Styrofoam plates. Family members were spread out over the house nestled close to any flat surface they could find to use as an impromptu table. The children were slurping their orange Tang through bright red straws and Dairy Queen cups.

Aunt Flappy rarely used glasses, she simply washed the Styrofoam cups people brought over from the Dairy Queen on Route 84. To say the least, Aunt Flappy was frugal and Ronald remembered this small detail. He was in charge of sneaking the ice in the freezer in place of the numerous ice cubes already in Aunt Flappy's icebox. Not only did Aunt Flappy wash the Dairy Queen cups, but she also recycled her ice cubes. The stern old lady gave specific instructions before anyone put their cup in the sink, or *zank* as she called it. They were expected to run water over the used ice cubes, drain the water and promptly place the ice cubes in the icebox. Near the end of the meal Aunt Flappy spoke out.

"Make sure y'all put 'dem 'dah ice cubes in the ice box befo' y'all put 'dem cups in da zank. He dat dranketh from da water and ice cubes that I give dem will never be thirsty again. You hear what I'm sayin' to you, boy?"

"Yes Aunt Flappy," the children replied.

"Can we ride with Phillip to the store mama?" Clem excitedly requested of his mother.

"Can I go too, mama?" Benny chimed in and made the same inquiry to Sheila.

"Did y'all eat some of my peach cobbler?" Margie replied.

"Nawh, but we ate some of Granny Osee's and some of Aunt Mag's," Benny answered.

William and Ronald, the inseparable golfing buddies, practically spit their food out of their mouths because of their on-going inside joke. They both confessed to each other that Margie made the worst peach cobbler in the family. Margie, having heard them laugh and joke about it before, looked over at the two snickering buddies and gave them a piercing straighten-up-and-fly-right look, and that's exactly what the two did.

"Well, y'all go ahead, but don't be out there too long. Make sure Phillip brings you all back here and don't go over to that motel," Margie demanded.

"I'm going as well, if you don't mind. Even if you do mind, thank you very much." Kenneth, their West Coast cousin, interjected.

Kenneth and his family didn't have the opportunity to attend many of the family reunions because of the long distance from Seattle they were required to travel in order to get to the Hope. Of course, they couldn't afford to fly all four members of the family from Seattle, so they were forced to drive and the children didn't do well on the two-day journey. This year, however, they all made it.

Kenneth was an articulate, bright, but cunning little boy about the same age as Benny and Clem. However, they were three diverse peas in a pod. The chubby fair skinned boy was a sight to witness when he strutted along with a pigeon toed walk. His father, who was a master barber, always kept Kenneth's shag styled haircut neat and trimmed. All of his girl cousins and their friends thought he was very cute and simply adored his full toothy smile.

Phillip piled his young energetic cousins into his sky blue '67 Dodge. The younger cousins loved being around the older Phillip. He was the closest thing to a big brother they had. Even though his car was an older model, the young boys loved it because it was a symbol of independence, a symbol they couldn't wait to have for themselves.

"What y'all little jokers up to these days?"

"Nothing," Benny answered. He and Clem were waiting to see what they could learn from their cool older cousin. Kenneth on the other hand seemed to be at ease and comfortable around the older family member.

"I'm just checking out the scene and watching out for these jive-ass turkeys in the country," Kenneth spoke out. Benny was taken completely by surprise. He had heard plenty of adults use profanity and heard some of the older kids in his school use it. This was the first time someone he knew, and near his age, had ever used it around him. They all waited for the reaction of the cousin in charge.

"What you know about some jive-turkeys, little cuz?" Phillip asked with a smirk of approval on his face.

"Yeah these are some suck my son-of-bitch ain't they cuz," Clem tried to join in. Everyone in the car looked at him strangely because of his awkward delivery. Clem hadn't had much experience with cursing. "All these white nigger honkies make me sick. All they try to do is son-of-a-shit."

"Clem," Phillip said.

"Huh?"

"Shut up! Who taught you how to cuss?"

"I saw it on Good Times," Clem replied.

"You a Good Times lie. They don't even cuss on Good Times."

"Sometimes they say damn," Clem said in his own defense. "And plus I be listening to my Daddy's Richard Pryor records, and he got a Willie and Lester record, too. They be sayin' titties and stuff."

"My Daddy got a Richard Pryor record called *That Nigger's Crazy* and they be cussing too," Benny interjected, trying to be included in the dialogue. Kenneth kept his cool demeanor. He clearly had something else on his mind.

"Don't y'all be goin' back to Ant Flappy's house talkin' 'bout I let y'all cuss," Phillip requested as they pulled up to the Piggly Wiggly grocery store.

"Okay, slobber dobber!" Clem said as he pulled on the door handle and tried to exit the front seat of the car. Just as he did, Clem felt a strong yank on his shirt collar. Phillip dragged his cousin over to the driver's side of the car and burned his skin with a set of cold dark eyes being hovered over by a pair of thick downward slanting eyebrows.

"Boy don't you *ever* call me that again unless you want a big fat knuckle sandwich for lunch, you hear me?" The boys were quiet. Suddenly the jovial mood turned very serious. Benny questioned whether they should even go into the store with Phillip. Just as Benny and Kenneth sat back in their seats awaiting Clem's outcome, Phillip smiled.

"I'm just jiving, little cuz." Phillip broke out laughing. "I really had y'all scared didn't I? Y'all got to stop bein' sissies man. Come on, let's go in and get some air-freshener for my ride."

After they entered the store, the boys were convinced that the near miss of terror was actually over. Phillip went off to the left section of the store to find the automotive accessories. The three amigos walked to the right and looked at the small yet acceptable toy section.

It was getting late in the evening and rain began pelting the small country town. People began running into the store for shelter, including some young teenage girls who knew Phillip and recognized his bad ride outside the store. Phillip immediately focused all of his time and attention on the girls. In turn, the three amigos focused their attention over on the candy section.

"Girl, I can't believe how fast that rain came down. It was like the Lord just dumped a big bucket of water on this little town," Sheila said to Margie and her cousin Isabelle as they entered the Piggy Wiggly.

"Oh, I know. Wasn't that something? Well, as hot as it is down here, we can sho' use it," Isabelle replied. "It's hotta than five, five hundred-pound fat women fightin' over Fritos at a Friday Night Revival."

Isabelle's two-person audience began laughing uncontrollably.

"Isabelle, you ain't got no sense girl," Sheila attempted to say between laughing hysterically and wiping away tears.

"Don't blame me, it's Aunt Flappy's fault. I got her silly gene in me."

"Speaking of which," Margie alluded, "Mama was telling me that Aunt Flappy ain't doing too well."

"What's wrong? Is she getting sick?"

"No, Isabelle, she's just gettin' old. You know that old bat is gon' live to be as old as Noah," Margie replied.

"Well, what we need to do? Put her in a old folks home, get her some blood pressure medicine. What she need, some Witch Hazel, Vicksas, or something?" Isabelle inquired.

"What in the world is Witch Hazel and Vicksas gon' do for an aging old woman," Sheila responded.

"So what she need, some BC powder?"

"Isabelle!" Sheila said, raising her voice in frustration.

"What, I'm just tryin' to help?"

"Sheila, leave her alone. Isabelle, we just need to come down and visit more often and people that live here need to stop by and visit on a regular basis. And I'm not talking about that old raggedy handy man that has that house looking like a circus.

"He did a good job on that squeaky front door, though," Isabelle said. Sheila shook her head in amazement at Isabelle's simple-minded mentality.

"Lord help the long lost children," Sheila mumbled to herself.

"Before we leave, Isabelle, we need to stop by and have a talk with everybody to try and persuade them to go and sit with Aunt Flappy from time to time." Sheila was no longer interested in the conversation, so she turned to walk up the aisle and proceeded to pick up the breakfast groceries for the next morning. As she looked up towards an aisle closer to the rear of the store, she saw three small familiar faces. One of the faces was attached to a pair of hands. The hands were attached to pieces of candy. The candy was being dumped into one of the little boy's pockets. When she moved closer, she recognized Benny and his cousins Clem and Kenneth. Benny's head was buried in page forty-three of an issue of Jet Magazine. Kenneth and Clem were standing close to the Brach's candy-by-the-pound shelf not realizing they were being watched. Sheila turned towards her sister to inconspicuously get her attention.

"Margie, look down there. Those boys have lost they damn minds."

Margie took off in a mad dash towards the trio because Margie knew if she didn't stop the boys, someone else would, and who knows what anybody else would do to the youngsters.

"Man, Kenneth, you a genius. This the kinda stuff they be teachin' you in Seattle? Because if it is, I'm gon' move up there with y'all," Clem asked of his newly found best friend. While in the toy section, Kenneth convinced Clem to take part in his candy business.

"Everyone that attends my school does this. It's how we make enough money to purchase collector's items Hot Wheels cars. I have two corvettes that cost five dollars each."

"For real. Man you must be loaded. You get all that money from selling candy?"

"Of course. You buy these items for one cent and then you take them to school and sell them for five cents. The good stuff you sell for twenty-five cents. By the end of the day, we could have two whole dollars. We can make way more than that with these old country kids down here. And we could do it a lot faster if Benny helped us out. What's wrong with him, is he chicken or something?"

"Nawh man his mama just real strict; she don't be playin'. My mama don't play either but she be lettin' me do more stuff than Benny's mama does. Uncle Freddy and Aunt Tiffany be whippin' you at home?"

"Yeah, but what's that got to do with our business? My older brother used to get whippins more than I do, though. They were real tough on him, but he's in college now. You sure Benny's not going to help us. Do you think he'll snitch on us?"

"Nawh he ain't gon' help just let him read his magazine. He always looking in Jet for the best records that came out or that half-naked lady on page forty-three. He ain't gon' tell on us because we ain't doing nothing wrong." Clem explained to Kenneth. Then he paused because he was confused by Kenneth's next actions. "You got to put that candy in a bag and take it up to the cash register before you put it in your pocket Kenneth."

"Shhh, be quiet. We'll make more money this way; it'll be all profit. Plus all these country folks aren't going to notice, because I'm too slick for them."

Benny was oblivious to the scheme his cousins were carrying out.

"Man, you beddda not get caught. You gon' get in trouble if you do," Clem said. Then he put his hands in the front pockets of his Wrangler jeans to determine whether he had enough room to stuff candy in them as his cousin was doing. Although Clem was hesitant, he was a sucker for a challenge as well as going along with the crowd. Clem walked over to the shelf of candy and tried to imagine which kind of candy he would like to sell. Butterscotch and caramel corn, he thought. The excited boy had visions of Hot Wheels cars and comic books, he even visualized a brand new tall orange flag for the back tire on his bicycle. Clem was going to be rich. His prosperous visions were quickly interrupted by another snatch on his collar similar to the one Phillip gave him in the car. This time Phillip had gone too far. Clem didn't care how much bigger Phillip was. It was time for him to stand up to his older cousin. As he turned and tried to break free of the increasingly tight grasp, Clem was deathly shocked to see his mother's face above the hand clutching his shirt collar. Even more disturbing was the site of his Aunt Sheila and cousin Isabelle walking down the aisle closing in on the boys. Margie's eyes were bucked wide open and her nostrils looked as though her nose was going to burst open and burn someone's head off with fire. Clem began trembling from the fright of being jerked and from the sight of his mother's face. Benny and Kenneth stood frozen in their places wondering what repercussions they would suffer for being in the same store with Clem at this point. Clem tried to speak.

"I didn't tak..."

"I'm gon' beat cha' when we get back to the house. Let's go!" Margie blurted out in one quick breath. With one swoop, Clem was being dragged out of the store, with the groceries left behind. Benny was dragged by his mother, and Kenneth was dragged by Isabelle. Phillip witnessed the drag race commotion from the soda section and decided not to make his presence known. Besides, he could get in just as much trouble for allowing them to do whatever they had done.

On the way back to Aunt Flappy's house, Isabelle's station wagon was quiet with the exception of the knocking engine rod that caught the attention of every pedestrian she passed. No one spoke. No one dared speak. As they knocked along the road, flashing lights could be seen ahead. The rain was beating down on the streets now. Approaching the flashing lights, they saw a car that had lost control and smashed into a utility pole. They passed the accident, and noticed the streets were fearfully black. Clem perked right up when he saw the latest development in his new found gloom. If all of the lights were out, then his mother wouldn't possibly whip him tonight. Perhaps she would wait until the morning and there might be a chance that she would forget or forgive him. Either one was fine with Clem just as long as he escaped this moment.

Pulling into the path that led to Aunt Flappy's house, everyone in the car noticed that no lights were on in the house. A compete blackout. Sheila entered the house first with everyone following behind her.

"Why is everyone sitting in the dark? Nobody knows where the candles are?" Sheila asked.

"In the beginning God looked out onto da darkness and he said I'm lonely! You listening to me, boy?" Aunt Flappy wasn't disturbed by the power outage just as long as everyone could hear her. Isabelle spoke to everyone and commented on the rain that evening. Margie's voice, however, could not be heard after the door closed and the six shoppers were all inside.

Just as the family members in the house settled down to sit in the dark quiet, a strange racket was emerging from the back room of the house. Although no one could see their hands in front of their faces, each person turned to where they thought the noise was originating. Suddenly, a small light could be seen peering from the kitchen. The occupants of the living room were frightened when the shadowed ghost like face came rushing from the darkness. Preparing for whatever terror the figure was sure to inflict upon them, everyone began feeling his or her way towards the front door. As the figure moved closer to the frightened body of people, they were able to make out the seemingly goolish face. It was Margie. In one hand she held an old kerosene lamp that had been stored away in one of the back rooms. In the other, she held a long and slender object. Margie had somehow felt her way to the back room, lit the lamp, and found one of the many switches Aunt Flappy kept behind her bedroom door. No one was frightened anymore, except Clem. He knew his rear end was now a hot commodity. Surely Clem thought he had been saved by the blackout, but nevertheless his mother was determined to carry out the punishment under any circumstance.

"Come here, boy, don't try to hide from me!" Margie exclaimed into to areas of the house she illuminated.

"What he do, chile?" Granny Osee asked in a state of shock about what was transpiring in the now dimly lit and confused house.

"He down at Piggly Wiggly stealing candy like a little thief that's what he did!" Margie answered as she grabbed Clem and turned him around so that she could see his backside. Margie released the death grip from the boy's arm and began delivering swift strokes to her mischievous son, and he immediately began the evasive whippin' dance. It seemed that the blackout was still working to his advantage because as he danced about shouting and crying, he was able to eluded solid strokes from his mother's rod. Margie struggled to make solid contact with the bouncing bottom, and in an effort to make progress, she began swinging wildly.

"Ouch, shit girl! You hittin' me wit dat damn switch!" an adult voice cried out. Although Margie could light the areas she wanted to see, the commotion of chasing Clem and trying to keep the kerosene lamp stable, made her lose control.

"Mama, I didn't do nothin'!" Clem yelled out continuing to dodge any serious licks.

"Margie get off my foot!" Sheila yelled to her sister. The punisher continued to whip, bump, and stumble.

"Yikes, you hit me in my titty!" Isabelle screamed with her distinct country twang.

"Hey! That's my eye you almost poked out, put that stick, down, Margie. You can't see nothin," William instructed his wife. Margie was leaving a path of destruction that no one could clearly see, but only hear and catch glimpses of as she flung the lamp about the room. The house was in a complete state of comical chaos now. Bystanders, who were far away from the center stage of rambunctious rhetoric, began contributing to the debacle.

"Margie, you hit my dog," someone said jokingly.

"Girl, you don' knocked my teef out my mouth. You gon' buy me some brand new teefus," another adult jested.

"You made my false eyeball pop out of my eye socket!"

"Ouch! You got that switch stuck up my booty, girl."

The house was in hysterics. Everyone was laughing and the laughter was roaring when the lights suddenly came back on. Margie could see her family members near the kitchen holding their stomachs and gasping for air after having laughed themselves practically unconscious. The people she had actually bumped into couldn't help but smile because of the shenanigans performed by the family hecklers. Even the children were laughing. But Clem was not sure if the lights meant that his mother's attempted target was easy prey now, or if she was too tired from her switch exercising that she would retreat. Margie looked at Isabelle who was clutching her breast and at William who had his hand over his eye. Breathing heavily and staring at the room and the characters in this instant side-show, she placed the lamp on the table, broke the switch, and stomped off to the back room where she remained, without even performing a curtain call.

Chapter 6
Explanations

The following morning, some of the children at Aunt Flappy's house arose before the adults to catch the early morning cartoons. They all loved School-House Rock.

"I'm just a bill yes I'm only a bill
And I'm sittin' here on Capila Hill
Well, it's a long long journey why
I sit here and wait and I'm eatin; and cooking
and I'm cleanin' my plate.
But I know I'll outloud someday 'cause I hope and play..."

"Y'all don't even know the words, you old doodie heads," Cynthia snobbishly said to her boy cousins. "It goes, So I'll sit here and wait. 'Cause I know I'll be a law someday. So I hope and pray that I will, but today I am still just a bill. Y'all dummies just makin' up words as y'all go along. No wonder y'all be gettin' in trouble, 'cause y'all so stupid."

"You da one stupid," Benny replied back. "Anybody that try to make cakes for wooden people in a old stupid Easy Bake oven, can't talk about nobody being stupid."

"Yeah, why don't you go somewhere and splash around in yo' old stupid jellies. Them da ugliest shoes I ever seen. When did you get here anyway? We thought you wasn't comin'," Clem added to his insults showing Cynthia that she was in for a battle if she'd planned on teasing the spirited boys.

"My daddy dropped me off last night and he went to see his friends in Texarkana. Y'all need to go brush y'all stanky breath and comb them kuckle-bugs out yo' heads. That's why y'all got green stuff growin' out yo' mouth. *They call me yuck mouth and I don't brush, oh I like my teeth like this.*" Cynthia mocked the boys by making a monstrous face while she threw a yuck-mouth smile in their direction.

"Gon' somewhere Easy Bake booger eater," Clem yelled.

"Yuckmouth!" Cynthia said, retaliating to her name-calling opponents.

"Girl, you make me sick," Benny said.

"Then go to the hospital and see a doctor," Cynthia replied.

"Ugh, I can't stand you!" Benny was becoming more and more frustrated with Cynthia.

"Well, if you can't stand me you ought to try and sit me." The smart alec little girl was too sharp for the boys.

"Up your nose with a rubber hose," Clem said, digging into his TV show arsenal of insults. Now it was a battle to the end between Cynthia and Clem.

"Kiss my grits!"

"You old fish-eyed fool."

"Watch it, sucka! The truth may set you free, but it ain't gon' clean yo' teeth."

"Girl, I'm tired of yo' lip. I'm 'bout to bust you in yo' eye wit my bionic arm."

"If you really want to hurt me, you can just breathe on me wit' yo' bionic breath."

"That's it, you dead girl!" Clem yelled as he rushed towards her with his fist balled. He surely meant to deliver a punishing blow to his enemy, but just as he was within a right jab's distance away, he heard the familiar voice of wisdom pressing in their ears.

"Do unto others as you would have them do unto you. You hear what I'm sayin', boy?" Aunt Flappy peered around the corner of her bedroom, which led into the living room where the young verbal warriors were fighting. Aunt Flappy made the statement and eased her way back into the kitchen to have her ritualistic morning coffee then a plug of tobacco. The kids were silent while they watched the commanding old woman drag her feet along a path to the back of the house. Suddenly, she stopped as if something was missing. Aunt Flappy turned around to the kids and looked in their direction but not directly at either one of them.

"I said do unto others as you would have them do unto you. You hear me boy?"

Benny realized they had omitted their part in this mechanical conversation that all children of the family were obligated to know.

"Yes, Aunt Flappy," the children said. It was at that moment, the kids realized Aunt Flappy was not merely yelling out comments and scriptures as though she were a walking talk box waiting for some one to drop money in her slot. Aunt Flappy was very cognizant of what was happening around her and had actually been delivering messages all of this time. The old lady, after receiving her response of gratitude, turned around and started back towards the kitchen as though nothing had ever happened.

"What's wrong with that old bat?" Kenneth asked. The new participant of the family reunion didn't know about the prestige and respect Aunt Flappy commanded. The other kids did not yet fully understand the significance of Aunt Flappy either, but they did know you weren't supposed to say anything bad about the woman, or her mannerisms.

"Man you crazy?" Clem asked. "Don't be callin' Aunt Flappy no names. You gon' get us all in trouble like you did at the store. Remember? I still got yo' number for that, too. Don't think I forgot."

"Oh man, that was just a little mistaken identity. Anyway, what's up with Aunt Fatty?"

"Her name is Aunt *Flappy* and you had bedda start respecting her before I tell Uncle Freddie on you," Cynthia demanded.

"You know what, I think you're a big snitch!" Kenneth replied.

"You know what, I think you don't know nothin' about me or this family 'cause y'all don't never come to the family reunions, so you can't talk," Cynthia said in attempt to set the record straight about Kenneth's disrespect for Aunt Flappy. In actuality, the wise know-it-all girl was correct in her assessment. This was Kenneth's first real family reunion. The only other time he attended was eight years ago, and he was only two years old at the time. The western cousin was in an unfamiliar setting and had no idea what the native customs were.

"So why don't you country mice tell me how it is."

"First of all, I ain't country," Benny was the first to reply. "And you ain't supposed to say nothin' about Aunt Flappy."

"Why not?"

"Cause she's Aunt Flappy, that's why," Clem explained.

"And what does that mean?"

"It means you don't talk about her. That's what it means," Cynthia added.

"But why not?" Kenneth was desperately searching for an answer to this puzzle his cousins had a firm grasp of but the significance seemed to elude his understanding. Benny, Clem, and Cynthia focused their attention on straightening up their Saturday morning mess of Sugar Smacks cereal and Tang orange drink. Neither of the three realized the depth to which they understood the concept of respect for Aunt Flappy.

"This is stupid."

"Stupid because she old?" Cynthia attempted to appease Kenneth.

"But Aunt Bessie Mae is old and no one says *yes Aunt Bessie Mae* after she speaks." The three seemingly aware cousins were suddenly lost for a reply or explanation. Cynthia made an attempt.

"Aunt Bessie Mae is a different kinda old. You see, Aunt Bessie Mae is a mustache face lady kinda old and Aunt Flappy is a pretty gray hair kinda old. When you old and got a mustache, it means that you kissed too many boys when you was young 'cause they beards and mustaches used to be rubbin' all on yo' face while y'all was kissin'. When you gray hair kinda old, it means that you was good when you was little 'cause you washed yo' hair a lot and always took baths and that's why yo' hair get gray because you washed all the black out. I'm gon' have gray hair and be old like Aunt Flappy not like Aunt Bessie Mae 'cause I don't even like kissin' boys because they all stupid like y'all." Cynthia gave the boys one of her famous barrette clacking head turns and sat down to enjoy the rest of her Saturday Morning by singing along with the cartoons.

"*When it's three, you can see. It's a magic number.*"

"That's the dumbest thing I ever heard," Kenneth commented.

"She don't know what she talkin' about, man. I don't know why she think she know everything," Clem said, raising his voice towards the girl who was enthralled in the television and perfecting her ignore routine on the boys. Cynthia however, briefly responded to Clem's comment in between stanzas of her cartoon recital; she could never let them get the last word in.

"*Man and a woman had a little baby. Yes, they did. They had three in the family.* Girls are smarter than boys. Everybody know that," Cynthia interjected quickly then returned to her cartoon recital. "*And that's a magic number. Three, Six, Nine, Twelve, Fifteen, Eighteen.*"

"Anyway Ken," Clem started. "Yeah we gon' call you Ken from now on. See Aunt Flappy got mo' money than Aunt Bessie Mae, that's why you can't say nothing bad about her. If you do, she's gon' give somebody money to come and run you over with a tractor. Phillip told me one time this man came and called Aunt Flappy a old witch just like Evilene on the Wiz. Aunt Flappy gave somebody money to put the man in her outhouse, and he stayed here until the dookie smell made his eyes pop out. Aunt Flappy told him wasn't nothin' ugly but him now and he wouldn't be able to see how ugly he was. One time Hope didn't have no rain and the president of Hope came to Aunt Flappy and asked her to buy the city some water from the river and she did it."

Cynthia looked over at Clem with a look of *how dare you tell that story over mine.* Kenneth was getting nowhere with an answer and now he was feeling as though the journey hadn't even been worth starting.

"This is so stupid," Kenneth stated.

"It's not stupid," Benny answered. We might not know why we not supposed to say anything about Aunt Flappy, but we know what's gon' happen if we do say something bad about her. She probably did something in her life that make people not say stuff about her. Aunt Bessie Mae might'uv done something, too. We too little to know what it is though. If you want to know, just go ask them. But I don't care why. I'm just not gon' say anything about her 'cause my mama told me not to.

"Ah you just a little scaredy sucka because yo' mama so strict," Clem responded.

"I ain't scared and I ain't the one that got a whippin' in the dark last night with no lamp either," Benny replied.

The kids were silent with the resolution of Aunt Flappy's respect. Their inquisitive minds turned to deeper and more meaningful activities that were now on the TV. From the West to the South, Clem, Cynthia, Kenneth, and Benny were on one accord, and little off key singing with their favorite cartoon.

Hey! Hey! Hey!
It's Fat Albert.
And we're gonna sing a song for you.
And you might learn a thing or two.
We'll have a good time with Bill and all his gang.
Learning from each other.
While we do our thing.
Nah nah nah, gonna have good time.
Hey! Hey! Hey!
Nah nah nah gonna have good time.

Chapter 7
Insightful Instigation

Two years had passed since Benny last witnessed the violent incident between Ryan and his father, Joseph. The neighbors played together often but Ronald always kept a careful eye on the boys when they were together. Ronald was never further than a wind sprint away. Today Benny was playing with Ryan and his new dog. The two chums were enthralled over the small creature, and Ryan was thrilled about having a living-breathing thing, which he could command.

"Oooh man, what's his name?" Benny asked.

"Jimbo."

"Come here Jimbo. Here Jimbo." Benny called to Ryan's puppy German Shepherd. The pet was a birthday present from his mother. "Man you lucky. My daddy won't even let me get no dog. He talkin' about they cost too much money and stuff."

"You can get a free dog. People be givin' 'em away."

"For real, Ryan?"

"Yeah, my cousin got a free dog one time. People be havin' dogs that be havin' puppies they don't want, so they give 'em away."

"If I tell my Daddy that, maybe I can get one, too. What's this red spot on his back?"

"Aw, that ain't nothing. I'm just trying to train him and sometime he be actin' up, so I got to teach him not to do stuff like pee on my shoes and try to bite me."

"Whatchu do to him?"

"I put this chain on his back, so he won't do it again."

"Don't he get mad and try to bite you?"

"If he do, I whack him on the mouth with the chain and he won't do it no' more."

"Man, that dog gon' be tough. Ain't *nobody* gon, try to come in y'all yard while y'all gon' somewhere."

"That's right! Jimbo gon' sick 'em and he might kill 'em."

The two boys continued to pet the oddly submissive dog when Benny heard his father's stern voice calling from the backyard.

"Benny!"

"Huh? I mean, Yes?"

"Come here Benny," Ronald requested of his son. As Benny approached his father, he immediately began his new proposal for a dog. After talking with Ryan about the no-pay-pet-puppies, he thought he had a good chance.

"Daddy, Ryan said we can get a dog for free. He said people be having dog's that be havin' puppies and they don't want 'em and they be tryin' to give 'em away. Can we find some of those dogs? Then it won't be no money or nothin'."

"First of all, when did you turn into a little yellow and black bug and sting people. I told you to stop using *be* so much like it's a verb. You sound like a crazy bumblebee. The man ain't gon' never give you a job talkin' like that. I told you we not gettin' no dog. I don't care if they is free. You still got to buy dog food, a dog house, take it to the vet, get dog toys, and somebody got to get up and feed him everyday. And as soon as you forget to do it, I promise I wouldn't feed him, because he would be on his way to the country. Now me and ya' mama gon' go to the store. We'll be right back in about five minutes. So come on in the house until we get back and don't let nobody in on ya'."

"Aw Daddy, can't I play wit' Ryan and Jimbo?"

"Who is Jimbo?" Ronald asked, trying to think of another kid on the block he hadn't met.

"Jimbo is Ryan's German Shepherd. He just got him last week."

"I should have known something had to bring about this new wantin' for a dog after I don' told you no the first time. You don't need to be over that crazy man's house anyway."

"His Daddy ain't home but his mama's there," Benny pleaded.

Ronald hesitated trying to think of a quick response as to why he couldn't let his son stay. His young definitive son seemed to have covered all of the bases.

"Don't go in them folks house. You stay outside and play with the dog until we come back."

"Okay!" Benny yelled as he tried to return to his previous activities.

"Benny!" Ronald yelled out to the fleeing boy.

"Huh?" Benny said, turning to face his father.

"Don't let me come back and find you inside them people's house," Ronald warned while giving Benny a scornful look.

Keeping his father's last words in mind, Benny ran out of his yard and into the weed filled lot next door. Returning to the spot where the two boys were playing, Benny was disturbed by a painful sight. As he approached his next door neighbor, Benny could see that Ryan was no longer stroking, petting, and caressing the small energetic pup, but now he was beating the dog with the infamous chain he had referred to earlier. Benny was confused by the spectacle. He wondered what had transpired in the short time since he'd left up until now. What could the dog have possibly done to provoke such a brutal beating? Ryan was hitting the dog unlike he described to Benny. This was not discipline; this was a problem.

"Damn dog, I told you to sit! Why can't you ever do what I tell you to do boy? You just stupid. When I say sit I mean sit!" The dog had no place to run in the small backyard. All the animal could do was yelp and hope that the beating would stop.

"Ryan!" Benny tried to get his neighbor's attention. "Ryan, did he bite you or something? Ryan!"

"I'm gon' kill this dog! He ain't doin' what I told him to do." Ryan shouted as he delivered one more crushing blow to the helpless dog. Barely breathing the dog lay against the fence panting for his life. Benny thought the whole scene was disturbingly familiar as if he had witnessed this act before. Suddenly, Benny realized Ryan was punishing the dog as Ryan's father had punished him in this same backyard. Benny wondered if everyone in Ryan's house was getting beaten, especially his mother. If this was happening to a dog, what was happening to a humble woman. At that moment, Benny wished he had taken his father's advice and remained in their own house.

"What you do that for, man?"

"Do what?"

"Beat yo' dog like that."

"Man, that dog got to learn that when people tell him to do something, he's got to do it. He's got to learn some responsibility."

"But he just a little puppy dog! He might not know what you talking about."

"I don't care how old he is. That dog is gon' do his share in the house.

"What kind of share? All he can do is bark, pee, and dooky."

"That ain't no excuse. I been working in this house since I was five years old and he can do it too." It was apparent that Benny and Ryan were involved in entirely different conversations. Ryan had assumed the role of a mean parent that came from nowhere.

"All I know is, if I was a dog and somebody beat me like that, it wouldn't make me want to sit. I'd want to run away or bite somebody."

"Let him run away. Shoot, that's one less mouth I got to feed. Besides sometimes fear is the only feeling that makes a person do something."

Benny was beginning to think five minutes was going to feel like a lifetime, and he was afraid his parents had been swept away by some clearance sale and had forgotten all about him.

"If I had a dog I wouldn't be doing that to him."

"Well, yo' dog wouldn't be nothing but a bad little mutt if you didn't."

"You ain't got to beat nobody to make them act right," Benny said all of sudden realizing he had just contradicted his parents theories.

"This a dog, man. This ain't no person."

"But still you ain't got to beat 'em. Do you like it when yo' Daddy beats you?"

Ryan was quickly silent now, knowing he wasn't supposed to discuss what went on in his house. His father threatened him with grave danger if he ever told people about his punishments.

"Well," Benny continued, "do you like when you get a whippin'?"

"That ain't none of yo' business so you bedda shut up before I beat *you*?"

"It is my business because you my friend. And I ain't scared of you beatin' me because my daddy said if anybody ever beat me up he was gon' go and beat they Daddy for not teachin' their kids how to stay away from fighting. So unless you want yo' daddy beat up, you bedda not hit me."

"Man you lyin'. All I got to do is hit you and yo' Daddy gon' come and beat my daddy up?"

"Yep."

"How hard I got to hit you?"

"You bedda not hit me at all!"

"Okay, okay, I'm just playin'. What if we play like I hit you? You think yo' Daddy'll still beat my daddy up?"

"Man, nawhh. You act like you want yo' daddy to get beat up or somethin'. Do you?" Benny stared at the confused neighbor and noticed Ryan couldn't look him in the eye. Ryan was silent again and this time distant, as though he were reflecting over times he cared not to remember, but could never forget. Ryan looked at the frightened dog that was now either in a deep sleep or dead at the hand of the unforgiving blows of the chain. Noticing small movements around the dog's stomach, Ryan was glad the animal was still breathing.

After ending his lengthy pause, Ryan finally said to Benny, "I don't know. I just wanted to see if yo' Daddy was gon' beat him up like you said."

"Nawh you wasn't. You wanted yo' Daddy to get hurt for real."

"No I don't, and you bedda not tell him either."

"I ain't gon' say nothin' to yo' Daddy because he might beat me too," Benny replied. "Why you get whippins all the time like that and why yo' daddy beat you so hard?"

Ryan, still mindful of his father's threats, kept his head down as though his father had just mentally hit him. Desperately wanting to share his thoughts and expressions about his father, Ryan quietly spoke and defied his father's command.

"I guess he just don't like me like yo' mama and daddy don't like you."

"Why you say that? You don't know my Mama and Daddy," Benny rebutted back. He was offended that the boy would make such a statement.

"Don't they be whippin' you?"

"Yeah, but that don't mean nothing?"

"It do mean something. You just said you ain't got to beat nobody to make them do stuff," Ryan replied sharply.

Benny was now caught up in his own contradicting observations of his parent's behavior. It was then that Benny began to doubt his parents' intentions.

"That don't mean that my Mama and Daddy don't like me, because I know they do. My Mama and Daddy love me."

"How you know?"

"Cause I do."

"Do they tell you?" Ryan was interrogating his friend. Benny was nearing his confession of guilt as he visualized the last time his parents made the three word offering that many people were denied. Struggling to pick out one particular event in which his parents made the comment, Benny withdrew in defeat.

"Man shut up. You don't know what you talkin' about!"

"The P.H.O. lady know what she talkin' about," Ryan offered.

"What P.H.O. lady?"

"The People Helping Others lady that be coming to our class and talking to us about stuff.

"Whatchu mean?"

"One day she told us, after Mrs. Hicks left the room, that parents ain't supposed to hit they kids," Ryan replied, almost as if he were holding on to the woman's proclamation.

Benny quickly darted his attention to Ryan's eyes. This was an amazing discovery to him. Was there actually a grown up in existence that believed kids weren't supposed to be punished?

"For real? What else did she say?" Benny wanted all the information he could have about the woman. He even wanted to know if she wanted to adopt any more children. What did she look like? How old was she? Could she make peach cobbler? Would she come over and talk to other grown-ups? Thoughts ran amuck in Benny's mind.

"She said that if yo' parents ever tried to hit you again, we were supposed to tell them that kids aren't supposed to be hit and tell yo' Mama and Daddy that she said so."

"For real!" Benny paused for a moment. He began to think this was a wonderful revelation. Now all he wanted to know, was had there been a test proven guinea pig or even worse, a sacrificial pig. "Did you tell yo' daddy he wasn't supposed to hit you?"

"Nawh!" Ryan's enthusiasm for the situation was wiped away by the mention of his father.

"Why not?"

"I 'on't know?"

"You gon' tell him the next time he try to do somethin' to you?"

"I 'on't know. Quit asking me! Why don't you do it?" Ryan responded, daring his neighbor to test out the theory.

"I am, because if the P.H.O. lady said it, then it must be right."

"For real! You gon' do it?" Ryan said looking at his neighbor with new admiration. Surely Benny's statement and actions would set a precedent for all kids their age. Anyone bold, or stupid enough, to tell their parents not to give them a type of widely used punishment was going to be a hero, especially if the parents relented and decided against the act.

"Yep, the next time my Mama or Daddy try to whip me, I'm just gon' tell it like it is, because I got they number now," Benny said as though he had just been given a badge of courage from the Wiz. The inspired young boy was now ready to take on the world that resided within his house. Poking his chest out proudly and enjoying the respect Ryan was pouring on him, Benny altered his arrogant attitude when he heard a voice that instructed him to be back home twenty minutes ago.

"Benny!" Ronald called out to his son.

"What!" Benny shouted back disrespectfully. There was no response from his father until a few seconds later.

"Benjamin Dempkins!" Ronald called out with more authority and with more agitation this time.

"Yes sir?" Benny answered.

"Time to come home. The street lights gon' be on in a little while."

"Okay," Benny said.

Ryan gave Benny one last look to remind him of the commitment he'd just made. Benny took a huge swallow and began walking back to his side of the fence. The temporarily empowered young boy jumped the fence and landed firmly on two feet as if he had landed on enemy territory and was preparing for battle. Little did he know, this battle would be short and swift.

Chapter 8
Be Thankful, Be Very Thankful

"Mama these high top basketball shoes gon' make me jump higher than anybody on my team," said Benny.

"They should make you jump higher than anybody on this earth as much as I had to pay for them," Sheila replied.

"It's not that much, mama, just twenty-two dollars."

"Just twenty-two dollars? Now correct me if I'm wrong but I don't think you go to work on Monday morning, do you?" Sheila jovially asked her son.

"Nawh, mama, you know I don't have a job. But when I do, I'm gon' buy me a new pair of shoes every week," Benny answered back, admiring his new shoes. He couldn't stop staring at the white cloth and canvas high top shoes with the sky-blue swoosh on the side. They were Benny's first pair of brand name shoes. His mother had always bought his shoes from the TG&Y bargain store. The only shoes they sold were Skips, Wows, or Blast Offs, all of which made him the laugh of the Boy's Club basketball team. *Ain't nothing wrong with them shoes,* his father would always say. *If you can play you can play in anything.* This time Benny was going to get the last laugh at practice. He convinced his mother to get the new shoes before practice so that he could show them off at the Boy's Club.

"Benny, you'd better be glad your daddy started working all of that overtime down at his job, or we wouldn't have any extra money. And we certainly wouldn't have an extra twenty-two dollars."

The satisfied boy was oblivious. He was already taking jump shots and making lay-ups in his mind. He was still making the lay-ups in his head when his mother dropped him off at the Boy's Club where he jumped out of the car and waltzed through the building with a new attitude.

Benny noticed the stares of all the other boys as he made his way back to the gymnasium. A few of the boys made comments such as how hip and how live or cool the shoes were. For the time being, Benny was definitely the envy of the kids at the Boys' Club. His coach even noticed his shoes and teased him a little bit but soon relented when he noticed Benny practicing harder and running faster. Even the better players on the team had to elevate their playing ability for the energetic and instant star. The coach urged the other players to play harder and keep up with Benny, which made him even happier. Benny was on top of the world and he was standing on top in his brand new pair of basketball shoes. Suddenly, Benny began to wonder how much better he could play if he had a pair of leather Nike's like the Ice Man, George Gervin wore. If he could play this well in canvas shoes, then he could probably touch the backboard with the leather shoes he had admired while his mother was at the cash register. Benny pondered the thought until his mother picked him up from practice at 8:45pm.

"Mama, I was killing 'em at practice today! The coach started telling everybody to play like me because I was doing real good in my new shoes."

"Ooh baby, that's so good. I'm proud of you. So are going to score a whole lot of points for your mama this Saturday?"

"Yeah, I'm gon' try. But you know what'll make me score a whole lot more points?"

"No. What baby?"

"If I had those leather ones that was at JCPenny's next to these on the shelf. I don't like these shoes that much because I can't get up high like I need to."

"What did you say?" Sheila asked her son in a harsh manner.

"I said I don't like these now and I want the leather ones."

"Did you get those shoes dirty?" Sheila asked Benny becoming angry by her son's selfish attitude.

Benny was too busy basking in his basketball greatness to realize his mother was not at all happy.

"No, they still clean, mama."

"Then take 'em off because we're going back to the store right now! I am *not* paying twenty-two dollars for shoes that somebody thinks aren't good enough for him! I knew I shouldn't have bought those shoes anyway. Twenty-two dollars for some shoes. I must have lost my damn mind!"

Benny was baffled by what was taking place. All of a sudden his plan had gone terribly wrong. Not only was he going to lose the chance to have the premium shoes, but he was going to lose the best shoes he'd ever had.

"Mama, I'll take these. I like 'em," Benny said quickly.

"Do you still have those shoes on your feet? I said take them off! Right now,

Benny!"

Suddenly Benny felt a rush of emotions running through him and they all seemed to strangely originate from his feet. All he could think of were the comments all of his teammates would make when he came to play in the game on Saturday. Now Benny hated basketball, the Boy's Club, and Nikes. He sealed his hatred with a tear streaming down his face. Sheila was deathly quiet. Benny knew that all of the begging and pleading in the world couldn't bring his shoes back to him.

After the DJ on the car radio finished playing *Ladies Night* he announced the time. *It's 8:55 in the Circle City and you're listening to the dynamite sounds of Smooth Daddy Silk on KOKY 1440 AM.*

Benny's only hope was that JCPenney's would be closed when they arrived and perhaps his mother would forget about taking the shoes back the following morning. Even better, he could get them dirty and the store wouldn't take them back. It was now a race against time for the preservation of his shoes. Only now, there was an entirely different woman in the driver's seat. His once road-rules-observing mother was now a bat out of hell traffic terrorist. Sheila ran through a stoplight and cut off an older woman driving a brand new Chevy Nova. Sheila's green Cutlass had never been such a blur on the streets.

The shopping center was within the temporarily insane mother's cross hairs and she was not about to lose focus, or her twenty-two dollar refund. Just as the manager was about to put his key in the front door of the store, Sheila spun her car into the parking lot, accelerated towards the curb only to slam on the breaks and skid right near the sidewalk. The manager thought he was about to be held up by a mad woman. Sheila emerged from the green speed capsule waving her receipt in the air with one hand and a new basketball shoe in the other. She yelled to the manager, "Wait right there, mister. I still got one minute before this store closes and I want my damn twenty-two dollars back!" Sheila had just lost her sense of rationality, and Benny had just lost his first pair of name brand basketball shoes.

"Because he was being ungrateful that's why!"

"You didn't have to take the boy's shoes back to the store, though, Sheila."

"Ronald, I paid twenty-two dollars for those shoes and I didn't feel like Benny appreciated it, so he didn't deserve to have them. Twenty-two dollars is a lot of money, you know."

"What did he do that was so bad you had to take the shoes back? Now he's gon' be embarrassed as hell when his friends on the team see him. The boy not gon' be able to hold his head up."

"I don't give a dookie-dog-gone about him being embarrassed. He's got to learn to appreciate what he has. When I went to pick him up from practice, he had the nerve to say, *Mama can I have the leather shoes? They'll make me jump higher and I don't like these canvas high tops no more,*"Sheila said in her best imitation of Benny. "Those leather shoes were forty-five dollars! Is he crazy?"

"Is that what he said?" Ronald asked.

"Yeah!"

When Sheila arrived home that night, Ronald could see right away she was upset. Unfortunately, Benny got to Ronald first to tell his side of the story and made Sheila out to be the enemy. Benny was becoming quite skilled at plotting his parents against each other.

"Benny!" Ronald called out in his thunderous *you're in trouble* voice.

"Yes?" Benny answered, hoping that he was being summoned so that his mother could tell him she had made a terrible mistake and they would return to the store and get Benny the shoes he wanted. To Benny's dismay, this was not the case as was revealed to him when he entered his parents' bedroom.

Sheila was staring at the television, purposely looking away from her ungrateful son. She had a *boy-you're–gonna-get-it look* about her, and Benny could smell it from across the room.

"Ya' mama said you was actin' up at the Boy's Club, talkin' about you didn't appreciate what she did for you," Ronald said.

Benny was puzzled by his father's statement, since this wasn't the conversation they'd had just moments earlier. Benny felt swindled, and no one seemed to be on his team anymore.

"But Daddy," Benny attempted. "I thought you were… but you said that… what about when you said Mama shouldn't have done that?" Benny noticed his mother glance away from the television towards him with a disdained look. This was no time for Benny to try his hand at Mama versus Daddy. He felt they were obviously against him.

"I'm not talkin' about what you told me earlier, I'm talkin' about ya Mama spendin' all that money on some shoes and you not appreciatin' it. Don't you know we can go down to the soup line right now and I'll find at least twenty people that'll be happy just to have *one* of them shoes? It's some people that ain't gon' never ever have no shoes at all and you up here talkin' about you don't like some twenty-two dollar shoes. Have you lost yo' mind?"

Benny was in awe. How had he possibly gotten himself into this situation? Where did it all start? More importantly, when would it end? All he remembered was lacing up his spectacular new shoes and creaming everyone at practice and now he was facing charges in the Lion's Den.

"I wasn't even doing nothing bad and Mama took my shoes back to the store. Everybody else at my school got Nike shoes and don't nobody have to wear those old raggedy shoes from the TG&Y store. Why I got to wear those stupid shoes?"

Again Sheila gave Benny a bitter look, this time to let him know he was increasing his chances of not escaping the room untouched.

"Boy, I ain't thinkin' of what other folks is doing and what they got," Ronald explained. As usual, the more intense Ronald got into a conversation the worse his grammar and diction became. You bes' be worried 'bout what I say and ya' mama say. Because 'dem other folks ain't bit mo' got nothing to do wit' you dan a man on the moon."

"That's stupid, Daddy, just stupid. I don't see why y'all couldn't get me those shoes. I don't ever get nothing because y'all make me *sick*!" Benny was completely frustrated with his parents, to the point that he was becoming arrogantly disrespectful.

"Boy who you *think* you talkin' to?" Ronald asked.

"I'm talkin' to you that's who!" Benny was over the edge now. Sheila gave Benny another look of the day. This time it was an *are you crazy* surprised arched eyebrows look.

"You done lost yo' damn mind, boy! Do you want me to whip yo' butt?" Ronald sternly asked of his son who was inevitably headed down that road.

Then, Benny recalled the commitment he had made to Ryan regarding the P.H.O. lady. He was beginning to think that this would set the precedent for all of the kids in the neighborhood. Tonight, at this very instant, Benny thought he could set the standard for discipline. Although very nervous and somewhat hesitant, Benny decided he had nothing to lose.

"Nawh, because you not supposed to whip your kids." *There, I said it* he thought to himself. Benny breathed a sigh of relief then gasped a breath of fear. The room was silent except for the local ten o'clock news on the television. Sheila didn't look at Benny this time, instead she kept her eyes on the television as she spoke.

"What did you say?" Sheila asked in disbelief.

Benny paused for a moment wondering to himself what he had done. A now humbled and fearful Benny chose his words carefully. His only hope was to justify the comment with the validation of the P.H.O. lady.

"The P.H.O. lady said you're not supposed to whip your kids," Benny replied as humbly as he could.

Sheila was absolutely livid. No longer was the distant mother consumed with ignoring her son by watching television. The once contained woman, jumped across the bed and made a swift leap to the side of the room where Benny was standing trembling in his own regret. Sheila yelled out a few babbled words until she reached her destination.

"What... Get... You... Where... I'm gon... Give me a belt!" Sheila exclaimed. Benny regretted his attempt at breaking the mold. He was now concentrating on perfecting his whipping dance. There wasn't much space to run in a circle, so this would take a well-executed performance. Sheila delivered seven sharp, quick wacks on Benny's backside. Seven was enough for Benny, enough to make him lose his mind again. Benny, while running and crying, reached back and popped his mother square in the jaw with his fist. Sheila dropped the belt in a state of shock and amazement. Although she wasn't hurt, she was stunned by her son's defiant actions.

"Boy... You... I... If... Get...I'll knock yo' little tale out!" Sheila momentarily forgot she was disciplining her son and rekindled visions of street fights as a little girl in the neighborhood.

"Sheila, go downstairs," Ronald said, realizing that the situation was out of control.

"This little nappy headed sucka don't know who he dealin' with now! I was the second grade sucker punch champ at Horace Mann; I'll hurt his little butt!" Sheila wasn't a concerned mother anymore, now she was a schoolyard psycho.

Ronald wanted to ensure that his wife regained her composure and that his son realized the error of his ways, especially for hitting his mother.

"Baby, I know you want to feed him a knuckle sandwich, but go on downstairs and cool off."

"I give him my old rope-a-dope!" Sheila was hysterical, and a tad bit crazy.

"Sheila, downstairs," Ronald demanded. Still fuming, the unruly mother retired for the evening.

"Daddy I didn't mean to..." Benny started a quick attempt to rectify the disaster, but his father abruptly cut him off.

"Lay across the bed, Benny."

"But Daddy I..."

"Boy, if you don't get yo'self across that bed, I swear you gon' be beggin' for ya' mama to come back in here," Ronald said. "Let me tell you somethin', boy. Don't you *ever* in yo' whole live long life ever hit a girl or a woman. Do you hear me?"

"Yes," Benny answered timidly.

"And as long as you want to keep breathin', walkin' and talkin', don't you *ever* think about touchin' my wife. How you gon' sit there and have the nerve to hit somebody that carried you inside they body and soul for nine months? If that ain't the most ungrateful thing I done ever seen, I don't know what is. Do you know how many little kids would love to have a mama so they can hug and kiss 'em. Now yo' little mannish tail want to hit ya mama. You must be out yo' rabbit mind. You 'bout to get another whippin. Half of it is gon' be 'cause you hit ya mama, and the other half is gon' be 'cause you hit my wife. The next time it ain't gon' be no whippin'. I'm just gon' send yo' little tail right down there to the county jail and you can see what they do to a man's booty down there."

Benny faced the reality of being out-of-line as well as being disrespectful, so he laid still on the bed. He hated this type of whippin'; no possibility of doing the whippin' dance here, and if he dared cover his backside with his hands, that would bring about a feeling worse than the whippin' itself. Succumbing to the fate of his father's wrath, Benny accepted the six strong wacks his father administered. All Benny could think about was how much he hated the P.H.O. lady and how he hoped he would meet her one day because he owed her not one, but two whippins. Things would be different very soon, he hoped. For quite some time he'd heard that teenager's didn't get half as many whippins as grade school kids. Now that he was nearing Junior High, Benny hoped his whippin' days would soon come to an end.

1983–1984

Chapter 9
Teenager's Transitions

"Benny, I know this is your big day, and I want you to have fun now that you're in Junior High School. But, baby, I need you to be careful. Don't sit down on the toilet seats at school, and don't be the last one in the hallway between classes, okay?"

"Mama, I know all of that."

"If there's something about the school you don't know, ask Clem, okay? You know to stay away from those kids that might be smoking cigarettes, right? Make sure you bring all of your books home to study, okay?"

"Dog, mama, we're not gon' have homework on the first day."

"Well, bring a few of your books home anyway, okay?"

"Ma-maa," Benny whined, slightly frustrated with his mother's instructions.

"Do what ya mama say," Ronald added. Since Ronald was promoted to Field Foreman, he had been given Mondays off, time he treasured and devoted to developing his golf game. As soon as everyone was out of the house, Ronald was on the golf course. Benny left the house much earlier now that he was in Junior High School, so that meant earlier tee times for Ronald.

"Benny, when you get home make sure you don't turn the TV on until you finish your homework," Sheila further instructed the anxious teenager.

"Even when the ABC After-School Special is coming on?"

"I don't care if the Harlem Globetrotters are playing Fred Sanford. You do what ya mama tell you boy!" Ronald said, becoming more impatient with his son's recent questioning of authority.

Benny discontinued his line of questioning and listened carefully to his parent's instructions. If he was ever going to get out of the house, obliging his parents was his only way he would make it.

"Now sweety, don't be nervous and remember to do your best and always pay close attention to what your teachers are saying. You'll do just find. And remember, C's are unacceptable."

"Okay, mama," Benny replied politely.

"Don't you be goin' down there fightin' either," Ronald said. Benny was disturbed by the fact that his father would insinuate his participation in violence. For the most part he had a clean record. Amongst his friends in the neighborhood, he was getting in much less trouble than the others. His grades were typically better than those of his friends, and his teachers always told Benny's parents of his enormous potential. In Benny's own estimation, there should have been no cause for his father to make the unwarranted comment.

"Okay. Can I go now before I miss the bus?"

"Ooh baby, I'm sorry. We're just talking like school is going to wait on us. Yeah, go on down the street to the bus stop and have a good day, Benny," Sheila said as her son took his first step towards his first day of Junior High School.

Benny marched out the door and Sheila watched his new Jordache jeans trot farther towards the bus top. With every stride, she saw his white socks peek out between the home-made hemmed jeans and his new brown shoes. Benny and his friends called them boat shoes. Although his light green shirt was too big, he insisted on wearing it. It was the only J C Penney fox shirt of its kind in the store. All of the teenagers were wearing the short sleeved collared shirts with some type of emblem on the breast. Those that were fortunate enough, had Polo or Alligators shirts also known as IZOD. The next logo level, which was barely acceptable amongst the junior high social standards of teenagers, was a fox. Benny barely made the cut. He considered himself very lucky when his mother found the pair of irregular Jordache jeans on the clearance rack.

"Ronald, your son is starting his first day of Junior High," Sheila commented to her husband as he gathered his golf equipment. "Doesn't seem like it was too long ago that he was going to kindergarten? Soon he'll be starting High School and then he'll be off to college."

"That boy needs to get his act together before he can even think about going to college."

"What do you mean? He's not doing anything that's going to hurt his chances."

"All I know is that he needs to get his act together."

"What act, Ronald? What's he doing? I mean, specifically."

"For one thing, the boy too damn disrespectful. You sittin' there tellin' him what he need to do at school and how he need to get his lesson and he steady want to talk back to you."

"I didn't feel that way at all, Ronald. He's just anxious because it's his first day in Junior High."

"So now you gon' take his side and it's okay for the boy to be disrespectful, huh? He ain't too old to get no whippin'. That's what you need to be tellin' him."

"Oh yeah, it's time for you to go play golf, because I see you're being very irrational and you must be forgetting I am not a teenager and you don't need to tell me what I should be telling my son."

"What's wrong wit' *you*? I'm just tryin' to talk to you and now you gettin' all mad. Is everybody is this house gettin' crazy. What y'all been eatin'?"

"Yeah, everybody in this house is crazy. Everybody except for Benny and me so, that leaves you. We're not eating anything that's making us crazy."

"You mean we not eatin' nothin' at all. I can't remember the last time it was somethin' on the stove for dinner when I got home from work."

"What did you say, Ronald?"

"I said you ain't been cookin' like you used to. Seem like you always gone off to some art class or something."

"Well, maybe you could cook sometime. Half the time you come home so stuffed with hot dogs from the golf course, you don't want to eat. I don't know what's wrong with me going to my art decorating class. I never say anything when you're at the golf driving range or drinking beer with your golf buddies, now do I?"

"Look, I ain't got time for this; I'm late as it is. We'll talk about this at dinner—I hope."

"Don't test me, Ronald Dempkins, and I hope you come home with a better attitude."

Sheila and Ronald had been arguing over such trivial matters lately. Just as they were basking in the glow of Benny starting junior high and it turned into an argument, other normal conversations sprouted into painful thorned roses of confrontation. Now more than ever, Ronald seemed to come down extremely hard on Benny for behavior Sheila viewed as normal teenage frolicking. Although Sheila never suspected something was changing in her husband's life nor her marriage, she was not pleased with this foreign element that seemed to be plaguing her household.

Upon Benny's arrival at his new school, he was shocked by the overwhelming size of the structure. Of course, he had the same intimidating feeling when he began the third grade and all of the sixth graders seemed like gigantic monsters to him. Now once again, Benny was at the bottom of the cool and hip totem pole. The new junior high schooler felt like a mushroom as the other students trotted through the breezeways of school. Benny attempted to not get stepped on by the oncoming and merging traffic. Although the earth had just introduced a new morning, the outside temperatures were already predicting a boiling summer day. The heat was, however, motivation for the students to expeditiously arrive at their next class as opposed to standing in the breezeway and socializing, only to find themselves tardy and at the mercy of unforgiving teachers. Fresh paint, as toxic as it may have been, wafted through the school. It was obvious the maintenance personnel had only recently completed the finishing touches for the new school year. Beige lockers lined the green breezeways this year. Every new school year prompted a new attitude and a new color scheme to match. It was the principal's method of introducing the students to a fresh way of thinking. Principal Wise believed if the students felt as though they were attending a new school, then their attitude towards learning would be new.

To the seventh graders, like Benny and some of his friends, the school couldn't have been newer. Benny watched as the older students slapped hands and laughed with each other during their brief reunions. Girls admired each other's Calvin Klein jeans and the young boys judged whose hair was the waviest. A group of boys standing near their lockers were furiously brushing their hair as if the act would magically produce a few more waves. Students, who were still wrapped up in the ever-changing whirlwind of teenage fads, were comparing their Jheri Curls. It was the same typical curl conversation; who's was the longest, the curliest, the wettest, and who's looked like a little perm instead of a curl.

Benny noticed a few familiar faces from the sixth grade, but he was not familiar with their mannerisms. He saw Stephen, his co-conspirator in the *girl with the glue* incident, and some other boys fondling girls as they attempted to walk by the cabal of boys. After the girls passed by the teenage vultures, the boys resumed their positions and placed their hands over their immature crotches as though someone threatened to steal them if they weren't covered up. Stephen noticed Benny and motioned him with the universal *what's up* nod as if to suggest that Benny join the group in their mischief. The activity of the boys was strange to Benny and the glue episode still had a reserved space in his mind. The bell rang providing Benny with a desperately needed escape route. Not sure of his new fellow classmates, Benny hoped that Stephen wouldn't be walking through the door of his new homeroom. There were empty seats all around Benny and he took one of them located in the middle of the class. Stephen was sure to come and sit next to Benny, which would have made for a long and uncomfortable semester. The teacher of the class was about to close the door when she began talking to a student walking down the breezeway.

"Are you in first period Social Studies, young man?" she asked. "Well you'd better hurry up and get in one of these seats before the tardy bell rings or you'll be in early morning detention hall."

Benny knew he was doomed. He thought for sure the teacher was talking to Stephen and as soon as he saw Benny, Stephen was certain to come and plop down right next to him. Thoughts of phone calls to Sheila and punishments from his father formed clear pictures in Benny's cautious mind. Just as Benny was beginning to think about how he could quickly get up and move to a more populated area in the class, a voice spoke to him accompanied by a smack on the back of his head.

"Thought you could hide from me, huh dude?" Ryan said to his neighbor placing his books on the desk next to his neighborhood comrade. Benny had never been so happy in all his life to see Ryan. Although the boy had been behaving rather strange lately, Benny preferred Ryan to the trouble-tempting Stephen any day.

"Good morning class, my name is Mrs. Lasker, and I'd like to welcome each and everyone of you to Johnson Junior High School and to Social Studies homeroom," the energetic and seemingly friendly teacher announced. Mrs. Lasker was a pale skinned rosy cheeked woman. She maneuvered through the chairs as she attempted to make contact with each student. After her third baby, Mrs. Lasker had found it very difficult to keep up with the strict exercise regimen for shedding her baby weight. The woman's medium length blond hair swirled around her head as soon as she turned corners in the classroom making sharp cuts at the ends of the rows of desks. Mrs. Lasker was just tall enough to peer over the shoulders of the five rows of students during any given test period while she sat at her desk. Only a few of the sprouting boys in the school were tall enough to confront her eye to eye.

As the new junior high school students settled in to what they thought was apparently an easy push over, Mrs. Lasker quickly changed her tone and her approach.

"Now let's get this out of the way right now, so there will be no misunderstanding. I do not tolerate any funny business. When I get home, there are three children waiting for me whom I love very dearly. If they get out of line, I have no trouble solving the problem on their little behinds. Now, I'm sure I will grow to love each and every one of you as if you were my own. Therefore, I will have no trouble solving your problems like you were one of my own children at home. The only difference is that you have bigger problems and bigger behinds, so it may take a little longer, and a bigger paddle. Are there any questions?" Mrs. Lasker said, this time using her sweet innocent demeanor—at least that was the image her voice portrayed. The students were completely bewildered by the two distinct personalities they had just witnessed. Only one student dared to even murmur a sound. From the middle of the room near Benny, there was a rebellious laugh under one of the student's breath.

"Hmph," Ryan remarked.

"Is there a problem, uh...Ryan," Mrs. Lasker said, as she read the boy's name from his registration card.

"I ain't got no problem, but you gon' have a problem if you try that mess on me," Ryan replied boldly.

"Excuse me, young man?"

"Ain't no excuse for you, lady."

The room filled with quiet disbelief. Only this time, Benny was thankful that he was far removed from the simmering trouble soon to erupt into boiling pot of problems. Mrs. Lasker, very familiar with the desk arrangements, dashed through the students en route to the soon to be ex-homeroom student. Upon her arrival at the disrespectful youth, she quickly grabbed his right arm. She assumed that the boy was right handed and if his right hand was grasped, then he wouldn't be able to try anything foolishly violent. Whisking the boy to the front of classroom, she pulled Ryan over to the door and pressed the intercom for the office.

"*Office*," a voice called out after a few seconds.

"Yes, this is Mrs. Lasker in room 172. I'm sending up a student, who doesn't wish to be in my homeroom any longer. His name is Ryan something. He didn't wait long enough for me to call the roll before he chose to become disruptive. He's leaving now. Do with him as you will." Mrs. Lasker politely ended her conversation, opened the door, forced the boy out into the breezeway, and swiftly slammed the door behind him. She turned to the rest of class without making eye contact. Mrs. Lasker walked over to her desk and adjusted a few papers as if nothing had happened. Pulling out a pencil and a small green book, she spoke. "Brandon Alexander?"

A student near the front of the classroom began rambling uncontrollably at the sound of his name. "I didn't do anything Mrs. Lasker. I don't even know that boy. Why am I getting in trouble? I didn't mean to throw that piece of paper out of the window on the bus. I promise I'll go and pick it up."

"Calm down, sweetie. I'm just calling the role. All you have to do is say here or present. You don't have to confess all of your sins to me," Mrs. Lasker replied, smiling at the energetic boy. She realized that the class had received her message loud and clear.

Benny was stunned and at the same time amazed at the opening action of this triple feature called Johnson Junior High.

Chapter 10
Deeply Devoted

Sunday mornings brought about the same routine for Ronald and William. They left their wives bright and early so that they could arrive at the golf course and make the early tee time. The first people to tee off always got the early bird special—buy one get one free. The two comrades would have finished half of their round before the women had themselves and their sons ready for church. Margie hardly ever bothered to ask her husband to accompany them to church after a huge argument they'd once had at a family dinner.

William was a firm believer in his philosophy of what you cannot see does not exist; therefore, he didn't feel the need to sit up in a church on Sunday singing and praying. During their conversation, Margie told her husband that she couldn't see his love so maybe that did not exist. William exploded in the middle of dinner and in the presence of Margie's entire family. He told her that if she couldn't see his love, then she could take her blind behind to someone who could show it to her because he could think of plenty of women that had 20/20 vision for him. The conversation summarily ended, along with any future possibilities of William attending the Sunday services.

Sheila, on the other hand, made a point of asking Ronald if he wanted to attend church as part of her Saturday night ritual. Just before the lights went out and the fondling did or did not occur, Sheila turned to her husband and asked, *Baby, are you going to church with us in the morning?* The reply was always the same, *Not tomorrow, me and William got a early tee time.* In the winter, when the golf course was consumed by cold and covered in a blanket of frost or perhaps snow, the reply was *Nawh baby, William coming over to watch the game today.*

This Sunday, William decided to try a new golf course for a little challenge. Ordinarily they made the drive over to the Douglass golf course where most of the black golfers played. Ronald was uneasy about the course as soon as he walked into the pro shop to check in for their tee time. There were stares and whispers as Ronald entered to door. He immediately wanted to turn around and leave, but then he thought to himself how great it would be to score close to the course record and brag about the great feat afterwards in the club house. He overcame the uncomfortable greeting they'd received and decided to play. Ronald did notice that one party in the club house was not whispering, but they were staring rather oddly. Sitting in the corner, at a small table, two rather alluring women were gawking. Both women were wearing their blond hair in conservative, athletic looking, long ponytails. Obviously, they were serious golfers and not just on the course to frolic around and tell their bridge partners about the wonderful time they had playing terrible.

"Y'all hit 'em good today, gentlemen," the taller of the two blond praying mantises said as Ronald and William walked by.

"Thank you, ladies. We plan on doing just that," William said as he smiled back at the seemingly forward woman. William, however did not receive the same warm smile back in return. He was being ignored because the woman's eyes and thoughts were adhered to Ronald.

"What time y'all teein' off, fellas?" the more provocative woman inquired. She had a southern drawl that filled the quiet corner.

"8:05," Ronald responded, trying not to be rude by ignoring the lady.

"Well, what a coincidence, Cheri and I are teein' off at 8:13. Are you boys gonna hold us up or are you gonna let us play through?"

William, who was still all teeth answered, "Well etiquette says that faster players should be allowed to play through, so if you catch us, we'll gladly let you play through unless you want to play with us."

Ronald made a quick turn in the direction of his playing partner to show disapproval of William's statement. He wasn't alone, the more silent of the two ladies quickly raised her head from the scorecard she was preparing and hit William with a *you must be crazy* glance.

"After all," William continued, "this is a gentlemen's game." The peering lady finally looked away from Ronald and acknowledged William's presence.

"Sir, in case you haven't noticed, we are not gentlemen by any means," she replied, standing erect and displaying her full size chest, which might interfere with her golf swing. "But we'll see what happens when we're near the ninth hole."

"All right then, you all have a good day," William added trying to make one last effort at innocent flirtation.

"Oh, we will, I'm sure. By the way, my name is Sally Reynolds, and this is my sister Cheri," she said extending her hand to William. She finally realized that William was the warmer of the two.

"It's a pleasure to meet you, Sally. I'm William and this is my good friend, Ronald."

Ronald acknowledged the ladies existence with an almost courteous nod and left Sally's extended hand searching for a reception that never occurred.

"I guess the gentleman aspect of the game doesn't start until after you've teed off," Sally remarked sarcastically.

"Don't worry about him," William said. "He's an intense player and right now he's concentrating on how he's gon' get back the money that I'll be taking from him."

"Well, good luck to the both of you, and we'll see ya at the ninth hole turn," Sally replied.

"Okay, nice meeting you both," William said as he followed his fleeing golf partner out to the first tee box.

"Why did you want to come all the way out to Country Lane Golf Course to play, William? You know I like to play the Douglas Golf Course," Ronald said.

"See that's your problem Ronald. You don't ever want to change. You need new challenges and new scenery every now and then. You shoot par on the first hole every time for three years. It's time for you to try something new for a change. Don't be so stubborn," William said, challenging his friend.

"What did you say?"

"I said don't be so stubborn."

"Why you say that? Have you been talkin' to Sheila?"

"Nawh, why would I be talking to Sheila. I got a hard enough time talkin' to my own wife," William answered. Ronald stood with his golf club in his hand mulling over the familiar conversation taking place. Only this time it was not the usual nagging that Ronald got from his wife. This nagging was coming from his friend who had no reason to lie.

"Yeah, I know what you mean man. It seems like I can't do nothing right no more. Every time I even think about doing something, Sheila comes down on me for something. I don't know how much more I can take, Will."

"Are you sure she's coming down on you or are y'all just constantly at each other's throat lately?"

"Nawh man, she's the one that's always gettin' on my case."

"So if I ask her, is she gon' say the same thing?"

"Nope. Because the first thing she gon' say is *Ronald, why you running out telling people our business*?"

"Now that's funny because, I don't ever remember Sheila actin' like that," William said in a suspicious and probing tone.

"Well hell, maybe she wouldn't say it like that but she would say somethin'."

"Umm huh. Maybe she wouldn't say it like that, you say? Are you sure she would say it at all? You can be set in yo' ways, man.

"Go on somewhere, ain't nobody set in they ways," Ronald denied.

"Oh really?"

"Yeah really. Now come on. Let's play."

"Okay." William paused. "I'm gon' tee off first today."

"Like hell you are. You'll tee off first if you ever win. I'm teeing off first like I always do.

"What's the big deal? It's not like you ain't gon' get to hit. It's just a five second wait."

"It's a five second wait that you'll have because I'm first. I won last Sunday, so I'm teeing off first."

"What if I walk up to the tee and just hit?"

"You might *get* hit if you do."

"So you gon' hit me over the first tee shot, huh?"

"That's my box."

"But you ain't stubborn, are you?"

"What?"

"You heard me. You about to beat me over the head with a three-wood because I want to tee off first, but you saying you not stubborn."

"That ain't got bit mo' to do with me bein' stubborn than the man on the moon!" Ronald replied with one of his famous lines.

"You tell me how can your own wife say you stubborn and then your golf partner say the same thing."

"Why you all of a sudden worried about me and my wife? You need to be taking care of your own house!" Ronald replied with a damaging deliverance of words.

"You know what?" William began. "I'm gon' pretend like I didn't even hear that. I know you good enough to know that when you get mad, you gon' start talkin' crazy," William said, pulling a new golf ball out of his pocket and pulling a white tee from behind his ear. He knew that his actions would keep Ronald quiet. If there was one thing Ronald respected, it was the rules and etiquette of the golf course. William stood sternly over the ball concentrating on his its planned flight as well as punishing his friend for the insensitive comment he made. When he was ready, William brought his club back, paused at the very top of his swing, and delivered a crushing blow that sent the white dimpled object soaring down the middle of the fairway farther than either of the two men had ever hit a golf ball before. William held a picture perfect follow through, careful not to let the amazement of his own shot become obvious to the waiting Ronald. Ronald, however, was not concealing his wonderment for the shot. The once arrogant man stood behind the posing William with what seemed like a fifty pound jaw-bone hanging open and his mouth just on the verge of salivating.

"Damn, Will," Ronald said. "Remind me never to say anything about yo' wife before we tee off." Once again the two chums were a laughing duo. Ronald hit his ball thirty yards shorter than William and the golf gurus began their traditional Sunday morning round.

"Are we playing for, the usual dollar and fifty cents?"

"I don't know, Ronald, I think we might try something a little different today. Sort of hungry, so I figure I'd let you buy me a hot dog. Let's play for a hot dog today," William replied.

"I guess you countin' on beatin' me today huh, William?"

"What you talkin' about? I beat you every Sunday."

"Oh is that a fact?"

"Now, there has been the occasional time that I felt sorry for you and let you beat me," William said, driving his sword of sarcasm deeper into Ronald's delicate ego.

"I'll tell you one thing. I'm gon' take this scorecard and mail it to Margie. Seem like the only way I can keep you honest, is to make sure I got yo' wife involved in something. You know good and well, I'm always a good five strokes better than you are."

"Well, besides his own pride, all a man got is his dreams, so at least let me have my little dreams about beatin' you," William replied as the two buddies broke out into laughter on the first tee box of the golf course.

William and Ronald were playing at about the same level. When the two buddies reached the seventh hole, they were tied with 30 strokes each. The men were playing with so much concentration and intensity that neither of them noticed the two gawking ladies behind them.

Cheri and Sally stood waiting behind Ronald and William on every hole, as though the men were slowly dying prey and the women were buzzards waiting patiently for a feast of some sort. After Ronald made par on the eighth hole, the beer cart came around to refresh the people playing golf. Of course, the beer and drinks from the cart cost a small fortune not to mention the extra tip, which was traditional on the golf course. Unknowingly, William and Ronald had the misfortune of being approached by Chip.

Chip was new at the golf course and had been led, to believe that he was being paid on commission. Chip was determined to be, in his mind, the top concession salesmen—therefore he wasn't taking no for answer.

"Hello gentleman. Could I interest you in a beverage or a snack?"

"No thank you young man we're just fine", William responded as he walked away from the cart and towards his ball. Ronald was sitting in the cart marking his score and trying his best to stay focused on the game. Chip, the hoodwinked salesman, had other intentions.

"Sir, what about you? How about a refreshing RC Cola?"

"No thank you son."

"Oh I got it, trying to watch the weight huh? I've got just the thing, a Tab. Just one calorie you know?"

"Son, I'm not thirsty and I'll get some water when I am, okay," Ronald replied a bit irritated now.

"Well why didn't you just say so. You're in the mood for a snack? Here's a nice Fig Newton."

"Young man, I got to admire yo' determination but you startin' to get on my damn nerves."

"Oh I know just the thing," Chip was oblivious to Ronald's comments as well as his festering anger. "A big jumbo hot dog with all of the fixins." The ambitious young worker began piling ketchup, onions, relish, and mustard on to a steamed hot dog that he'd pulled out the hot box of his cart. As Chip made his move to close the sale and present Ronald with his masterpiece frankfurter, Ronald got out of the golf cart in order to escape the boy's pestering. Without looking, the two crossed paths and Chip accidentally smashed the monstrosity of a meal onto Ronald's chest and regretfully watched it slide down his new shirt. Ronald's first inclination was to snatch the young man and shake him until he looked like the disaster on his shirt, but he just wanted this antsy person out of his sight.

"Oh sir, I'm so terribly sorry. Please let me clean that off for you," Chip said, taking a napkin and spitting into it for wetness.

Ronald blocked his own upper body, denying Chip access to it.

"Young man, if you don't get as far away from me as this golf course will let you, I don't know how I'm gon' hurt you, but I will hurt you. Please don't let me hurt you, okay boy?"

Chip was astonished by the man's sudden change in attitude, nevertheless he proceeded to leave. Before he left, however, Chip felt compelled to leave his most challenging customer with something useful.

"Sir, just for your information, there's a bathroom about
fifteen yards to your left down that paved path." Ronald waved to acknowledge the statement. "Sir, I'm really very sorry!" Chip shouted from a distance.

Ronald didn't acknowledge him this time. Instead, he muffled his way to the bathroom that Chip mentioned so he could get cleaned up, get back on the course, and get his head back in his game.

The bathroom wasn't a bathroom at all. It was more of a remote sitting room in a fancy restaurant similar to the one Sheila was always begging Ronald to take her to. A fresh pine scent filled the entrance of the spotless area. The mirrors were cleaned, the urinals could easily have been mistaken for drinking fountains. Marble tile covered every squared inch of the floor in a color to match the nicely decorated walls. Ronald, still in awe, glided back towards the rear of the restroom where a part of the area was sectioned off, obviously for more personal activities. After removing his shirt in preparation to scrub out the stains, he heard the entrance of someone else into the immaculate room. Thinking that it must have been William, he yelled out to him about the unbelievable rest room.

"Hey man, can you believe this place? I ain't never in my life seen no john this clean before, have you? This right here by itself is worth the price of the green fees. Hell, the Queen of England could cop a squat in here and not realize she wasn't on her Royal Throne. Man, if Sheila saw this she'd want to redecorate all our bathrooms. Shoot she'd probably want to redo the whole house!" Still diligently scrubbing at the impossible stain, Ronald didn't notice that his buddy never commented on the restroom nor had he commented on any of Ronald's other remarks. Ronald assumed that William was upset about not making par on the last hole and was concerned about getting humiliated on the back nine. Ronald kept scrubbing, until he felt what he couldn't believe was William's hand rubbing his backside. Ronald was appalled, shocked, afraid, and then mad as hell. *What could William have possibly been doing? All of this time and he didn't know that his faithful golfing buddy, not to mention brother-in-law, was a tooty fruity.* He decided that he was going to kick all of the fruit right out of William's behind and begin with an elbow to the jaw followed by a crushing uppercut. Ronald turned to begin the brutal punishment to his soon to be former golf buddy. As he clenched his fist fully intending to deliver a weltering blow, an unexpected sight greeted Ronald. Before him stood a pale display of warm flesh a few breaths away from drooling over Ronald's half-exposed body. It was the woman from the pro shop that had been so openly flirting with the two men earlier. She was standing before him with her blouse unbuttoned. The exposed woman was smiling an evil, but desirable, crooked grin the Mona Lisa would have admired. The woman moved closer to Ronald and in his state of confusion and slight fear, he stood paralyzed, staring at whatever part of her body his eyes happened to be focused on—her breasts. Taking advantage of Ronald's temporary lapse of movement, she planted herself against his exposed torso and grabbed his crotch. An awkward and wrong feeling immediately jolted Ronald back into reality, like a flash of lighting or a bloodstream filled with high-octane adrenaline. His heart was racing and his brain was crashing into a brick wall. The feeling of his privates being handled by a strange woman startled him. Ronald jumped back and pulled away. She followed him.

"What the hell do you think you doin' lady?" Ronald asked, uncertain if he was angry, offended, or just pleasantly surprised.

"Why Ronald, you're a grown man. I shouldn't have to answer that question, unless of course you're intending on playing a game of Mama's little baby."

"Ma'am I don't think you know this or not, but we in a public bathroom," he said, still unsure of his current emotions.

"Don't be silly, there aren't any more groups in front or behind us for at least twenty minutes. No one's coming in here, sweetie."

Ronald could now feel his fear winning the internal emotional race between his brain and his loins. "Lady, I don't know about you, but I ain't crazy and I know what's gon' happen if somebody walks in here and sees us out here in the open."

Moving even closer to her intended prey, she grabbed his butt, which seemingly initiated an advance from Ronald.

"Well, that's more like it, we can sneak into one of these stalls in the back, and I promise to be quiet," the seductive solicitor commented.

Now Ronald was feeling something take the lead in his extemporaneous mental marathon.

"Look lady. I know what's gon' happen here," he began. "If you don't get your way, you liable to start rumors about me. Or worse, you might run out of here with yo' shirt open. And if you do run out of here, I'm thinking you gon' run out of here yellin' what I did or didn't do to you. Either way, I figure I can't win. Is that right?"

"Sugar, are you gon' keep talkin' or are we gonna go into this back stall and screw each other's brains out."

"What other choice do I have?" Ronald said, feeling trapped in an inevitable situation. The woman's bare breasts was not helping matters one single bit.

"Honey, life is about choices and you've got plenty of them right now. But the more you keep talkin', the more you lose."

"What choices do I have?"

"Oh let's see, there's on top, on bottom, from behind, you do me and I'll do you...." Ronald swallowed whatever moisture he found his throat. There was mostly a dry feeling of doom and he swallowed that too. "Come on, honey, we're running out of time now," the woman urged, as she placed Ronald's hand on her breast and grabbed his other hand to lead him to her lair of seduction. All of a sudden, the half-naked woman didn't look like a woman at all. She now took on the appearance of a snake attempting to entwine Ronald in a weave of deception and dishonesty, all bundled in a scrumptious forbidden fruit. The woman, sure she had convinced her object of desire to agree to her request, halted her stride when Ronald stopped in his tracks and left the woman pulling on a seemingly immovable object.

"What's wrong honey? You nervous? This is gonna be over before you know it."

"No, I ain't nervous at all... I want to make my choice now.

"That's more like it. What's it gon' be? But make it quick."

"I choose to keep it together and keep it out of the trash."

"I'm not sure what that is, but it sure sounds kinky."

"I'm talkin' about my family."

"What?"

"I'm talkin' about my family. I'm talkin' about my life."

"Oh hell. Feelin' guilty about the little woman?"

"Let me tell you one damn thing. I don't really care if you run yo' little pale butt outta here yellin' rape, because I'd rather sleep wit' my peace of mind in a jail cell for fifteen years than sleep with my wife in dishonesty and bad trust for the rest of my life. You can't make me do it. You can't make me look at my boy in the face and teach him about respecting women like some damn hypocrite. My woman might not be the best woman in the world, but she's the best woman in my house, and that's where I gotta go back to every day, my house. Lady, when my house ain't in order, there ain't no way I can go out in the world everyday and try to live a righteous life. I ain't gon' let you make me dirty up my house. I just ain't gon' do it. So you go ahead and do what you got to do. Go ahead on and start yellin' because I really don't give a damn. Go ahead on you witch!"

"You stupid son-of-a-bitch. You mean you'd rather be falsely accused than get some of this premium piece of ass."

"I mean you ain't comin' in my house, that's what I mean."

"You dumb bastard; no wonder y'all ain't gonna never get nowhere because you can't take advantage of the situation at hand. I can ruin your little worthless life right now by walkin' out that door and just tellin' one person what you did to me. Do you realize that?"

"Yeah, I figured you'd do somethin' like that. Y'all been doing it for years."

"Why you presumptions ungrateful bastard. I ought to crush you right now, you do not scoff me like I'm some ten dollar whore! I am Sally Reynolds and I am never denied what I want. You will give me what I want or you will pay!" Now the pale body was raspberry red as though she were being instantly painted by an angry artist. Ronald reached into his pocket, pulled out three golf tees, a ball marker, and the two dollars he carried with him just in case William got lucky and won the match that day.

"Well lady, I got a few dollars, some tees, and this marker. I can send you a check in the mail but I can't promise you it ain't gon' bounce. I ain't got ten dollars on me now though. Since I didn't use yo' services, this ought to be a bargain."

"Why you sarcastic little... how dare you talk to... you've got the audacity to stand before me and ...." The invisible artist dipped the brush into a brighter shade of red and laid on another coat. "I always get what I want, do you understand me?"

"Yes ma'am. I understand and I think you oughta wait for the next man with no shirt to come into the bathroom, if you want to screw a man in the toilet. I'm about to do like Wal-Mart give you a good buy. I'm splittin'."

Ronald exited the facility and was sure that his life, as he knew it, was about to end. Walking back out to the course, he expected to hear the violent screams and outburst of false accusations, quickly followed by the rush of security guards swooping him back to the clubhouse where he would wait for the police. William was standing at the water fountain seemingly contemplating how he could get back into the game. Ronald noticed Cheri, the other woman, driving her golf cart down the cart path repeatedly looking at her watch as though she were keeping track of a planned routine.

"Man, you didn't get that stain out? That shirt is soaking wet. You can't wear that. I got my windbreaker in my bag if you want it," William said.

"I need to go and call Sheila right quick."

"For what? They still in church."

Ronald was completely oblivious to his wife's activities for the day, and oblivious to everything after the incident in the bathroom, he was still waiting to feel the repercussions.

"Let's skip this hole and start on the eleventh," Ronald requested of his buddy.

"Why? We not gon' get a hot dog at the club house? Man, what's wrong with you today? You act like ..."

"Take the damn cart to the eleventh hole or take me home, dammit! I'm not gon' ask you no more, you here me!" Ronald exploded at his unsuspecting friend.

William was frightened by his partner's attitude, but rather than make anymore judgments, he obediently drove the cart to the eleventh hole. Again, Ronald noticed the other half of the troublesome twosome off in a distance. Cheri looked at her watch one more time, nodded her head toward the watch, and drove the cart at full speed toward the path leading to the restroom where he saw a now fully clothed, but red-faced Sally get into the golf cart. Ronald sat waiting for his demise.

"Wow, you're usually not dressed by now. It must have been a real quickie this time," Cheri said to the embarrassed woman getting into the golf cart.

"What did you say?"

"I said it must have been a *very* quickie."

"What would you know about a quickie. You haven't been with a man since they were giving them away in Africa."

"Now that's unusual," Cheri said sarcastically. "You're not usually in such a bitter mood after your little ninth hole workout. Did he disappoint?"

"Oh, just shut up and drive the damn cart, will you?" the denied temptress exclaimed. Cheri sat next to her sister consumed in confusion. Usually when her sister returned from her routine ninth hole rendezvous with men in the restroom, she was refreshed, pleasant, and satisfied. Today she was irritable, evil, and refused. "Why I don't believe it," she said. Cheri suddenly realized what must have happened. "Say it isn't so. You mean to tell me that the praying mantis missed out on a feast. The black widow wasn't able to strike. This is unbelievable, Sally. That man turned you down didn't he?"

"Are you going to drive the cart or are you going to sit there like a cackling hen going on about some obviously impotent or homosexual Negro? I never heard of such of thing. The nerve of that beast tying to lie about being faithful to his wife and family. What a blatant lie."

"Yes, imagine that, a man being honest to his wife. How ludicrously absurd," Cheri said, pouring on the cynicism. She did as her sister requested and drove the cart while smiling with satisfaction to herself and for Ronald's family whom she'd never met but for whom she was very happy.

Chapter 11
Conviction

"Come on, Benny, we'll be over to the store and back before the first bells rings. Nobody'll ever know we gone," Ryan said.

"I don't think we're supposed to be going over there," Benny answered. "I heard a boy was going over there last year and the principal met him at the door on his way back. They said the principal took all the stuff he bought from the store, sent him home for three days, and he couldn't get none of his money back. They said he bought thirty three dollars worth of stuff and he couldn't get none of it back."

"Did the principal give him his stuff back when he came back from suspension?" Ryan asked.

"I 'on't think so," Benny replied.

"Well, ain't nobody gon' take my stuff."

"You don't know that."

"Yes I do, because I'll put somethin' on somebody if they try to take stuff I bought with my money."

"Somethin' like what?"

"Like I'll drop this atomic elbow on him like Hacksaw Jim Dugan."

"Man, you crazy," Benny told his neighbor and constant disruption in class. Although Benny was transitioning into junior high school well, like many other teenagers, he was faced with distractions. Ryan was his number two distraction, teenage girls was his first.

For quite some time Ryan had been trying to hire Benny as an accomplice to his morning journey over to the grocery store before school began. All of the students knew that once they were on school property, the rules prohibited them from leaving the grounds until school was dismissed. Most of the students thought it was such a waste to have a store so close and not be allowed to venture over during lunch or before school. The staff's main concern was children being injured in the store's parking lot or possibly being abducted during their journey to and from the store. Of course, there were a few select students that decided to make a career out of the forbidden act labeled, store running. Whether it was permitted or not. They could be found trotting back across the football field to the school before the tardy bell rang.

During lunch, the store runners were quite obvious because their lunches were always different from the other students. Some of the runners had jumbo hamburgers, french fries, and large bottles of pop. Then there were the ever-enviable desserts—Suzy Q's and Honey Buns. Some days, the runners were even bold enough to buy enough food to sell to the students. Often times, students lined up just to get a small piece of one of the scrumptious desserts.

Aside from store running, another extremely popular event was the occasional pencil-popping tournament. The runners bought packs of jumbo size pencils that the school bookstore did not sell. Entrants from all grades scampered to the back of the building during lunch to have their turn. The object of the game was to break someone else's pencil with your own pencil.

Talent and acquired skill was required of the bold participators. Girls gathered around to see the different styles of pencil popping that the boys had perfected. There was the pull back and jump method where the popper pulled his pencil back near the top of the eraser with one hand and created as much leverage as possible with the other hand near the bottom of the pencil. When a slight crack off the wooden tournament tool was heard, a boy would jump in the air and land just as he released the pencil delivering a swift pop onto his opponent's pencil.

Others had an eye-high-good-bye technique where they requested their opponent hold the pencil up high enough so that a pop could be made horizontally to the pencil instead of vertically. The participants were not yet scientifically astute enough to realize that no technique was better than another. Realistically, a good pencil popping round never lasted more than three pops, and amongst most veteran poppers, the first pop usually won the round. With a long line of anxious participants, a crowd of spectators, and a box full of pencils, the juvenile organizers hosted quite a spectacular event. More than any trophy or prize could ever symbolize, the winner simply won the title and bragging rights as the pencil popping champion of the school.

All the runners and pencil poppers ever wanted, and received instantly, was notoriety and popularity. And that was all Ryan sought more than anything else, to be wanted and appreciated. He didn't feel either of those at home. His father constantly yelled at him and beat him, while his mother watched, doing nothing. Occasionally, she tried to intervene, which typically got *her* yelled at as well.

The lonely boy didn't want to walk this path alone. Ryan needed a partner, and Benny was slowly becoming popular because of his manners and his knack for schoolwork. A few girls noticed how good his test scores were and aside from good grades, he was very respectful and courteous to everyone he met. Benny, also, knew when he was crossing the fine line between being a nice person and becoming a teacher's pet. When Benny felt himself venturing out into the dark and lonely land of teacher's petdom, he'd commit some small act for which he'd get reprimanded as well as reminded by a teacher that they were very surprised at his actions. Back on the dark side of peer pressure safe and sound, Benny would think to himself.

Ryan wanted the potential filled Benny to partner with him on his periodic expeditions. Someone to validate his actions in the eyes of the other students. Someone to take the fall with him in case anything ever went wrong.

"So what you gon' do Benny?" Ryan asked.

"Man, I don't know about all of that. What you want to be a store runner for anyway?"

"Why not? All of the girls like the runners, and they be gettin' those good lunches whenever they want one."

"And sometimes they be gettin' caught," the cautious Benny replied.

"You always worried about gettin' caught. You scardy or somethin'?"

"I 'on't care what you say. My mama already told me if I go to jail, don't call her to come and get me out."

"You crazy. They don't be locking juvees up. All they gon' do is call yo' mama for you, and since you ain't eighteen, she got to come and pick you up because she responsible for you."

"How you know all that? You been to jail before?"

"Nawh, I heard some boys talkin' about it. They said it don't even be hard doin' no time in juvee. You just gotta watch yo'self and don't let nobody try to punk you."

"I ain't even got to worry about that, because I ain't goin'," Benny said with an overwhelming resilience. "My Granny Osee's peach cobbler is too good for me to miss out on, and I know they don't have that in jail."

"Whatever. So we gon' run over there or not? Come on, let's go!" Just as Ryan submitted his final plea to his uncertain neighbor, the bell rang and all inappropriate activity was canceled for the day. "See there!" the disappointed Ryan exclaimed. "Now it's too late. Man, you talk too much. Next time we just need to run on over there and hurry up and get right back. We ain't gon' mess around with all this talkin' next time, alright?"

"You got that right. We won't have to talk about it because I ain't goin', not tomorrow, not ever, so don't ask me again."

"You weak," Ryan said adding insult to Benny's rufusal. "You just a little weak old punk."

Benny, surprised by Ryan's sudden disgust, realized he couldn't stand idly by and be insulted by the boy, even though they were neighbors.

"I got yo' punk, Nigga."

"What you call me, you little weak punk?"

"You heard me, Nigga," Benny replied knowing full well that he couldn't back down from his instant enemy. He walked towards Ryan as his neighbor returned the gesture. The boys were now in a face off, and both were on the verge of being late for class.

"I don't know who you think you're talking to, but I'll kick yo' ass right here, boy," Ryan said, offering the first threat.

"I ain't scared of you," Benny said, attempting to make his lie as believable as possible. Benny only hoped that Ryan wouldn't put his hand around his throat. If he did, he might feel Benny's racing pulse which signaled his fear.

"Didn't you two hear the bell ring?" A loud authoritative voice called out in their direction. "What y'all waiting for, an invitation to learn? Keep waiting, because you're not going to get one, but just in case, why don't both of you wait for the invitation in your classrooms, or would you prefer to wait in the Vice-Principal's office?" The squared-off duo turned towards Coach Deeks, the head football coach and PE teacher. He stood in the breezeway which he seemed to fill. The brown-skinned towering man was almost four-feet wide and having width that size, his height didn't matter, but his speed did. None of his players could catch him on the football field; therefore, no one wanted him to catch them in the hallway. Benny's fear was temporarily redirected, first to Coach Deeks, then to thought of having his mother bring him to early morning detention. Benny chose Coach Deek's first offer, getting to class on time.

"How long will you be gone playing golf today, Ronald?" Sheila asked.

"Umm, I don't think I'm gon' play today."

"What?"

"Did I stutter? I said I'm not gon' play today."

"Excuse me. Could you get out of my bed and please return my real husband?"

"You need to be thankful instead of always tryin' to be funny about stuff."

"Oh, I'm very thankful! It's just that I thought that since Benny spent the night at Margie's, you would surely be playing golf or at least be at the driving range. Don't get me wrong, though, I'm very thankful."

Since Ronald's temptation on the ninth hole, he had lost some of his passion for golf. Playing golf was Ronald's means of escaping the frustrations weekdays had to offer, and now his fluffy green Utopia had been scarred by someone attempting, in his mind, to destroy his home.

Although his first inclination was to call his wife after the incident occurred, he later decided against informing Sheila at all. He didn't want her to feel as though she had to concern herself when other women approached him and offered sexual advances. In Ronald's estimation, Sheila considered him a simple, yet strong, man that didn't appeal to women other than herself. And that was all the assurance he ever wanted his wife to have. After having no repercussions from denying the woman, Ronald didn't feel the need to talk about what happened. He was, in fact, utterly amazed the woman did not run out of the bathroom telling the world, that she had been brutally raped. To this day, he wasn't completely sure that the police weren't going to make a special guest appearance at his house or his job to present him with brand new pair of one size fits all locking bracelets. After reviewing the conversations from his wife's perspective, he could definitely understand why she had some concern about his lack of enthusiasm for playing golf that day. After all, it was a government holiday and there was no obligation to Benny since he was visiting Clem.

"Are you *really* thankful or just a little thankful?"

"Oh, I'm *very* thankful, baby," Sheila said, transforming her suspicion into a seductive lure. Opportunities such as this, an empty house at the introduction of a new day, were indeed rare. There would be no need to keep quiet during passionate activities. When the opportunity presented itself, the two starved lovers took full advantage.

"How thankful are you?" Ronald asked.

"Very thankful."

"Is that, very nice thankful, or is that a, Thanksgiving with all the trimmings thankful?"

"It's this thankful," the now passionate wife offered as she slowly caressed the trail of her husband's hair leading to his slightly bulging appreciation for his wife's affection. Oblivious to the boisterous sounds of their lovemaking, yet totally consumed with each other's love and desire for the other, the husband and wife released within each other and were both sexually and sincerely satisfied. They slept in one another's arms well into the afternoon. However, after the lovemaking ended, the love would soon come to an end as well.

Chapter 12
What Just Happened Here?

"I need to go to the store, baby. You want to come?" Sheila asked after having been physically filled.

"If you want me to, but I just wanted to hang around and do some things I been needin' to do for a while," Ronald answered.

"Like what?"

"I don't know, I just think I need to do some things."

"Some things like what?"

"I said I don't know. I just want to hang around," Ronald replied, a bit more agitated this time."

"Ronald, is something wrong?" Sheila's suspicion was blind to the morning filled with lovemaking.

"Why does something have to be wrong? We just made love, and I thought you really enjoyed it. Now something got to be wrong?"

"No that's alright. I'm sorry I brought it up. Just forget I ever said anything about it."

"I don't think I want to forget about it now; let's talk about it. You the one that always wants to talk, so let's talk."

"No, really, we don't have to. We've had a good morning let's not spoil it."

"Sheila, you can't just bring somethin' up and then try to drop it on the floor like a bad egg. Why you think something wrong?"

"Ronald, please."

"No, Sheila please. Tell me what you think is wrong." Ronald became more persistent each time. Sheila's attempts to evade the conversation were futile.

"It's just..." she finally relented. "It's just that you've been acting sort of different the last couple of weeks."

"Different like how?"

"I don't know."

"You got to know if you think I been different, so you must know how I'm different."

"Ronald, don't cut me off. You're the one that kept pushing, so you should at least be patient when I'm trying to finish my statement."

"So now I'm impatient and different."

"You know what, Ronald? It's obvious that you're missing something and that's probably why you're acting the way you are, so let me know how and when I can accommodate you."

"What's that supposed to mean?"

"It means that what happened this morning was obviously because I was convenient and maybe you'll do better when you do some of your things you haven't done in a while."

"What you sayin'?"

"I'm saying that this was the first time we've made love in over a month, and I wonder if you find me as desirable as you used to. And if you don't find me desirable, I wonder is there someone else that is more desirable to you than me?"

"What?"

"You were the one that wanted to push the issue, Ronald."

"You think I'm screwing around after what we just did?"

"This morning was phenomenal, and I'm not complaining one bit, but you were the one that started the discussion."

"No, I just wanted to know how I was different."

"And if you recall, I was willing to let it go."

"Well, it's really gone now, ain't it?" Ronald said.

"Can we talk about something else?" Sheila asked.

"Yeah, let's talk about who I could be screwin'."

"This is ridiculous."

"Is it? Why is it so ridiculous that I got to defend my honor and my trust."

"I'm not asking you to defend any of that. All I'm saying is that our love-making, as wonderful as it is every time, is sporadic lately like something has happened."

Ronald was quiet for a moment reflecting on the incident at the golf course. He was convinced that it was best not to mention anything, because his wife would have more suspicions and wonder why he didn't tell her earlier. He was also concerned that, at this point, his wife might not even believe him.

"All I know is that I shouldn't have to defend myself on something like that and you probably don't need to question me like that ever again. So know where your place is."

"Excuse me?"

"For what?"

"What did you say to me?"

"I said don't question me again?"

"No, you said something about being in my place or something *crazy* like that." Sheila was losing her calm level-headed mentality and bringing to life her country family reunion spicy back talk.

"Well...," Ronald hesitated, realizing he had ventured into dangerous waters. "...You know, I don't think you should be asking me about my activities. It's not yo' place."

"First of all, I don't have a place. Not a place that I'm supposed to be kept in like some little concubine or some little turtle that peeps out when it's safe. My place is next to you as a supporting member of this family. Yeah, I'm submissive according to the word of God, but I ain't supposed to be stupid. You obviously have me mistaken for Sharon Stupid or some other tramp. But I'll tell you right now, I will inquire, ask, probe, or poke when I think that there may be a potential breakdown within this house. My house! The house that I contribute to as much as you do and I ain't contributing to be in no place. So until I feel that this house is in order, I will question you and your actions. Yeah, I trust you, but when I think the trust is in jeopardy, I'm gon' take some action. Ain't nothin' or nobody gon' take what I sacrificed and worked hard to keep together."

"Oh, so you the only one that's been working and you the only one that pays the bills, huh?"

"Ronald, you missed the whole point of this conversation."

"Then why don't you tell me the point then, since I don't know nothing. Let's see, so far I'm changing, I don't know nothing, and I'm screwin' around, does that sound about right?"

"Since you're being such a butt-hole about everything, don't forget that you want me to stay in my place like some slave."

"Woman, you gettin' on my last nerve."

"Me! I'm gettin' on *yo'* last nerve! You're the one that wanted to keep talkin' about this. I begged you to leave it alone. Now I'm not begging, I'm insisting. If you want to continue this useless conversation, you're going to have to finish it with someone else, because I can't look at your face and say good things at the same time right now."

"Where you think you goin'?"

"I'm done. Don't ask me anything else."

"I can ask you whatever I want to. You don't tell me what to do," Ronald said, offended by his wife's dismissal of his concerns. As she walked towards the front door to leave the house, Ronald followed her and extended his arm to reach for her. He turned Sheila around so that he could look into her eyes before she left. In her anger, Sheila violently snatched her arm from Ronald's grasp and turned to give him another severe tongue-lashing. She could feel a few profane words beginning to rear their ugly vowels and consonants in preparation for the verbal beating. Just as she inhaled to begin her sassy sermon, they heard the sound of keys in the door, which interrupted their growing anger. The doorknob turned and magically, like a small brown leprechaun approaching to bring sunshine into a gloomy day, Benny appeared with both dimples in full view.

"Hey, mama and daddy! What y'all doin'? We about to go somewhere? Did y'all have a good day off? I thought we had a crazy house, but Aunt Margie and Uncle William got some loose screws," Benny said comically.

Instantly, Sheila found relief in the one product of she and her husband that could bring them joy. She smiled, not just at her son, but *their* son, who in just a few words lifted the mood and made the difficult times worth tolerating. Had it not been for the ebullient son coming through the door, the situation in the house could have been potentially harmful to everyone there.

Ronald's stone-covered emotions didn't allow him to smile and rejoice in his son's innocence, but he felt an extreme relief that Benny interrupted the argument. Looking down at his son, he saw reflections of himself and wondered how he had gone from a young boy to an overbearing husband who passionately satisfied his wife in the morning and upset her to the point of leaving him in the afternoon. Ronald was thankful for his family. Sheila cherished being a member of her family. Benny made being a part of this family a precious gift. If any member of the threesome was ever to leave, the foundation was sure to collapse.

Chapter 13
Influence

“Where do you want to go for lunch, Margie?” Sheila asked, blabbing into the telephone receiver.

“Sheila, girl, I don’t even know. I’m so excited to be able to get away and have lunch like some big shots, I can’t hardly believe it.”

“Isn’t that the truth? My boss actually let me out of my cage for once. You know, I really need a break from my co-workers. As much as I depend on them, just a few hours a day out of the office soothes my nerves.”

“Oh, that reminds me, one of the girls from the shop next door wants to tag along with us. You remember me telling you about her? The one that just about took her husband’s right to breathe when she caught him messing around on her. She’s cold-blooded girl. I think you’ll like her.”

“Oh, yeah, I remember you telling me about her. She sounds like a bad sister; I can’t wait to meet her. I don’t mind at all.”

“Good, we’ll see you in about twenty minutes,” Margie enthusiastically responded hanging up her phone.

Occasionally Sheila and Margie were privileged to get away on a lunch outing. If they were fortunate enough to hit the time off lottery or their managers were away, the two giddy girls would plan to splurge at Bonanza or Shoney’s.

Usually the lunch conversation consisted of how their co-workers probably needed to be invited to somebody’s church. Neither of them dared extend the invitation, because their co-workers were likely to interrupt the sermon and began asking questions for clarification on some of the characters in the Bible. Other times, the conversation consisted of their husbands and wonderful children, although lately the content wasn’t always about how wonderful their husbands were.

Sheila arrived at Shoney’s before Margie and her friend, so she was standing in the parking lot when Margie and the cold-blooded sister pulled up in a Cadillac Fleetwood Coupe-de-ville. Upon seeing the luxury car, Sheila began wondering if the automobile was a result of the ugly divorce that the lady had gone through. At least they'd have some new and interesting material for conversation this time.

"Girl, you like my bad ride?" Margie broadcasted across the parking lot, just barely giving herself enough time to open the door and get out of the car. She couldn't contain the excitement of driving her friend's car to the lunch rendezvous.

"Don't you wish," Sheila said greeting her with a jolt of reality after they made their way towards the restaurant.

"I sho' do, honey. That car has everything. The seats moved back and forth with the push of a button and so do the side view mirrors, chile. It's got a cassette player in it, too, and some nice soundin' speakers! I thought that I was bad when we got an eight-track in our car. And you ain't gon' believe the way she got like some wood lookin' stuff on her dashboard and on her steering wheel. Girl, don't you won't to go for a ride?"

"I wish I could. In fact I'd like to ride right on away from here and into some place where I can get away from it all."

"You get in that big Caddie, turn on that nice cool AC, put on some Cameo, and you'll definitely be away from it all."

"How you doing?" Sheila said, extending her hand to the sharp but casually dressed woman. "I'm Sheila. Can you please forgive my rude sister for not introducing us?"

"Hi Sheila. I'm Chandra. It's nice to meet you, honey. Your radio of a sister has told me so much about you."

Chandra was dressed in tight fitting Calvin Klein jeans and a red silk blouse that was tied up near her waist exposing just a hint of flesh. It was enough to convey the message that she was available, but not cheap. Perhaps the lunch invitation prompted the energetic divorcee to match her wardrobe to her car. Bright red strappy high heels showed off her newly painted red toenails. Chandra was red hot, as was her new, single woman—men can't hurt me—but they can help me pay bills mentality.

"Oh please, don't believe one word she mutters out of that mouth of hers," Sheila said.

"No, all she did was say good stuff about you."

"Then honey, you really shouldn't believe that, because I try to keep all my good stuff away from her so she won't know it, won't know how to get to it, and won't know what to do with it if she finds it."

"Oh listen at you, ain't you just a no good bag of nothing?" Margie said, referring to the snide harmless remarks."

"I see you know your sister well."

"Both of y'all hefas can kiss my black greasy behind. I let y'all two cackling hens meet one time over lunch, and y'all just lifelong bosom buddies. Why don't y'all sadity sisters hurry and take y'all tails in the restaurant so somebody can pick up my check."

The twosome began laughing at Margie's instant attitude and entered the restaurant taking their seats. Everyone in the restaurant was scoffing down their meals, rushing to get a quick away-from-work meal while at the same time enjoy a little time for conversing. Most of the patrons were doing more scoffing than conversing. The waitress came over, took the ladies' orders and vanished, leaving them free to have a juicy conversation.

"So, Chandra, you work in the shop over near Margie's office?"

"Um hm. I used to sit around all day and do nothing except for watch the *Price is Right, General Hospital*, and *Donahue* until I found out that my husband was making house calls everywhere, except at his own house. So I came into some, ooh what a bad mistake that was sneakin' around on me money, and got me some booth space over at Beauty Boutique until I build up enough clientele to open my own shop."

"Your husband was a doctor? Wasn't that exciting?"

"He *was* a doctor," Margie said barging in. "Now he's a *broke* doctor. Ain't that right, Chandra?" She laughed hysterically and slammed her hand on the table enjoying her joke more than anyone else.

"Margie! Have you have lost yo' mind?"

"Oh that's alright. I'm not bothered by it at all. Your nut of a sister keeps me sane and laughing most of the time anyway. But yeah, you're right. It probably was interesting for all of those sluts he was probing, prodding, and giving free breast exams to. As for me, he was as boring as toe jam waiting to be cleaned."

"That's really unfortunate," Sheila responded.

"What? That he was like toe jam, or that I have to rely on your sister to keep me going."

"Well yeah, that too, especially you having to be motivated by Miss Nappy Headed New Growth over there. But I was really talking about the situation with your husband, I mean ex-husband."

"Look, let that be that last make-fun-of-Margie comment of the day or I will go to the back and ask the cook to put some saliva sauce in y'all salads."

"I bet you won't," Sheila insisted.

"Why not? You think I won't?"

"Because the waitress is bringing out the salads right now," Sheila answered after seeing the waitress appear from the kitchen with three Chicken salads.

"Dag! Wait till next time," Margie said to her sister. "And anyway, all that gettin' away from it all you were talking about, I do it every month."

"Now where can you possibly go every month?" Sheila asked. "You're just as broke as I am."

"I get away right next door. Girl, Chandra can do some hair, and she has a special on a facial plus your nails. She makes you feel like you're getting the red carpet treatment or something. A few hours in the shop, and I'm satisfied. If she could get some naked men dancing in there, I might not ever go home."

Sheila and Chandra interrupted their eating to laugh at the comical Margie.

"Your sister is a mess," Chandra replied, politely covering her mouth and preserving her table etiquette. "It's not all that fancy anyway, but I do plan to have an extensive salon after I get my steady clientele. Hopefully, I can get a masseuse and some other lavish things, so it will be really nice. In the mean time and in between time, I try to do the best with what I have."

"She's just being modest, Sheila. I guarantee if you walk in there, you'll leave saying to yourself I don't need to get away anymore because I'm just now returning," Margie added, now wolfing down her food like everyone else in the restaurant.

"Yeah, you should stop by one day, Sheila. You'd better get in while I can still give you a discount, when the customers start rolling in, I might not be able to give you the special hook up price."

"Oh I know how that is, supply and demand. What, are your hours?" Sheila asked somewhat hesitant. Perhaps taking a pampering session at the boutique was her own admission of a problem in her personal life.

"Just call and make an appointment, or you can let me know now when you think you might want to do it and I'll let Miss..." Chandra paused as Margie looked up from her barrel of salad to stop the insult with her eyes. "…excuse me, this fine young woman sitting here inhaling her lunch, if the time is okay."

"Girl, just go ahead and go on over there, "Margie insisted with a mouth full of food. Swallowing she added, "You were just saying how you need to get away from everything."

"Yeah, but as nice as it sounds, that's not really getting away. And besides I was just talking crazy; I wasn't really serious."

"What's the problem, Sheila, you having a hard time at work?"

"Oh those fools at work don't bother me, honey. I don't listen to half of the things they say anyway," Sheila said with conviction.

"Well, what is it then?" Chandra asked, probing further. Sheila looked down at her picked over salad. "It's just..." Sheila's conviction yielded to her hesitation once again. "Nothing, it's nothing," she murmured, picking up her fork and torturing her salad further by toiling in it, but not eating.

"Sheila," Chandra said, placing a concerned hand of newly gained friendship on Sheila's eating hand. It signaled her to stop what she was doing and communicate openly. "I can see that there's something bothering you?"

Suddenly, Sheila realized she hadn't shared her feelings with anyone except Ronald, and that moment of sharing all but ended in disaster. This might be her last and only opportunity to vent her emotions. Reluctantly, she gave in to Chandra's kind inquires.

"I really don't like talking about things in my house but…"

"Is Benny doing drugs?" Margie asked.

"No girl, it's nothing like that. But what's been bothering me a little bit is that…"

"Oh chile, you about to lose yo' house. Lord Jesus!" Again Margie's speculation halted the confession.

"Are you going to let me talk, or are you going to play the guessing game?"

"Go ahead on girl. I wish you'd hurry up though, I'm gon' eat yo' salad if you don't."

Sheila irritated by her sister's actions, quickly slid the plate over to her in an effort to keep her quiet. Chandra, however, was still focused on her new friend's problem.

"Sheila, what's bothering you?" Chandra asked sincerely.

After pausing for a moment, Sheila finally made her concerns known to someone outside of her family, "Ronald has been acting a little different lately."

"Is that it?" Margie began. "I thought it was something major or..."

"Margie, be quiet. Please!" Chandra insisted.

"Excuse me!" Margie's haughtiness erupted.

"What do you mean *different*, Sheila?" Chandra asked.

"Little stuff like, he hasn't been there as much lately. I don't mean been there as in being at home," Sheila clarified. "But not there as in kind of distant and quiet lately. Almost like he would rather be somewhere else or be doing something else." Chandra sat back in her chair and folded her arms, assuming the pose of an experienced listener.

"Why are you looking like that, Chandra?" Sheila asked, noticing Chandra's reaction.

"No reason, it just sounds all too familiar."

"What do you mean?"

"I'll tell you what, let me ask you a few questions? That's of course, if you don't mind?"

"No, go right ahead. I'm interested in what you have to say."

"Okay. First, when you say lately, do you mean that all of a sudden your husband came home and he seemed to have a different attitude?"

Sheila pondered over the question for a while. "I guess so. Maybe it wasn't one day, or all of a sudden, but it wasn't over a long period of time either. Why?"

"Just curious. What about arguments? Overall, do the both of you communicate alright or is it kinda knocking heads?"

"It's funny you should mention that because just recently it seems like normal conversations turn into fights, and I mean over little things. As a matter of fact, earlier this week we had just finished doing something we both enjoy tremendously and..."

"Why don't you just say y'all was freaking. Ahh, Freak Out!" Margie said, blurting out the old R & B song.

"Anyway," Sheila said, trying to ignore her sister's interruption. "Like I was saying, afterwards I asked him to go to the store with me and he told me he had some things to do or some errands to run and it turned into a big argument."

"Right after you two had ... you know," Chandra said.

"Yeah."

"Did you ask him where he needed to go?"

"Yeah!"

"And what did he say?"

"He said he just needed to go and run some errands."

"Were you suspicious at all?"

"A little."

"Did you tell him that?"

"Yeah and I also told him that I felt he was acting a little different."

"What did he say to that? He didn't get defensive, did he?

"He sure did. How did you guess that?"

"Wild guess," Chandra answered cynically.

"Then he just lost it when I mentioned that there..."

"That there might be someone else," Chandra said, finishing Sheila's sentence.

"Yeah how did you know that? Have you ever met Ronald?"

"Not directly, but it sounds like I was married to him for a little while."

"What!"

"That's exactly how things starting turning around in my marriage, small things like you mentioned. At first, I was a fool, thinking it was something I was doing wrong. For a long time, I went on trying to accommodate all of his feelings and not thinking about my own."

"Girl, you can't stop all that right there," Margie said. She'd completely devoured all of the food left stranded by the conversation. "Are we talking about Simple Simon Ronald? Go to work and play golf Ronald? Plain everyday nothing exciting Ronald? Don't nobody want Ronald but you, just like don't nobody want William but me. That man ain't making no house calls, because he don't want to be bothered touching somebody else's doorbell. He stays to himself all the time. Are y'all crazy?"

Since Margie didn't have anything valuable to add earlier in the conversation, the women weren't very interested in her theories now.

"Sheila," Chandra began again. "You really need to come and see me, but until you do there are some things I want you to look out for. I'm telling you all of this from experience, okay?"

"Alright."

"Take notice if you walk into the room and he hangs up the phone quickly."

"That's silly, he hardly ever talks on the phone."

"Sure, that's fine, but like I said, I'm only telling you this from experience. You don't have to go along with this if you don't want to."

"Alright, I'll look out for that. What else?"

"Be very concerned if a normal conversation turns into an argument, like you said earlier, and try to pinpoint what ticks him off in the argument. Sort of like when you said he exploded when you mentioned someone else may be in the picture. And the most important thing, although it may sound far-fetched, watch out for him not eating his favorite dish and changing his sleeping position in bed at night."

"Lord have mercy, y'all have completely flipped out. While you at it, check his drawers, and if his skid marks go side ways instead of up and down; take note of that too. Y'all have lost it, " Margie said, emerging with her unwarranted comments again.

"Margie, please. This is serious," Chandra said.

"No it's not. It's actually quite funny. Ann Landers and Pimp Po' Peter patient number one in here having a counseling session at Shoney's about a man who ain't seen another woman other than you since his mama had him."

"Don't mind her Sheila. Remember what I told you, and please call me. More importantly, come and see me, alright? It's time for me to get back to the shop because I've got a two o' clock with a new client. Seriously Sheila, watch out for those things. I'm only telling you this from experience."

"Okay Chandra," she replied. Sheila was mentally taking notes on the advice she had been given. "I need to get back to work, too. It was very good to meet you and I'll be giving you a call real soon, girl. Thanks for everything," Sheila said compassionately to her new friend for what she believed was a sincere interest in her well-being.

"I've got to go, too, because that AC in the Caddie is callin' my name," Margie said.

"That girl is too much; I don't know why you fool with her, Chandra."

"That's exactly why, because she's too much fun."

"Y'all know you love me. Bye girl," Margie said to Sheila, as the women got up from their table and made their way to the cash register, then to the parking lot and back to the work force. Seemingly, Sheila now had two jobs, her nine to five and keeping peace in her own house. A visit to the salon might be just what she needed, or didn't need.

Chapter 14
Unproven Theories

"Chandra, thanks for seeing me on such short notice, I really need a touch up bad. My new growth is old and dead," Sheila said.

"Oh, don't even mention it. I'm just surprised it took you so long. It's been what, about a month since we all had lunch together?"

"Yeah. I guess it has been awhile. A part of me wanted to come a long time ago, that was my new growth part. Another part of me was afraid to come and get some of that insight of yours."

"Girl, please. I'm sure you've got your head together more than you realize."

"Funny you should say that, because if I did, I have a feeling I wouldn't be in your chair today or any other day, for that matter."

"Oh, so what you're sayin' is, I ain't good enough to do your hair unless I'm giving free advice for a peaceful life. I need to add my counseling fee to your bill when I'm done," Chandra said jovially.

"Chandra, you're a mess. You and Margie are two peas in a pod."

"That nutcase is in a league by herself. What did you want to get done today? I've got Jheri Curls on specials, plus your first bottle of chemicals is free."

"Mmm, that is a good deal. But, I don't want to hear Ronald's mouth when I get home talkin' about, *What you do that for? Wasn't nothin' wrong with the way you looked before.*

The other ladies in the salon seats looked over at the seemingly independent and secure woman. Sheila was a new face in the shop so that meant that she got the five-minute quiet. Everyone in the shop kept quiet for the first five minutes of her entrance and let her spill her guts so they could eavesdrop and assess her situation. It wasn't a sudden silence either. The windows of the shop had a dark tint and people could be seen walking up to the door, but the people approaching the shop could not see in. To any new patrons, the salon was a dark glass wall. It was almost an undesirable and uncomfortable sight from the outside.

Once the door was opened, the welcoming committee was a greeting of hair chemicals and flowery aerosol air freshener. Beautiful ferns hung from an extended rail behind each of the five parlor chairs. There was more uniformity than individuality at all the booths because the owner thought it looked more professional. Pictures, although different throughout the shop, were the same size and all hung from the same height on the walls. Photos of beauty products and hair models were confined to their special section on a back wall. The only disorganized display was the hundreds of magazines scattered everywhere. If a woman entered the shop and did nothing else but get her hair done, she definitely had the opportunity to catch up on the latest home tips, recipes, love advice, fashion standards, gardening, and movie reviews.

Each night after closing, one beautician took her turn at organizing the magazines only to have her creation destroyed within five new customers the following morning. When the nosy women saw Sheila through the tinted glass doors, all of the magazines assumed the, *get-the-scoop* position. They covered their faces with magazines to give the perception of an involvement in something other than whoever was on center stage, which at this time was Sheila. All the women, who were Wednesday regulars, took their own mental notes and prepared to assemble a case study on the new patient.

"Well, how's it been going?" Chandra began.

"You know, I don't know what it is about people walking into the doors of a place a business that makes them lose their mind. Maybe it's something in the air. And it seems like it's ten times worse down at the DMV. When people walk through that door down there, they just throw away whatever home training their mama may have given them."

"Mmm, you must have read my mind, Sheila."

Ah hah she's insightful with a slight sense of humor. The swimming sharks, with faces still covered, were making careful observations.

"Oh it's not just the folk that walk through the door, it's also those maniacs that I work with. They seem worse than the customers when you get them in the break room or back in the records room. You know Chandra, I could have sworn that Dr. Jeckyll and Mr. Hyde died years ago but now I realize, that he and all of his cousins are workin' down at my office."

"You're a mess, Sheila," Chandra said, making the small talk larger.

Seems like she's got a lot of patience, but it looks like something is on her mind and she's hiding it. Come on and push her Chandra. Now the sharks were swimming, generalizing, and speculating.

"So how's it going, really? I know you needed your hair done, but you wouldn't have waited this long if things weren't going the way you'd like them to."

"Are you a hairdresser or a mind reader? You're thumbing through the pages upstairs, girl."

"I keep tryin' to tell these people when you rub enough scalps you can pick up brain waves through your hands."

"Oh really?"

"Truly."

"Well, what do those waves tell you about what's going on in my head?"

"Funny you should ask that, because I just felt them tingle."

"Mmm, tingle on girl, what are they sayin'?"

"Well, to be quite honest, I was concerned about those three observations that I asked you to be on the look out for around your house and around your husband."

"Really?"

"Yeah, really," Chandra replied back sharply trying to intensify her line of questioning. "Are you going to make me guess, or are you going to let me know what's going on in your life?"

The whole shop was dead quiet now except for the sounds of KOKY playing *Little Red Corvette*. Usually, the popular song caused an impromptu party wherever it was played, but this time it was merely the background music for a developing drama.

"Now why do you want to hear about my pathetic little life. There's nothing to tell really. Just another day in the life of an average Black woman."

Oh no, it's real bad. She's in denial. This ought to be real good. Chandra sho' ain't gon' let her get away with that. The sharks brought the magazines down a little lower and turned their ears towards the two conversationalists.

"Just another day in the life, huh? Well, what about the items we spoke about in the restaurant and the things I told you to look for?"

"I really didn't think about what you told me after I left the restaurant. When I got back to work those heathens took so much of my brainpower, I didn't have the energy to concentrate on what we were saying. But really girl, it's no big deal. Like I said it's just ...its' just another day." Sheila stared out into space for a moment trying to determine whether to release or recant her built up confession of concern. "It's just another day in the life of an average Black woman...that can't seem to communicate with her husband and stays at odds with her son who seems to be developing into a young man that she can't talk to and acts like he's keeping things from me because when I ask him things I never get a straight answer, but he always tries to turn the tables and make me think that I'm doing him an injustice by trying to communicate with him. That's all, nothing major."

In one simultaneous motion, all of the sharks pushed their fins through the water by throwing their magazines down onto their laps and shooting a let-me-tell-you-what-I think glance towards Sheila.

"Gosh. I didn't know all of you cared so much," Sheila responded sarcastically, breaking the ice.

"Now what is this you said about turnin' the tables, Sherry?" asked a lady sitting the farthest away from Sheila.

"It's Sheila. And what did you say your name was?" Sheila responded trying to insinuate that she hadn't given the woman clearance to join the conversation.

"I'm Delores," the skinny woman replied. Delores was taking advantage of the Jheri Curl special. She wanted to get one more in before the wet drippy look began it's slow decline into fashion history. Her dark black hair blended in with her dark black skin. Delores drooped her left leg over the right leg as she crossed her walking limbs settling them into a more comfortable position. It seemed that Delores enjoyed curly things because when she crossed her legs, her curly ruffled ankle socks were revealed along with a distinct grey ash line on her ankles. She obviously lotioned after her purple ruffle socks were stretched up as high as she could pull them. Of course no curly ruffle sock set would be complete without the matching curly purple ruffles down the outseam of her denim jeans. Delores didn't wear ruffles above her waistline. That would have clashed with her purple and red rhinestone blouse and this outfit couldn't dare to be insulted by a clash of any kind. The red in her blouse, matched her thick red loop earrings that dangled down to her shoulders. Delores was a walking long and lanky last season clearance sale.

"Honey, let me tell you what I know about turnin' tables because my man tried to turn the tables on me like he a busboy or something." The shop broke out into giggles of agreement. "Talkin' about, *I don't know why you always asking me if I like yo' meatloaf. Don't I always eat it every bit of it?* He ain't foolin' nobody because my mama always told me if a man don't like your meatloaf, then he must be eatin' the slices off of somebody else's potroast. So I always ask him does he like my meatloaf even if he does eat every bit of it. Girl, don't let no man turn no tables on you. When he do, then you change the tablecloth on him." The shop wasn't giggling anymore they were confused by the analogous nonsense Delores spewed.

"Sharon, don't pay her no mind," another woman sitting closer to the door interjected.

"My name is *Sheila*, thank you."

"I'm Doris. And that woman's common sense gets blinded by the colors on her outfit sometimes." The rest of the women laughed at the quick verbal jab Doris gave Delores.

"I know you not talkin' because you look like you just jumped off the pages of Fashion Follies," Delores said, defending her wardrobe's honor. Delores' defense was justified because Doris was making a single-handed attempt to preserve the jumpsuit and had no room to insult anyone else's attire.

Frequenting Hancocks Fabrics for the latest do-it-yourself patterns, Doris was a sewing machine disaster in motion. Of course, fashions eventually came back around again. The jumpsuit might make a valiant effort to be placed in closets once again, but when that happened, the jumpsuits probably wouldn't have thirty-four pockets like Doris' did. She insisted on having a pocket for as many years as she was old. Not only was her striped jumpsuit covered with pockets, but she sewed designs, animals, and phrases protruding out of her pockets. Her left back pocket had the word THE sewn onto it and her right back pocket had the word END sewn onto it. Whenever Doris walked around, THE END swished and swayed along for everyone to see. There were pockets on her thighs, pockets on her knees, and even pockets on her elbows. A picture of a pair of dice was sewn into the large pockets across her chest and beneath it was a caption that read, **Try your luck.**

"Delores, I look good and I know it, and if you forget, just look on my side pocket because that's where I sewed it," the expressive woman rhymed back to her glamour colleagues. "Now listen, if your man ain't actin' right, then you need to remind him all the time of your beauty, your essence, and other men's attraction to you. People have to see things, hear things, and read things. Why you think I have all of this positivity on my clothes? Not because I'm crazy, I assure you." Delores was having her hair dyed for the fourth time this year.

"See Sheila, that's the main reason why I need my own shop. There is no tellin' what kind of clowns come in here on any given day," Chandra whispered.

"Did you just call me Sheila? Is that my name? I was confused for a minute; I'm glad you cleared that up for me," Sheila replied jovially.

"You need to quit girl. Now come on. What about the observations I asked you to make."

"I told you already, I forgot what you told me."

"Mmm-huh. Let me help you remember."

"What about his phone conversations? Does he jump off the phone when you come home or enter the room?"

"Not really. He usually only calls his friend William to talk about golf and sports. Every now and then he doesn't like for me to see or hear him on the phone talking about golf, so he gets off the phone when I'm around because he thinks that I don't like him playing golf."

"But you're sure that he's talking to William. That's Margie's husband right?"

"Yeah, that's his golf buddy."

"And when he gets off the phone, does he leave the room or does he sit around and talk to you?"

"You have to understand, Ronald's not much of a talker, he only..."

"Wait a minute. He's not much of a talker but he's always on the phone talking to William, and when you come around, he jumps off the phone?"

"He's not *always* on the phone."

"Sounds to me like you need to make sure he ain't talkin' to Willimena instead of William. I don't know about no William, girl, but I had a froggy man like that. Always jumpin' off the phone and always jumpin' up to go somewhere else when I came home," a woman named Katherine sitting in the chair next to Sheila said.

"So what did you do Katherine?" Delores asked.

"Look chile, I am talkin' to Shebra not you," Katherine responded. Sheila turned and looked up at Chandra baffled at the fact that none of the women had addressed her properly. Chandra tried to contain her laughter and gave Sheila's head a light push to resume her position for her hairstyling.

"Since he was moving so much I sat on him to make him settle down," Katherine responded.

If Katherine had sat on anybody, they would have probably been broken down instead of settled down. She was on the larger side of the weight scale, however, she wore her weight well. The casual hairstyle she was having touched up complemented her large bones. Adorned in a loose fitting dress, Katherine seemed very comfortable with her weight. She remained consistent with the theme of giving useless advice.

"I can't take much more of this Sheila," Chandra whispered again in her Sheila only voice. "Okay, so what about your conversations? Can you have a normal conversation without it blowing up in your face, or does everything you talk about seem to turn into a duel?"

"Now that can't really be a sign of anything can it? He's a man and they just don't communicate very well."

"Do you talk or do you argue?"

"Well, it's a little bit of both, but if you don't have disagreements then something is wrong."

"Yeah that's right, but is there something in particular that usually sets him off?" Chandra probed.

Sheila thought for a moment, seriously reflecting on a few of their previous quarrels.

"Well he is rather sensitive about me asking him to reveal his inner emotions."

"Explain what you mean." Chandra asked in the most psychiatric way she could. The sharks were on the edge of their seats now.

"Now that you mention it, we were having a conversation about my mother and father. Ronald was telling me how he admired the fact that my parents had been together for so long and that they must know everything there is to know about each other. I used that as an invitation to see how he felt about people knowing their mates. When I asked him what he was really passionate about, he looked at me like I had asked him had he taken a bath that morning. He just erupted talkin' about, *What you mean passionate? You tryin' to say that I'm not satisfying you enough? Is something wrong with me and I don't got no passion in my life?* It was amazing, almost like another person had shown up when I tried to get inside of his head and his heart."

"Shequita my dear, its sounds like your darling husband has a case of the peek-a-boos,"another nosy woman interjected.

"Sheila! It's Sheila!" Chandra exclaimed back at the intruding group.

"Whatever darling, but it's obvious the peek-a-boos is what's wrong with your man and that's my prognosis.

"Sonya, what the hell are the peek-a-boos?" Katherine asked.

"Must I keep reiterating that my name is pronounced *So'nee-ah*?" the woman articulated.

"Um-huh, every since you moved and you don't live *so nee uh* the projects, you done changed yo' name," Delores joked. The shop exploded into laughter. One woman that was siting directly across from Sheila, and hadn't destroyed her name yet, gave a slight chuckle. She had been glancing over at Sheila during the conversation and was the only one actually reading her magazine.

"Yes, yes, yes. Laugh as if none of you have a care in the world, but darlings the poor woman has a serious problem. The peek-a-boos, my darling, are what a man has when he has something to hide, and your husband, dear child, is looking for the best hiding place and you're just sitting there counting to one hundred hoping that you can find him when you finish counting. What you should be doing, is peeking while you count so you can find out where he's been." Sonya, or *So'nee-ah* as she proclaimed, was a pure soultress. Dressed in hot pink, she peacocked around the shop and she even peacocked in her seat. Before she allowed her stylist to start on her hair, *So'nee-ah* took a full five minutes to find the perfect position to sit in so everyone could observe her exuberance. The well-endowed woman made it a point to show off her bodily gifts to any audience she could get. Her hair appointments were unnecessary because her long silky black hair was washed regularly and never out of place. Although the appointments were completely useless, there was the matter of the weekly waxing she needed. *So'nee-ah* had a hairier upper lip than most of the men at the neighboring barbershop.

"Like I was saying *Sheila*!" Chandra said, enunciating her client's name. She was trying to adjust all of the mistakes the self proclaimed counselors made during their free and unsolicited sessions. "What about the behavior patterns that I told you were somewhat off the wall, but very important?"

"You mean... about eating and sleeping?" Sheila said, after momentarily searching for the answer.

"Exactly! You ought to be ashamed of yourself talking about you forgot what I told you. A slight case of convenient amnesia, huh?"

"Anyway. Everything in that department has been pretty normal," Sheila said, then recalled the incident she and Ronald had involving potatoes. Sheila recanted her statement. "You know what? Come to think about it, he made a big deal about mashed potatoes all of a sudden. And it was the strangest thing because ever since we've been married, he's always insisted that his potatoes are baked and just the other week he went crazy because we never have any mashed potatoes. When I tried to talk to him about it, he left the table. Ronald never leaves food on the table. He doesn't believe in wasting food, but that doesn't mean anything, does it? A person can change his mind whenever he wants, can't he?" Sheila said, searching for a confirmation. She never got it. All Chandra gave her was a blank stare of concern.

"What about sleeping?" Chandra asked.

"Well that doesn't count? You can't tell anything from that because he hurt his back last month and he has to sleep on his stomach now."

"Is that what the doctor requested that he do?"

"Uum, he never really went to see a doctor about it he just…"

"So he made the change on his own, huh?"

"Yeah, I guess you could say that."

"So he *has* changed the way he sleeps."

"Kinda. Yeah, I suppose you could say that he has," Sheila said, attempting to follow Chandra's lead.

Chandra turned the salon chair around so that Sheila's back was facing the nosy neighbors and she was facing her client. Chandra bent down, moving in close to Sheila so that she could keep her words safe from the conversation predators.

"Sheila, listen to me very closely. I'm telling you this as a friend and as a person who has been through this before. The first thing you need to do, and whatever you have to do to get one doesn't matter, but you seriously need to get a Private Investigator. I'll help you out with a loan if you need it."

"A Private Inv…" Sheila blurted out before Chandra shushed her.

"Sheila, I know it sounds a little far-fetched, but you need someone to collect the facts and collect the evidence on what your husband is doing."

"My husband's not doing anyth…"

"Look, I've been through this before and one of the toughest things for me to do was to admit to myself that my husband might actually be cheating on me. Once I faced that reality, it was no problem for me to go ahead and take care of business. But it took me so long to wake up and realize what was going on, I almost lost. I don't want that to happen to anyone else, especially to someone that I consider to be a friend. Then after you get your PI, I know it's difficult but then you need to get a lawyer. Try to get a white man so it won't look like you're out just for the money. And lastly you need to keep my number close by. I've done this and there's no reason for you to go through this alone."

Sheila was speechless. Nothing Chandra just said could possibly be accurate, she thought to herself. But each one of the items Chandra warned her about had all come to pass. Sheila was just about out of explanations for Ronald's actions. All of her reasons were bottled up and ready to be tossed out to sea. Suddenly, visions of an empty house and weekends without her little Benny appeared. Family reunions would now be filled with speculation and peach cobbler gone to waste because there weren't enough mouths in her home to eat it all. Sheila felt ill and her day of pampering instantly became a day of disgust. She didn't want to look beautiful anymore, especially for a man like Chandra had described. As

Chandra prepared to take Sheila over to the sink suggesting she get a wash and rinse, the saddened woman declined and asked Chandra to postpone the appointment until next week. When Sheila rose from her seat and began to solemnly gather her things, the other women in the shop shook their heads in disgust for the newest member of the lonely-hearts club, except for one woman. A quiet and humble lady who had been sitting calmly just on the other side of Sheila was looking at her. The woman was not a regular as the others were. Sheila turned in her direction and the woman laid her hand on Sheila's arm as she walked near the table to get her purse. Sheila was startled by the woman's gentle and comforting touch.

"Oh, excuse me, I didn't mean to bump into you," Sheila said, politely trying to give the woman a chance to admit that she was wrong for reaching over and touching her without reason.

"That's quite all right, Sheila." *Finally someone got my name right,* Sheila thought. "You didn't bump into me at all. I hope I didn't make you uncomfortable by touching you, but I just had to get your attention before you left. I hope I'm not being forward but, are you and your husband on equal playing fields, spiritually? You eat together and argue together, but have you ever prayed together? Once a man and woman get married, you are bone of his bone and he is flesh of your flesh. If something has changed with him, it's changed both of you and if you step out on faith, together, you might find out what is. I just wanted to drop that in your spirit. I hope you don't mind."

Sheila had no answers for the woman. She had answers but they couldn't be formed to make any sense after the load of rationale the woman deposited in her head. All Sheila could manage was. "No, you're not being forward at all. Thank you." Sheila thanked Chandra for accommodating her abbreviated visit, and exited the shop. The sharks were shaking their heads and the comforting woman bowed her head and said a small prayer for Sheila.

Chapter 15
Talking

"Hey Ronald, are you going out to that golf place so you can hit those little balls this evening?"

"Nawh Mr. Jackson, not tonight. I'm tryin' to cut back."

"And it's about time, too. Good, I need to talk to you about some things, you got a moment before you go home?"

"Yeah, I can stick around for a few minutes I guess."

"Okay, come to my office after you get cleaned up."

Ronald's mind was suddenly flooded with questions about why his supervisor, Karl Jackson, could possibly want to talk to him. He didn't think he had done anything wrong. There was only the one incident when he took a nap during his lunch break, but sleeping on the job was almost a normal routine, especially in the summer time with the heat and long days out on the road. There were no rumors of cutbacks or layoffs, although one of his coworkers was fired last week for poor work performance and insubordination. Ronald didn't think he fit any of those categories, yet he still worried about what the topic of conversation would be once the door in his superior's office closed behind him. Wasting no time getting cleaned up and change out of his city uniform, Ronald walked though the dingy locker room adjusting his clothes and buttoning his shirt afraid of being late for the impromptu meeting. He reached the front offices and noticed a few people were still at their desks, perhaps completing assignments before they left for the evening. As he walked through the areas practically everyone spoke to him commenting about how they hadn't seen him in awhile. Most of the front office people knew Ronald from his picture on the employee of the year plaque, which was placed in the reception area as well as in the locker room. Ronald was highly regarded and well liked by the city workers. His work ethic and dedication were unmatched. If he'd had a college education, he'd very possibly be Mr. Jackson's manager. Right now, Ronald felt like Mr. Jackson's prey and he didn't like the fearful feeling of being swallowed whole.

"Mr. Jackson, you wanted to see me?"

"Oh yeah, Ronald," he responded, temporarily puzzled by Ronald's presence. "That was fast, I forgot I'd asked you to come in ."

"Well, I rushed over as soon as I could. You want me to go back and wait a little bit longer or come back tomorrow?"

"No, no, that won't be necessary; please have a seat. I'm just wrapping up some of this never-ending paper work. I tell you the truth, Ronald, sometimes you have to wonder why we cut down all the trees for paper to write down information that we just throw away eventually anyhow. Seems like there should be a machine or something to keep all this information on. Whoever invents something like that is gon' be living high on a hill somewhere. In fact, I hear that by nineteen eighty-seven, the city will have computers for us."

"That's good. In the meantime, people got to work, so I guess they'll be keeping those paper-making places open for jobs."

"You're right on that one, Ronald. Did you know you have a keen common sense philosophy that I think every so called smart person should adopt."

"Oh I don't know about that, Mr. Jackson. I just know what I know and try to find out what I don't," Ronald replied, as he wiped his sweaty palms on his pants.

"See that's what I respect about you most Ronald, no beating around the bush, and no puttin' on airs for no reason and..."

"Mr. Jackson," Ronald interrupted, "no disrespect, but did I do something wrong? Am I about to lose my job?"

"What?" Mr. Jackson seemed shocked by Ronald's comment. "Why, no! Is that why you thought you were being called in here? I'm sorry if I gave you that impression. I guess I should have prefaced my request with a little bit more information, shouldn't I have? No, Ronald, by no means are you in danger of losing your job. You're probably one of our most valued workers. Man, I'm sorry if I put you in an awkward position."

"That's okay," Ronald replied keeping his hands still now. His palms began to dry.

"However, I am concerned about you personally, though, not just as it relates to your work performance, but as someone who cares about what happens to you."

"How do you mean?"

"I've just noticed some differences in your attitude both physically and mentally."

"What's that supposed to mean," Ronald inquired, slightly offended and puzzled.

"Don't take it personally, Ronald, but I've noticed a considerable difference in your stride so to speak. You used to walk through the locker room with enthusiasm and now it seems like you're only going through the motions. At one time, you were the first one to take a seat before the morning assignment meeting. Now it's not unusual to find you standing against the wall in the back. Like I said, it's not affecting your work performance, it's just that I'm concerned about you man to man and not supervisor to worker. I even noticed that you don't talk about golf as much anymore. Is everything okay at home?" Mr. Jackson gave Ronald a minute to absorb everything he'd just mentioned. He sensed that Ronald didn't enjoy being put on the spot even though they were the only two in the office.

"Why is it just 'cause I don't won't to play golf, everybody think's something is wrong with me?"

"What do you mean everybody?"

"First my wife, then you. It's just a stupid game, and if I don't want to play then I just don't want to play. It doesn't mean I'm going crazy."

After years of being a foreman, Mr. Jackson had become very skilled at reading people's emotions based on their statements and reactions. He sensed that because Ronald's wife had obviously picked up on the changes in Ronald's demeanor, there were possibly some difficulties at home.

"So you and your wife aren't on the best terms right now?" Mr. Jackson asked, realizing that his inquiry had touched a soft spot.

"How'd you know that?"

"I didn't, that's why I asked."

Look, you must have heard something 'cause I didn't tell nobody," Ronald said, not realizing he was furthering his own confession.

"Ronald, I give you my word that I haven't talked to anyone about your personal life, but I think what you're missing here is the fact that you're becoming very upset because I asked if you and your wife are having problems. Now, I'm no psychiatrist or anything, but to me you're sending out signals, which show that their may be a problem. Again, I have to reiterate that I'm not trying to be nosy and pry into your personal life. I'm merely offering you help and an ear if you need it," Mr. Jackson said baring down on Ronald's soul, which seemed at this moment to be an empty place.

Ronald was quiet for an instant, staring at the floor as though the courage he needed to face his problems lay somewhere beneath his feet or was perhaps lost in one of the crevices of the hardwood panels of the office.

"Mr. Jackson," Ronald said, "you got a wife?"

"Yes, I do Ronald. Been married for seventeen years as a matter of fact."

"Have y'all had y'all share of troubles and good times?"

"Why, yes we have Ronald… yes we have."

"Then you know what I'm going through without me sayin' another word, don't you?"

"Ronald, one can only assume that you and I have had similar experiences with our wives. As for guaranteeing they are all the same, we'll never know unless we talk about them."

"Seems like everybody want to talk to me for somethin' or another now a days. First some old floozy, then my wife, and now you. I guess I'll be gettin' a call from Phil Donahue pretty soon."

"What did your wife want to talk to you about?"

"Oh just the same old woman stuff, talkin' about she's seen some changes in me and all this. She even had the nerve to ask me if was I messin' around. Can you imagine that?"

"To tell you the truth, Ronald, it's not uncommon for a woman to think about her husband tippin' out when his normal routine changes."

"But what's so big about me not doing something for one time. What's the big deal?"

"That just it man, when we think something is no mole hill, a woman may see it as the Rocky Mountains. We just think differently, always have, and always will. You know it took me a while to get used to it, but what I found that helped my marriage most was just talkin' to my wife about everything. Now I'll be the first to admit that I'm not the biggest advocate of communication, but it's sort of like going to the dentist, you're gon' have to do it sooner or later, so you may as well do it when you're healthy."

"I don't get it."

"Healthy communication, brother. If you don't talk about the little things now while there's no problem, eventually you'll have discussions about big things that have gotten out of control. You need to talk with your wife and don't just talk to her, talk with her."

"Well, I'm not sure if that's gon' help anything."

"There's only one way to find out."

"We'll see. Besides, I never said me and my wife was havin' a problem anyway," Ronald said defensively.

"No, you didn't say it, but we sure did talk about it quite a bit."

"See that's what I'm talkin' about. All of this nonsense got us talkin' about something that wasn't a problem and didn't need discussin'."

"Maybe you're right, but still, it never hurts to communicate with people."

"Mr. Jackson, I got to get out of here before it gets too late but the one thing I will say is what I always believed, and that is, talk is cheap."

"Okay, Ronald, thanks for taking the time out to sit and talk. If you don't mind, I'll leave you with my own unique spin on your cliche. That is talk is cheap, but a healthy lifelong relationship with a loved one is priceless." Ronald exited his supervisor's office with the man's parting words weighing heavily on his mind and even heavier on his heart.

1985–1987

Chapter 16
New Interests

"Yo' mama let you talk on the phone this late?" Benny asked his potential girlfriend Lawanna.

"My mama sleep, boy. I keep tellin' you, after ten o'clock I just about got the whole house to myself, but you don't want to act right, so I guess you'll just miss out on a good thing," Lawanna asked.

"What kinda good thing do you mean? Like a Miss Goobar?"

"Uuuh, what kinda rap is that you trying to play. I swear Benjamin Dempkins, if you wasn't the cutest tenth grader in class I wouldn't even try to mess with you."

"Aw come on, girl, you know I'm all the way live, don't you?"

"Ooh please, will you give me a break. That ain't even live. Yo' rap is weak and you need some help. You know what, you better be glad that yo' mama and daddy gave you those dimples 'cause if you didn't have them, you wouldn't have me."

"So I got you now?"

"No, not yet."

"But you said..."

"I know what I said and now I'm sayin' when I get ready. You got a lot to learn about girls because we can't be rushed."

"I'm not tryin' to rush you. I just want to see what it's like."

"What what's like, boy?"

"You know what I'm talkin' about."

"I might know what you talkin' about, but I think you need to say it."

"I always say it, but you don't never do nothing."

"That's because I'm not one and you are."

"What am I?" Benny asked.

"You know what you are."

"What am I?" Suddenly Benny's phone clicked.

"You know, a virgin." The phone clicked again only this time louder.

"So what are you gon' do about that?" Benny asked.

"What you want me to do?"

"Everything."

"Everything like what?"

"Everything that you know how to do," Benny insisted.

"You can't handle this cause you'll drown and mess around and get turned out."

"What do you mean drown?"

"You don't know what drownin' means?"

"Like in a ocean?"

"Boy, you got a lot to learn."

"So when you gon' start teachin' me?"

"Do you always beg for stuff that you..."

"Wait a minute, hold on..."

"What is it? Benny? Benny?"

"I'm not on the phone, mama... what... who said something about a virgin? When, just now? ...Mama you're not supposed to be listening to my phone calls. That's an invasion of privacy. Hey Lawanna, I gotta go. I'll call you tomorrow or see you at school," Benny said abruptly, then quietly hung up the phone.

"What do you mean invasion of privacy, little Mr. lawyer? And since you're so in tune with the law, I'm sure you know that you've just committed perjury which is punishable by jail time."

"What do you mean perjury?"

"First you said you weren't on the phone and now you're saying that I'm not supposed to be listening to your phone calls that you supposedly weren't making at this time of the night."

The trapped boy looked into his mother's eyes and awaited his sentencing. His only rebuttal was a pitiful little, "Huh?"

"Don't huh me, Benny. I told you to stay off that phone past ten o'clock, haven't I?"

"Yes."

"I'll tell you what. I'd better not have to make anymore surprise inspections for phone calls or it will get ugly around here. You weren't talking to that little pissy tail gal Laquanda, were you?"

"No, and her name is Lawanna."

"No, her name is little underage hooker with a book bag," Sheila sharply offered.

"Why you say that, mama?"

"Cause I've seen that little trash walking around this neighborhood. And you're not the only one she's seems to like."

"What do you mean?" Benny was baited by his mother's conversation and her hook was jabbed deep into his emotional interest.

"Uh huh, that's what I thought. She's got your nose open so wide that your eyes are completely shut. I know the only reason you're trying to court her is so you can have sex with her."

"What?" Benny was appalled by his mother's bold honesty.

"You heard me. Doesn't she live over on the south side?"

"Yeah."

"I hope you don't think you're taking my car in that neighborhood to pick her up for a date and try to get in her little coochie in my back seat."

"Nawh mama. I don't know why you keep sayin' that," Benny replied offering the best dishonest denial he could possibly find. Sheila's boldness completely threw him off guard and shocked him into denial. It was almost as if she had heard all of his conversations between him and his self-proclaimed girlfriend. Sheila was seemingly inside of Benny's head, or at least maybe she had been there before.

"Mmm-huh. Don't think this is my first time around the block. I've been there and back and seen it all, so I already know what this Lackawana is all about."

"Her name is Lawanna, mama."

"Her name is fire and I hope you don't get burned. I don't approve of that girl at all, Benny, and I don't like you calling yourself dating her or whatever you think it is you two are doing."

"But what's wrong with going with her. Just 'cause she live on the southside doesn't make her bad.

"I didn't say that makes her a person bad. Frankly I don't care if she's from the southside or if she's from Siberia. It's her that I don't like, not where she's from."

"But you don't even know her."

"I know her kind, though, and she's not the kind of girl you need to be dating or courting or whatever you call what you're doing. I call it whoring around and one thing is for sure, you'd better not be doing it in my house."

Benny turned away from his mother, partially because of his disappointment in the opinion Sheila expressed for his girlfriend. Also because he didn't want Sheila to see the guilt on his face for making out on the couch after school one day before anyone got home from work. Deciding against a clever rebuttal, Benny decided to give his mother the victory this time in what was becoming constant debates of right and wrong.

"Benny go to bed and don't let me pick up the phone again after ten and hear you on it, because I will embarrass you and whoever you're talking to. I would prefer that you not talk to that girl, Lassie, or whatever her name is." Benny made no attempt to correct his angered parent this time. He decided that the fastest way to end this one-way conversation was to keep it going one way—her way.

"Okay, mama. I'm sorry; I'll try to do better next time."

"Don't you even try to patronize me, because I don't have much tolerance for this developing attitude of yours."

"But mama, I…" he attempted.

"Don't try, me boy."

Benny remained silent until his mother exited his room.

Since his entrance into high school, Benny and Sheila had suddenly become warring tribes and household rivals. As Benny matured and became more involved in new activities and met new people, his ideas and thoughts developed into complete contrast of those that his mother believed in. She seldom approved of girls he chose to pursue. None off his female preferences were up to Sheila's standards. His mother wanted young ladies that were pure, pretty, and intelligent. Benny wanted an intelligent girl, a pretty girl, or a semi-pure girl, but not all in the same package. If there was no room for improvement, he felt there was no chance of he and a girl growing together. Although the theory was far-fetched, it was an approach he learned from one of the nighttime soap operas. In fact, Benny learned all of his lessons about romance from television. He thought there was very little to be learned about relationships from the example Sheila and Ronald set.

"Ronald, you need to talk to your son… Ronald!"

"What?" Ronald grunted as Sheila's interruption made him depart his deep slumber.

"I said you need to talk to your son."

"What's wrong with him?"

"Nothing's wrong with him yet, but if you don't talk to him, he's going to turn into a whoremonger, then maybe he'll become a drug addict, and then he'll just be nothing more than a street pimp."

"What's wrong with you, Sheila?"

"Why does something have to be wrong with me just because I'm the only one that's concerned about the development of our son."

"I'm not talking about that. What's wrong with you waking me up over some nonsense when I told you I had to get up at four o'clock in the morning."

Sheila paused at Ronald's audacity totally dismissing what she thought was an urgent matter.

"You know what, that's fine. I just won't talk to you ever again about Benny, and we can go and visit him together when he's in the state penitentiary in a few years."

"In the state pen, for what?"

"I don't know, for being a whoremonger or something."

"Lord have mercy, you act like the boy can't be a young man. You better be glad he chasing after all these skirts and he ain't chasing no pants legs. Hell, every boy go through the same thing. It ain't nothing new for a boy to want to try and do something with a girl when he that age. He just need to make sure he knows where the drug store is so he can get some of them rubbers. That's what you really need to be worried about." Because of the silence, Ronald assumed he'd finally gotten through to his wife and she'd seen his side for once. However, Sheila wasn't responding because she couldn't believe what her husband just attempted to sell her.

"What did you just say?" Sheila asked, angrily.

"I said, what you need to be worried about is...," Ronald began, attempting to repeat his statement.

"Oh, I heard what you said," Sheila interrupted, "I just can't believe you said it. And I really can't believe you tried to pass that nonsense off on me."

"I'm just saying that..."

"I know what you're saying, but if you're smart, you wouldn't say it to me again. Cause what you're actually saying is that it's okay for men to pursue multiple women at one time. That's what I'm hearing."

"Here we go again."

"Yeah that's right, here we go again! Let's go again, because that's all we seem to be able to do consistently, go again. And speaking of which, where have you been going lately when you say you're going to the driving range or going to run some errands."

"That's exactly where I've been going, to the driving range and to run some errands."

"I thought you had suddenly lost interest in golf."

"That was for just a little while."

"So now all of a sudden you're back into it and you're going to play more than ever, huh?"

"What's wrong with that?"

"I don't know. You tell me what's wrong with it. What's wrong with losing and gaining interest like it's the weather changing. Then you tell me what's wrong with having a philosophy about men pursuing multiple women and it's just a part of life, and then tell me with what's wrong with feeding that poison to a young boy. And when you tell me what's wrong with all of that, I'd like for you to tell me what's wrong with our marriage, and I don't care what the answer is, I want you to be honest. Be a man, Ronald. Be what you're trying to make your son, a whore mongering man. Tell me what's wrong with that because I'm tired of looking for what's wrong in this house. I just want to find out what's right, if anything, and make some peace. But you know what, I don't think it's going to happen because in the other room is a young boy that thinks it's okay to disobey the rules of this house and date girls just so he can get him a little piece of her action. And in this room, in our bedroom, there is a grown man that condones this disrespectful and disgraceful attitude. So here I am, the crazy woman in the house and the only person who seems to realize that there is a problem. After you tell me what's wrong with all of that, you can fix the leak in the bathroom cause, I'm obviously not the right person to fix our house and keep it in order, so maybe I shouldn't even be here!" Sheila, completely exhausted by purging her feelings, wept openly and buried herself within whatever comfort she could find. Unfortunately, the only the comfort she found was her pillow, now soaked in her wet emotions. There she swam in her tears until she floated away into a restless sleep for remainder of that night's darkness.

"Did you get a whippin' last night, Benny?" Lawanna asked.

"Nawh, for what! I don't get whippins, girl, what's wrong wit' you?"

"Cause yo' mama caught you on the phone after it was late."

"I can talk on the phone as late as I want to."

"Mm-huh, that's why you had to get off the phone, huh?"

"My mama just wanted to talk to me about somethin' that's why I had to go."

"Benny, you ain't got to lie to me cause I already know the game. Talkin' about you don't get whippins. You tryin' to tell me you ain't never got no whippin' in yo' life. The way you act, I bet yo' mama and daddy used to be on yo' butt all the time, didn't they?"

"Yeah I got whippins when I was little, but I don't get 'em no more cause I'm too old."

"Don't say that around my granddaddy cause he'll tell you in a minute you ain't too old for him to take a switch to yo' behind, and he'll get up out of his wheel chair and whip you too. When was the last time you got a whippin', Benny?"

"I don't know probably about when I was thirteen or maybe when I..."

"Thirteen? That was only two years ago!"

"Yeah, probably, I can't remember the last time."

"What did you do when you was that old to make you get a whippin'?"

"Why we keep talkin' about whippins, Lawanna? I thought we were gon' finish what we were talking about last night."

"I forgot what we was talkin' about last night. I been to sleep since then. Don't you know a woman can't concentrate on little things when she's getting' her beauty rest? Besides, I think you gettin' a whippin' when you were thirteen is better than talkin' about you tryin' to get some action."

Benny quickly looked at Lawanna with a shocked expression covering his face, "I thought you said you didn't remember what we were talkin' about last night.

"I don't remember. Is that what we were talkin' about? It was just a lucky guess," Lawanna refuted, searching for a lie to keep her evasive moves intact. "You always talk about that anyway that's why I said it."

"If we stopped *talkin'* and started *doin',* I probably wouldn't talk about it anymore."

"Never mind that. Tell me why you got a whippin' when you were thirteen. That's almost like a grown man gettin' a whippin'. What did you do?"

"He burned a rubber chicken in his mama's oven and tried to make them eat it for dinner with some mustard and bacon grease for gravy."

Benny turned to see the familiar voice that appeared out of nowhere. Before he turned to find the culprit, he realized only one person in the school had the knowledge to convict him of his mischievous adolescent crimes as well as know firsthand about the swift punishment his father had delivered.

"Hey Clem, where you been hidin'," Lawanna called out in a more affectionate tone than Benny had ever received from her.

Benny noticed the sudden interest Lawanna had for his cousin, but he concealed his discomfort for her actions.

"What's up, cuz?" Benny said enthusiastically, attempting to be more interested in Clem than Lawanna was. If he couldn't get her full attention, then she certainly wasn't going to give Clem more attention than he could.

"Nothin', Benny. You didn't tell Lawanna about the time yo' daddy to' yo butt up 'cause you tried to cook that rubber chicken?"

"I didn't try to cook no rubber chicken. All I was tryin' to do was pass a little time until the other chicken thawed out."

"So that's why you tried to put some fake gravy on it. You got to put some kinda baste on a dry bird like that. Don't you know anything about cooking?" Clem asked.

"It sounds like you don't either, talkin' about basting a rubber chicken. What were you thinking?" Lawanna asked.

"Look, I knew what I was doing. If I would have had just a few more minutes, everything would have been cool. Was it my fault that the gravy started..."

"Nawh, you wasn't even close to getting away with it," Clem interrupted. "See Lawanna what had happened was..."

"Aw maaan," Benny mumbled as he noticed a few of Lawanna's friends coming over to join Clem's storytelling hour.

"His mama told him to take a chicken out before he left for school, so it could be thawed out when she got home for work. All he had to do was go in the kitchen and take the chicken out of the freezer as soon as he got out of bed. But knowing my cuz he probably got up, started watching cartoons, eatin' Fruit Loops..."

"Wasn't nobody eatin' no Fruit Loops. I eat Flinstone Fruity Pebbles," Benny interjected and, to his surprise, the girls found him amusing."

"Them Fruity Pebbles good, Benny. I be eatin' those every morning too," one of the girls said, validating Benny's statement.

"Anyway," Clem continued, "Benny forgot to take the chicken out, until his mama called home after school and asked him to soak some potatoes so that she could peel them as soon she got home. Benny runs and takes it out of the freezer. That chicken was hard as a rock so he starts running it under some hot water. It only took wonder boy about five minutes to know that the hot water wasn't gon' work so he takes the chicken and puts it right next to the hot water heater in the basement."

"No you didn't, Benny!" another one of the girls exclaimed.

"My daddy too cheap to buy one of those fancy microwaves," Benny said. "If we had a microwave, all of that would have never happened."

Again the girls chuckled at Benny's senseless humor.

"Nawh, it would've never happened if you took the chicken out like yo' mama told you to." Clem's one liners only got a few more laughs than Benny's had. "While the real chicken is in the basement next to the hot water heater, Benny tries to think of a way to make his mama think that he started cooking the chicken before she got home. Even though he ain't never cooked a chicken a day in his life, he gon' tell his mama that he started cooking the chicken. This fool goes up to his room and gets one of those rubbers chickens, you know like the magicians use?"

"Uh-huh," they all chimed.

"Benny, the brain, takes the rubber chicken and puts it in a pot and sticks it in the oven with the heat on four hundred degrees."

"Nawh it wasn't," Benny said, objecting as if he were in a courtroom. "It was three hundred and fifty degrees."

"That's not the point. It was on and it was a rubber chicken," Clem replied. "So he thinks he's in the clear until my Aunt Sheila comes home early and Benny is standing next to the hot water heater waiting for the real chicken to thaw out. He forgets about the chicken in the oven that's just about to catch on fire. Aunt Sheila walked in the house, saw her oven smokin' and went off. She yelled down to Benny to get in the kitchen, and you know what Benny said when he saw all that smoke?"

"What?" the curious girls asked.

"This nut says, *Mama ,you burnin' another dinner? Daddy said you need to use Stove Top stuffing*."

The small audience broke out into laughter like an uncontrollable plague.

"Benny, you so crazy," one of the girls said in a funny but somewhat affectionate tone.

"How you think of stuff like that, Benny. If it was me, I would have just broke down and begged my mama not to put me on punishment," another girl asked.

Suddenly the girls' attention was focused on Benny's mischievous acts. For the moment, Benny was completely disregarding his interest in Lawanna and enjoying being showered with instant fame.

"Y'all know what came next, right?" Clem said, putting the final touches on the masterpiece story he was creating. "Benny's trademark whippin' dance!" Clem jumped around in a circle imitating his cousin's elusive moves against punishment. Benny, offended by his poor imitation, interrupted him.

"That ain't no whippin' dance. If you gon' do it, you got to do it right," Benny explained, attempting to create a little self basting for the ham he was now becoming. Stretching his legs in mock preparation for perhaps some sort of exercise, Benny began jerking and popping like a cowboy on a bucking horse and then he covered his backside—the key defensive maneuver. His strides became rhythmic while he illustrated the curtain call of his whippin' dance. The young girls were completely enthralled with Benny's performance. Clem had unintentionally propelled his cousin into premature high school popularity.

Everyone seemed to enjoy his introductory showcase with the exception of Lawanna. Her routine of tease and torture wouldn't be effective much longer with all of the new interest in her guinea pig. If Lawanna didn't do something drastic and do it soon, she'd be looking for a new subject, and the few cute tenth graders were either seriously committed to their books, holding on to their junior high school girlfriends, or already being teased and tortured. Lawanna was not quite finished with her tenth grade toy.

"Benny, stop being so silly. Let's go to my locker, because I got something for you," Lawanna announced pulling Benny away from his brief stardom. Benny, the poor love struck puppy that he was, faithfully obliged, but not before he got one last laugh from a quick whippin' dance exit. Lawanna wagged her flirtatious tail in hopes that Benny would not be far behind her, and he wasn't. When they finally reached Lawanna's locker located in a secluded section of the hallway, Benny asked, "What do you have to show me? It's all most time for..." Lawanna ended the conversation by beginning Benny's first experience with a French Kiss. He'd always heard about them and seen some of the students sneaking around doing it, but he never imagined that his first one would be with an older girl in a hallway at school. He liked it; he liked it very much.

Although Benny didn't have much practice with the act, Lawanna didn't seem to care or didn't notice his lack of experience. She pulled away from Benny who was standing at full attention and with everything that could stand at full attention. His eyes remained sealed shut.

"What was that for?" Benny asked after the kiss concluded.

"That was for being patient. Now when do you think you can get some?"

"I don't know. That's what I've been asking you for the longest time."

"Nawh boy! I knew the answer to that question a long time ago. I mean when can you get some rubbers?"

Benny's expression was anything but cool and collected. His hasty motion signaled right away that Lawanna's statement had thrown him off guard.

"I can get some real soon."

"Okay, if you can get some real soon, then you can get some real soon."

Benny stood at even fuller attention—everywhere. A cool breeze ran through his body and expanded through his skin covering him with goosebumps.

"Soon, like when?" Benny said, darting back with his response.

"Soon, like Saturday, when my mama is at work."

As desperately as Benny wanted to rejoice and celebrate in the hallway, his goosebumps and full attention kept him calm.

"Alright then, I'll see you this Saturday."

"You gotta be there by twelve cause my mama leaves for work at eleven thirty okay?"

"Alright, I'll be there if you can do something for me?"

"Something like what?"

"Like gimme one more kiss," Benny answered as the bell rang through the hallways.

"Just one quick one," Lawanna said, while Benny prepared himself for another French Kiss. Instead, Lawanna gave him a teasing peck on his lips. It was as innocent a kiss as one family member might give another one, but it excited Benny to the point of oblivion. It would have to hold him over until the much anticipated Saturday. Benny was cool, instantly popular, thanks to Clem, and about to have his first experience with a girl. Life was great, at least for this moment.

Chapter 17
Man Talk

Ronald and Benny were driving through the last part of what had been a heat punishing Saturday. Although the sun was slowly retiring, it showed no mercy on Ronald's old Ford pickup, which had no air conditioning. Ronald never even considered getting a more modern truck. He just drove faster so more air would circulate through the cab, even if it was hot air that could peel skin off if anyone that sat in it for too long. Now that Benny was older, the disagreements between he and his father were fewer. It seemed as though the two could talk almost as friends when they were alone. Ronald was facing the reality that his son had been in his home for fifteen years and the father-son talks they'd had weren't enough to fill a small basket of broken dreams. Ronald hoped he could salvage whatever was left of their diminishing time together and have some significant impact and influence on Benny's life.

Benny enjoyed the times with his father lately. It gave him some relief from the frequent arguments he'd been having with his mother. Ronald and Sheila kept their own disagreements concealed, so Benny was not aware of the fact that Sheila was struggling with her relationships amongst the men in the house. Benny was older and had an ever-changing mentality. He was developing his own philosophies about people and society. Sometimes his philosophies weren't in accordance with those of his mother. They weren't inappropriate, just different from Sheila's.

Sheila was not prepared for Benny's new interest in girls, nor was she prepared for the types of girls Benny was interested in. Sheila wanted Benny to date a church girl who always carried her books and kept her pretty dress ironed and clean. The fact that this type of young lady was rare didn't matter, Sheila always found flaws in Benny's potential girlfriends, even without meeting them. She might not appreciate the way a young girl requested to speak with Benny when Sheila answered the phone. Maybe a girl said *May I speak to Benny* when Sheila was waiting for her to say *please.* Maybe a girl did say please and Sheila was waiting for the caller to introduce herself before she began speaking. A perfect girl, as euphoric as she may have been, had yet to make her presence known to Sheila.

Benny preferred having a father-son talk rather than butt heads with his increasingly overbearing mother. Ronald promised Sheila he would talk to Benny about his interest in girls and specifically about his growing sexual interest. Sheila hoped that Benny would simply grow up and wait until he was married to even think about sexual encounters, but denial and false hope plagued her reality. Sheila, unable to communicate her feelings about premarital sex to Benny, turned to Ronald for help.

"You still gettin' yo lesson everyday?"

"Huh?" Benny was preoccupied with remaining still to limit the energy he exerted in an attempt to keep himself cool in Ronald's mobile oven.

"Yo' lesson. Are you still gettin' yo' lesson everyday?"

"Yeah."

"Yo' grades still alright?"

"Yeah. I got a 3.1 on my last report card."

"Aw that's good! You know what college you want to go to yet?"

"Nawh, but Coach Dirks is trying to get some of us to take a trip up to Tennessee State when we get in the eleventh grade."

"Aw that's good, that's good," Ronald said, as he searched for a way to break the heat filled silence. There was no easy way to initiate the discussion, and Ronald was no expert in open communication. Ronald was wishing for a little bit of his supervisor's, Mr. Jackson's, communication skills right now. But Ronald realized that Benny was his son and the words he used to talk to him were his and his alone, no matter how awkward they came across.

"Yo' mama wanted me to talk to you about them little girls that's been callin' the house."

"What about 'em?" Benny said, preparing to defend himself.

"Well, you know you gettin' older and the girls are gettin' older. We just want to know what y'all doin'."

"You mean what we're doing on the phone?" Benny knew where the conversation was headed, and he was trying to elude and confuse his father the best he could.

"Look, don't act crazy, Benny. You know what I'm talkin' about."

"What? You said girls are callin' on the phone and you want to know what we're doing?"

"Benny, I'm talkin' to you like a man; I ain't talkin' to you like no little punk or nothing like that." Ronald's frustration was building, not because of Benny's comments but because communicating was again proving to be extremely difficult.

"Then say what you got to say?"

"Well hell, are you screwin' them little girls or what?"

"What did you say?"

"You heard me. I said are you and these little girls doing sex?"

Benny was appalled that Ronald could even find the audacity to raise a question like that. Who did he think he was, his father or something? Ronald was relieved that he had thrown the question out to serve as a sword marking the beginning of this battle.

"Man, I can't believe this," Benny said.

"You can believe it and you can say *aw man* all you want to, but like I said I ain't tellin' you like a punk, I'm tellin you like a man. Cause if you is doin' stuff, you need to know where you can go and get some things so you won't be gettin' them girls pregnant."

"What?" Benny had a new perspective on the conversation now.

"Boy, you on drugs or something? Can't you hear when I talk to you?"

"Yeah I'm listening? I was just confused about what you just said? You know when you said go and get some stuff so they wouldn't get pregnant?"

"Yeah, they called rubbers. You ain't never heard of rubbers?" Ronald asked, then realized that he himself should have been his son's educator for matters such as this.

"I heard of 'em. I just never talked to you about it?"

"About what?"

"You know, about that kinda stuff."

"Well, yeah, I know but that's why I guess ya mama wanted me to talk to you?"

"So you'll buy me some rubbers?" Benny dared to make the unusual request of his father and peered over at him awaiting his response.

Ronald was quiet. He looked briefly over at his son. Ronald looked again and visualized his infant son lying in the seat, as innocent as he could be while still wrapped in a blue blanket from the hospital. He looked over again and saw his son taking his first steps then stumbling only to get up with great resolve and try to walk again. He looked again and saw his five-year-old son attempting to throw a football back to him. The ball was so big it nearly toppled him over. Then Ronald saw his ten-year-old son riding a brand new bike down the street, seemingly riding off into the distance, and never to return and then suddenly making a turn at the end of the street and paddling back towards him. He looked again and saw his son running down the basketball court scoring baskets and immediately looking up into the stands to see if his father had witnessed his rare scoring opportunities. Ronald had been watching, just as he had been watching this fuzzy faced boy look into his eyes and ask him this thing. Asking him to do this task for him that would either help him or hinder him. Ronald wanted to tell his son that he'd buy him the package of condoms so he could start being a man, but in that same instant, Ronald wasn't completely comfortable with the task.

"Daddy?"

"Huh?"

"You gon' buy 'em for me?"

"How many you gon' need?"

"I don't know, about twenty."

"Twenty?"

"You don't think that's enough?"

"Do you even know twenty girls?"

"Nawh but I'm gon' be meetin' a whole lot more."

"Is that a fact?"

"Yep," Benny replied as confidently as he could, with a hint of haughtiness.

"And you gon' use a rubber with every girl you meet?"

"You suppose to use a rubber, ain't you?"

"What I'm asking is, are you planning on doin' something with every girl you meet?"

"Aw, I didn't know that's what you was talkin' about. Probably most of them. You know it depends on how they look."

Ronald was not particularly surprised by his son's comment, because he probably had the same mentality at that age, but he was still uncomfortable with his own son now displaying the reckless attitude. Ronald felt as if he were bearing witness to the reoccurrence of an historic and catastrophic event.

"Look, Benny. I'm only gon' tell you this one time and one time only because I been exactly where you been, so I know what's at the end of this road you on. Now you, as old as you are, ain't nobody married, so it ain't like y'all supposed to be with each other for the rest of yo' life. And so, well you know it's kinda like you can court whoever you want to cause y'all young and y'all trying new things out."

"See that's what I'm talkin' about. So I can have a girlfriend and still have another kinda girlfriend too, right?"

"It's been done a whole lot of times and I know plenty of people that's done it. You know when I was about yo' age, I had more than one girlfriend."

"For real! Daddy, you was a Playboy."

"A playboy? Is that what y'all call 'em now, playboys?"

"Yeah that's what they... I mean that's what we are. What did y'all call 'em."

"Wasn't no mistake about it. We was lady's men. If you was a lady's man, you was the cock of the walk."

"What?"

"Cock of the walk. You know the main man, the big cheese, numero uno."

"Aw, you was dope?"

"Whatever that means. But yeah, I had me a few young ladies."

"Did mama know you had a lot of girlfriends when you were my age?"

"Boy, are you crazy? Yo' mama probably wouldn't even have talked to me if she knew how wild I was when I was your age?"

"Yeah, I think that's the best way to do it. I'm just gon' have my fun now and have me one real fine girlfriend and then just have a few on the side, you know, in case the main one doesn't work out. Is that how y'all used to do it?"

"Yeah, that's exactly how we used to do it. Yep that's exactly how we used to do it," Ronald said, gazing aimlessly out at the road in front of him. He reflected on the mistakes he'd made and speculated about the ones that he was sure his son would make. As they passed through the traffic light, Ronald pulled over into the parking lot of the Mr. Dan's Hamburger Stand.

"Are you gon' take me to the drugstore after we leave here?"

"Yeah, if you think that's what you really want."

"What do you mean?"

"I mean if you think that's how you want to start yo' life."

"Start it like what?"

"Like disrespecting yo' wife."

"But you just said that as young as I am, nobody's married to each other."

"Yeah, that's right, but one day you will be married, and you've got to take all those women that you've been with to bed with you and yo' wife. 'Cause everything that you do and everybody you see, yo' wife is gon' be where you rest yo' head and keep yo' heart."

Benny was shocked by his father's rare, yet thought burdening philosophy.

"Me and my friends used to run through girls like they was front doors. In and out, we didn't care about who we were with or how long we was wit' 'em."

"See that's what I'm talkin' about. I knew I was just like you, daddy."

"Yeah you probably like me but you better make sure you don't end up like me."

"What you talkin' about, Daddy?"

Ronald paused for a moment, "Man, being with all them girls didn't do nothin' for me but mess me up. See, when you sleep with too many women you lose somethin'."

"Somethin' like what?'

"Like you just don't have a fire inside of you like you had at one time. You know how when you eat too much Mr. Dan's, then you don't want any for a long time?'

"Yeah."

"That's what I was like. I used all my appetite up before I got married to yo' mama. And sometimes I can't love yo' mama like I want to."

"So you don't love mama no more?"

"Oh, I love yo' mama more than anything in the world. Sometimes I don't think she believes me, but I do. I mean the physical love not the mental love."

"What's the difference?'

"You might be just a little too young to understand all of this that I'm saying. But what you need to know is, although it might feel good now, it may not feel good later. The bad thing about it is that you not gon' know how bad it hurt until later. So the best thing you can do is try and plan ahead. See, I didn't have nobody to teach me all of this what I'm tellin' you now. And like I said, I ain't tellin' you like no punk or nothin'. I'm tellin' you like a man who done lived and learned and regretted."

"What do you regret?" Benny posed a wounding question to his father and watched him develop a meaningful answer. Ronald nurtured his thoughts for awhile and then educated his son.

"I regret not being right for yo' mama. I ain't sayin' I treated her wrong or nothing, but I mean being right, talkin' about being pure and not having so many other girls before her. What me and yo' mama got now is real and it means a lot to me. But sometimes I feel like the most important part of me and the most special part, she got to share it with all those other girls I had. And now I love yo' mama so much I just want her to have it all, and I want it to belong to her and her only."

"So what you sayin', you cheatin' on mama?"

"Nawh boy what I'm sayin' is... it's kinda like... well, let me tell you like this. As far as yo' mama is concerned, I'm a used car. I'm in good shape, but I been driven by other women, who done steered me in a lot of different directions. Now I just want to go in one direction—wherever yo' mama is going. But I got so many miles on me that I been to most places she wants to take me and now those places won't be special between both me and her."

"So what you sayin', is I don't need to get twenty. I should start off with about ten rubbers?"

Ronald shook his head in disgust and slight amusement at his son's sexually motivated ignorance.

"Nawh, son what I'm saying is, when you get married, it ain't no better gift you can give a woman than yourself. I mean your whole entire, pure self. Look, I know you young and I can't keep my eye on you all the time, so I can't run behind you and make sure you doing what I already know is right for you but you might not know it's right. Think about this for a minute, Benny. Think about graduatin' from high school, walkin' across the stage, goin' to college, having the time of yo' life, meetin' new friends, and gettin' a job. Now think about gettin' a job next week, buyin' diapers, goin' to class, goin' to work, then graduatin' high school. Think about walkin' across the stage and watchin' yo' friends go out to a party and you babysittin' your baby. Think about goin' to school close to home so you can help yo' baby's mama. Now think about fightin' over who's last name the baby gon' have and then think about graduatin' from college and gettin' married to a girl you not sure you love, but marryin' anyway cause you think makin' a bigger mistake is the right thing to do. After you take all them thoughts, think about how many rubbers you want to buy. If you can imagine yourself sleepin' with some little girl, then you can imagine yourself walkin' down the street with that same girl pushin' a baby stroller. If you can't, then you ain't ready for what comes wit' buyin' rubbers."

"But I thought you said that when you was young…"

"Benny, I keep tryin' to explain to you that just because I did it, don't make it right. It makes it a learning experience. If I had to do it all over again, I wouldn't be running around like I did. What I'm trying to tell you is that I made a mistake by bein' with all those women, and since I made the mistake, you ain't got to."

Benny sat petrified by the lessons his unassuming father was instilling in his soul. He had never heard his father speak as open-heartedly as he had just now. Benny was attentive and his head was marinating in his father's hidden wisdom.

"So I guess this really means you not gon' buy me no…"

"Benny, don't ask me about them damn rubbers no more! I done said what I had to say. And from here on out, the decision is gon' be yours whether you take my advice or not. And it's also gon' be yo' responsibility for taking whatever steps you gon' take about my advice."

"Alright, daddy. Can I ask you about buyin' something else?"

"What is it now, boy?"

"You gon' buy me a Mr. Dan hamburger? Man I'm hungry. I ain't tellin you like no punk or no sissy. I'm tellin' you like a hungry young man," Benny said humorously mocking his father.

"Boy, you know what?"

"What's that?"

"You need a job."

"I'm gon' need a car so I can get to work."

"You gon' need a job so you can buy a car."

"Daddy?"

"What is it now, I'm going to get some hamburgers."

"You think that you and mama gon' stay together forever?" Ronald looked away from his son and contemplated the state of his marriage and the problems he and Sheila were having. After a short silence, he replied,

"Forever is a long time, Benny, but it's even longer when you spend it by yourself."

"What chu' mean yo' mama is at home?" Benny asked Lawanna.

"I mean she sittin' in there on the couch watchin' TV."

"I thought you said she was gon' be at work today."

"She was, but she called in sick."

"Then tell her to go to the hospital and then go to work."

"Boy, are you crazy? Why am I gon' tell her that?"

"Cause we got something to do."

"I know, Benny, but my mama home so we can't do nothing."

"Man, see Lawanna, you said we were gon' be by ourselves today," Benny whined, throwing an immature temper tantrum."

"Why you acting like a baby?"

"Why you acting like a tease?"

"What you call me?"

"You heard me. That's all you been doing with me all this time anyway is playin' like a little tease. I bet yo' mama ain't even in there and it's probably somebody else we go to school with, ain't it? Let me see," Benny said as he forced his way through Lawanna's front door.

"You can't come in my house like this."

Benny was disappointed to see a grown woman sitting on the couch watching TV just as Lawanna said. He was expecting to see a boy lying there naked or under the covers waiting for Lawanna to return. There was no boy, only a woman dressed in a sky-blue hospital uniform. The logo on her uniform read 'Golden Arms Senior Care'. She had obviously made an attempt to make her way into work, because she was dressed and ready for duty.

Lawanna's mother was an assistant at a senior citizen's home and worked the weekends for extra overtime money. Lawanna was home alone often because of the numerous hours her mother worked. Benny felt foolish having barged in on the resting woman, so he blanketed her with polite manners.

"Hello, Mrs. Baker."

The resting woman turned away from her television program and focused her attention on the young boy that had entered her house.

"Hello, young man."

"My name is Benjamin Dempkins, and I'm a friend of…"

"Benny, I know who you are. Lawanna talks about you all the time," the woman interrupted, which threw Benny off guard, while at the same time pleasantly surprised him.

"Really?" Benny said, looking towards a blushing Lawanna. He smiled with the comfort of knowing he wasn't being lead on an emotional goose chase.

"Oh yeah, honey. I was wondering when you were gonna stop by so that I could meet you baby."

"It's nice to meet you, Mrs. Baker."

"Oh sweetie, it's nice to finally meet you, too and I didn't know you was such a sweet young man."

"Thank you."

"Oh please," Lawanna interrupted, "Give me a break! Mama, Benny and me going outside for while," Lawanna announced, rather than asking for the permission to do so.

"All right, honey. Benny, you come back anytime and talk to me, okay?"

"Yes mam. I'll be back," he said, staring at Lawanna to make sure she'd heard Benny's open invitation. "I'll be back for sure," he repeated again, this time loud enough for only Lawanna to hear. "So you been talkin' about me huh?"

"Oh, don't get froggy, you can stop jumpin'. I may have mentioned you once or twice, but don't think it's a everyday thing."

"I see your mama knew my name, so that's more than once or twice."

"So what, boy! What you wanna do, move in wit' us? Dag!"

"I'll move in with y'all for about two hours, so I can sleep in your room."

"Please. Just tell me when you coming back over here and make sure it's a day when my mama gone."

"I don't know. When can I come back? You tell me."

"Just come back next Saturday," Lawanna replied nonchalantly.

"I can't make it next Saturday."

"And why not?"

"Because it's Labor Day weekend and we got our family reunion down in the Hope next Saturday."

"You can' t miss it?"

"Miss it? You crazy? That's peach cobbler from all over the family. I ain't stupid."

"What y'all be doin' at y'all family reunion?"

"I don' t know, probably the same thing y'all do."

"We don't have family reunions."

"What?"

"I ain't never been to one."

"What? So how does everybody stay in touch?"

"We don't."

"For real?"

"Nope."

"Man, that's a trip. I thought everybody had family reunions."

"Nawh, everybody don't. So you gon' bring me back some peach cobbler?"

"What you gon' give me if I do?"

"Some Lawanna cobbler."

"You sure it's not no tease cobbler."

"Goodbye, and go home."

"Okay, okay, I'm sorry", Benny said quickly, attempting to heal Lawanna's offended wounds.

"I ain't gon' tell you no more to stop calling me a tease."

"Alright, I ain't gon' do it no more."

"You bedda not."

"So what about the Saturday after next?"

"Mmm, I guess so."

"You guess so?"

"Yeah, I guess so."

"That's it, you just guess?"

"Don't get cocky just cause my mama know your name."

"She like me too."

"No she don't."

"Yes she does."

"Look, whatever. I got to go wash the dishes. I'll see you at school Tuesday."

"Alright then. So make sure yo' mama get to work that Saturday, so me and you can get to do our work."

"We'll see about that, Benjamin Dempkins."

"It must be something about this house because all the women that live here love to say my name." Benny said, and darted off the porch before Lawanna could fire her reply in his direction. Benny was off and running down the street and running as fast as he could towards the Saturday after next.

Chapter 18
New Generations, New Branches

"Aunt Isabelle, yo' little boy is a Tasmanian devil runnin' around here," said Benny.

"Now wait a minute little Benny, cause I still remember when you got yo' butt to' up because you was begging for some Captain D's."

"Aw, that was when I was little."

"You mean little like my baby Jeremiah?"

"I wasn't that old when I was acting up, was I?"

"Let me tell you somethin' boy. You and that little heathen Clem came out the womb talkin' about, *Hey man you better not slap my behind no mo' and stop looking at my mama's coochie.*"

"Aunt Isabelle, you need to stop clownin' like that."

"I ain' t lyin'. Y'all wasn't no better than Jeremiah."

"But look at him," Benny said as he pointed to one of the new family editions picking his nose and dipping his finger in the bar-b-que sauce. "He's poisoning Uncle Seefer's secret sauce."

"Jeremiah! Boy, if you don't come away from there!" Isabelle ran over to her son in an attempt to rescue him from the sauce, or perhaps rescue the sauce from him.

Benny's Aunt Isabelle, who was really Benny's cousin, and her husband Seefer had faced the reality of not being able to have their own child. When the opportunity arose to adopt the infant boy of a teenage girl who was said to have links to their family, Isabelle and her husband seized the opportunity. Members of the family speculated who the teenage girl might have been, but Granny Osee quickly shut the lid on any further gossip. She told everyone that the child was God's baby and that God gave the baby to Isabelle and Seefer. Aunt Flappy confirmed that statement with a boisterous, *And behold thou shalt conceive in thy womb and bring forth a son and shalt call his name Jesus—but y'all call him whatever you want to.*

There were many new faces at this family reunion, many of whom were little children or were new husbands or wives. Benny worked through the family crowd filled with stubble faced old ladies asking for cheek-scratching kisses and stoop-down-to-me hugs. Benny obliged them all and made his way over to his dependable family reunion partner, Clem.

"Man, look at all of these people. I don't even know who half of them are."

"Me either. Somebody was callin' my name and I walked by them and they almost cussed me out talkin' about they used to change my diapers and now I can't stop by and speak to them."

"Who was it?"

"I 'on't know. Somebody talkin' about I'm yo' Uncle Sho Shack."

"Uncle Sho Shack?"

"Yeah, there he go right over there standing next to that little boy that I ain't never seen either," Clem announced, as Benny's attention was drawn to a short old man wearing a derby style hat accessorized with a long purple feather. He was sporting slacks with cuffs that were large enough to hold pocket change, a wallet, and maybe a few snacks. The gap between the bottom of his cuffs and the top of his shiny red shoes exposed orange glittery socks, even more so while he entertained his one-person audience with what Sho Shack thought was a shoe-shine tap dance. The choreographed nightmare was more reminiscent of the funky chicken done on a bed of hot coals. Never the less, the small boy was mesmerized by the performance and that was all the motivation Sho Shack needed.

"Who is that little boy that Sugar Shack is tryin' to scare away?" Clem asked.

"I thought you said Sho Shack, and that little boy is Jeremiah, but I'm gonna call him little Jerry," Benny answered.

"Sugar shack, rat pack, Big Mac attack, whatever his name is. Where did that little rug rat come from?"

"That's Aunt Isabelle's and 'nem son," Benny answered.

"Aunt Isabelle and ' nem had a son? Ain't they too old to be having kids?"

"I think they adopted him."

"For real? I ain't never had no adopted cousin before," Clem said.

"How you know?"

"What chu mean?"

"I mean how you know I'm not adopted?" Benny answered.

"I just do?"

"You wasn't there when I was born, so how you know I'm not adopted?"

"Are you?"

"Yep?"

"For real?"

"Nope but what if I was? I'm still yo' cousin and you still like hangin' wit' me. Just cause somebody is adopted don't mean something is wrong with him."

"I ain't said it was something was wrong with them." Clem replied.

"Well you was actin' like Jerry got a problem or something."

"Nawh, he alright. Just as long as he ain't as bad as you were."

"Man, please, you was the one always makin' me get whippins," Benny said in his own defense.

"Yeah, uh huh, you need to go and get yo' little cousin, 'cause Uncle House the Shack man, or whatever you call him, tryin' to chase Jerry down and get his hat back from the boy."

Benny threw a glance in the direction of what was once a performance stage only to see it empty with the exception of a blazing trail being led by the new edition followed by yesterday's news, Sho Shack.

"Little Jerry, stop running and give him his hat back!" Benny demanded.

Every family member gathered under the pavilion, gave their attention to the surprisingly authoritative voice of Benny, particularly Jeremiah. The small boy instantly responded to the nickname Benny bestowed upon him. The two engaged each other with a look of respect and then concern. Jeremiah responded to Benny's care of his well being and the command of discipline he had issued. Benny saw in the small mischievous stranger, a trait he himself was very familiar with. The two were separated by a generation but connected by character. Jeremiah produced a pouting puppy face as though it were his post scolding routine.

"Don't give me that lost puppy face 'cause I can make one better than you."

Jeremiah looked up at Benny and suddenly realized he wasn't dealing with any ordinary big person. His pouting was bumped aside by a grin that forced its way to the surface for Benny to see.

"Whatsth yo' name Mistha?" Jeremiah hurried his words out around his lisp. He could talk just as fast as he could run from an old man looking for his hat.

"I'm yo' cousin Benny, and you don't have to call me mister 'cause I'm not a grown man yet."

"Aw, you know my name?"

"Yep?"

"Then what you me call Jerry fo'? My name that isth ain't!" Jeremiah's mouth lost the race it was in with his brain resulting in a babbled statement of confusion.

"Wait a minute, slow down and speak clear."

"Ughh." Jeremiah sighed in frustration because he'd made perfect sense to himself.

"I sthaid, why you call me Jerry that'sth not my name."

"It is now. You can't be at the family reunion and not have a nickname if you're little."

"Did you have a nickname when you was little?"

"Yep, and I still do."

"What isth it?"

"Benny."

"What'sth yo' real name?"

"Benjamin Dempkins."

The little boy stared in amazement at his big cousin and new friend. Jeremiah probably hadn't had a conversation this long in his entire life. Suddenly he sprang out of his attentive position spreading the good word to his mother, Isabelle.

"Mommie, my nickname isth Jerry? Call me Jerry, okay," Jeremiah announced to Isabelle as he ran through the pavilion in order to make his proclamation official. The other family members were quite stunned at Benny's maturity and ease with the smaller child. Sheila stood in the distance smiling with pride at her son.

"Hey, you finished baby-sittin' so we can go shoot some hoop?" Clem asked as he walked over to the Sesame Street hero. Clem's mouth was oozing with bar-b-que sauce and he was licking his fingers in between gulps of RC Cola.

"Man, hold on, I haven't even had time to eat yet. Why you go over there and eat without me?"

"You was over there playin' father knows best."

"All you had to do was wait. You act like you got a job and you got to go to work or somethin'," Benny told his insensitive cousin. He was disappointed Clem didn't see the importance of interacting with their young cousins.

"You bedda go on somewhere. You act like that's yo' son or something'."

"That ain't got nothing to do with it. You just selfish."

"Nawh, you over here playin wit' little kids actin' like a little punk."

"I got yo' punk. If you see a punk, spit on one," Benny angrily responded. The conversation was heating up and gaining more attention from the other family members. Clem and Benny were lifelong playmates, so no one was rushing over to interrupt the commotion.

There was no need to stop the boys, because the latest arrival to the family reunion had just silenced everyone in sight. No one was speaking or moving when they witnessed the unbelievable spectacle making a grand entrance to the gathering. Although this was the family reunion of new editions, some editions were less welcomed than others. Jeremiah took a back seat to a soon to be family member.

No one noticed Jeremiah's misbehavior or showed much interest in the dispute between Clem and Benny. Everyone turned away from the peach cobbler table that was being attacked with forks and knives just minutes earlier. As if it had been orchestrated, the tape recorder even reached the end of its last song, and now there was only dead silence overtaking the aroma and good times that surrounded the family festivities.

"Mommie, who'sth that lady with the big belly?" Jeremiah, although completely innocent, was the first one to break the silence.

"Shhh, Jeremi… I mean Jerry don't talk so loud," Isabelle said, quickly covering her son's inquisition. "That's your cousin Cynthia."

"Can I go over there sthee if sthe wansth to play?"

"No, go play with your cousin Wayne, but you two had better stay out of trouble, you here me?"

"Yesth." Jeremiah disappeared into the heat with his cousin Wayne who was a new edition himself five years ago. Meanwhile, Benny and Clem were still standing close to each other. The two were wishing they had continued arguing instead of feeling so uncomfortable watching their pregnant cousin stand in the entrance of the pavilion seemingly helpless and alone.

Benny wasn't sure where his discomfort originated. Perhaps because the sight of this pregnant young girl had just destroyed his expectations. Cynthia was the cousin who was sure to surpass he and Clem by becoming a largely successful woman. This round-bellied youth was surely not that same aspiring young girl. This couldn't be the cousin that teased him and laughed as he reluctantly walked out to the tree retrieving switches. Then Benny realized that the reason for his discomfort was because he didn't see his cousin standing there with an expectant womb. What he actually saw was Lawanna standing there, and then he saw all of the other girls thrilled by his whippin' dance whom he thought about persuading to do it with him. Benny wasn't so interested in Lawanna's house when her mother wasn't home anymore. He wasn't interested in the rubbers he and his father had talked about. Benny's primary interest at that time was getting his cousin to a seat, so she wouldn't continue to feel as though she were a freakshow. His long-term interest was ensuring that he would never put a young girl on display as his cousin Cynthia was.

As usual, Cynthia's father had dropped her off. Benny walked over to his deserted cousin so that that he could begin reminiscing and later begin inquiring.

"Hey, cousin Cynt. I ain't seen you since y'all moved out of town. How you been doin'?"

Cynthia was startled by Benny's words. She was sure that the first person to speak to her was going to embarrass her in some way. Benny's greeting was like a pair of arms embracing her. Finally someone was treating her like family instead of like a foreigner.

"Hey, Benny. You still gettin' all those whippins?" Cynthia was searching for small talk until the conversation inevitably turned towards her belly.

"Nawh, not me. But you used to get quite a few when you was little, so don't get crazy. You want me to get you somethin' to eat? Come over here and sit down. I'll get you something to drink. What you want a Tang, RC Cola, what?" Benny was being overly hospitable, almost as though he felt responsible for Cynthia's condition.

"Benny, you don't have to do all of that. I'm pregnant; I'm not about to die.

Calm down."

Benny desperately needed that icebreaker. With the comment, Cynthia conveyed that she was open about her situation and good-spirited as well. The concerned cousin paused for a moment and thought about what he could say to ease her pain. Instead, he decided to go with the direct approach.

"Cynthia."

"Huh?"

"How'd you get pregnant?"

"If you don't know, then yo' mama and daddy need to…"

"No I mean… but I thought you didn't like boys and didn't…" Benny wasn't quite sure want he wanted to say nor was he aware of how idiotic he'd sounded. "I guess what I mean is, didn't you know about rubbers and stuff?"

"Yeah, I know about rubbers. I know about foam, pills, diaphragms all that stuff. We was using a rubber and it broke."

"They can break?" Benny almost invited everyone else to join their conversation with his outburst. Although people pretended not to notice, they were all gawking and holding conversations about the new outcast.

"Yeah boy, you didn't know that?"

"Nawh, didn't nobody tell me they could break."

"Benny, you still stupid as ever," Cynthia said, jabbing Benny with an insult for old time's sake.

Benny couldn't help from thinking to himself, *you're the one with a watermelon in your belly, so I can't be too stupid.*

"What did yo' daddy and 'nem say?"

"They said don't expect them to be live-in baby-sitters and that I had to come up with a plan for when I go to college."

"They not gon' watch yo' baby when you go away to school?" Benny asked, amazed by the stern attitude of Cynthia's father.

"Nope."

"Man, that's cold blooded."

"Not really. I mean it's gon' be my baby and my responsibility, so why shouldn't I have to take care of it?" Cynthia sounded as though she had spent many tears convincing herself of the statement she'd just made.

"Well, is the boy gon' help you?"

"I 'on't know. I really don't care what he does."

"What's his name? Does he go to your school?"

"Why you all up in my business. You need to get you some business!" Cynthia put up her emotional jailbars so no one could get in and she couldn't let any feelings out.

Same old Cynthia, Benny thought, *tough and terrible*. Still, he felt overwhelming sympathy for her.

"Cynthia, yo' kids gon' be bad. I already know it."

"If they are, they gon' get a strap across they backside, too."

"You gon' whip yo kids?" Benny was shocked that Cynthia would even consider such an act after they had all grown up loathing whippins and vowed never to whip their children.

"Yep, I'm gonna get in their tail as soon as they cross the line," Cynthia announced with a bold confident voice.

"As much as you hated gettin' whippins, you gon' do that to somebody else?"

"Yeah, if I get a wor'some child like you."

"I wasn't bad at all, just a little excited about most things," Benny offered in place of the truth.

"Oh yeah? Then why did Aunt Sheila beat yo' butt for pouring tree sap in that lady's peach cobbler?"

Benny thought for a moment, reminisced, realized, and then laughed.

"That was just one thing. That lady don't know how to make peach cobbler no way. I was doing the family a favor by getting rid of it."

"Uh huh. Aunt Sheila almost got rid of the skin on yo' back side too, didn't she?"

"Y'all need to be thanking me for that. Everybody would have been eating nasty peach cobbler."

"Oh, we should have thanked you alright. Thanked you for the entertainment."

"Go on somewhere, girl."

"I tell you one thing, though. You had the most whippins trophy, but those little boys over there are making you look like an angel. Now those boys are acting crazy. Whose kids are those?"

Cynthia's statement prompted Benny to turn to see who could have possibly been exhibiting the antics that made Cynthia call him an angel. Unexpectedly, but not unbelievably, Benny saw his new cousin and a not so new cousin causing trouble. Jerry and Wayne were standing behind a tree near the pavilion where some of the older family members were sitting. Benny noticed that two older members were rubbing the backs of their necks as though insects were biting them. In between their supposed bug bites, they talked to each other about the insect epidemic.

"Chile, deez here bugs is 'bout da worse I done ever seent 'em," a gentle gray-haired woman declared.

"Um just about to be ate up out here," the other elder replied. "Bugs must thank um some kinda black watermelon or somethin'. I can't hardly stand it no mo'. Ouch! There go another one. Where deez here bugs don' come from?"

"It's prolly all dis rain we got. My knees been itchin' too and that always tell me somethin' ugly comin'. I guess I bedda get da Witch Hazel out when we get back at da house," an older man said rubbing his knees and scratching his neck.

After observing the situation, Benny noticed that the two desperadoes would make an appearance just before the older family members thought a bug had bitten them. A few minutes later, Benny watched more closely as the boys came from around the tree and threw small pebbles and rocks at the necks of their dumbfounded victims. The pebbles were small enough and thrown with just enough velocity that it simulated a quick sharp bug bite. Benny yelled the boys' names just as they were about to graduate from the small pebbles to more dangerous stones. Jerry and Wayne held larger rocks in their hands, which were the size of marbles and were preparing the next phase of their amateur attack.

"Wayne, Jerry, I got yo' numbers, both of you!" The two culprits were startled and exposed. Benny thought no one was paying any attention to the young boys, so he was surprised to hear the discernable voice of Aunt Flappy from the other side of the pavilion.

"Little heathens, let he who has sinned cast the first stone, and y'all been chucking them rocks for twenty minutes. Y'all bedda get on away from here! You hear what I'm sayin' to you boy?"

People turned to look at the boys as they dropped the rocks and ran around the pavilion to hide themselves between the parked cars imitating an action movie narrow escape. Instead of leaving Cynthia and chasing the fleeing suspects, Benny was suddenly trapped by the colorful outfit and undesired enthusiasm of his Uncle Sho Shack.

"Hey, what cha say there, youngsters? I ain't seen nare one of y'all since Jesus wore loafers!" Sho Shack, regardless as to how close he was standing, always shouted like he was on stage and felt the need to project his voice. Always an entertainer, Sho Shack lived in his costume. To everyone else it was a costume, to him they were normal work clothes. His orange socks were exposed as usual because his slacks with the red rhinestones down the seam were being suffocated in his crotch because of his homemade suspenders. One side of the suspenders was made of paper clips. The other side was constructed of rubber bands. Sho Shack carefully maintained his prized suspenders and also used them as a backup sewing kit. In case he tore his clothes or he lost a button, Sho Shack would pop off one of his paper clips and repair any clothing item in whatever manner he could with an instant alteration remedy. He once considered making a safety pin belt but thought that would look too tacky.

If his tap shoes separated at the soles, which they routinely did, the rubber bands came off and were stretched around the wounded shoe. One of Sho Shack's biggest fears was the thought of his suspenders becoming snagged in his tuxedo T-shirt during a performance. If it were before or after a show, he could handle it, but Sho Shack was a skilled improviser of the arts. This being the case, Sho Shack always kept a spare tuxedo T-shirt tucked safely inside his green derby hat which adorned with red and blue battery-powered lights. The hat was added especially for his night shows. It was an obvious attraction to Jerry, who'd tried to steal it earlier.

As a young boy, Sho Shack found some pictures of a tap dancer in Harlem. He was completely overcome by the agile poses, splits, and the elevation of the dancer's jumps. Sho Shack, never having seen the entire routine, made a dance out of the three pictures he saw. In between the images on the photos, Sho Shack inserted his own creative concoctions, which resembled bailing hay and slopping hogs. His show was atrocious in everyone's opinion, except his own. When the people laughed at him, he simply perceived it as gratitude for his attempted art.

Having perfected his debacle dance, Sho Shack took his performance on the road. Fortunately the road was only twenty miles long. The star-struck young boy built a dilapidated stage with a roof in case it rained and hitched it to his father's tractor. He drove from house to house offering to put on his show in the self-made shack. After making a few rounds, and once in a while traveling an extra three miles, he picked up the name Sho Shack. He never really made a living as a performer; in fact, Sho Shack couldn't even make a dying out of performing. Down in the country, he was the closest thing to an entertainer black folks could find. In his prime, he'd performed at all of the juke joints in the surrounding counties.

"Uncle Sho Shack you gon' do yo' new dance for Cynthia?" Benny said, encouraging the eager old man to put on his ridiculous show.

"Oh yeah I got a new move for you . It's called the Sho Shack Shuffle. Just let me know when you ready for it."

"We're ready whenever you're ready, Uncle Sho Shack."

"Nawh, don't put it on me cause I stay ready, so I won't have to get ready, boy. Watch out now!" He pointed at his two new audience participants. First he slapped the bottom of each shoe three times to signal the beginning of his ritual. Then, without hesitation swished and swayed from left to right pouring out an imaginary bucket as though he were feeding hogs, then he stopped suddenly and reached in front of him only to pull back up and reach back down again like he was bailing hay. The proclaimed new Sho Shack Shuffle was the Sho Shack Slide reborn with a different name and for a different audience. Benny felt the need to encourage the old man who was obviously caught up in what he thought were his glory days.

"Hit it... Uncle Sho Shack! Hit it... Uncle Sho Shack! Get up... Uncle Sho Shack! Get up... Uncle Sho Shack!" Benny cajoled in a rhythmic pattern. Cynthia could only laugh from embarrassment for her uncle, and that was the only applause the colorful performer ever wanted, a smiling face, even if it was at his own expense.

When Sho Shack danced, it was only a matter of time before the crowd exited, and today was no different. As Sho Shack neared his finale, the family members began leaving the pavilion and getting in their cars in preparation to return to the hotels or to the quiet country setting of Aunt Flappy's house. Benny was still snickering when he saw Cynthia leverage herself to one side in an attempt to pull the rest of her bloated body from the chair. As she pulled herself up, Benny came to her aid and wrapped his arm around her back and pulled her up.

"Whew! Thank you, Benny," she said.

Benny realized that this was probably the first nice thing Cynthia had ever said to him. Likewise, he also stumbled over the fact that helping her up was probably the first nice gesture he had ever done for her.

"No problem. Are you comin' over to Aunt Flappy's house?"

"Nawh boy, what I want come over there wit' y'all for?" Cynthia said, quickly transforming into her old self again.

"I don't know. I just thought you wanted to come over there cause that's where everybody is gon' be, and it's some more peach cobbler and ice cream." Benny watched as Cynthia's interest tried to run out of her mouth and exclaim that she would love to go and spend time with the family. Just as quickly as her emotions tried to show their true intent, they relented back into the reality that some of her family would probably look at her differently. Benny watched his cousin's emotions change and then become her falsely spoken words.

"Nawh, I'm just gon' go back to the hotel with Jessie and 'nem cause I'm kinda tired."

"Okay, we'll all be at church tomorrow so maybe we'll see you there," Benny said, making one last attempt to include his cousin.

"Maybe."

"Okay, see ya Cynthia."

"Bye."

Benny watched as she waddled out onto the gravel parking lot towards a car of a family member who'd consented to give her a ride back to the hotel. Again, Benny saw the vision of Lawanna cast within his cousin. When she was near the car, Cynthia turned back to face Benny. His eyes widened as he saw what was surely the face of Lawanna climbing into the car. His vision confirmed the possible fate his father had tried adamantly to warn him about. Their special Saturday seemed closer than ever now, and Benny wanted to run in the opposite direction, for as far as he could and as long as he could. Then Benny saw Jerry climb into Isabelle's car. In that afternoon Benny found himself serving as a father figure to Jerry and a comforting companion to Cynthia. Although he had served both roles well, Benny knew he was not prepared to assume those types of responsibilities. As his family members left the pavilion, which was a failed heat barrier, Benny exited the place that had just instilled a lesson in him, which would never be learned in a classroom.

Most of the family members who had returned to Aunt Flappy's house were either sitting on the front porch, sleeping in the many abstract bedrooms, or playing in the yard. The older family members, with the exception of Aunt Flappy, were fast asleep while Sheila, Ronald, and a few cousins sat on the porch playing spades. Clem, Benny, and the teenage cousins, who were now too old to run around the yard, were standing around talking about sports, dating, and high school. The newest generation was set loose in the yard, the same way wild piglets would scavenge through the mud.

Jerry and Wayne, bored with the trivial dealings of the other kids their age, disappeared into the house for a while and then emerged again near Benny, Clem, and the older kids.

"Cousin Benny, what y'all doin'," Jerry asked.

"We takin' care of grown folks business, so y'all need to get on away from here," Clem lashed out at the unwanted visitors.

"If y'all talkin' about grown folks business, then why y'all not over there with the grown folks?" Wayne said, jumping in for his accomplice launching a stinging verbal attack on Clem.

"Who you think you talkin' to?" Clem asked.

"I'm talkin' to you. You big baboon!" Wayne said with authority.

"You want yo' little tail beat into the ground, don't you?"

"Let me tell you somethin'...." Wayne said, mustering up every bit of courage he'd ever known about in his short-lived life. He paused for a moment, perhaps trying to decide whether to risk his life by responding to the giant in front of him. Wayne looked around and decided to go for it. "Kiss my booty!"

All of the teenagers roared in laughter. Not because the statement was funny, but because someone so small had the courage to offer such a bold phrase. Clem now faced the humiliation of the small delinquent insulting him. This was the same territory where Clem had once urinated on a frog's head to get attention. Wayne was attempting to defame Clem's reputation as one of the top cousins in the family. Clem decided to be an adult and make an example out of the new mouth of the family. While everyone continued to enjoy their hysterics, Clem unbuckled his belt, and in one swift yank, pulled it from all of the belt loops on his pants. Wayne's courageous face dwindled to a meek look of fear. Clem reached out to place his little cousin's arm in the whippin' clasp of his left hand. Wayne quickly realized the challenge at hand. He was about to get whipped by someone who was not one of his parents and more importantly, someone who was not an adult. With that in mind Wayne had only one option left—running! Just as Clem's clutches drew closer, Wayne sprinted backwards away from his cousin and made an about-face to allude Clem for good. Wayne would have escaped if perhaps he had another eighteen inches on his little legs. Yet his best attempt to run was futile because Clem made five giants steps to Wayne's miniature twenty little steps and captured the boy. Angered now that Wayne disrespected him more by giving chase, Clem was hot and full of adrenaline.

Surely, Wayne was doomed by the belt. Clem drew back the belt to commence his cousin's punishment and started the delivery, when suddenly Cousin Pearl peered out onto the front porch from her deep slumber and yelled to everyone she could possibly reach, "Flappy, oh Flappy! Those little nappy-headed son of a guns done hid my fake titty! Make that boy bring me back my titty!"

Sheila, Ronald, Margie, William, and the other adults were flabbergasted. For a moment, they thought that their family member was reaching the end of her senility and had completely lost her senses. Then, as they observed her irate mannerism, everyone saw that she only had one sag in her nightgown instead of the usual two. The duo of desperadoes had slipped into the elderly's slumber palace and taken the old woman's prosthesis. Just as the family deduced what unbelievable dealings the boys had done, another snoozing elder appeared from inside.

Uncle Tyrone poked his head out the door and attempted to flap words between his lips and gums, "Dem dare lirl headens done tole my teefus."

"What?" Benny yelled back, trying to clarify what the old man mumbled.

Granny Osee got up out of her chair to take charge of the developing mayhem.

"He said them there little heathens done stole his teeth. Wayne, Jerry bring y'all little tails over here fo' somebody beat the hot piss out of the both of you."

The adults were looking at the toothless old man standing next to his lopsided mammary-glandless sister. Suddenly, sounds from within the house became progressively louder. Repetitious thuds resounded towards the front door. It sounded as if someone were beating a wild animal to death with rhythmic swings of a baseball bat. As the thuds became louder, and everyone looked towards the front to see what was about to be revealed. Cousin Waldo managed to hop his way to the front door. That was the noise which had bewildered everyone. Each mouth in the yard, on the porch, and within visual distance of the front porch follies, dropped wide open, except for Wayne and Jerry. They had already gotten a sneak preview of the show, because they were the producers. The two boys were not at all shocked to see the elderly man leaning up against the wall to keep his balance on his one good leg which had been abandoned by his prosthetic limb.

"I don't know who done did this, but whoever done took my damn wooden leg better make sure I get it back in two seconds or um gon' take somebody out to the watermelon patch and spank dey tail with the biggest and hardest switch I can find."

All eyes were now on Wayne and Jerry, but before anyone could make a Christmas-shopping rush towards the boy's behinds, Granny Osee stepped out into the yard and parted the sea of young and old as though she were Moses.

"Granny Osee, let me take care of him, I already got my belt off. You ain't got to do nothing," Clem offered as he tightened his grasp of the sobbing little boy.

"Clem, you bedda let him go, cause you ain't but a couple years away from the last whippin' you got, boy."

Clem obeyed while the other teenagers stepped away from the wrath of Granny Osee.

"Wayne, Jerry didn't I tell you to get over here!"

The adults turned all of their cards face up to show that they were more interested in the developments in the yard than they were in making their books for that particular hand.

"Now let me ask you something, and I don't want even the slightest *smell* of a lie on the breath of either one of you, and you'd bedda not utter or stutter one drop off anything but the truth or you'll get *two* whippins, one from me and one from God. Do you hear me?" Granny Osee's voice and demeanor were so commanding that even the adults found themselves nodding their heads in submission.

"Yes ma'am," the boys replied simultaneously.

"Now, am I to believe that the two of you snuck into the back bedrooms and took Pearl's prosthesis, Tyrone's teeth, and Waldo's wooden leg while they were all asleep?"

"He cometh like a thief in the night, you hear what I'm sayin' to you boy?" Aunt Flappy yelled.

"Yes mam," the two softly replied.

"Well, the both of you turn right around and walk back to Aunt Flappy's old outhouse behind the kitchen. I'll be there in just a few minutes with a switch for each one of you."

Jerry and Wayne erupted into tears and sobs of fear. The adults on the porch gasped at the thought of Granny Osee coming out of whippin' retirement for the two young boys. Over the years, Granny Osee had become the savior from the switch, and it had been a few generations since she was the deliverer.

On the way back to their fate near the outhouse, the boy's sobbing weakened to tear-filled sniffles. But when Granny Osee reached over to the small tree next to the outhouse, the boys opened the valve full throttle on whatever mechanism controlled their sobbing and crying. Granny Osee grabbed a couple of three-foot switches and clasped them near the bottom. In one single motion, she jerked her left hand up the switches and swiped every leaf and small branch from the sticks. The limber, bare sticks waved around in her hands as she pointed them at the boys.

"Granny, you gon' whip us?" Wayne whimpered out through the gasps of air that made up his panic stricken breathing. Wayne looked over at Jerry who followed his lead.

"Granny, you gon' whip usth?" Jerry said, mimicking his cousin hoping he had a plan to escape their great grandmother's judgement. Neither of the two contemplated running, for they knew that Clem was still in the front yard with belt in hand, still itching for the opportunity to rectify the disrespect Wayne imposed on him earlier. Granny Osee composed herself, held a switch out in each hand and looked sternly into the boys' eyes and posed a question.

"Do you two think you should get a whippin', or do you think that y'all haven't done nothin' wrong?"

"We was just havin' fun," Wayne replied.

"Yeah, we wasth justh havin' fun," Jerry said following his leader.

"Do you think that it's fun to do bad things to people and to steal?"

"No," they both said simultaneously.

"Would you like someone to do bad things to you?"

"No."

"Then why did you do what you did to your elders?"

"What's a elder, Granny Osee?"

"Yeah what'sth a eller?" the duplicating Jerry asked.

"It's someone that's older than most people and someone that you should be nice to and respect."

"Are you a elder, Granny Osee?" Wayne asked.

"Are you Granny Osee?" Jerry said.

"You can think of me as an elder but that's not what we're talking about. We're talking about you two and what you did today to some other elders. Now Jerry, pick out the switch that you want and Wayne you do the same thing."

Again the boy's opened the floodgates in their eyes. This time, they knew that the inevitable was reaching its arrival.

"I don't want none of them, Granny Osee," Wayne pleaded tearfully.

"Me either Granny Osthee, I don't want one," cried Jerry.

"If y'all don't quit acting crazy, and pick one of these switches, I'm gon' go out to the front yard and get yo' cousin Clem. I hope y'all know that he ain't gon' ask what you want, he's just gon' start whippin' you wit' his belt until he gets tired. Now which one do you want?"

Wayne lowered his head realizing he'd failed in conniving his way out of the situation. Slowly, Wayne walked closer to Granny Osee, with Jerry right behind, and pointed at the long slender switch. Jerry pointed to the same one Wayne had picked, but Granny Osee paid him no attention.

"Wayne, take this switch in your hand that you picked, and Jerry you take this one that you didn't know that you picked. I want you to put these switches under you bed tonight. From now on, when you think about doing something bad, I want you to think about those switches, cause the next time either one of you even so much as sniff some kind of trouble, I'm gon' get two mo' switches twice as long and twice as thick, then I'm gon' make sure that you boys wear these switches on yo' backsides like a pair of trousers. Do you hear me?"

"Yes, Granny Osee," the relieved but confused boys exclaimed.

"And don't y'all go runnin' around here talking 'bout Granny Osee didn't whip us either, cause if I hear that from somebody, the next thing you gon' hear is yo' cousin comin' around to the outhouse ready to tear a hole in both of y'alls behinds. Now gon' in the house, wash yo' hands, sit down at the table and get some peach cobbler, and there had better not be one crumb left on a plate.

"Okay, Granny Osee," Wayne said rushing towards the house before she changed her mind. This time Jerry was slow to act and Wayne had a huge smile on his face.

"Thank you for not whippin' usth. I love you," Jerry said.

"Granny Osee loves you too, but that don't mean I'm not gon' whip you. That just means I'm might not whip you today. Now if you catch me on a Wednesday, it might be a different story", Granny Osee responded jokingly.

"What's so special about Wednesday?" Wayne asked.

"The same thing that's special about that switch in your hand, nothing, unless somebody decides to do something with it like I will if you don't get in that house like I told you to."

Jerry darted off to join his cousin who was already elbow deep in the peach cobbler. Granny Osee looked on as she watched this newest generation walk away from her and into the house, which had hosted many generations.

Lawanna and Benny finally arrived at the moment that Benny had perhaps waited for his entire teenage life. The previous unexpected visitor, who just so happened to live at Lawanna's house and pay all of the bills, was safely tucked away within the confines of her Saturday nine to five.

"Benny, I really like you, even though you probably think that I'm a tease or somethin'."

"Nawh, I don't think that you're a tease, girl, just a little slow," Benny said submerging his real feelings from Lawanna.

"Slow!" Lawanna said, obviously offended. "No, yo' lil' young behind didn't call me slow. I got your slow alright cause..."

"Wait a minute, Lawanna, don't get carried away, cause if you do, you may have to get carried off." Benny was seemingly more mature and confident. It was as though perhaps something had occurred in his life that instilled a jolt of rational behavior in him. Lawanna was confused while at the same time impressed. "Lawanna, I know that I've been talking about this for a long time and I probably been begging you for it, but... I don't think this is such a good idea anymore." Benny said. His sexual fantasies were still clouded by the site of his ostracized cousin at the family reunion. Lawanna wasn't in Benny's family, but surely there was a family somewhere that wouldn't have a problem ostracizing another pregnant, unwed, teenage girl. Benny didn't feel the need to be a contributing factor in such a feat.

"So what are you saying you don't want to do it at my house? Then where are we gonna do it?"

"We're not gon' do it at all, cause I don't want anything to happen."

"Anything like what?" Lawanna asked. Her offensive side was slowly giving way to her reason and understanding.

"Like you getting pregnant."

"I thought you bought some rubbers."

"I did, but anything could happen. It could come off, or it could break and then what are we gonna do?"

Lawanna paused for a moment. The all-knowing girl even surprised herself when she couldn't produce one of her ready-rapid answers. "I 'ont know."

"Neither do I. My cousin Cynthia is about our age and she came to the family reunion we just had, and she was pregnant."

"Who was the daddy?"

"That ain't got nothing to do with anything, Lawanna. I'm tryin' to tell you that when she came to the picnic, everyone looked at her like she was a stranger and nobody wanted to talk to her. It seemed like people didn't want her to be there. And people looked away from her and walked away like if she would get too close to them something bad would happen to them. Everybody treated her different. All I could think of, was something like that happening to you and that it would be all my fault because I did it to you. You probably won't believe me, but I really like you and I don't want anything bad to happen to you."

Lawanna was shocked by Benny's confession of honest emotions. She was used to the boys typically coming over and not talking much at all. Most of them just wanted to know when her mother was leaving for work and when they had to be out of the house. Lawanna was unsure if she should thank Benny or laugh at him. She chose neither. Lawanna was speechless. Benny had so swiftly taken control of the so-called relationship that she was completely comfortable with what he was doing, so he kept doing it.

"Lawanna, I hope you don't think I'm crazy, but I don't think we should do anything. You can call me what you want and tell people what you want, but I like my chances of not getting you pregnant if we never do anything, so I'll see you later." Benny walked away from the stunned Lawanna and towards the locked door. He unlocked the door to the house as well as any opportunities he was in danger of losing by committing the long awaited act. Benny walked down the street and couldn't stop wondering what his cousin Cynthia was doing right now.

Chapter 19
Ryan's Revenge

"So what you gon' do now, Ryan?"

"I 'on't even know, Benny. I was tryin' to see if my teacher would let me take my test over, but she be trippin' all the time."

"You should have told me you had a problem in Algebra. I ain't no genius but I could have at least helped you a little bit."

"I don't need yo' help. Ain't nothing wrong with me. You act like I'm stupid or something. I'm sick of this. If one more person tries to tell me I need some help in school, I'm gon' put them in a reverse spin and break they back."

"Look, you can talk all that noise you want to Ryan, but I been knowin' you since yo' daddy used to chase you out the house beatin' yo' tail all over the back yard, so don't act like…"

"What you say, faggot?" Ryan asked Benny. Ryan stretched his fingers out as he did before all of his high school wrestling matches. He was preparing to grab Benny by the throat and toss him outside of the imaginary circle, similar to the ones on the wrestling mats at school.

"Hey, man, I didn't mean to make you mad or nothing," Benny relented, still maintaining his resolve. "I'm just talkin' like I know you. Don't get all mad at me for tellin' the truth. And you'll probably get me right quick with all of those fancy wrestling moves you got, but you bedda get me good and get me before I get to a stick or a brick, cause if you don't…well, you just bedda get me first."

Benny's relationship with his next door neighbor had always been about them squaring off and testing one another's toughness. Every since they were ten years old they were always jumping in each other's face, usually over nothing significant. They always waited to see which one would blink or throw the first punch. Now they were both in high school and in eight years, neither of their eyes so much as twitched and not one clenched fist had come as high as their waists. Benny was hoping that this would be just another stare down and nothing more, because Ryan had become somewhat of a wrestling maniac. After realizing that football was not physical enough nor violent enough, Ryan joined the wrestling team and broke the team captain's hip during his first tryout. Since then, the team had crowned him with the name *hippo*, and designed a dangerous and potentially illegal move after him called the hip-hugger. In an attempt to live up to his nickname, Ryan was a diligent weightlifter. Most days and weekends, he could be found in the weight room at school. His weekend workouts were more of an escape from his still abusive father and his defenseless mother. Now that Ryan had failed Algebra, he was sure to be removed from the team and probably miss his senior year wrestling competitions.

"You know what, I ought to put you out of commission and hurt you real bad, you know that?" Ryan said, threatening Benny once more.

"You bedda do it before I get to that stick, that's all I got to say." Benny held fast to the tradition of lowered, clinched fist and immovable eyes. This would have been the worst possible time to flinch and he hoped that this was not the beginning of the end of their stare downs. Ryan was in an entirely different weight class now. The one hundred and eighty pound young man would have demolished Benny's wiry one hundred and five-pound frame.

"Whatever," Ryan said, signaling that the stare down had thankfully come to an end. "What makes you think you know so much about math and all that junk. You must have turned into some kinda nerd or something."

"It ain't got nothing to do with me being a nerd. My mama and daddy don't play when it come to homework. Come to think of it, my mama 'nem don't play when it come to anything, I don't really have a choice when it come to doing my homework," Benny said.

"My daddy ain't really said nothing to me except, *You did yo' lesson for the day*, but he wouldn't never check it or nothing. I just always told him that I did it, even if I did half of it, or none of it," Ryan said.

"Well, you can't blame that on yo' daddy. That's yo' own fault for not doin' yo' homework. Are you gon' tell them that you got a F?"

"Nope. They gon' find out probably tomorrow when the report cards come home."

"What 'chu mean tomorrow? The report cards came home today in the mail."

"What?" Ryan said in a panic plagued voice.

"My mama gave me mine as soon as she opened it up."

"What you get?"

"Why you wanna know?"

"Cause punk, I just wanna know. You ashamed or somethin'?"

"Nawh, I ain't ashamed. I just think that my grades belong to me and not to everybody else," Benny said in an attempt to humbly keep his success in school from his failing neighbor.

"Just tell me what you got," Ryan said.

"I made the B honor roll, but I had easy teachers this year," he quickly added, not wanting to be the supplier of salt for Ryan's wounds.

"Man, you make me sick; how you get so smart?"

"I ain't smart. I told you, I just do my homework or my mama gon' be on my butt. And after a while, it was just a habit."

Ryan lowered his head and drowned himself in thoughts of what he could have done differently to avoid the pit into which he had suddenly been dropped. Looking for someone to blame, he could only see himself. Although his parents didn't demand the studious activities that Benny mentioned, ultimately he realized the choice was still his own. Ryan's mental trip back over his life was interrupted by the all too familiar commotion of the back door opening and his father storming out immediately after.

"Ryan!"

"Hey, here comes you pops man; you gon' be alright?" Benny instantly gave his neighbor and friend every bit of concern he could find within the realms of his emotions. "Let me know what I can do for you, alright?"

Ryan didn't respond verbally, but his expression told of his feelings and gave a hint to his fate at the hands of his father.

"Ryan! Don't you hear me callin' you, boy?" Get in this house now and don't take yo' time doin' it!"

Benny watched as Ryan and his father entered what he had labeled the house of hurt. Ryan gave Benny one last glance. It was a look Benny had never seen, but always feared. Benny saw in Ryan the look that was sure to follow one of their stare-downs, if there was ever going to be a physical confrontation. Benny often imagined what it would be like to take their ego escapades one step further and exchange blows. He realized that the expression on Ryan's face was the look he would have given him before Ryan lunged pain into his chest cavity or dropped a burden of hurt on his jaw. Benny was very concerned now, but not for Ryan. He was more concerned for Ryan's father.

Once inside the house, Ryan saw his mother performing her normal stay-out-of-it routine of fidgety housecleaning. She'd spend two minutes or more washing the same dish over and over although it was sparkling clean and sanitized. Sometimes she'd sweep the same spot on the floor before realizing she was daydreaming about what she could do to intervene in her husband's abusive behavior.

Her daydreams were always laced with the memory of the first time she'd tried to stop her husband from scolding Ryan. Touching her temple, she painfully remembered the incident which forced her to be admitted to a hospital. The daydreaming stopped as did her thoughts of interceding the father and son altercations. Joseph was pacing back and forth in the kitchen a few feet from the back door holding a piece of blue paper. Ryan recognized the form. It was the same form he always loathed getting from school—his report card.

"What the hell is this?" Joseph asked angrily.

"Looks like a report card to me," Ryan replied, trying to sound unconcerned. Joseph flamed up and charged over to Ryan with a backhand drawn. When Joseph was within arm's length of Ryan he delivered the blow across Ryan's face. Instead of the collapsing young boy Joseph had become accustomed to seeing, he saw an unmoved young man with flaring nostrils and closed eyes. Ryan stood erect as though Joseph had never even touched him.

"Don't you get smart with me, boy! I'll knock you into next week and you won't come back until next month. Now why you bringin' home all of these bad grades? I ain't tryin' to raise no dummies in this house." Joseph waited for Ryan's response. "Boy, do you hear me talkin' to you? What the hell is wrong with you? You on drugs or somethin'? Is that what's wrong with you? Come here and let me look in your eyes to see how red they are." Joseph raised his hands to Ryan's face in an effort to examine his pupils, but instead he was prohibited by a pair of hands surprisingly stronger than his own.

Ryan would not let his father touch his face. As far as Ryan was concerned, his father had just touched him for he last time. "Oh, so you bad now, huh? You think you grown. Well, I show you what it's like to be grown."

Ryan' s mother took a half a step forward thinking that now might be a good time to retry her intervention. Then she took two steps backwards after feeling the physical pain in her head. It was a reminder of the brutal beating her husband had given her years ago. The pain reared its ugly head every time the light was too bright or she was in a stressful situation. Then her brain seemed to erupt into an excruciating migraine headache.

Joseph was so close to Ryan, he could have slapped Ryan with his breath. The unsuspecting father threw his hands back over his head preparing to throw them forward and grab his son like a bag of groceries that could carelessly be tossed around. Ryan, noticing the maneuver from his wrestling matches, anticipated his stepfather's next motion and prepared for battle. When Joseph threw his hands toward him, Ryan blocked the landing by throwing his arms inside of Joseph's grasp. He threw his arms outward forcing Joseph's arms away from him. At the end of the motion, Ryan curled his arms around Joseph's arms and clenched them under a vice-like grip in his armpits and leveraged Joseph's arm's into a straight rigid position. Then with a crisp and swift thrust, Ryan pushed his father up at the joints of his elbows producing two powerful snaps that broke both of Joseph's arms. Ryan wasn't at all phased by the torture he'd inflicted on his father. Joseph screamed when he felt the unbearable pain bestowed upon him by the person who was once the recipient of beatings in the house. Today Joseph's arms was the addressee of this a hurtful message and Ryan was the return address.

"Oh God, what the hell are you doin' boy?" Joseph cried out with tears in his eyes. "What the hell you do that for, Ryan? What's wrong with you?" Joseph was still in Ryan's clutches with his joints beginning to protrude through his skin. Ryan looked into the man's flowing eyes and saw nothing. Nothing that could bring any compassion or sympathy for this abuser who was now the abused. No sorrow for the man existed in Ryan's present state of mind. As his father stood before him groveling and begging, Ryan's heart turned cold and his intentions became ruthless. He freed the ailing man only to catch his withering body before it descended to the spotless kitchen floor. Joseph hoped that the gesture was a means to repair what he had done and to help him to recover. Ryan, however was merely setting Joseph up for the proverbial kill. He grabbed his father from behind and Ryan strapped his arms around Joseph's waist as if he was some sort of seatbelt. However, Ryan was not looking out for the safety of his father, but for his inevitable destruction. Elevating his father into the air and placing the side of Joseph's hip against his own stomach, Ryan began his father's fast descent towards the floor. When the soon-to-be discarded body was half way through its flight, Ryan jumped over and maneuvered so that he could land directly on his father's hip during impact—it was his infamous hip-hugger move. Ryan had perfected the malicious move with tackling dummies and one other time accidentally, or so he claimed. A linebacker who stepped on his foot in the cafeteria and suffered the painful consequences as a result. But this was the first time Ryan's adrenaline was fueling the hip-hugger move. Both bodies collided with the kitchen floor and between the two masses and the kitchen floor, something had to give, and it did—Joseph's hip. There was a pop, which was similar to Joseph's elbows being broken, but no one could process right away that Ryan had just broken Joseph's hip. Ryan, however knew that his patented move was reliable and consistent. He was sure that his intentions had come to pass and Joseph would soon realize it as well when he attempted to lift himself from the floor.

"Ryan, what are you doing, sweetie?" he heard his mother make one of her rare vocal occurrences. "Why are you doing this?" She had denied herself the privilege of the truth for so long, she was now convinced that the agonizing man lying on the floor could do no wrong.

"Why did *you* do it? Why did you let him do it to me and why did you let him do it to both of us mama? He ain't perfect! Look at him! If he was so good and perfect, he wouldn't be laying there on the floor like a little girl. Look at 'em, he can't even get up. Get up!" Ryan yelled at his father. "I said get up, you punk!" Ryan was taunting his victim. He walked closer to the shivering man and kicked him in his spine as though the pain he had already inflicted was not enough. Ryan knelt down over the man and delivered a sharp blow to his temple. Ryan was suddenly having visions of all of the beatings he had been receiving for years. Now it was his time to return the favor. Ryan continued to kick his father and pound his fist into his skull, while his mother stood nearby crying, perhaps for revenge or perhaps for fear—she cried while Joseph bled. Ryan was interrupted by a splatter of blood across his own face and thought maybe he had cut his fist and was concerned for his own well being. He jumped up and ran over to the kitchen sink and began to clean his wound. As the water washed the reality onto his hand, Ryan could see there was not a single scratch on his hand, only a small hint of swelling. Thinking to himself that he was sure there was blood somewhere, Ryan mentally retraced the events leading up to sink and when he turned around to visualize the moment he had walked away from his father, the delirious young man was compelled to look down. He saw an unconscious body in the middle of the kitchen floor and he saw the source of the blood he'd felt. Joseph's head lay still in a pool of blood from the beating Ryan delivered to his now mangled face. Ryan looked over at his mother who was paralyzed in confusion and fear. She saw Ryan walking toward her. The timid woman sheltered herself from what she could only imagine would be a new and improved beating, perhaps worse than the ones Joseph used to administer. Instead she was greeted by a concerned soft voice, the one that she remembered from Ryan's younger years.

"Mama, which one you gon' call first?

"What are you talking about. Call who?" his mother asked, still confused and dazed. "The ambulance or the police?" Ryan's concept of reality had suddenly returned. He began thinking to himself that they both were more than likely to show up—one taking his father and the other probably taking him.

Chapter 20
Differences

"Man what was he thinking?" Steven Wilburg asked Benny.

"That's just it. He wasn't thinking. Ryan was just reacting to all of the stuff that his dad had been doing to him for all those years. I knew he used to get whippins but I never thought it was abuse. My mom said that his Dad used to beat Ryan's mom, too."

"So is his dad's back at home now?"

"No, he's still in the hospital cause he was in a coma for a little while."

"Where's Ryan?"

"He's in juvee hall, but I don't think that he's gonna to be there very long, because my mom was saying something like he was provoked and that because his dad used to abuse him his actions were justified. The only problem is that they have to get his mom to testify and say that he was abused and my mom said that she probably wouldn't because she's so afraid of her husband... did I just hear your mom call your name?"

"I don't know, probably. Man, that's pathetic! I feel like choking my dad to death sometimes just because."

"What are you talkin' about? Your mom and dad have never even laid a finger on you your whole life. I doubt if you even know what a belt is if it's not around your waist."

"Yeah and they'd better not try and touch me, or what Ryan did will seem like a loving day in the family after I get through with them. Do your parents ride you all the time about coming in at your curfew and nag you when you come in a few hours past it?"

"Are you crazy? If I come in even five minutes after curfew my dad is all over me and I can't go out for about a month," Benny replied.

"And you let them do that to you?"

"What do you mean let them? Like my dad always tells me, *Boy, I pay the rent around here and when you start paying the bills and paying some rent, you can start comin' and goin' as you please. But until then, if you're not here when I say be here, don' t come back here.*

"They can't do that!"

"Do what?"

"Put you out or not take care of you. It's against the law or something isn't it?" Steven asked.

"Are you smoking dope? You think I would even think about sending my mama and daddy to jail? Where would I live, in a foster home or a shelter or somethin'? Be for real. See it's different for white people. The stuff yo' mama and daddy let you do, I'd be strung up, tarred and feathered, and then my mom would whip me on television in front of the whole nation."

"That's child abuse!"

"That's what *y'all* call it. Everybody at my family reunion call it the Book of Proverbs."

"What does that mean?"

"It's one of the books in the Bible, and some times when me or one of my cousins used to get a whippin', my Aunt Flappy would always yell out a Bible verse from the Book of Proverbs talkin' about sparin' the rod and spoilin', the child," Benny explained.

"What?"

"If you don't whip yo' kids then they'll be spoiled, that's what the Bible verse means."

"My mom and dad know better than to put a hand on me and I'm not spoiled at all."

Steven's mother called upstairs to his room informing him that he should be getting ready for dinner, but Steven, living in his conversation with Benny, was intentionally ignoring his mother until she came up the stairs and opened his door.

"Well, hello, Benjamin. I didn't know you were here. Steven didn't say he was having company over, and of course, he never asks for permission. But you're welcome anytime you want to come over. How are your mother and father doing?"

"They're doing fine Mrs. Wilburg. Thank you very much for asking."

"How's school going?"

"It's going okay. I have to take Calculus next year when I'm a senior and I'm a little scared."

"That's great! Calculus is pretty hard, all those derivatives and integrals. I'm sure you'll do fine. Are you still on the honor roll?"

"Yes ma'am, but it's getting harder, especially with the advanced classes that my mom makes me take."

"It's good for you, Benjamin. Would you like to join us for dinner?"

"I would, but my mom has plans for us tonight."

"I understand. It was great to see you again and don't be a stranger. Steven, did you not hear me call your name five times from downstairs?"

Steven couldn't possibly respond to his mother in a polite manner now. She had committed the unforgivable parenting sin. Mrs. Wilburg had just complimented a visitor and then turned to ask a question in such a way to make Steven feel inadequate.

"Mom, why did you come in my room without knocking on my door first?"

Benny was somewhat shocked at his friend's response to his mother.

"I would not have even had to come up here if you would've answered when I called you."

"Next time yell louder. What are we having for dinner anyway?"

"We're having roast in a brown sauce, russet potatoes and asparagus tips."

"Jesus Christ, mom. I hate that gourmet crap. Didn't I tell you not to make that stuff anymore? I feel like barfing already."

Benny moved away from Steven expecting his mother to do a flying leap and drop an atomic elbow across Steven's forehead. When the wrestling action didn't happen, Benny was bewildered.

"Steven, do you know that there are hungry people all over the world that would kill to have a meal like this and all you can do is complain?"

"Send it to the starving people of the world because I'm going to kill someone if I have to eat that crap."

Benny continued to stare in disbelief at the unfolding drama. He had a flashback to the black-eyed peas that had gotten him into so much trouble years ago. Benny was thinking how, Sheila would have jumped on top of him and shoved a funnel down his throat forcing him to eat every crumb on his plate for the comments Steven was making. Then Ronald would have forced Benny to drink some beet juice out of a twisty straw if he dared objecting to eating a meal someone prepared. Benny was definitely in a completely different home.

"You know something, Steven Wilburg," his mother began. "I'm glad that Benjamin is here to witness how you really behave and treat your parents. And as far as dinner is concerned, don't go in my purse and take my keys and money to go to Taco Bell. I will not tolerate it tonight. And this time I really mean it. Wait till your father gets home."

Uh oh, Benny thought, *there's gonna be an action packed night after all.*

"Mom, dad's not coming back from California until Sunday."

So much for the action Benny thought.

"Well...well this time I'm not going to forget and I am going to tell him about your behavior and disrespect."

"Yeah, yeah, yeah, mom. Be sure you lock my door on your way out, so you can't let yourself into my room whenever you feel like it."

"One day, young man, one day," Mrs. Wilburg mumbled as she exited the self-proclaimed private kingdom.

"Now what were we saying about Ryan," Steven asked as though no conversation with this mother had ever transpired. Benny, on the other hand still had his eye attached to the door. He was waiting for Mrs. Wilburg to come back into the bedroom like a maternal hurricane, whipping the nonsense out of his longtime, but very different, playmate.

"Benny…Benny!" Steven called to the baffled Benny.

"Man, is yo' mom feelin' all right?"

"I know. Isn't she pathetic, just bursting in my room like she owns the place. But she's not sick, she's just a nag."

"Then, are you sick?" Benny was desperately searching for an answer to the whirlwind in this household, which was clearly the antithesis of his own.

"What do you mean?"

"I mean, you talk to your mom like that all the time?"

"No not all the time. Whenever she's not spasin' out, we get along, but as soon as she starts acting like she runs the place, then we have problems."

"See, that's exactly what I'm talkin' about right there!"

"What?"

"I would have been strung up for even thinkin' about talkin' to my mama like that!"

"Like what? That's how we always talk. It's nothing unusual."

"Unusual? You got to be crazy," Benny said allowing the Ronald in him to seep out. "Let me ask you somethin'. Do you remember that time we got in trouble when you put glue in that girl's seat and I told you not to do it, but you did it anyway?"

"Yeah! Now that was funny! What was that little tramp's name? Does she go to your high school?"

"Never mind that. That's not the point. What happened when your parents found out about that?"

"Oh man, my dad was pissed at me. He sat and lectured me for..." Steven looked up at the ceiling searching for the exact occurrences of the event. "It had to be about a half hour at least, maybe forty five minutes."

"Yeah and…."

"What do you mean and?"

"And then what?"

"And then, he fell asleep on the couch like he always does. My dad works a lot of hours, so he can't stay up all night."

"What happened when he woke up?"

"You mean the next day?"

"The next day, the next hour, the next week, whenever he woke up."

"What do you mean what happened? He went to work, it was a week day probably."

"And that was it?"

"Yeah, that was it. You act like something else was supposed to happen. Tell me what happened to you since you think that was easy," Steven responded.

"Man my mama was all in my face for about an hour and when my mama is on you, your brain just melts cause she can get all up in your head and stuff. Then after she was through, my daddy came home and he was all over me tellin' me how wrong I was and that I was in big trouble for having my mama called while she was at work and he sent me to bed feelin' all bad because..."

"See you got the same thing I did, all they did was talk to you, so what makes my punishment so easy?"

"Like I was saying. He sent me to bed and then the next morning I didn't get no alarm clock wake-up call. I got a butt wake up call 'cause my daddy came in my room the next morning and woke me up with *his* favorite and my *least* favorite belt, the black bomber."

"No way! While you were still sleep?"

"Yep, and then I had to go over to that little girl's house and apologize to her for something *you* did. Then on top of all that, I had to get her a new dress out of the money that my parents were gonna use for my birthday. Man my mama and daddy didn't play that stuff and still don't."

"So what, are you still mad about me getting you in trouble or something?"

"Nawh! That ain't got nothin' to do wit' nothin'," Benny's ethnicity was raging out of him and his articulation was not so clear. "I'm just stunned at the fact that you talk to yo' mama like that."

"She knows that I love her, she just eeks me out sometime."

"You need to check yourself because that ain't right."

"Oh give me a break, Benny, since when did you become so pure? I bet you aren't so pure when you guys at your school get a little bit of this in you." Steven reached in his nightstand and pulled out a Hot Wheels box. Inside the box was a plastic kitchen bag with a bunch of green leafy particles inside.

"What is that?" Benny asked in a voice to convey that Steven had the audacity to even try to pull out a bag of weed in his presence.

"Yeah right, like you don't know what this is? Come on, it's cool. All you have to do put a wet towel under the door and no one will ever know."

"Fool, is you crazy? You gon' do that mess in yo' mama house?" Benny's ethnicity had completely escaped now.

"What? I told you it's cool that's why I told her to lock my door. Why are you being a pain about it? It's just a couple of joints." Suddenly, Steven was startled by his mother's distant voice.

"Steven, you need to get down here right this minute, dinner is ready and you *will* be eating, even if you don't like it!"

Steven darted over to his door and yanked it open. "Mom, give it rest okay! I said I'm not eating because the food taste like crap, and it looks like crap. Now get that through your head and leave me the hell alone, you got it? Good!" Steven grabbed the backside of the door he'd just thrown open to make his performance of ultimate disrespect and gave it a huge push. The door slammed and all of the small items and pictures in his room rattled with an aftershock of the commotion.

"God, she makes me sick sometimes," Steven muttered to himself, and Benny.

Benny was not the least bit receptive to his friend's actions. He burned Steven's eyes with his own and awaited for his Ronald to make his way out of his soul. Finally his father's thoughts and philosophies made their way to Benny's lips. He spoke to his friend, perhaps for the last time.

"Steven...boy...you don' lost yo' damn mind." Benny turned his back on his friend and walked downstairs past Mrs. Wilburg with every bit of respect that her own son could not give her, then he exited the house where disrespect dwelled. The two playmates had grown up and grown apart. Benny's backside made its way home and was beginning to reminisce about all of the lessons the whippins had taught it. He felt the urge to run home and tell his parents thank you, I love you, and I appreciate you. At the same time though, he felt sorry for Steven because he would never know how much he was hurting his mother, though it was plain enough to Benny. The thoughts about Benny not whipping his own children were slowly fading away with his youth. No parent, he thought to himself, deserved the disrespect Steven gave, and no kid, he also knew, deserved the abuse that Ryan's father had delivered.

The maturing boy was determined to find the healthy balance that lied in between the two. Benny realized that his parent's careful and constant nurturing had produced a bountiful fruit in him, yet he had no idea that his parent's marriage was experiencing a matrimonial drought.

Chapter 21
Reasons And Excuses

"Baby, it's supposed to rain tomorrow. Are you coming with us to church?"

"Nawh, cause it might clear up by noon, and we can play about nine holes before it gets too late."

"But, Ronald, it's gonna be cold outside isn't it?" Sheila replied.

"We done played in colder weather than this before. Besides we gon' be walkin', so we'll keep warm that way."

"Just go ahead and say it."

"Say what?"

"Say that you just don't want to go to church," Sheila answered in disgust at her husband's usual dodging of spiritual endeavors. Realistically, Sheila didn't think today would be any different from any other Sunday, but every since the woman at the beauty shop, the thought wouldn't leave her mind. She and her husband rarely attended Sunday service together. They belonged to a small church, only about fifty members, so people never inquired about her husband's absence. Everyone merely rejoiced when Ronald did make one of his rare cameo appearances and didn't miss him when he wasn't there.

"It ain't that I don't won't to go to church, it's just that...well like I said we can get a few holes in before it's too late."

"What is it, Ronald?"

"What is what?"

"What is it about going to church that you just can't tolerate? Is it the fact that you have to go with me? Cause if it is, I'll find another church so you can go to church with your son before he goes to college. You think you might like Eastern Star Baptist Church? That's how much I love you and this family, Ronald. You know how much worship means to me, at least I think you do, and for you, I'll do it somewhere else other than the church where my entire family has grown up. Is that what I need to do?"

"Why we always got to go through this every Sunday, Sheila? Huh—why?

Ain't it enough that I believe in God? You know it's some people out there that won't even say that they believe in God. You in here worrin' me cause I don't go to church every Sunday."

"*Every* Sunday?" Sheila responded in wonderment of Ronald's inaccurate statement.

"It seems like we have this conversation all the time and you always know how it's gon' end up, so I don't even know why you start in on me."

"You know something? I don't know why I start either, but I have a funny feeling that it's because I probably love you and I care about you and your pitiful soul."

"My soul?"

"Yeah, that old pitiful soul that's slowly burning out deep inside you."

"What's that supposed to mean?"

"If you don't know, I'll never be able to explain it to you. I just hope you're happy with the example that you're setting for your son."

"So now you sayin' I'm a bad example for Benny, huh?"

"No, I never said that, so don't try to put words in my mouth, okay? All I'm saying is that what Benny sees and what he's *been* seeing is that every Sunday his father gets up to go play golf while he and his mother go to church. Now when he gets married and his wife wants him to go to church, how do you think he's going to feel about the importance of attending church with his wife?" Sheila injected the words into Ronald like bad medicine, and he was frozen as though he had just been given a huge dose of the worst tasting truth serum. After he swallowed, Ronald searched for his justification although he realized his argument had been fatally wounded.

"Why does it have to be all that, Sheila? Why it ain't enough that I just believe?"

"What are you talking about, all of what?"

"All of me going to church and you wantin' me to be at the church all the time. It ain't like I don't believe in God cause I do. And I think that Jesus is good and all that other stuff. Why can't you be at ease with that? Now I could see if I was a atheist or somethin', but I ain't. I mean I usually make it when it's important, cause you can't say that I'm not there on Christmas and Easter and all them other times."

"How many times have you gone to bed mad at me or mad at Benny?"

"You mean this week?"

"No, I mean this month, this year, whenever?"

"I don't know, maybe a few times, but what does that got to do with this?"

"Do you know how to make me submit myself to you?"

"What you talkin' about?"

"I mean submission, me doing anything you ask me to do?"

"Anything?"

"Anything in the entire world?"

"Ain't no woman crazy enough to do that, and that ain't got nothing to do with church, and even I ain't got to go to church to learn that."

"Oh really?"

"Really?"

"You know if you don't go to a car lot, you'll never know what kind of new cars are available and you'll be stuck driving a car that's unsafe or worse illegal because it spits out too much smoke. And it if you don't go to the DMV to renew your license, you'll never know what new requirements there are for drivers."

"Yeah, and ,so?"

"So if you don't go to church, you'll never know the new messages pastors are trying to give to the community and to the families."

"I already know. It's the same record, different label. Jesus died for our sins come on down the aisle and get born again, the doors of the church are now open, now we'll have the benediction—oh and don't forget the three offerings in between," Ronald said rushing out his insensitive reply.

"Ronald, I don't know what to say anymore?"

"Say what you know. I'm right"

"You're not right, you're ridiculous? And not only that, you're irrational because that's the most closed minded statement I've ever heard you make and I've heard you make a lot of them."

"What's so ridiculous about the truth."

"You know what I...nothing."

"What?"

"Nothing, Ronald. Don't worry about it?"

"So now you mad, huh?"

"No, I'm not mad. I'm scared. I'm scared that you have no idea what's going to happen to our souls. I'm scared that our marriage will never meet its full potential because there's so much more that you're missing. I'm scared that you think it's okay for a man not to go to church with his wife, and you think that's okay for Benny to see. But most of all, I'm scared that I think for some reason you have this strange idea that I want you to do this for me when all I ever wanted, all this time, was for you to build your own spirituality for yourself so that the man I so deeply love can know a love so much more greater than I could ever give him." Sheila exited the room and continued her Sunday routine of preparation for she and Benny. Ronald, burdened with the thought provoking weight Sheila had dropped on him, went back to bed and tried to wrestle with his own argument, because Sheila was victorious in the one they'd just finished.

Benny and Sheila rode to church the next morning in a disturbing quietness.

Benny could sense that something tumultuous was disturbing Sheila's normal Sunday morning drive. She wasn't listening and singing along with the gospel music playing on the radio as she usually did.

On any given Sunday, Sheila would nearly sideswipe another vehicle because she was so enthralled in the spiritual sounds of the gospel radio shows. Today, she was simply a melancholy mess taking up space in the seat next to Benny.

"Mama, why you so quiet? Sheila didn't respond. "Mama…mama!"

"Huh?" Sheila answered from her entranced state.

"Why you so quiet?"

"Why are you so quiet? Is that what you meant to say?"

"Mama, I know how to speak proper English, sometimes I just don't feel like doing it."

"So you're saying I nag you too much? What is it with you and your daddy that makes a simple question into an integration. All I'm tryi...."

"Mama, mama whoa whoa slow down. I never said you nagged me."

"You act like it."

"I'm glad you always correct my grammar. When we had our English assignment about proper grammar, I made good grades because it was all just common sense. It makes sense to say there *are* people instead of saying there *is* people, so I'm not complaining at all, Mama.

"Well… it's good to see that there are some people who appreciate it when someone is looking out for their best interest."

"Oh I see, you must have tried to make daddy go to church again. You should know by now that's a lost cause."

"Now why would you say that, Benny?"

"Because you know daddy don't like, I mean *doesn't* like going to church. That's just how he is."

"And what about you? Just how are you? Do you go to church because you want to or because I make you?"

"I guess both."

"What do you mean both? It's one or the other."

"Not really cause..."

"If you had your choice, would you go to church every Sunday or would you stay at home and watch TV?"

"I don't know; I'd probably do both."

"You mean go to church and then come back home and watch TV?"

"No, I mean go to church some Sundays and then stay home some Sundays."

"But you'll never know what you're be missing on the days you're at home."

"Mama, Reverend Deshon always preaches about the same thing. He just changes the title, but the message is always the same."

"What do you mean?"

"You know, he always talks about Jesus dying for us, God is able and please come join the church. It's the same old thing since me and Clem been sleeping on the back pew when we were ten."

"Did your father tell you that?"

"No, we hardly ever talk about church."

"Then what do you talk about?"

"You know, man talk?"

"What kinda man talk?"

"I can't tell you cause you're not a man."

"Neither are you, little boy."

"Nuh uh, that's not what the minister said."

"What minister?"

"The minister at The Light of The World Christian Church. He said that everyone male under the age of eighteen was considered a man-child. They told us that we should all be trained to walk upright and take our places as strong men who can love a wife like Christ loved the church."

"What? Who... When did he say that? First of all, when did you go to the Light of the World?"

"Remember that time you went to a conference? Some kids from school went there on youth day and it was live! They got drums, keyboards, saxophones, and everything in there. We were kickin' it. And the preacher had everybody into it. He was telling jokes during the sermon about how the Bible was dealing with everyday life and then a whole lot of people went down the aisle after it was over. More people went down the aisle than people go to our church. Why don't you ever go to that church?"

"All those bells and whistles don't make a church, Benny." Sheila paused trying to counter her son's discovery of a spirit-filled church. "Just because our church is small doesn't mean it's not a good one, it just means..."

"It means it's boring."

"It is not boring; it's just traditional." Traditionally boring Sheila silently admitted to her self. She never stopped to think about the reasoning behind Ronald's refusal to attend the small church. True, there were no fireworks at their church, but in Sheila's opinion, a church was a church. That alone should have been reason enough for Ronald to accompany her, even if it was a tad bit on the boring side. She was quiet again, but Benny had more questions.

"Mama, why didn't you and Daddy ever get a divorce?"

"What? Why would you say something like that?"

"I mean every time I see y'all talking, it's always an argument or it's about to be an argument."

"Benny, people argue, that's part of being in a relationship. If people agreed on everything we'd all be running around here with no differences and no means of creativity or expression. Just because someone argues doesn't mean something is wrong. Didn't you and that hot girlfriend of yours argue when you were together?"

"Yeah and that's why we're not together anymore because we always argued. We broke up."

"It's not that easy when you're married, and you need to stop switching girlfriends like you're buying cars."

"What do you mean by that?"

"I mean when a new car comes out people want to go and buy it and get rid of their old one just because it's old. Then after they buy a new car and drive it for a while, they realize all they have is something to get them from place to place and they should have kept the one that they had."

"So that's why you never got divorced?"

"Once you get married and have children, you'll understand, but right now I don't think you have a concept of what a real commitment is. All I can tell you is that I love you and your father more than life itself, because I want to love you and I need to love you. One day you'd better hope and pray you could love someone that way because if you don't, you'll die a lonely old man. And as long as you live on this earth, don't ever let me hear you say anything about me and my husband getting a divorce."

Sheila was severely quiet now, as was Benny. The car turned onto a street next to the church. There weren't enough church members to warrant a parking lot. Benny was accompanying his mother into the boring church and Sheila was taking her son into the traditional church where her entire family was raised. Sheila and Benny were both in the same building, yet they were in two completely different places. The caring mother was raised in the building and nurtured under traditional spiritual ways of its congregation. Benny, however, was a young boy in a modern world, whose soul needed a bigger stick in order to stir it up. He had become mature and he was very observant. What the young man observed, was the different directions his parents were traveling. Blinded by the sights of college and a new life, he could not see that he was the bond that could bring them back together. Benny had failed to observe that his family was slowly falling apart.

Chapter 22
Leaving The Nest

Benny was finally leaving his childhood home. He had been given a scholarship to Tennessee State University. During a spring visit, Benny and his parents had visited the campus and he was overwhelmed with the enormous size of the institution. Although the school wasn't the largest in the city, it was colossal from Benny's perspective. Once they arrived on campus, Benny almost gave himself whiplash trying to take in the sights, mostly the beautiful women walking around. He knew instantly that this was where he wanted to become a man. Benny felt as though he could learn everything that a man needed to know about life, people, and the world around him.

During their visit, there was step show taking place on campus where the various fraternities and sororities displayed their skills of a stomp like dance—some even used canes. Benny was especially interested in the students dressed in purple and gold. Later, he learned that they were called Omega Psi Phi and were considered to be an unruly bunch, but very unique in their own way. Tennessee State was known for its rich football history and for its outstanding engineering program. Oddly enough Benny had chosen Tennessee State for neither of those two reasons. Having always been interested in his small cousins and fascinated by human behavior, Benny was leaning towards a major in psychology or early childhood development.

He and his family had the opportunity to meet with some of the staff members in the psychology department. In the morning, they met with a woman named Fannie Doss who was a kind and simple older woman. Ms. Doss had a very effective down-home approach to counseling, but still reserved the scientific methods and theories to back up her applications. Later in the afternoon, the family was addressed by Dr. Perry who was a Ph.D. from Georgia Tech.

Unlike the stereotypical Ph.D., Dr. Perry had a little bit of *mama* in her also, but she was an astute and patient observer. Dr. Perry and Ms. Doss were the two main ingredients that made up the recipe for a nurturing and professional psychology department. It was no surprise that both of the women were thrilled, yet at the same time intrigued that Benny wanted to major in psychology, especially with a minor or emphasis in early childhood development. Most of the psychology majors at Tennessee State were female. Sheila had her concerns as well. Unsuccessfully, she had tried to persuade her only son to major in Mechanical Engineering. A degree in engineering would all but guarantee him a nice job with a good salary. With his good math grades, he was certain to do well. Benny refused to even visit the engineering department. He knew that once he saw the computers, gadgets, and gizmos the students were developing, he would become starved for interesting technology, and the department would definitely be his meal ticket.

Ronald didn't attempt to influence his son either way. Not familiar with college majors and their job markets, Ronald simply admired his son's conviction and educational achievement for being accepted into college, with a scholarship no less.

Now Ronald and Sheila were driving Benny to TSU, the sight of his symbolic first flight away from the nest. By no means were his parents kicking him out. During the drive to Tennessee, Sheila asked Benny every fifty miles if he was sure that he wanted to leave home. *You can always go to school at home your first year if you want and then transfer to TSU,* Sheila kept saying during the entire trip, each time with tears. Benny didn't help the matter at all. His response was the same each time. *So are you all going to send my bus ticket here for my trip home Christmas?* Sheila couldn't believe he wasn't considering coming home for Thanksgiving, since Christmas was four whole months away. Sheila had never been without Benny for more than a week. She never knew what to do with herself when he went away to sleep over camps in the summer. *How would she live four months without her little Benny*, Sheila thought to herself for the duration of the trip.

When they arrived on campus at eight o'clock in the morning, it was just as Benny remembered it. He wanted to be the first one in the dorm, so he could have his choice bed. The campus was so much more alive now than when he had visited in the spring. Cars were parked on the lawn and people were unloading bags and footlockers. Upper classmen were walking around with blue and white shirts that read *Peer Counselor* on the front and *Ask Me* on the back. The fraternities and sororities were out early helping students with their belongings and providing refreshments and directions to local stores for last minute shopping. They all made very good first impressions on their new potential members. Benny was a blur to them, however. Before the helpers could even make their way over to him, Ronald with Benny's help, had all of his things unloaded and sitting outside the door of his dorm room.

Although the room was only on the second floor, Sheila still insisted on taking the elevator, just to make sure it was safe enough for her precious son to be carried up and down the floors of the dorm. Once on the second floor, she saw her two men all the way at the end of the hall waiting patiently and laughing. *At least this is easy for someone* she thought walking down the freshly painted hallway. She handed the key over to Benny and watched as he opened the door to what seemed like a pathway leading further and further away from her. With each step towards getting Benny moved in, she realized it was another step of Benny moving out. The tears were building up in the ducts of her eyes and her constant blinks were futile sandbags trying to hide her feelings.

Inside the small dorm room, the environment was unbelievable. The same smell in the hallway was much stronger inside the room. Paint fumes couldn't be diluted in the confined space and the rectangular box impersonating an air conditioner was barely operable, so the windows were closed. There was only recirculating air permeating from the clanging unit. The drawers next to the closet were obviously adopted from two separate lumber yards because the closets were light brown and drawers were dirty dark brown. A large mirror, recessed into the wall above the drawers showed the evidence of previous residents. There was still tape residue and small traces of permanent markers that the cleanup crew could not seem to remove.

Benny's decision to arrive on campus early and choose his bed was a good one. Now he could choose between a little wobble and no headboard or a tremendous wobble with a headboard. He chose wobble free nights and was thrilled about it. The small enclosed room was paradise to Benny. It meant freedom, independence, a new life, and numerous challenges. In his eyes, the small hotbox was the equivalent of his own private mansion. Before he'd even unpacked, Benny had mentally placed his books on the two-person desk, hung his favorite posters on the wall and even set his small Wal-Mart easy-to-water-plant near the window.

"Mama, can you take my clothes out of my clothes box while I get my bathroom box."

"How am I supposed to know which box is which Benny? I didn't pack them," Sheila said with a hint of an attitude. Every opened box, every item placed in the room was one step closer towards Benny's departure. Subconsciously, she was doing all she could to prolong the inevitable good-bye.

"Mama, what are you talking about? Each box is labeled and all of the contents are described in the outline taped to the side of the box. You were standing there watching me when I started packing two months ago."

"Look, don't get smart boy. I can read."

"I can read too," Ronald interjected. "And yo' story says that you don't want the boy to grow up. You don't even want him to move out of the house. Seem to me like you ought to be glad that he leavin', cause he could be stayin' at home doin' nothin' but eatin' up all of the food."

"How about this? I'll just go and sit in the car until you two have all of this taken care of! Just let me know when you're ready to go, Ronald. Benny, I'll see you Christmas, since I don't want anybody to grow up and leave home!" Sheila left the room with her wet cheeks leading the way. The sorrowful mother hoped that she wouldn't be the one to break down and go back into the room saying what a mistake it was for her to explode like she had. For once she hoped that one of them would be sensitive enough to realize that this was a very difficult time for her. She hoped it was Benny, but unfortunately for Sheila, Benny was consumed by his new adventure and new found freedom. The only feelings he was concerned with were his own filled with joy.

After the parent orientation, Sheila, Benny, and Ronald had a very quiet dinner followed by a very emotional goodbye. Ronald gave his son the, *don't get into no trouble* speech, while Sheila simply hugged her little Benny for what seemed like a lifetime. She wished it could have been an eternity. Sheila held on to her son for as long as she could—released him—looked into his eyes and said,

"Benny, you'll never know how much you mean to me and my life. I love you baby."

Chapter 23
What Happens Now?

On the drive back to Indianapolis, the car once filled with suitcases, boxes, midnight snacks, and lively music, was now occupied by two people and their silence. Sheila and Ronald began their drive in the same manner most of their time together was spent—with no talking. Noise of the tires communicating with the pavement was the only conversation taking place. Sheila was looking forward to seeing new billboards approach the car so that she would have something to read and think about. As pathetic as it was, Sheila had never been so happy to learn about a Motel 6, which was seventeen miles ahead at exit 34b. Her preference was to read the billboards rather than talk to Ronald. She just didn't want to risk crossing the emotional line that was becoming shorter and shorter leading up to her husband's fuse box. She knew the ride would be much longer if she'd spent most of it arguing about anything that came out of her mouth. Not only was the ride uncomfortable, but the thought of what their home would be like once they returned, was making her nauseous. In Sheila's opinion, Benny was the glue that held the family together. She believed in commitment and her belief would not let her leave or quit anything to which she'd committed herself. By no means was Benny going to be subjected to a one-parent home. Now that Benny was away, Sheila was going to have to face the reality of a motivationaless marriage. What was her reason for remaining committed now? Ronald seemingly was not fully committed, so why hold on to a rope that wasn't anchored to anything, or anyone? Sheila was wrong about the trip being shorter without arguing. Whether she and Ronald spoke to each other or not, the ride home was getting longer with each mile they traveled, and home would be an empty entity without Benny there to bring joyous moments with his funny antics. Sheila and Ronald would not have to discipline Benny, which was how they always met on common ground. Without joy and commonality, maintaining their relationship would be a constant test of tumultuous emotions.

Ronald felt completely alone driving the car. As the return trip progressed, the interstate was slowly becoming consumed with darkness. Soon he would not be able to see his wife sitting next to him, and the loneliness would be even more overwhelming. Ronald thought that Sheila was distraught after seeing her son off on what was not the most pleasant of good-byes. He didn't think it would affect her to the point where she wouldn't speak to him. Quickly, he tried to retrace his thoughts, his actions, and his words, double checking to see if perhaps he'd done something inappropriate while on the campus. Finally he arrived at a clear record for today, at least as far as he could tell. Before they'd gotten in the car to begin the journey back home, Ronald swore to himself that as soon as Sheila said something to him, anything at all, he was going to be pleasant for as long as he could. And if she said anything that upset him, Ronald was prepared to politely change the subject or agree with her just to keep the peace. With Sheila, neither of the two endeavors would be an easy task. So far, he hadn't even seen a chance to change the subject; he hadn't even changed the radio station. No chance for any type of change so far. Even for the solemn Ronald, the quiet was a bit disturbing.

He attempted to break the awful silence, "You miss him already?"

"Huh?" Sheila said trying to concentrate on the Antique Mall and Flea Market billboard whizzing pass the car.

"Benny. You miss him already, don't you?"

"No, don't be silly. We've only been on the road for an hour and a half," Sheila said in a somewhat harsh tone, then realizing she'd probably just opened the door for a Mr. Hyde or Dr. Jeckyll personality or whatever Ronald wanted to explode with. Surprisingly, Ronald turned his head back towards the road. Sheila's eyes followed his actions and waited, but nothing happened. Not even a head shake of disgust. *Still*, Sheila thought, *I'll be more careful next time.*

"Is that why you keep readin' those signs like they books or magazines?" Ronald asked.

"What do you mean?"

"I mean that you ain't never been that interested in restaurants, hotels, and flea markets yo' whole life. You 'bout to break your neck trying to read every word before it pass by. I can slow down if you want to read all of 'em. I don't mind at all," Ronal said gently, teasing his wife. He was regretful as soon as he finished the last word of his sentence thinking that Sheila may view the observation as an attack. *Next time*, he thought to himself, *I'll be more careful.*

Sheila didn't take the observation as an attack at all, because Ronald's silly snickering of a smile gave him away.

"Leave me alone, boy. Talking about reading a book. I'm gonna read your book."

They turned to each other and giggled, and it seemed as though a cloud of tension was released into the air vents and flushed outside of the vehicle far away to some other part of the interstate.

"That sounds good to me, but why don't you skip the beginning of the book and get right to the sexy parts," Ronald replied hinting with a back door approach about his intentions.

"The sexy parts huh?" Sheila loosened up just a little, although most of her thoughts were focused on Benny and what was in store for her at home. The other portion was thinking about Ronald's next move. "You're just gonna to skip right past the opening action, the build up, forget about the plot, not even think about the climax and go straight to the smut, huh?"

"Who said anything about smut? I said the sex scenes, you know the lovemaking parts."

"Oh I see, so you've gone from sex to lovemaking?" Sheila joked with her husband trying to reel him in. At the same time, she was keeping a safe distance away.

"You know it's sex in the books, but it's lovemaking in our own personal book."

"Is that a fact?"

"That's a fact Jack."

"And what pray tell is the name of this heart gripping novel?" Sheila asked.

"Hot and Heavy Highway Love."

"What?" Sheila said before she erupted with laughter.

"You heard me. Hot and Heavy Highway Love. What's so funny?" Ronald said, laughing a bit himself. Repeating the phrase allowed him to hear how ludicrous the concocted title sounded, but he was still focused on his task.

"Heat Up the Highway with Hot Grease…is that what you said?" Sheila asked making a mockery of her husband's creativity.

Now the atmosphere was relaxed, and the couple laughed and teased each other in ways they hadn't done in quite some time. They were both very much at ease with each other. Ronald decided to make the next move. When he saw the approaching rest area sign, his mind and his hormones went into overdrive.

"Where are you going, honey; do you have to use the rest room? Are you tired, you need me to drive some?" Sheila asked, as she noticed Ronald slowing the car and pulling over to the exit ramp.

Ronald couldn't remember the last time his wife called him honey. The passion light was turning yellow and fast approaching green. He knew his wife was an advocate of spontaneous lovemaking. His idea of pulling over at the rest area and making love in the back seat as they did in high school, was sure to win her over.

"No I'm not really all that tired. Are you tired?"

"A little, but I can drive if you need me to," Sheila replied. Ronald was carefully feeling out her mood. There had been a lot of time and tension between the last session in which the two had been intimate. "Why are we parking way back here? The restrooms are near the front."

"I wanted to park back here so no one could see us."

"See us doing what?" Sheila said, shying away from her husband as he turned off the car and leaned over to nibble on her ear.

"See us doing what we used to do when we first started dating."

"Oooh, Ronald Dempkins, you so nasty."

"I know. Why don't you come on over here for a minute?" Ronald said trying to nibble again

"Stop, boy; I'm ready to get home." Sheila was giving her best hard-to-get routine.

"We'll get there soon enough, baby; just come here for a second." Ronald was spreading it on extra thick now, caressing his wife's arms and prying his way into more sensitive areas.

"And what's gonna happen when we get home," Sheila said as seriously as she could under the influential circumstances.

"The same thing that's gonna happen right now." Ronald slipped his hand inside Sheila's blouse and watched the light turn green as she gave a moan of what he perceived to be acceptance.

"And what's…what's that." Sheila was not remembering the hard-to-get game very well.

"What you're about to get and what you been gettin'."

"What I've been getting?" Suddenly, the light turned yellow again. Ronald was amazed at how quickly Sheila went from moaning to misunderstanding his intentions.

"Yeah, what you been gettin'."

"And what is that?"

"What do you mean?"

"What have I been getting? Are you referring to attention, affection, care, what? What do you mean, what I've been getting?"

"Sheila, why you gon' do this? Why you always got to turn something nice into something ugly?"

"You know what, Ronald. I'm not even going to answer that question, because I see it's just going to be a gateway for you to express yourself and that's just going to result in an argument so…"

"Just cause I…"

"Let me finish!" Sheila demanded.

Ronald became as quiet as the night was outside of the car. The intensity in Sheila's eyes frightened him, not a fear of what she might do, but a fear of what could be disturbing his wife so. "Just let me finish," Sheila repeated. Pausing for a moment, she started again. "I'm not going to answer your question, but I am going to allow you to answer one. And it's not just for me, it's for both of us, Ronald. Okay?"

"I'm listenin'."

"What's it going to be like when we get home?"

"What are you talkin' about, Sheila?"

"What's it going to be like when we get home? What's going to be so different about us and our marriage. I mean, with Benny gone, what motivation do we have for being a family?"

"Wait a minute just cause Benny...."

"Ronald, I don't know if you realize it, but for the past year or so, most of your conversations in the house have been with Benny. And I'm not faulting you for being a loving father, but the only time we talk is when we're fighting or we're talking about Benny. Whether you know it or not, Benny has been what's kept us together."

"How you figure that?"

"When was the last time we took a trip somewhere together?"

"What you talkin' about, we takin' one now."

"My point exactly; why are we taking a trip now?"

"Cause we had to take Benny to..." Ronald stopped himself not wanting to admit out loud that Sheila's observation was accurate.

"Uh huh, that's exactly what I'm talking about, Ronald. Can you think of the last time that we sat down and talked about something, as a couple?"

"See, that's why I don't think you know what you talkin' about, cause we just had a talk the other night at the table."

"And what were we talking about?"

"We was tellin' Benny the stuff he needs to stay away from when he got down here to school," Ronald said, quickly realizing he had proven yet another point in Sheila's theory.

"Once again, Ronald, we were with Benny, talking about Benny, and talking to Benny. I'm very concerned that we won't be communicating at all when we get back home; then when we stop talking period, what is our marriage going to be about? What are *we* going to be about?"

"Now ain't you overdoin' it just a little bit, baby? You act like we can't talk to each other no more."

"That's just it. I don't think we can talk to each other; I don't think we know how to, at least not without it becoming an argument or a fight. And what's worse, I can't think of what started all of this or why it even started. We used to not carry on this way," Sheila said in a voice that pleaded for answers she hoped that Ronald could supply. "Can you help me?"

"Help you do what, Sheila? I don't know what you lookin' for."

"Where did all of this start, the fighting and the way we talk to each other? Was it somethin' I did or didn't do? Was it something I said? How long ago did I do it? I want to make it right, but I don't think I can if I don't find out what's wrong."

"Nawh, baby, you didn't do nothin' wrong. I don't even know why you thinkin' like that."

"Then what is it!" Sheila shouted in frustration.

"I don't know!" Ronald returned the same frustrating tone. He turned the key in the ignition, put the car in drive, and returned to the monotony of the interstate. Sheila stared at him for a while, disappointed that he couldn't give her any of the much needed insight. "I was hoping you weren't going to say that, Ronald. So, do you think we have any other choice?"

"What, a divorce?"

"No! That's not what I was thinking at all. Is that what you want to do?"

"Nawh, I thought that's what you meant."

"No, I meant getting some help. I think we need some counseling."

"Some what?"

"I think that if we want to salvage whatever is left of our marriage, we should try and get some professional help."

"For what? Ain't nothin' wrong with us."

"But you just admitted that you have no clue why we're acting the way we are. And I don't know why either. So what else is there?"

"We don't need no counseling; that's for crazy folks."

"That's not true. People that have difficulty finding their own answers seek counseling all the time. And it's not necessarily because they're crazy, or have issues, I should say.

"Look a' here, I ain't got no *damn* issues, I don't need no answers, and I ain't goin' to no counselor, no head shrink, no mojo lady, or nobody else!" Ronald proclaimed.

Sheila began to tremble, because she felt that Ronald had just stated he had no intention of finding a resolution for their current or future problems. Sheila now felt that at this very moment, Ronald had given up on their marriage. Then, the cloud of silence and tension, which exited the car back at one of the previous billboards, caught up with them and slowly slipped into the back seat and became a permanent passenger. Sheila seemingly had placed a bookmark at one of those billboards of the interstate, because she started where she'd left off, enthralled with the billboards advertising hotels, restaurants, and antique flea markets. The informative signs racing towards her then away from her, were the only solace she could find at this instant. Her only son was gone, and her husband had never been as far away from her as he was at this point in their marriage. Like, the billboards, Ronald was racing away from her faster than she could take notice and he was beginning to move faster and further away. It appeared he had no intentions of returning, ever.

Chapter 24
Discoveries

Benny was doing very well his freshmen year. All of his inhibitions about not succeeding in college were banished when he received a 3.7 on his first semester midterm report. The department heads noticed his academic excellence, as well as an extremely high level of maturity for such an amateur at college endeavors. He held very good conversations and was actually a logical and influential debater. Ms. Doss approached Benny before the Christmas break and propositioned him with the opportunity of serving in a Counselor-In-Training position, or CIT's as they were commonly called. These prestigious volunteer jobs were usually reserved for juniors and seniors who needed internships for their senior projects. As luck would have it, there was one open spot and not a qualified junior or senior in sight, so Ms. Doss and Dr. Perry were compelled to give Benny a once in a lifetime opportunity. Benny, of course, jumped at the chance to get his feet wet in his chosen field of study.

The available CIT positions were in Drug & Rehab, Family Crisis, and Child Abuse & Neglect. Benny was assigned to the Child Abuse section. His first choice was in Drug & Rehab, but the majority of his work had to be done at the Correctional Facility located in Madison, and Benny didn't have reliable transportation. Actually, he had no transportation. Thinking of his deranged yet comedic family down in Hope, his next logical decision was Family Crisis, however it required twenty-five hours per week of group therapy. Benny's eighteen hour class schedule wouldn't allow him to complete the therapy, attend class, sleep, and eat, so he was left with compiling research for current and previous Child Abuse cases. He also answered phone calls for potential Child Abuse and neglect emergencies from the hours of seven to nine in the evening, for the Help Our Children Protection Agency. The agency was within walking distance of the campus except for cold winter nights when the bathroom down the hall wasn't even within walking distance. Benny rode the city bus on those nights.

Most of the calls Benny handled were limited to pranks and kids frustrated that they had just received a whippin', although they probably needed one. Every once in a while a legitimate abuse or neglect case would make its way to Benny's ear. No matter how trivial or serious, every call had to be documented, which made him feel more of a secretary-in-training than a counselor-in-training. Benny was beginning to wonder if there was really a need for counseling in the area of child protection.

"Help Our Children Protection Agency," Benny said, answering an incoming call.

"Is this the Child Abruse place?" a quiet voice, with not-so-great diction asked on the other end.

"Yes, this is Child Protection Agency," Benny answered, preparing a new case documentation sheet.

"*Yeah that's the place I dialed the number didn't I? Gon' and say what you got to say!*" Benny heard another more mature voice talking in the background, perhaps standing very close to the caller.

"My mama just whipped me," the younger voice managed to sniffle out.

"*Now speak up so they can hear you. Ain't nobody gon' understand you if you keep on cryin', and I told you once before that you bedda stop cryin' before I give you sometihin' to cry about!*" The older voice was getting louder and more domineering now.

"Can y'all come and get me?" Benny didn't know what to make of the call. Apparently, a young child had been punished and afterwards the same child had threatened to call the authorities. From what Benny could deduce, their parent had dialed the number for them.

"Have you been abused?" Benny asked.

"Yeah, my mama in here tryin' to whip me for nothin'."

"Tryin'! Oh, I did more than try! And I'm gon' try some mo' as soon as you get off the phone. And I didn't do it for nothin' either. Gon' and tell them peoples what you did, since you want to put all our business in the street anyhow!"

"Do you have any bruises or marks on your body?" Benny probed professionally.

"Just my birthmark on my ankle."

"No, I mean any marks as a result of the suspected abuse.

"What kind of abuse?"

"Suspected. When your mother spanked you, did she leave a mark on your body?"

The voice was quiet, obviously performing a quick examination."

"No," the voice said after a while.

"*Well, you gon tell 'em? Go 'head and tell 'em that you was at school puttin' yo' hand in some little girl's panties. You didn't tell 'em that, did you? Em mmm. Why don't you tell 'em that you made a F in PE and you always gettin' in trouble on Thursdays right after y'all watch a film in class. Go 'head tell 'em everything, cause I'm tired of it... Boy hang up that damn phone and get in yo' room and clean it up like I asked you to before I go berserk up in this here place.*"

"I gotta go," the young voice said.

"Before you go, if you give me your name and address I'll document the incident for future reference," Benny tried to say without laughing in the boy's ear.

"Nawh that's all right."

"*I know it's all right! You got five seconds to... gimme that phone.* I'm sorry to have bothered you, sir or mam. Y'all have a blessed day in the Lord," *Click.* The powerful distant voice had transformed into a soothing and gentle person before the phone was hung up.

"In the case of an emergency please call 911 and..." Benny said, trying to present his procedural last comment. Once off the phone, Benny covered his mouth and began laughing. He tried not to let his laughter escape his own work area. While closing out his documentation, the phone operator next to him was ending a call herself and was confused by Benny's amusement for such a serious task.

"Is there something funny about children getting abused? Cause if there is, I'm sure Dr. Perry would love to hear about it. If you want, tomorrow morning I can tell them that you're over hear laughing at abused children." The young lady sitting next to Benny was a boiling pot of attitude, and it seemed someone had just added a pinch of anger for taste.

"No, there's nothing funny about child abuse at all," Benny said in his best Sheila Dempkins School of Articulation voice. "However, there's a difference between child abuse and a mama gettin' on her child's butt."

"Oh really? And how can you be so sure which was which on that phone call you just had," she said in a matter-of-fact tone.

"Cause the lady dialed the number for her little boy."

"Who, the mother? No she didn't?" Benny's co-worker said in amazement.

"Yes, she did."

"How do you know?"

"Cause she was standin' behind him and I could hear everything she was sayin'. " Benny said, forgetting about his articulation also. The two were slowly becoming informal.

"No she didn't."

"Standing right there talkin' about, *Yeah, that's the right number. I dialed it, didn't I?*"

"Now see, that's what I'm talking about. Some of these thugs running around here need a mama like that. And not to mention a daddy," Benny's co-worker testified.

"I know what you mean. My mama and daddy didn't play at all."

"Please, your little well-mannered tail? You probably never got a whippin'," the young lady replied. She paused for moment, then faced Benny squarely and said, "My name is Karmin. I'm sorry if I was rude to you earlier, but I get real serious when it comes to kids."

"I understand. I'm Benjamin Dempkins, but most people call me Benny."

"Like Benny Hill or Beni Hana?"

"Watch it Carmine Ragusa from Laverne and Shirley. We're gonna do it— Give us any chance we'll take it, Give a steady rule will break it. We're gonna make our dreams come true." Benny sang, retaliating with a few bars from the Laverne and Shirley show.

"See there, his name was Carmine and I'm Karmin, but I'll give you an eight out of ten for the quick comeback.

"Okay, I'll take that." Benny made the brash Karmin smile, and he enjoyed all thirty-two pearly white characteristics of her gleaming happiness.

Karmin was a velvety smooth dark brown-skin sister and her white teeth contrasted her flesh beautifully. She was a rather thin girl, not runway model thin, but no potential fatty features thin. Her hair was short and feathered and she possessed a very professional look, which Benny liked.

"So were you a trouble maker?" Karmin asked.

"No, I wasn't really a troublemaker; I was more of a trouble finder. No matter where I went and no matter what I did, somehow I always ended up being with some kid that was causing trouble. When my mama and daddy found out, it was on all night long. There was one time when this girl had on a brand new dress at school. I was about..."

Karmin's phone rang and she put up a hold-that-thought finger to Benny. Her smiled disappeared. A professional voice matching her professional look took center stage as she prepared a documentation sheet. Benny observed the serious approach Karmin took towards the caller. The call could have been a simple inquiry for information on child abuse or a request for a pamphlet. Benny couldn't decipher because her phone persona was filled with intensity. He picked up a few pointers for his own calls. *She must be a graduating senior* Benny thought to himself. Now Benny was intrigued by the phone call *and* the operator sitting next to him. Checking his watch, he saw it was 9:15. Karmin was very good company, but volunteers didn't get paid, so overtime was out of the question. Benny initiated his leave by closing his documentation pad, placing it in the file cabinet, and locking up the confidential information. Karmin was consumed with her phone call. When Benny returned to gather his books, there was a post-it note left on his back pack that read:

Call me tonight so we can discuss your butt-beatings.
You seem like you have issues 320-3620. --Karmin

That was the smoothest forward move Benny had ever seen or even heard of. Karmin definitely had class and Benny wanted to be taught. He just hoped she wouldn't mind him being such a young pupil.

༺༻

"Hello."

"What do you mean I have issues?" Benny asked Karmin.

"That didn't take long," she replied, glad that Benny had taken the bait and called that same night.

"What?"

"The phone call."

"I'm just following directions."

"Is that a habit of yours or a result of years of getting your behind strapped?"

"What?"

"Following directions."

"Oh, probably a little of both. Without direction, one knows not where to go and when to stop when they get there."

"Profound, who said it?"

"Said what?"

"That quote you just recited."

"I did. Just then."

"I mean from whom did it originate?'

"From me…no wait a minute I think it originated from Sho Shack."

"Sho Shack? Never heard of him. What has he written?"

"Sho Shack? He's not much of a writer. He's more of a southern philosopher."

"What are his main theories and observations."

"Girl, you're way too analytical. Sho Shack is my uncle down in Hope, Arkansas." Benny giggled while Karmin rested in her silent frustration for taking the bait so far out to sea.

"See. I told you."

"Told me what?"

"You've got issues. Trying to push your family members off as twentieth century philosophers."

"Well, he is a philosopher, to some extent. You should meet him one day."

"I'd love to, but I have no urge to submit myself to the watermelon pits of Hope, Arkansas. If you have issues I'd hate to see your ancestral mentality."

"What do you expect from an immature freshman."

"Yeah, right. Don't even try that. You are not no immature freshman.

"Yes, I am. I hate to disappoint you. What did you think my classification was?"

"Oh, I knew you were a freshman, but immature you are not. I already know about you, young squire. Dr. Perry doesn't let just anyone work in the CIT program. If you were immature, you would not have even been considered. You mustn't give yourself a negative self-assessment. Issues I tell you, issues," Karmin replied jovially. Benny was shocked, that Karmin didn't mind him being a freshman, but she'd also done her homework on his background.

"Look, don't try to give me a psychosomatic complex about my state of mind cause..."

"Watch out, he knows his terminology too!" Karmin interrupted. "But you still have issues because you called me right away. Let's meet tomorrow in the student affairs office to discuss the history of your childhood discipline."

"Student affairs?"

"Yeah, that's usually where we study. It's the quietest place on campus at noon because everyone else is hanging out in the plaza. Stick with big dogs and you'll find this stuff out."

"The big dogs being you I assume."

"Bow wow wow, yipee yo yipee yea."

"Do you often behave like animals at night because I can probably get you an appointment with the counseling center if you're having mental problems.

"I'm sure you can, because you've got the hotline number on all of your books in case you flip out, right?"

"Touché," Benny offered.

"I know. Tomorrow, student affairs. Be there or keep your issues to yourself, she said." Benny was attracted to Karmin's quick wit and snide sense of humor.

"Hey, before you go, I want to ask you something?"

"It's too early to get serious, Benny. Perhaps premature steps towards commitment brought on by suppressed feelings and fears of loneliness?" She was also a bit presumptuous.

"Please. Give it a rest," Benny said. "What was your last call about, was it a real incident?"

"Nope. Someone just wanted a pamphlet," she replied nonchalantly.

"But you were all into it like you were trying desperately to arrive at a prognosis."

"Benny, like I told you once before, I'm very serious about nurturing and protecting children, because if we aren't, you just might be the one that gets a bullet in the head because of some violent past a child has been subjected to. I mean, we never know what the conditions of each call are, so I take each one as serious as the next." Karmin's words dropped onto young impressionable Benny like an anchor plummeting through the deck of his ship. His loveboat was slowly sinking. "Tomorrow—noon—goodnight."

"Good night," Benny replied hanging up the phone. Yes, a very good night. *Perhaps we can spend some of these good nights together*, he thought to himself.

Chapter 25
Comparisons

Trying desperately not to seem overanxious, Benny took his time and intentionally found some distractions on the way to the Student Affairs office. If he was too prompt, Karmin might accuse him of being in a rush to see her again. If he was late enough, she might think he wasn't interested in seeing her. Benny preferred the latter. At twelve thirty in the afternoon, he approached the supposed sanctity of study, but was surprised to find that there was nothing of the sort in this office.

The upper classmen were sitting around the room perched on desks and wolfing down sandwiches and snacks while listening to the AM talk radio show with Dr. Lucy. They were amazed at the simplicity of the caller's problems, yet their ability to present them as life-ending circumstances. The problems ranged from not wanting to see a friend because they'd stolen some music from their collection, to wanting a divorce because the dog meant more to one of them than anything else. Realizing the ease of counseling such simple problems, the students felt compelled to take a study break, thinking that they were studying too hard for such an elementary task.

"This doesn't look like the hall of knowledge you talked about yesterday," Benny said walking up behind Karmin.

"Well, well, well, if it isn't my own personal case study," Karmin replied. "You're a tad bit late. Did you know I get paid by the hour whether you're here or not?"

"That's funny, we never discussed a fee did we?"

"Counselors never discuss fees. It distracts from the seriousness of the appointment."

"I see. The money sort of makes it all real to life, huh?"

"You catch on fast," Karmin said, turning to the other students in the office. She gave them an *I told you he was mature* look. By this time the other girls had already sized up Benny and the only other guy in the room shook his head at the women and their ability to smell freshmen or 'fresh-meat' from miles away. "Let me introduce you to the most productive study group on campus. Everyone, this is Benjamin Dempkins, but he prefers to be called Benny. Benny this everyone."

"What's up people?" *Some introduction* he thought. He felt like he was at his mother's job being paraded around to allow everyone to pat him on the head.

"Benny works with me at Help Our Children. He's agreed to let me do a case study on his childhood discipline and its affects on his current state of mind," Karmin announced, flexing her therapeutic muscles.

"My state of mind is fine, and it may or may not be related to the family-centered discipline I received as a child. However, that by no means qualifies me to be injected with useless terms and technical babble like a guinea pig just to prove that my mama and daddy didn't play. The room was focused on Benny's comment and shortly after rang out with statements of confirmations for his self-confidence and ability to communicate his point."

"Alright, honey."

"Talk that talk, boy."

"Girl, you got yo' hands full with this one."

"Hey guy, that's how you lay it down right there. You're alright with me man."

Karmin gazed at Benny with a piercing look of disapproval, then with an apologetic smile. She was obviously dealing with a more mature person than she'd anticipated.

"What exactly do you mean by your parents didn't play?" Monica, one of the girls, asked.

"I mean they didn't play when it came to me gettin' my butt tore up."

"So are you saying you were abused?" Monica probed again.

"No, not at all. Of course, now that I think back, it may have been pretty close. I mean they never left bruises on my body or anything, but it was thick sometimes."

"Thick like what, how do you mean?" Monica seemed very interested in Benny's story.

"There was this one time, it's actually pretty funny now, but I have this Aunt Isabelle who's a big joker in our family. She's the one that's either the butt of the joke or telling the joke

"Hey, I got an aunt just like that only she's the butt of all the jokes too," Kevin, the only other guy in the room, interrupted.

"One year at our family reunion, I was playing with my Operation game. I was just about to get the wishbone out, when my aunt came over and smacked me on the back of my head saying, *I'm sorry, little Benny. I was just trying to operate on those naps and bee bee balls in the back of yo' head. Boy, yo' head shole is nappy!* She made me hit the side of the game, and the buzzer went off so I lost. Of course, everybody was laughing at me calling me kuckle bug. And in my family, when you get a nickname at a family reunion, it sticks with you for the rest of your life. In order for me to overcome my new label, I had to take swift and severe actions against my Aunt Isabelle."

"Was she young or something, because I know you weren't thinking about doing this to an adult," Karmin said.

"No, she was about as old as my mom, but she had taken my name *and* my chances of getting a prize for beating everybody at Operation. Shoot, she was messing with my bragging rights, and we don't play that in the country. She had to go down. Man, I went out to the back field were there were always some kind of critters running around, and I found me a prize-winning specimen."

"What kind of specimen," Kevin asked.

"I'm getting to that. After Aunt Isabelle went to the house and sat down for a while, I made sure all of my cousins were looking through the window while I brought Aunt Isabelle a nice tall cup of RC Cola. By this time, Aunt Isabelle had forgotten all about the little neck-smacking show she'd put on earlier, so she wasn't expecting any funny business. She turned that cola bottom side up and started slurpin' it down like it was the best she'd ever had. But then she started slurpin' on something that wasn't so smooth. To this day, I'm still amazed by the fact that she just about swallowed half of that mouse in her drink before she knew what was in her mouth."

"No you didn't! You need to quit lyin'," Karmin demanded.

"I'm not lyin', you can call my cousin Clem right now, and he'll tell you the same story."

"Benny, you put a mouse in your aunt's drink?" Tonya, another of the students inquired.

"You know, now that I think about it again, it was a baby rat with a long pink tail."

"Uuuggh," all of the women in the room said simultaneously, squirming at the mere thought of the devilish prank.

"Man, that's wild. What did your aunt do?" Kevin asked.

"She didn't do anything, she was too busy throwing up her lungs. But my mom jumped across the living room with an old spatula that my grandmother had sitting out on the table and started whippin' my legs like she was playing the hambone. All you could hear was me hollerin', breaking out in my whippin' dance and that spatula going flap-ta-da-flap, flap-ta-da-flap, flap-ta-da-flap. Then when I wouldn't stand still, she started smacking my butt with the spatula, almost like she was turnin' over pancakes or something. Man, I never even looked at another rat my whole life.

"See, that's one of those Black folks' whippins right there. You wouldn't know nothin about that, would you Kevin?" Tonya said.

"Excuse me?" the slightly offended red-haired student asked. "I hope you're not insinuating that just because I grew up in a Beaver Clever house and all of you grew up in a George Jefferson house, I didn't get my fair share of lashings."

"Yeah, right, Kevin." Tonya continued. I bet your groundings were gruesome weren't they?" she added sarcastically.

"They were! Look, you all have to get over these color barriers that you like to dance around. My mom used to beat me until I couldn't sit down. It was border line child abuse too, I think."

"Are you serious?" Benny asked in amazement.

"Serious? Man, I remember I lost my reading book when I was in school, and I thought that it was over at my cousin's house, so my mom drove me about thirty miles to get the book. When we got there, it wasn't there. So guess what?"

"She tried to spank you?" Karmin speculated.

"Spank, what is all of this spank you keep talking about? Anyway, then I thought it might be at my grandparent's house, so my mom, as mad as she was already, drove about fifteen more miles the other way and when we got there, you guessed it, the book wasn't there."

"Oooh! I would've beat you down for that too?" Monica said.

"My mom walked over to me and asked, *Where is the damn book, Kevin?* I said, *I don't know mom, maybe I left it at home.* The next thing I knew, my mom turned her back on me and then spun back around with the speed of some kind of demon. She slapped me so hard that I flew through the air over my grandpa's easy chair.

"What?" Benny asked, surprised.

"Yep, sure did. I just laid there on the floor squirming trying to play it off like I was dying or having a seizure, just praying she wouldn't hit me again. I was on the floor whimperin' and shakin' like a little puppy." Kevin laid against the wall and reenacted the puppy dog performance he'd just described. He squirmed and wiggled to everyone's amusement.

The crowd of supposed scholars were studying nothing. They were merely exchanging stories of their childhood experiences with discipline. All except for Jasmine, one of the students who listened to the stories and remarked only by strange stares of disapproval for the other students' lighthearted look at being punished. Benny chimed in with the group and gave an encore performance of his whippin' dance that guaranteed to bring down any house. His routine was suddenly interrupted by Jasmine.

"I'm sorry. I can't sit and listen to this ignorant and insensitive rhetoric any more," she announced, staring coldly into the laughing faces.

"Jasmine, what are you complaining about now?" Karmin asked.

"Why must I always be complaining and why aren't my comments seen as reasonable observations. Just because I have different views from you, doesn't mean my thoughts have no merit." Jasmine was a very serious student, especially when it came to her course work. Most of the time her large wire-rimmed glasses were hidden by a text book or magazine relating to her field of study. She was a small student with big opinions.

"So what do *you* think, Jasmine?" Benny asked.

Jasmine gave Benny a *don't patronize me because I don't even know* you look. Her eyes rolled and her mouth opened.

"What do mean, what do I think?" she asked. "This is not even a debatable issue. You all are in here making light of child abuse. How can you sit there as people who are even contemplating a career in the mental-health profession and joke around as though…"

Karmin interjected, "First of all, this is not child abuse because there are no marks and no long-term detrimental affects.

"How can you say that? That is so insensitive! You have no clue what effect physical or mental anguish can cause a child later in life. Not to mention that when abused children grow up, their first inclination is to beat their own kids because that's the only type of discipline we're, I mean, they're used to." Jasmine slipped and made a small confession that only Benny noticed.

"Look girl, you try raising some little nappy headed kids without gettin' in they butt every now and then," Karmin said. "It doesn't work! Especially in today's society! When you spare the rod, you spoil the child. Kids been getting their behinds to' up since caveman times and they're gonna keep gettin' straps on their butts until the end of time. In *our* culture and *our* community, kids get whippins. That's how it is. That's how it needs to be and that's how it's gonna be. It's obvious you must have gone to time-out when you shoulda been laying across yo' bed with a switch fixing yo' little attitude. That's what I got and that's all my kids are gonna get."

"Not mine," Benny offered in a humble voice.

"Say what?" Karmin asked, surprised at Benny's comment.

"I'm not gonna whip my kids. I didn't enjoy getting whippins, and I don't think my kids would enjoy getting' them either."

"Whatever. Make sure you keep them away from my kids, cause I don't won't to have to snatch up somebody else's kids cause their parents didn't correct them."

"You've just got the answers to all parental questions, don't you Karmin? You should go ahead and teach the curriculum, you know so much."

"I came out alright, didn't I?"

"Hhmmph," Jasmine replied.

"What's that supposed to mean?"

"It means that just because my mom beat me, or whipped me, as you like to so eloquently put it, doesn't mean that it was effective for my upbringing. You want to talk about marks and bruises. Marks are not the only tell-tell signs of child abuse. What if she beat me everyday but hit me in a different place every time? Just because there are no visible tracks, doesn't mean the road hasn't been traveled. That's what it's supposed to mean." The active room was quiet and still. "You know when I got a break from my beatings? Whenever my mother had hit me in every place imaginable, then she'd wait until my skin had softened up. Oh, she was careful not to bruise me. No bruises whatsoever. Lucky for her you know how to define child abuse, so my mother can wash her hands of any guilt."

"Jasmine I never knew...," Karmin attempted.

"I know you never knew, because you're talking like it's a damn joke and it ain't!" Jasmine's voice made up for her small size as it filled the room with discomfort, smashing the occupants against the wall with a blow of reality. "You can't just go by a rule or a guideline. You have no idea what's it's like to hurt on the outside and on the inside because someone you loved did this thing to you. She was supposed to protect me from harm, not bring harm to me. Don't sit here and justif..." Jasmine escaped from the room and from the embarrassment of sobbing hysterically before her friends and classmates. She left the room just as she had transformed it—quiet and still. Benny couldn't help but reflect back over his experiences growing up, but more importantly, what might be going on at home now. He felt the overwhelming urge to call his parents.

Chapter 26
Here and There

“How did everything go at work today Ronald?”

“Everything was the same as usual.”

“Nothing exciting happened or anything?”

“What you talkin’ about excitin’, Sheila. I said nothing happened.”

Sheila walked a tightrope during dinner. Determined to break through to her husband and communicate on some level, she seemingly changed the subject with every breath. Counseling was still in the back of her mind, and she hoped to bring it to the front so that Ronald would realize its importance.

“I was watching the news last night, and they were talking about the increased interest of golf in the black community. Have you noticed that when you and William go out?”

“Do I notice it? It’s so many black folks out there now, you’d think that it was night time on the golf course. William don’t play as much as he used to now that he’s spending more time with Margie.”

“Oh yeah, I see how he wouldn’t play as much now. He probably wants to spend as much time as he has left with her.”

“What you mean by that? You want me to stay home more?”

“No, not at all. I was just saying I realize how William would be compelled to stay at home now. I’ll probably start dropping in to see William myself.”

“So you sayin’ you not gon’ be home as much now?” Ronald searched for some hidden message in his wife’s conversation. Sheila was simply thinking, another breath, another subject.

“Do you think we should go down to Tennessee State for Benny’s first homecoming?”

“Who they playin’? I thought we was gonna have to go down to Hope and see about yo’ sister.”

“Somebody else can take care of that if we don’t go. I think they’re playing Florida A&M University.”

“Is that the school with the big fancy band and everything?”

“Yeah, they’re a little bit bigger that TSU’s band but Benny says TSU’s band sounds much better."

"When you talk to Benny?"

"I called him from work about three weeks ago to see if he received his money."

"Sheila, you don't need to be callin' nobody long distance from them people's phone. What you gon' do if they try to fire you for callin' long distance?"

"Ronald, I know the rules of my work place; that's why I used my calling card."

"So what you sayin' I don't know the rules of my workplace?" Ronald was insistent on getting to what he thought was the root cause of this line of questioning. Sheila on the other hand was out of breath, and out of subjects.

"You know what Ronald, sometimes when you're looking for something and you can't find it. That means that there's nothing for you to find. I'm just trying to make conversation. It is so bad that I would want to talk to my husband about little things? I might just want to hear your voice and nothing more. Just because I ask questions, doesn't mean I've got a hidden agenda."

"It just seems funny that *you* always askin' the questions."

"Then why don't you ask a few questions sometimes."

"When I want to talk, I just do it. I ain't got to ask questions."

"That's fine too, but you rarely say anything to me, so I'm left either sitting around the house in silence or poking you hoping that you'll wake up. This is exactly the kind of thing someone would help us with if we had counseling."

"There it is!"

"There what is?"

"I knew it was somethin' you was tryin' to slip in there. Now it's all comin' out in the wash."

"Oh please! You need to get off that. It's not even about that. It's about what we need to do to function in this house and in our marriage, so don't give me that 'eureka I discovered gold' stuff, cause you haven't discovered nothing!"

"That's what I'm talkin' about right there. That's why we can't do nothin' 'cause you always flyin' off when you don't like the way somethin' is," Ronald rebutted. He had to raise his voice to finish the sentence because the phone rang and Sheila darted away from her husband hoping she could be detained by the call. The disruption was an excuse for her to avoid any further discussion with Ronald.

"Hello. House Of Happy Times," Sheila said sarcastically to the caller.

"What is that all about?"

"Hey boy! What are you doin' callin' yo' old mama in the middle of the evening? Shouldn't you be studying or something right now?"

"Mama, I'm a college student. Studyin' is my life." Benny instantly lifted his mother's mood just by giving her his voice through the phone. Not only was she going to be able to exit Ronald's cross-examination, but she would also get to speak with her favorite person in the world.

"So you're dead now waiting to be resurrected by the study gods?"

"You got jokes, huh mama?"

"Amongst other things."

"Oh, what else you got?"

"I got bad news about your aunt."

"Who, Aunt Margie."

"Well..." Sheila hesitated about Margie and William's situation. She didn't want to drop all of the developments at once.

"It's your Aunt Isabelle."

"What's wrong with her?"

"Nothings wrong with her. She's just in sort of a little trouble."

"What happened?"

"She...well she kinda got arrested."

"Arrested? For what?"

"Honey, somebody had the nerve to call the police on her cause her son was eating some grapes in the grocery store and she..."

"...Beat him like he stole something?" Benny interjected.

"Yep. You know the routine."

"I know it better than anybody."

"So some heifer had the nerve to call the police and report her for abuse."

"What? So what happened to little Jerry?"

"They came and took him and put him in protective custody."

"Mama, no! How did y'all find out all of this?"

"One of the neighbors that lives down the road from Aunt Flappy was in the store when it happened. She said that little clown had climbed up on top of the produce section, bounced across the bell peppers crushed the cauliflower, plopped down on the plums, and just started picking off grapes and eating them."

"No, he didn't," Benny said, trying not to laugh at such a serious matter.

"It's alright to laugh. I fell on the floor laughing too when I heard about the little monster."

"So what's gonna happen to Aunt Isabelle now?"

"I'm not sure, but they said somebody went down to the courthouse, to see her and they said she was so upset she couldn't even speak. We might go down there if we don't come to your homecoming."

"Don't worry about homecoming because that's much more important. I've got three more homecomings to go after this one."

"That's so considerate of you. Look at my baby tryin' to grow up and become a man in college."

"Awh mama, please," Benny said. "So y'all gonna go down there and see about Aunt Isabelle and get her stuff straightened out?"

"Yeah, I guess so. I don't know what we we're going to do but rant and rave and act as ethnic as we can."

"That shouldn't be too hard for y'all."

"Watch it, boy. I'll reach through this phone with a belt if I have to."

"I know you will, that's why I'm about to get off the phone and go to the computer lab. How's my pops doin'? Still hittin' those golf balls?"

"Not like he used to. William doesn't play with him much either."

"Really, why not?"

"Uuuh..." Sheila hesitated. "I don't know Benny, you know how those two get. One minute they think they're on a professional tour or something, the next minute they hate the game."

"Yeah, you're right. I was thinking about signing up for the golf PE class in the spring, so I can learn how to play and then come home and spank Daddy on the golf course."

"Ooh, I would love to see that myself. He wouldn't know how to act."

"I said I'm only thinking about it," Benny reminded his mother. He paused for a moment realizing that his mother was rather short with his initial question. "So how are you and pops doing—collectively?" Benny emphasized.

"We're fine, boy. You know, we just like some little love puppies now that the house is all ours again," Sheila replied softly so that Ronald wouldn't hear her statement of obvious denial.

"Are you sure?"

"Yeah I'm sure, stop worrying about me and worry about yourself. And stay away from those little fast-tail girls."

"What fast-tail girls? You mean the ones that you've been trying to get me to stay away from since third grade?'

"What are you talking about?"

"Mama, you'll never be satisfied with a girl I date until I bring home the spittin' image of you," Benny teased.

"I don't want you to bring me home because I already got one of me. I'm all I can handle."

"Me too." Benny said, snickering at his mother's high expectations.

"Watch it."

"It's too late anyway.'

"Too late for what."

"I've already found a fast-tail girl."

"What?"

"I met a nice young lady who's an upper classman and has herself together."

"Lord have mercy, how many months pregnant is the tramp?"

"She's not pregnant mama."

"Oh Jesus. The skank done gave you some kinda disease hasn't she?"

"Mama, what are you talkin' about. She's very nice."

"I knew it! You're dating a white girl aren't you Benny?"

"What? Mama, are you losing it?"

"A transvestite!"

"Mama!" Benny snapped.

"I'm just asking. Something has to be wrong with her if you start out telling me how nice she is and this is only your first semester and she's an upperclassman."

"She's very nice and nothing's wrong with her. And she's Black."

"Mmm-huh. We'll see. Just remember you're up there to get a *de—gree* not a *fam–a—lee*," Sheila stressed her words so that Benny would catch her rhyming emphasis.

"You're a mess. I don't know what to say about you."

"I'm your mess, and I'm all you've got for a mess of a mother so that entitles me to be as messy as I please." Sheila regained her prim and proper composure as the conversation came to a close. She very seldom broke her articulate and astute persona, but when an issue arose about her son's well being or even potential well-being, she was known to transform into a different character.

"And I love you for your messiness. That's why I'm about to get out of your pocketbook."

"What are you talkin' about?"

"I'm in college I don't have any money. You know I'm using your calling card."

"Oh yeah, I forgot. Boy, get off this phone before you put me in the poor house. Hold on. Ronald… do you want to talk to Benny?"

"*Nawh, tell him I'll probably talk to him next week, I'm about to get in the bed*," he yelled from another room.

"Your daddy says he'll probably talk to you next week."

"Okay. I'll talk to y'all later."

"Bye baby, we love you."

"Love y'all too mama. Bye."

Sheila was relieved that the fulfilling warmth and unconditional love of her son saved her potentially ugly evening. Like so many times before, Benny was always there when Sheila's emotions needed salvaging. She feared that one day his phone calls wouldn't be enough and if Benny wasn't home, there would be no salvation for her, Ronald, or the marriage.

Chapter 27
Life In High Gear

Benny arrived at the computer lab and was barely able to find a computer. Last minute paper writers, as well as dedicated nerds, were all hard at work. Taking a proactive approach to his homecoming weekend, Benny finished all of his assignments early, so he decided to take a much-needed break by surfing the internet while other students were eating and practically inhaling caffeine and chocolate. He logged on and read an e-mail from Clem.

Clem had chosen to attend Butler University one of the local colleges in Indianapolis. He wasn't quite ready to take the big step of flying too far away from the nest. If Clem found out he couldn't fly, he wanted to be near his mama bird so that she could pick him up. Clem's e-mail to Benny said that he tried to surf the Web about the same time every night, and that if Benny was ever in the computer lab at that time, he should join Clem in his favorite chat room. A clock on the wall facing all the computer users served as judgment day for fast approaching assignment deadlines. It was 9:32 p.m. Clem might still be online, Benny thought. He disregarded all of his other e-mails and quickly entered that chat room. Once in the cyber-space chat room, he immediately noticed Clem's user name—Melc.

Both he and Clem always used their names spelled backwards for secrecy. They used all capital letters when they wanted to convey messages with strong emphasis, much like shouting.

Ynneb: *What's up cuz?*
Melc: *You tell me you're the one kicking it with all the babes.*
Ynneb: *Womenn are the sane everytwhere.*
Melc: *I told you that you should have paid attention in typing class.*
Ynneb: *What you meanm?*
Melc: *Your typing is terrible.*
Ynneb: *You understamb what I'm saying don't you?*
Melc: *Barely.*

Ynneb: *s up back at home?*
Melc: *Same old same old.*
FoxyT: *Want to see some nasty girls with big tits?*
Ynneb: *Private conversation pleese go awaay.*
FoxyT: *Are you stupid or just a bad typist?*
Melc: *Told yo. ROFL(Rolling On Floor Laughing) Let's go to a private room.*
FoxyT: *Cool!!*
Melc: *Not you! I mean Ynneb!!*
FoxyT: *Not that kinda party huh?*
Melc: *Did you get an invitation?*
FoxyT: *No not yet.*
Melc: *Keep waiting. Ynneb, let's be out.*

Private Chat Room

Ynneb: *You talk in theses thing s much?*
Melc: *All the time.*
Ynneb: *I can tell. You got oon the lingo down to a scicnes.*
Melc: *Benny please slow down with the typing you're killing me.*
Ynneb: *Okay Is*
Ynneb: *this slow*
Ynneb: *enough for you.*
Ynneb: *?*
Melc: *Not my fault you can't type.*
Ynneb: *Don't have all night. What's up?*
Melc: *Thought you could tell me.*
Ynneb: *How s school?*
Melc: *Easier than I thought. Guess what.*
Ynneb: *What*
Melc: *I play golf about once a week now.*
Ynneb: *WHAT????*
Melc: *Yep, it's a trip. I never thought I'd like it but it' s all right.*
Ynneb: *Uncle William got you you huh?*
Melc: *Yeah I thought that might make him happy and lift his spirits.*
Ynneb: *Never thought I'd see the day.*
Melc: *The day is here. What's going on up there? Your grades all right?*
Ynneb: *I'm doing alrihgt. Met this real cool girl.*
Melc: *That didn't take you long at all.*
Ynneb: *She'ss not really a girl she' s a senior.*
Melc: *WHAT???*
Ynneb: *Yep she s cooler thsan a fan.*
Melc: *I heard those old heads like to choose up on the new meat but I never*
Melc: *thought it would happen to you.*

Ynneb: *Why nott?*
Melc: *You must have told her one of those stupid whipping stories and she felt*
Melc: *sorry for you.*
Ynneb: *My stories aint stupid.*
Melc: *Which one did you tell her? The Rat Juice story or the whipping I got at*
Melc: *the store when Kenneth stole that candy.*
Ynneb: *She likes my conversttaion it doens t matter what I'm alking about.*
Melc: *Yeah right.*
Ynneb: *Who you messing with up ther now?Toni?*
Melc: *Nope she had to get dismissed.*
Ynneb: *Again?*
Melc: *This time for good.*
Ynneb: *Why? She didn' t like another one of your poems?*
Melc: *Nawh that was last month. She couldn't hang with consequences.*
Ynneb: *What consequences*
Melc: *The consequences of me spending most of my time with my pops.*
Ynneb: *Man you and Uncle William got close after you graduated huh?*
Melc: *Didn't have no choice. Don't know how much longer I got with him you know?*
Ynneb: *Why, you goin' somewher?*
Melc: *That ain' t funny.*
Ynneb: *What you talking about*
Melc: *This ain't nothing to joke about.*
Ynneb: *What?*
Melc: *You know what, don't play stupid.*
Ynneb: *Man what are yo utalking about?*
Melc: *I' M TALKING ABOUT MY DADDY DYING PUNK THAT'S WHAT!!!!!*
Melc: *IF IT WAS YO' DADDY YOU WOULDN'T BE JOKING NOW WOULD YOU????*
Ynneb: *What happened to Uncle William? What are you sying?*
Melc: *You already know don't you?*
Ynneb: *No what is it? Nobody told me anythingg.*
Melc: *You mean your folks didn't tell you?*
Ynneb: *Tell me what???*
Melc: *My pops got prostate cancer.*

Melc: *You still on line......*

Melc:	*Benny.....*
Ynneb:	*Please tell me you lyin.*
Melc:	*I thought you knew already.*
Ynneb:	*NO!! AIN' T NOBODY TOLD ME SHIT!!!!*
Ynneb:	*Y'ALL ECPECT ME TO KNOW EVERYTHING*
Ynneb:	*I'M HUNDREDS OF MILES AWAY*
Ynneb:	*AIN' T NOBOSY TELLIN ME NOTHIN' !!!!*
Melc:	*I'm sorry . I thought your mom told you*
Melc:	*She probably thought that I told you.*
Ynneb:	*I guess that what my mom was saying when she siad that*
Ynneb:	*my dad was spenind more time over y' alls house.*
Melc:	*Yeah people been real good about coming by.*
Ynneb:	*So when did all this happen and how bad is it.*
Melc:	*We found out last month. And it's spread up to his lung and liver. So he's*
Melc:	*not doing too good. You can't tell him that though cause he still want*
Melc:	*to golf a little.*
Ynneb:	*That' s why you atarted playin?'*
Melc:	*Yeah I figure I got to get as much time with him as I can you know?*
Ynneb:	*Man my head is messed up now.*
Melc:	*Sorry you had to find out like this.*
Ynneb:	*Not your fault.*
Melc:	*When you coming back to the crib?*
Ynneb:	*Christmas. Will that be too latee*
Melc:	*Nawh!!! He ain' t on his death bed yet Benny.*
Ynneb:	*You made it sound like he was.*
Melc:	*He gets sick every now and then but he's okay for now.*
Ynneb:	*I can' t believe this.*
Melc:	*You should call your pops and make sure he gets checked. He's getting to that age now*
Ynneb:	*Yeah I' m gonna do that.*
Melc:	*I need to roll, I got a paper due tomorrow.*
Ynneb:	*So do half of these fools siting in this lab.*
Melc:	*Do you have one due?*
Ynneb:	*Nope alerdy done it.*
Melc:	*I see why.*
Ynneb:	*Why*
Melc:	*Your typing is so bad it probably takes you a week to make corrections.*
Ynneb:	*I'm finished and you ain't.*
Melc:	*Alrihgt you got me.*
Ynneb:	*Hey keep your head up bruh.*

Melc: *Alright peace.*
Ynneb *I' ll holla at you .*

"Hey are you through yet? Say bruh you finished?" a student asked Benny.

"Huh, oh yeah my bad." Benny replied as he was awakened from his night time day dream. He found himself staring blankly at the computer screen where he had just been delivered the devastating news about his favorite uncle.

"I gotta get this paper done for Ms. Whitfield, bruh. She ain't no joke either," the anxious student remarked.

"I know what you mean. Let me log off and it's all yours man."

Benny logged off his session and returned the screen to the University's standard screen saver. He gathered his note pad and headed back to his dorm room. His thoughts were burdened with details of his family's problems and his absence from the scene. He knew there was no way he could have prevented any of the occurrences, but he couldn't help feeling guilty for not being able to give his support. Benny knew his family was a major part of his existence and his characteristics. When they suffered, he did as well.
His time was dead so there was none left to kill. He stopped in the lobby of the computer lab and gambled with a daring phone call to Karmin.

"Hey Karmin. This is Benny, what's up?"

"Well, well, well, what have I done to deserve this call, Mr. Dempkins."

"Are you busy?"

"No, just reading."

"You have company?"

"No. Is something wrong Benny?" Karmin asked, abandoning her cynical pseudo professional routine giving Benny sincere concern. She sensed stress in his voice.

"Does the offer still stand for the free counseling? I don't really have issues, but I do want to talk."

"Yeah, what's the problem?"

"I got a lot of bad news from home all at one time."

"What's going on, is everyone okay there?"

"Yeah, well, kind of...well, it's." Benny hesitated, searching for the truth, an answer, and then a confession. He found neither. "I'd rather not talk about it over the phone. You mind if I come over? I'm at the computer lab and it'll take me about thirty minutes to walk down there to your apartment. I really hate to bother you."

"No, it's not a problem at all. In fact, why don't you just stand outside and I'll swing by and pick you up. I'll be there in five minutes."

"You sure you don't mind?"

"I'm already walking out of the door. Make sure you're outside."

"Thanks Karmin, I really appreciate this. You're a pretty good friend after all."

"Not really."

"What makes you say that?"

"The counseling session isn't free. You will be charged for an hour's session. My rent is due."

"I should have known."

During the short ride back to Karmin's apartment, Benny opened up and told Karmin about his Aunt who'd been arrested and about his favorite uncle. Karmin in turn told Benny about all of the tragedies she'd heard about during her four years in school. Benny never realized that so many people and their families could make up such an enormous chalk board to scribble upon the lessons and pains of life. His two incidents seemed minimal to the stories Karmin shared with Benny.

Once they arrived at Karmin's apartment, Benny forgot that he was actually at college. Her spacious apartment was a fortress compared to Benny's low rent district dorm room. The scent of peach potpourri wafted though the air. It was obvious why Karmin studied on campus. The smell permeating Benny's nostrils was a pure sleep poison. He was reminded of the poison poppies from the movie The Wiz. Just like the characters in the movie, Benny was tempted to fall asleep forever. And it would have been a very comfortable rest on Karmin's floral patterned red and green sofa sleeper. Framed Black-Art from the art shop, Woodcuts, on Jefferson Street, hung on the walls and complemented the tall vegetation that occupied the corners of her apartment. Benny could hear faint crescendos of traditional jazz teasing its way through the speakers that were camouflaged by the numerous books on the shelves. Some were academic books, others were novels, and a few were financial management books.

"You've got a nice place. Are you rich or something?" Benny called to Karmin who had gone into another of the four rooms.

"Rich is a relative term. You can get something to drink or a snack from the kitchen if you want."

Benny walked into the peninsula shaped kitchen and noticed that the living room color scheme continued in the kitchen with her towels, bowls, and curtains. He was scared to touch anything for fear that he might leave something out of place. Inside the refrigerator, Benny was amazed at all of the food Karmin had. He saw leftovers from what seemed to be the remainder of a full course meal. There was orange juice, iced tea, and three different kinds of soft drinks. All Benny could think about was his one carton of Jungle Juice, which he kept by the window near the air conditioner so that its preservation could be appreciated on nights when the cafeteria was closed and he was out of change.

"Did you find anything you wanted in there? I need to go grocery shopping, don't I?"

"What?"

"It's that bad, huh?"

"Bad? I haven't seen that much food in one place since I left home. It's looks like you're about to have a family reunion."

"You're so silly. Did you find a snack or something?" Karmin entered the kitchen and watched Benny gazing in amazement at her food supply.

"I found a lot of stuff! How can you afford all of those groceries and this apartment?"

"Please, Benny. You'll have the same stuff when you're a senior."

"How do you figure?"

"My scholarship pays for my housing and I get a stipend for working at the hotline."

"Really! I thought that was a volunteer job."

"It is unless you win their Academic Excellence Scholarship Award. And at the rate you're going, they'll probably throw the award at you and beg you to take it.'

"Yeah, right."

"I'm serious Benny; you're the department's golden child. Everyone talks about how you're a fast tracker, and very mature for your age. And the shame of it all is that you're so humble you don't even realize it. It's sort of sexy if you ask me."

"Go on somewhere."

"That's exactly what I mean."

"What?"

"I'm trying to pay you a compliment and you don't even realize it."

"Okay, I'm sorry. Thank you for the compliment."

"Thank you for being sexy and available."

"What's that supposed to mean?"

"It means you're sexy and available, and that's good."

Benny was reaching for all of the maturity and cool he could find. It wasn't easy because Karmin, as forward as she always was, had never been forward with him in a private setting.

"I'd love a snack, but I ate in the cafeteria a little while ago."

"What about something sweet, want some dessert?" Karmin asked him with a smooth voice and seductive eyes.

"You mean some of you?" Benny asked, losing what little cool he had.

"I see where your mind is, but I was thinking about some peach cobbler."

"You got peach cobbler! I love peach cobbler!" Benny had already lost his cool and now his maturity was following suit.

"Settle down, big fella. I've got some in the freezer. It takes about 30 minutes to cook."

"What do you mean in the freezer?"

"It's that Mrs. Smith or Sarah Lee or something."

"Peach cobbler in a box?"

"Yeah. Would you rather it be in a bag or something?"

"There's no such thing as peach cobbler in a box."

"What are you talking about, Benny?"

"Man, peach cobbler is like a big family tradition back home. You can't call yourself a cook in my family and not know how to make peach cobbler. We have at least fifteen peach cobblers at every family reunion"

"So what you're saying is that I've pretty much insulted your ancestors by offering you this disastrous dessert."

"Pretty much." Benny said in a lighthearted manner.

"So how did this peach cobbler become such a rich tradition in the Dempkins family?"

"It's on my mother's side, and to tell you the truth, I really don't know. For as long as I can remember, whenever we get together, it's just been a big thing to have peach cobbler. But nobody makes it like my Granny Osee. She has some kind of secret stuff she put in hers. Granny Osee's cobbler stands out more than any of my other aunts, or anybody else that tries to get with her recipe. You should come down to one of our family reunions one summer and try..."

"Benny," Karmin interrupted."

"Huh."

"I want to be spontaneously intimate with you right now, so don't be alarmed when I walk over to you and kiss you long and deep. Then don't be surprised when I lead you back to my bedroom and seduce you to the point of insanity."

Benny starred at Karmin not knowing what to say or do. Fearful but anxious, he remained quiet. Karmin walked over and initiated the actions of her preceding announcement. As they began walking to Karmin's bedroom, old thoughts began to haunt Benny. He envisioned his cousin Cynthia's swollen belly at the family reunion. Then he remembered his father's words when he spoke of the women he had been with before he was married and how it ultimately lessened the passionate appetite he had for his wife. Benny kept thinking, but kept walking. Karmin was proceeding as planned and Benny was now thinking about Karmin, and nothing but Karmin.

Chapter 28
Appreciation

"How you holdin' up, partna?" Ronald asked William.

"Man, I ain't never been better my whole life," William replied optimistically.

"I guess if you gon' be a liar, you may as well be consistent with it."

"What you talkin' about?"

"You lied on the golf course all these years just to try and beat me by five or so strokes, and here you are lyin' on yo' deathbed."

"Ronald, go ahead on somewhere with that mess. I ain't never had to lie to get no strokes off of you. All I had to do was say something about yo' wife and yo' whole game was gone."

"I tell you what. All this medicine must have made you remember things funny or something, cause that ain't at all how I remember it." Ronald said, joking with his ill-fated friend. Ronald was one of William's frequent visitors and probably the best received. William carried on as though he had just been told he was going to go on living for the next five decades and he should enjoy life to its fullest. However, quite the contrary was the reality he faced. During William's last visit, his doctor informed he and Margie that his cancer was spreading so rapidly he could expect not to see his son graduate from college. He might not even see him begin his sophomore year at Butler.

In the early stages, William disregarded all of the doctor's orders for rest and healthy eating. Instead, he enjoyed playing nine holes or less with Clem. William's son had found new interest in the game he'd always tried to avoid playing. Clem was terrible, but from William's perspective, his son was the best person on the course simply because he was playing with him. William's spirits were untouched by his illness. The same ebullient person that succeeded or failed in life was the same person lying in bed or propped up against the chair. His attitude and strength helped everyone around him cope with his inevitable end.

"It don't matter no way, cause when I tee off on the eighteenth hole upstairs, I'll be looking down watchin' Clem spank you up and down the golf course carrying on my legacy."

"Mm-huh. I'm glad at least one of those knuckleheads picked up the game. I don't know what Benny is waitin' on."

"How's he doin' down there in school anyway?"

"His mama say he doing pretty good. He got some kinda job doing counseling with kids or something. Say he works late at night and works long hours too. I think he a psychiatrist already or somethin'. His mama said they pushed him up to the top of class or something like that, I don't know," Ronald said, misconstruing every fact his wife had ever given him about Benny's status in school. "I don't see how he gettin' nothin' done because he supposed to be real serious about this woman that he met at this job. She about to graduate and get one of those high payin' jobs. But you know how Sheila is, she tryin' to make the girl out to be some old hussy that's up to no good."

"Ain't nobody these boys bring home gon' be good enough for them, Sheila or Margie. They just like that."

"They make it sound like they about to get married already," Ronald said.

"Already! That boy ain't been in school but how long?"

"Just as long as Clem. He about to finish his freshman year."

"Yeah, that's right. I forgot he left the same week Clem was going to get registered. Boy, my mind ain't what it used to be, Ron," William admitted as he slipped into a fatigue spell. Ronald took notice of his friend's condition. He only called him Ron when there was a problem or he needed some type of help. Beyond fluffing his pillows and getting a drink of water or something, Ronald felt hopeless in accommodating his dear friend for any of his requests.

"What did your mind used to be, 'cause I can't remember?" Ronald offered, as a dose of fun for the obvious discomfort William was experiencing.

"If anybody know, it'll be you, buddy. We been knowing each other a lot of years, ain't we?"

"We got some years left yet. Didn't you just tell me you wasn't on yo' death bed just yet?"

"Mm-Huh. That was ten minutes ago, but this thing tries to wrestle me all day long. Sometimes, I just let the damn thing pin me on the mat and count to three. It's strong Ron…sometimes, it's too strong," he replied battling the pain.

"I hear ya' partna. That's what I'm here for, to help you fight it. I ain't leaving until we win," Ronald said, grasping his friend's hand. Just as he'd noticed many years ago while holding Benny in the backyard, Ronald realized that this was the extent of affection he'd ever shown his longtime friend in all the years they'd known each other. *Later was better than never*, Ronald thought to himself. He held his friend's hand in support and watched him slowly lose this round's battle with fatigue. William slumbered while Ronald stood over him and watched, thinking of the times they'd shared and the times they'd never have. William made a sudden comeback in this round as though he had a few more important things to say to his protector.

"It'll probably be Margie."

"What?" Ronald asked, then realizing William was probably delusional.

"You were wondering what I'm gon' miss the most."

"No I wasn't."

"Well, it'll still be Margie."

"Why do you say that?"

"She know the most about me." William was attempting to keep his statements short and meaningful."

"More than I do?" Ronald asked.

"We're different. She's special...know all my mistakes...forgave me for all of 'em...loved me in spite of 'em.

"That's what she supposed to do ain't it?"

"Yep...don't mean she had to though."

"I guess you're right."

"Margie and Sheila...they both long wives."

"What's a long wife?"

"Love you as long as you let 'em. Long as we keep bein' stupid. Long as we keep on livin'."

"You really think so?"

"Know so."

"How can you be so sure?"

"I can feel... Margie's love ending."

"Why you say that?"

"Cause...ain't gon' be living much longer."

"That don't mean..." Ronald started until he watched William slip off into another slumber battle. Ronald was thinking that just because a person wasn't alive doesn't mean someone won't love them. Then Ronald thought to himself, I'm very alive, and so was his *long* wife. However, Ronald didn't feel the long love William so plainly described to him, but he did feel that Sheila was still there, making conversation, making attempts, making a way to long love him.

"I knew that they wasn't gonna have anything substantial when we got there anyway. Those backwards rednecks down there don't know the first thing about the law and public policy. And did you see that trailer trash that had the unmitigated gall to call the police on somebody that disciplines their child in public. Now I bet you she would have been the first person to call the police talking about *these gangbangers are terrorizing my neighborhood.* Who kids does she think are gon' turn into gangbangers? The ones that don't have no discipline and don't get they little butts beat when they're young. We ain't trying to raise no murders, drug addicts, or rapist in this family. I'd like to go to her house and see how her kids runnin' everywhere talking about *Mommy where's my dinner?* She got some nerve!"

"Yeah Margie. I'm just glad everything worked out for the best and Isabelle is doing alright," Sheila said to her sister.

"And see, I couldn't believe the two of you just sittin' up there trying to be cool and collected the whole time. I wasn't even trying to hear that, because I wanted somebody's job and somebody should have been sued for that kinda of craziness. That didn't make no sense! If I ever get in trouble, y'all better stay at home and bring the hell raisers of the family, cause I think I would've hurt you if y'all came in there to get me, all polite and everything."

"Margie, everything doesn't have to always be done with an exclamation point at the end of it just to get something accomplished," Sheila said, trying to massage her words around Margie's explosive comments.

"Sheila, people need to know you've been in a room after you've gone, and unless you walk in there disrupting what was going before you got there, ain't nobody gonna give a damn about what you did while you were in there. They're certainly not going to notice you after you've left, so you may as well not have even gone in the room."

"Margie, you can have the same effect by going in the room and farting, but when it's all said and done with, people are only going to remember you because you stunk up the room," Sheila said in her defense. Margie stopped dusting the living room table and stared at her sister beyond her eyes.

"So what you saying, I stank. Is that what you're trying to say?" Margie's sense of humor had been lost somewhere between vacuuming the carpet daily and supplying painkillers. She would have normally come back with a snide and piercing remark making everyone in the room laugh with the exception of the victim. Sheila regretted the comment as soon as the period left her lips. She noticed how short-tempered her sister had become and took every precaution to be as sensitive as possible.

"No girl, stop being so sensitive. You know I wasn't trying to say that. I'm just trying to convey that...," Sheila hesitated realizing that her sister didn't need a debate right now, she needed support. "I'm just saying that you and I handle things differently, that's all, and we both can be very effective even though our approaches differ."

Margie turned away from Sheila in the middle of her statement and resumed her circular swirls with her dust cloth on anything that needed and didn't need dusting.

Margie had been increasingly verbose during William's illness. She kept herself busy and kept herself talking. Their house had never been so clean. The clothes had never been so fresh and crisply pressed, and even the small lawn looked as though it had been professionally manicured. Sheila could plainly see her sister was having difficulty coping and adjusting to this new yet temporary way of living. When she approached Margie with conversation about William, her response was generally limited to comments about their first months of dating. Margie refused to acknowledge that a happy and kind spirit even existed in this trying time of their marriage.

For the most part, Margie behaved as a hired nurse while she was around her husband. Her duties entailed supplying medicine and food, changing his clothes, and rearranging the room so that he wouldn't be consumed by the monotony of his setting. Once William told her that he never realized how routine the sun rising and setting was until he had seen it happen for three consecutive weeks from the same window. From that moment on, Margie vowed to make something different about their bedroom everyday. Margie was a nurse all day and evening until it was bedtime. Then she'd make her way into bed next to her weakened husband, kiss him gently on the lips, and talk him to sleep with stories of the beginning of their relationship. Margie was desperate to rekindle and hold on to their beautiful beginning. William always fell asleep smiling, and Margie would always fall asleep talking.

Sheila walked into the kitchen thinking she could help Margie straighten up, but of course, nothing was out of place so she elected to make some hot tea. Walking over to the sink and turning on the faucet, she filled Margie's teakettle with water. The black kettle even had swirl marks where it had been repeatedly polished and cleaned. When the kettle was full, Sheila turned the faucet off and heard squeak marks being made against a glass in the other room. *Margie is going to polish her house away*, Sheila thought. In between the polishing sounds she also heard faint sniffs, the same sniffs that people made when their allergies were being tortured.

"Margie, why don't you stop dusting, you know your allergies can't handle all this dust!" Sheila shouted towards the other room as she ignited the stove to a medium high setting. Suddenly she remembered that Isabelle was the sister with the bad allergies and Margie was practically immune to sinus problems. The sniffing grew louder and was approaching her direction. Sheila walked back into the living room holding her nose because she figured if Margie had stumbled over a dust bowl that made her sniff, Sheila would probably gag on the tiny particles. When she entered the room, there was no dust, only her younger sister sobbing, sniffing, and wiping her tears. Sheila rushed over to Margie and embraced her tightly in an attempt to squeeze all of her pain and troubles away.

"I'm here for you, Margie. You don't have to go through it alone, baby." Sheila sat and held her sister until she heard her attempt to speak. Sheila let her sister go and held her hands so that she could see her face, now drenched with tears of fear and hurt. "I'll help you Margie."

"He's..."

"It's okay Margie."

"He's leaving... and it hurts so much! I just wish I could stop loving him right now, so when he's gone, it won't hurt so bad. But I can't stop loving him, Sheila. I love him more now than I ever have in my whole life...I already miss him."

Sheila embraced her sister once again. The teakettle began whistling for attention, oblivious to the troubles in this home its warm liquids would never be able to soothe.

Chapter 29
Confessions

"Benny, really I don't mind going to your uncle's funeral with you," Karmin said, consoling Benny.

"I appreciate the offer, but I don't think you should be spending that kind of money for a quick trip, especially since I haven't worked out all of the details with my mom yet."

"Benny, you keep talking about your mom like she's an evil witch. How bad can it be?"

"It can be messed up when it to comes to her little Benny. Look, Karmin I'd love for you to come, but it's just not the best time. Besides, I'll be with my cousin Clem most of the time tyrin' to give him some support and stuff. My mom says he took my uncle's death pretty hard."

Benny and Karmin were spending more time together after they'd worked out their complexes about age differences. Karmin had become so frustrated justifying to everyone that Benny was very mature for his age, she all but severed her ties to her hypocritical friends and professors that showed unusual interest in the new couple. Karmin complemented Benny and vice versa. Karmin was so focused on graduating that she kept him studying diligently. The only time they spent together during the week was during her study period and working at the hotline. Benny kept Karmin just immature enough so that she could participate in pep rallies, bonfires, and football games. These were all activities she had avoided during her matriculation through school. Karmin had been completely out of touch with campus activities until she and Benny became an item. Although there was an unwritten rule of no sleeping over during the week, they were both guilty of influencing the other to bend the rule just a little. The slightly mature freshman that Benny enrolled as, was slowly becoming a very supportive and responsible man. And the determined senior who was on the verge of graduation with no obstacles, now had an obstacle, a strong sex drive and a supportive and responsible young man.

"Well, can I give you something before you leave?"

"Karmin, what's been wrong with you lately? We've been doing it practically once a day every week now."

"I don't mean that. See, you've still got issues. I want to give you a thought. I wanted to talk about it on the way to your house, but I see that's a closed door since you won't let me go with you."

"Trying to make me feel bad, huh?"

"Reverse psychology is still a viable option. But I want you to think about you and I," she said staring at Benny's chest. She held both his hands, and looked into his eyes and said, "I want you to think about me loving you."

"What?"

"I think that we've been seeing enough of each other to the point that I can openly admit to you that, I think I love you." Benny was quiet, uncomfortably quiet. "Don't get young on me, Benny."

"You know, I hate when you say that."

"Well I hate when you ...."

"You know something, I am young, so now what?"

"I still love you. Now what?" Karmin said, backing him into a verbal corner from which he was forced to answer his way out of.

"Karmin...I don't know if I love you or not because, I've never been in love with anyone before."

"And you think I have?"

"I don't know, have you?"

"Even if I have, does that matter right now?" Karmin answered.
Benny was feeling weighed down by all of the thought provoking burdens Karmin was placing on him.

"I guess not," Benny replied.

"I'm not asking you to marry me. I'm just putting what I assumed was a pleasant thought in your mental suitcase for your trip. Is that alright?" Karmin said in frustration. Benny was quiet but this time comfortably quiet.

"Yeah, I guess so... I mean yeah, it's fine. It's just that nobody, besides my parents, have ever told me that before. I hope you'll forgive me if I screw up the response. I'm very new at this."

"You're right. I may have been a little unfair. Just do me a favor."

"I'll try."

"Just have a safe trip, hurry back, and think about what I said while you're on the plane. Take my calling card and call me if you need to, cause you still have issues, you know," she joked walking away from Benny and retrieving her calling card from her purse on the sofa.

"All right, I'll do that."

"Do what Benny?"

"All of the above."

"Don't make any false commitments, because you know I'll make a checklist for you."

"Go ahead and make your checklist. Just make sure I get my gold stars when I get back."

"We'll see."

"No, *you'll* see."

"I love you."

"...That sounds peculiar."

"How does it feel?"

"...Not peculiar."

"I'll take that for now. Come on so you don't miss your flight."

❧

As Benny waited for his flight he watched one of the airport televisions that only showed news and sports. He began thinking about what Karmin was watching, and then what would she eat for dinner tonight. All of a sudden he found himself consumed with her well-being and her activities. Not obsessed, just concerned. Walking towards one of many fast food-restaurants, he immediately thought about ordering two combo-meals, one for him and one for his partner who he would not see for a few days. She was on his mind constantly, and not just today. Benny realized that he'd been having these fulfilling thoughts about her for sometime now. When he got to the counter and inadvertently ordered two hamburgers, Karmin had her answer and Benny had his confirmation. He scoffed down his preflight meal and watched planes take off, wishing he and Karmin could take a romantic flight somewhere together. Suddenly the gate attendant announced the arrival of Benny's plane, and a few minutes later the preboarding call was made. Benny now had the urge to give Karmin her answer before he left the city. What if he never made it home? What if the plane crashed and he died not telling Karmin how he truly felt? An instant melodrama began playing out in Benny's head until he stopped in his tracks and rushed over to the nearest pay phone. He quickly dialed Karmin's number without even thinking about which buttons to push. She was just walking in the door.

"Hello, hello," she said rushing her words in hopes that the other party hadn't hung up.

"You been jogging or something? Why are you out of breath?"

"I just got back, so I had to run inside and catch the phone. You miss your flight?"

"Nope. I missed you."

"Aww that's sweet. I'm gonna miss you too."

"So do I."

"So do I what? You already said you missed me."

"So do I, I mean... I love you too," Benny said, professing his love for Karmin. She was quiet, not exactly the response Benny was looking for. "You still there?"

"I'll always be here, Benny. For whatever and as long as you need, I'll be here. I'm glad you called." She was quiet for a few breaths again. "Are you sure Benny? You're not telling me this because you're getting lonely are you, cause I don't want a confused emotion type of love. Don't mistake love for lonli..."

"Karmin!"

"Huh?" she humbly jumped off of her platform of precaution.

"I said I love you." Again she answered first with a short silent quiet."

"I love you too, Benny. There's something else I want to talk to you about. Now don't confuse..."

"Hey, it's gotta wait until..."

"No, it can't wait."

"Then come pick me up, because I'm about to miss my flight."

"Benny..."

"I gotta go. I'll try to call you from home. See ya bye. I love you again," he rushed one more confession to Karmin and hung up the phone.

"Benny. I'm...,"Karmin had a choice of making her second confession to a dial tone or not making it at all. Neither Benny nor the dial tone would learn today, that Karmin was pregnant.

Chapter 30
Futile Changes–Fatal Choices

While at William's funeral, Benny couldn't seem to find the courage, or the strength, to sit any closer than the last few pews of the crowded church. He figured he would have a difficult time providing any support that Clem needed now. People who were supposed to simply view the casket and then walk back to their seats found themselves walking over to Margie and Clem to hug them, kiss them, or just give words of encouragement. Margie gave every well-wisher the same response. She stared at them sincerely only for a brief moment, cautious not to let them see her unbearable pain. A quick incidental smile to each person, then she glanced back down at her funeral program awaiting the next well-wisher. Margie appeared to be so much stronger than Sheila could have ever been. Sheila couldn't even manage a smile, nor could she make eye contact with any of the onlookers. While, Margie greeted people like a gracious host, Sheila's attention was focused on discarding her tear-drenched tissues. When a tissue would not suffice, she utilized Ronald's shoulder to hide her obvious pain and grief. Ronald didn't mind the intrusion of her grief, for it seemed as though Ronald wasn't cognizant of any of the ongoing events. He stared blindly at the pulpit, or whatever object was directly in his line of vision. Religiously, he looked at nothing in particular, envisioned himself inside the casket, blinked and made no recognition of anyone. Ronald's longtime friend, or at least his body, was lying inside of a box, because of an illness Ronald was very susceptible to, especially at his age. Suddenly things were becoming much more valuable to Ronald. He thought about how Benny would only be home for another day and there was no guarantee when he'd see his son again. The argument he'd recently had with Sheila seemed so trivial and useless now. He kept thinking about Margie sitting just a few spaces down from him and what it would be like when she returned home and her husband was completely gone. After the funeral, William would simply be a memory.

The last of the well-wishers made their respectful laps and the service was conducted somberly without many outbursts. Margie was a symbol of strength for all in attendance. She was determined to make her husband's departure a respectful one instead of a massive gathering of mourners. As the service concluded she gracefully walked over, placed one last kiss upon William's home going vessel, left the church, and her husband.

"You need me to make some dinner?" Ronald asked his grieving wife.

"No, thank you."

"You hungry?"

"No, Ronald, I'm not hungry right now."

"You want me to go out and get somethin' for later?"

"No, that's okay."

"You don't feel like eatin' take-out, food huh?"

"No, there's plenty of food over at Margie's, so there's no need in cooking or going out."

"You want to go over to Margie's later?"

"Ronald, please. Right now I don't want anything, but to sit in this chair and do nothing, is that okay?"

"I'm sorry, I was just trying to see if you needed anything," Ronald explained, slowly throttling back on his expression of concern. He felt compelled to relive every argument he and Sheila had ever had. The need to instantly make all of their wrongs, right had never been so desirable to him. In fact, Ronald never recognized any of the problems that plagued their marriage, but he did realize a desperate need to make every remaining moment with his wife pleasurable and memorable.

Suddenly, the concept of communicating was a refreshing alternative to silence and bickering. Margie and William had always been a mirror of comparison for Ronald and Sheila. Every since Sheila and Ronald's wedding, when Benny was just learning how to walk, William and Margie were there to serve as a guide for any path they might choose to walk. Now the image was smudged with a transparent vision of William. Clearly he had been there, but now he was merely a name that would always be associated with things in the past tense.

Ronald was preparing himself for his new attitude towards his marriage and his family as a whole. The very next time that Sheila requested something or so much as gave an inkling about a task, Ronald decided from this day forward, his wife would have it done for her. He thought of how he could be more open-minded and ways that he would agree to suggestions Sheila presented. For a moment, and only for a moment, Ronald considered making an appointment to visit a counselor at one of the local churches. In a few days, after Sheila recuperated and her spirits were lifted, Ronald was going to present her with the mindset of a new man and would begin by preparing dinner for her on Monday night. He had a few extra hours built up at work and Mr. Jackson, his manager, definitely wouldn't mind him taking a little time off, particularly if he knew it was for his family. Ronald was distracted from planning the menu by the faint sound of Sheila calling his name.

"Ron...*eg hem*," Sheila cleared her throat to produce enough volume for Ronald to hear her statement. "Ronald."

"Yes, baby. What do you need?" Ronald said as sincerely as he could.

"Will you do me a favor? If you don't mind, could you..."

"Yeah baby, just tell me what you want. I'll get it for you," Ronald said with expedient enthusiasm. Sheila wanted to smile at her husband's gracious willingness but she didn't find her smile, she only found herself giving a blank stare, a mundane voice, and a strange request.

"Could you look in the phone book and call Essie Crawford. Tell her I won't be in to work for about two weeks. I think I need some time off." Ronald quickly walked downstairs to the hall closet to retrieve the phone book, when, he halted and turned towards his wife. They had never discussed a vacation for this year, and even if they wanted to take a vacation, there was not enough time to give notice, so he was quite confused about his wife's request. However, he was already consciously committed to his self-proclaimed vow, so he followed through with the phone call.

Sheila's coworker was just as stunned as Ronald. Until the co-worker mentioned it, Ronald did not realize Sheila had never taken a day off from work in the past three years.

"I called her, and she said that she'll tell the people at work, but you still should call and talk to the office manager on Monday. Sheila, you feeling okay, baby?"

"I just want some rest. I don't think I've been getting enough rest lately."

"Yeah, you have been rippin' and runnin' for a long time now. Why don't you take a nap, and I'll lay down here beside you like I used to do?"

"No, why don't you go on downstairs and watch some TV, you don't have to stay up here with me. I don't think I'll be asleep very long anyway."

Although he wasn't walking this time, Sheila once again managed to halt his actions. For years, Sheila had always complained that Ronald was never around on lazy weekend afternoons to lie down with her as they did when they were first married. Now that Ronald had just extended the offer and been summarily rejected, he saw no alternative but to take his wife up on her suggestion. Dejected, Ronald walked downstairs, flipped on the television, and tried to ascertain who was the person upstairs that had seemingly come and taken control of his wife's body.

"Hey pops, you alright?" Benny asked, entering the living room.

"Hey man, how you doin'? I see you comin' from your second home—the refrigerator."

"I'm alright I guess. I'm more worried about you though."

"Ain't nothin' to be worried over my raggedy self for. It's good to see you back home." Ronald was running over with sincerity, which was very obvious to Benny. It was almost alarming. Benny looked his father over as if his inexperienced psychoanalytical skills could make an immediate diagnosis.

"You sure you're holding up?"

"Yeah, I'm fine."

"Is mama sleep?"

"Yeah, she said she just needs some rest. That's probably a good idea cause you know ya mama been doin' a lot these past couple weeks. She said she might take some time off from work."

"Mama! Take some time off from work?" Benny replied in wonderment.

"Yeah. Why not? You know she deserve it."

"I know, but mama never takes a day off," he said looking upstairs toward his parents room. Benny felt sympathy and concern for his mother. "That's not like her. I'm worried about that."

"It's nothin' big. You got enough to be worried about up there at school already. When you goin' back?"

"My flight leaves tomorrow evening. I'm gonna get Clem to take me to the airport. Mama probably needs to hang around at home anyway."

"Did you call Clem and ask him yet? You think he gon' feel like goin' anywhere?"

"I don't know. I'm on my way there now. I thought I'd go check on him in case, you know, he needs somebody to talk to. If he doesn't feel like it, I can find a way to the airport."

"I can probably take you, cause I ain't got to work this weekend."

"Okay. Let me see what Clem says and I'll let you know when I get back."

"How long you gon' be out?" Ronald asked, and then realized he may have come across as a bit overbearing to his nearly grown son. "I mean… I just don't want to worry and in case ya mama ask, I'll know what to tell her."

Benny appreciated his father's consideration for his maturity.

"I know pops, you don't have to explain it to me. It's almost eight o'clock now," Benny said glancing down at his watch. "I wanted to stop by the store and get Karmin a postcard, since she's never been to Indy before."

"Boy you and that girl getting' serious, ain't you?" Ronald said, smiling proudly at his son's new endeavors of manhood.

"She's nice. I'll say that much. We'll just have to see what happens. I should be back by twelve. If it's any later I'll call you."

"Okay then. Be careful. You need some money?"

"I can always use some money. I'm in college," Benny smiled with enthusiasm as his father pulled twenty dollars from his bulky brown wallet that was full of pieces of paper more than anything else.

Ronald walked his son to the door and watched him drive off into the night. He was grateful he could still see his son.

Benny took the change the cashier gave him from his postcard he'd purchased for Karmin and read it. *This is my city and my city is mine.* He thought the jingle was corny and thoughtless, but it was the most picturesque view of the city. The moon's gracious beams and the bright lights of the city illuminated the skyline in the picture. He searched for a thought so that he could scribble a simple message on the card. His first inclination was to write *Wish you were here...on top of me*, but then he thought about who might read the card; classmates, her parents, his parents, so he changed his mind and decided on:

The city is as beautiful at night,
as you are all day and each day.

Instead of waiting until he got in the car, Benny reached in his pocket to retrieve something to write with. As he looked down towards his pant pocket, a tall, lanky man hurriedly walked toward him. Benny was near his house and as far as he was concerned, this was still his neighborhood. It was somewhat odd that a person would approach him in the parking lot, but Benny thought maybe it was a homeless person approaching him for money. As the figure closed the distance between them, Benny could see the stranger holding some type of package. Walking towards his mother's car, which was safely guarded by a well-lit area, Benny saw that the man was no stranger at all and the package was a small baby joyfully squirming around in the man's arms.

"Benny Dempkins! What's up, playa? How you been livin'?"

"Ryan? What's up man. I didn't even recognize you. How you doin'?"

"Oh, I'm straight. Hey, can you give me a ride right quick over to Tonya's house?"

"Tonya...Tonya Jones? Is that who's baby this is? How old is he?"

"Nawh, it's our baby together and *she* seven months old. Can you run me over there right quick? The baby need to get back home so she can...uh, you know, she need to be changed and, uh I ain't got no diapers.

Benny was suspicious of his old neighbor's hasty request. He was surprised that Ryan had such an urgency to get his newborn home to be changed, yet he was at a grocery store making no attempt to purchase any diapers. Ryan kept looking around, as though he was looking for someone—or someone was looking for him.

"Why didn't you pick up diapers when you were in the store?"

"They didn't have none."

"What? A big store like that doesn't have any diapers?

"No. I mean they didn't have the kind I needed." Ryan replied altering his story. In between his obvious lies and inquiries for an expedient ride, Ryan sniffed with the demeanor of a flu plagued patient. It was obvious he didn't have a cold, although he did look quite ill. The bulky athletic build that once outlined his frame, had somehow withered away to a scrawny, and sniffling baby-carrying body. The infant soon lost its bouncing joy and became very irritable while in Ryan's arms. *Perhaps she really did need new diapers,* Benny thought.

"Where does Tonya live now?"

"Over off of fifty-sixth street. It's just five minutes from here."

"Five minutes doing seventy through a residential area! Man, that's almost on the other side of town!"

"Well, just take me up to College Street. and I'll get another ride from there."

"Who's gonna pick you up?"

"Uh, I'll get somebody. Tonya'll come get me."

"Then why can't she come get you now?" Benny probed, attempting to satisfy his suspicion. Ryan was becoming increasingly nervous the longer they talked. And his casual looks around and behind him evolved into steps in different directions. He was obviously trying get a better view of whatever he was on the look out for."

"Man, are you gon' give me the damn ride or you gon' interview me?" Ryan said halting his fidgeting. He looked directly into Benny's eyes. Now the baby was giving hints of a potentially irritating cry for comfort or attention. Benny consented to the ride, but only for the baby's sake.

"Alright, but you better hope that Tonya comes to get you, cause I got to go over to Clem's house."

Ryan was immune to Benny's words and consumed with his objective. Suddenly, Ryan stopped shuffling around and focused in on something, or someone, off in the distance. His eyes were immediately filled with fear and distress, and his nervous actions were redirected towards Benny.

"Where yo' car at, man? Right here? Is this the one right here, where you parked?"

"Calm down man, it's over there by the buggy rack," Benny said, pointing to the clutter of buggies that no one seemed to push completely into the buggy corral. Ryan picked up his pace, hurried over to the car, and immediately began pulling on the door handle. "Man hurry up, this child gon' start cryin' out loud in a minute, and then she gon' stink up the car." Ryan was being elusive now.

"Aw man, I can't give y'all a ride."

"What? What you mean you can't give us a ride, you bedda get in this car and drive us over to fifty-sixth!" Ryan exclaimed violently, sniffing an even greater volume of air.

"Hold up partna. I ain't got to do nothing," Benny replied in an attempt to make Ryan aware that he was not at his beck and call. "I'm doin' *you* a favor. I'm just tryin' to look out for your baby. I don't have a car seat so it won't be safe for her to ride with me."

"Is that all?" Ryan seemed relieved at the minor detail that was temporarily obstructing his goal. "I ride her around all the time without a car seat. We just put her in our lap and put a seat belt on over her. She'll be alright. Let's roll outta here before they get...before Tonya gets worried."

"All right. But if I get pulled over, y'all paying the ticket."

"Let's go, Benny, you ain't gon' get no ticket." Ryan said as he watched Benny enter the car and unlock the door for Ryan and his miniature passenger. Ryan sat the child in his lap and buckled the bundle in with him. "See, she safe, let's go, hit it!"

Benny obliged the request, started the ignition, put the car in drive, and headed out toward his altered destination.

Once in the car, the baby was growing more agitated, perhaps because of the seating arrangement or her uncomfortable wet clothing. Ryan attempted to quiet her by rubbing her head in between his constant sniffs.

"You got a cold or something?"

"Huh? Why you say that?"

"'Cause you sniffing like your nose running off your face."

"I just got bad allergies and sinuses."

"So how old is your daughter?"

"My what? Huh?" Ryan was extremely concerned with everything outside of the car and nothing on the inside of it.

"Your daughter. How old is she? What's wrong with you?"

"Nothing, man. I'm just thinking about something. She's seven months. Her name is Raytona."

"What?"

"Raytona. It's Ryan and Tonya put together."

"Her parents let y'all name her that?"

"Forget them fools; they didn't want to have nothin' to do wit' us."

"That's messed up, but that's just how some folks are."

"Yeah, they bedda not come around when she get older either." Ryan looked down at his daughter lovingly, but with a strange hint of regret. He sniffed over her and the baby cried a little louder and for longer periods now.

"You can't just shut them out like that, Ryan. If they...I knew it!"

"What? What is it?" Ryan asked, panicking and noticing Benny's dismay in the side view mirror. Flashing blue lights illuminated the darkness around them and were shortly followed by a brief siren urging Benny to pull over.

"I knew this was gon' happen when you put that baby in this car. I told you! You still gon' pay for the ticket."

"Just keep driving, they may be pulling somebody else over, drive a couple of miles," Ryan suggested out of desperation.

"Fool, you crazy? They right on my tail. Who else they gon' be pulling over?" Benny exclaimed to his passenger of inconvenience. Ryan slipped down in his seat attempting to go unnoticed during the traffic stop. Benny reached over to the glove compartment and retrieved the registration and insurance. He reached into his pocket to retrieve his wallet when an unexpected voice blurted out over the PA system of the police car.

"Driver, turn the ignition off and hold the keys outside the car with your right hand."

"What the hell is this?" Benny said. He had witnessed many of his friends being pulled over, but none were ever as abnormal or structured as the one taking place now. Looking in his rear view mirror, he could see another set of blue lights pulling up behind him. "Two police cars for a damn car seat?" Again he spoke out loud and then looked over at Ryan who possessed a solemn look of contemplation. Now Benny was getting very suspicious of his passenger and the baby, who after the boisterous police introduction, was wailing at the top of her lungs. The voice repeated the command.

"*Driver, turn the ignition off and hold the keys outside the car with your right hand. You have five seconds.*" Benny complied without haste and waited for more.

"*Hold your left hand out of the window...With your right hand, open the car door...*"

Now he feared for his safety, because it was late and very few cars were driving by that might serve as witnesses. "*Exit the vehicle and lie face down on your stomach.*"

Benny's fear was quickly becoming crowded by anger. As he obeyed the commands, he lay stretched out facing the blinding lights while the voice continued.

"*Passenger, hold your left hand out of the window, with your right hand, open the car door.*

Benny wondered how Ryan would maneuver the request with his daughter in his arms. Either he was thinking of a way to comply, or he was blatantly disrespecting the order because the voice repeated after a few moments had passed.

"*Passenger, hold your left hand out of the window...With your right hand, open the car door. Ryan, we've had surveillance on you all evening, and we know you're in the vehicle so hold your left hand out of the window. You have no seconds. Do it now, Ryan*".

Benny realized that this was not a routine traffic stop and it certainly wasn't concerning a child's car seat. He discovered what had been keeping Ryan's interest since he saw him in the parking lot. Benny could hear the passenger door open and the police called out over the PA again.

"Do not exit the vehicle until you are told to do so. Stay in the vehicle!"

Benny heard sniffing and the sound of the squeaky car door being opened. *Ryan, do not exit the vehicle or we will take forceful action to contain you...Stay in the vehicle... Stop or you will be fired upon...This is your last war...Wait! Hold it guys, he's holding something up in front of him.*" The voice softened when it spoke out of its procedural voice. Benny was lying on the ground close enough to hear their normal conversations.

"Oh my God, he's got a baby!" one of the officers yelled out. Ryan walked around to the side of the car where Benny was lying. He walked with his infant daughter extended out in front of him in order to deter the officers' actions and any possible shooting. His precious daughter was now being used as a bullet-proof vest.

"Hold it. Hold it. Jesus Christ, he's got the baby in his arms!"

Ryan moved towards the back of the car and out towards the oncoming traffic. Benny could now see the disturbing sight the police were describing over the loudspeaker. Ryan drew the infant closer to his chest as she screamed out in anguish and discomfort, not from pain, but from her strange surroundings. Benny remained stretched out watching the unfolding events. There was a long silence disturbed only by Ryan's rapid sniffles. The police were seemingly developing a new strategy.

"Ryan, we're going to send someone over to take care of your baby. One of the officers is going to take your child into protective custody. The baby will be alright."

"Y'all ain't doing a damn thing with my daughter! You bedda stay the hell back!" Silence linked Ryan's rebuttal and the police's next move. This time they attempted a more aggressive threat.

"Ryan, we know you've got the drugs on you. There is no way you're gonna win this one buddy. Now, you have a choice. You can let us take the baby from you and take her some place safe, or we can take other measures to ensure the baby is secure while we deal with you in other ways."

"Ryan, what the hell is goin' on. What are you doin'?" Benny shouted to his passenger. The situation had turned tumultuous, and Benny was caught up in this potentially disastrous scene. He immediately wondered what his consequences would be.

"I ain't tryin' to get locked up again," he said to Benny. "I been down at county one time and don't want no mo' faggots chasin' after me in a cell.

"You been to jail?" Benny asked in shock.

"Look, I gots to get mine one way or the other and even if I got to sell, then I just..."

"Ryan you have five seconds to comply with our demands or we will take swift actions."

"I told you I ain't doin' shit, so stay away from me!" Ryan screamed towards the flashing lights.

Benny could only watch in disbelief. The bold voice that had been administering the commands over the loudspeaker began giving individual instructions to the other officers that had arrived as backup. A few of his unamplified orders were just loud enough to be overheard by both Benny and Ryan.

"Let's go ahead and approach him from three angles, two sides and straight ahead. On the sides, you'll use your stun guns when you get close enough. I'll lead straight ahead. Keep your weapons drawn. There's no telling what else he's got in the baby's blanket. Do not, under any circumstances, harm that baby!"

"I heard you godammit! Y'all move in if you want to and see what happens!"

"Ryan you're leaving us no choice; we're coming towards you now!" the leader shouted this time without the PA. The plan commenced just as the leader had orchestrated and Ryan instantly protested their actions."

"Stay back I said!"

"Ryan, calm down man," Benny pleaded.

"Shut the fuck up, Benny! This is my shit! Y'all better stay back!"

The police slowly gained ground on the strung out suspect still clutching the screaming baby. They walked towards him as if they were predators relentlessly preparing to feast on their prey."

"Get back! Get back! Get the fuck away from me!"

The officers looked at each other but continued their advancements. "I said get back!" Ryan yelled as he kneeled down and placed the baby on the ground beneath him. The officers paused briefly thinking that Ryan was finally giving in. Suddenly, Ryan raised his hand high in the air, and then descended it with a crashing blow towards the screaming infant.

"Ryan, stop!" Benny cried out and covered his face.

"Get back! I said get back!"

"Stop or I will fire!" the lead officer shouted as the baby's screams decreased and became short gasps of air for life.

Ryan uncontrollably lifted his hand again, intending to stop the officers with the destruction of his own child. As he began the delivery of another painful blow to the already still infant, shots rang out and their impact forced Ryan back away from the baby and slammed him against the car. He fell to the asphalt screaming in pain.

"I told y'all to get back!" Ryan said crying and moaning. "I asked y'all to get back, please get back," he continued as the police officers rushed over towards Ryan restraining and then handcuffing him before doing the same to Benny, who was too devastated to even begin explaining his innocence in the entire episode. The lead officer hovered over the lifeless child, then knelt down to feel for any remaining sign of life or salvation for the baby's spirit. There was neither.

Chapter 31
Results And Reflections

"Why is all of this shit happening to me?" Benny asked, pouring out his emotions to Karmin.

"What do you mean, happening to you? You act like this is not going to affect me. Is that what you think? You think that because I'm graduating in the fall everything is right on time and my life isn't gonna be altered? Do you think I planned this? You think I'm just some kinda ho' that will use a baby to trap a man? You got me all messed up if you do because I don't need nothing not you, not your help not any..."

"Karmin, I'm not saying none of that. You're the one that's running on talking about what I'm thinking, and you don't have the first clue about what I'm thinking or what's going on in my life."

"I don't know what's going on in your life, is that what you're saying? We've been together for all these months and all of sudden I have no idea what's goin on in your life. Is that what your young mind is thinking?"

"My young mind?"

"That's what I said."

"Now I'm not the mature freshman on the edge of manhood that I used to be, huh?"

"If that was my initial diagnosis, then it couldn't have been more incorrect."

"And neither could mine."

"What are you saying?"

"I'm saying that I could not have picked up on the fact that, however old you may be, your mentality may as well be the same as all of these other hood-rats running around here."

"What the hell did you just say?"

"You heard me. Sometimes you act just as immature as anybody else when something doesn't go your way."

"You got yo' damn nerve, nigga!"

"Now see, that was a really mature response." Benny's frustration with the ensuing argument prompted him to spread on his combative sarcasm as heavy as he could. Karmin was not responding well to his attempts.

"Go to hell!"

"Thank you."

"For what."

"For proving my theory about your immaturity."

"You know what, you can get out of my apartment right now, Benny, because I didn't expect you to help me pay for the abortion anyway."

"What...What did you say?" Benny's sarcasm was erased by shock.

"Now you're the one that's hard of hearing."

"How can you make a decision like that?"

"What do you mean?"

"You never even talked to me about it?" Benny said with humility and concern. "I mean I'm just now finding out about you being pregnant and you've already made this decision?"

"Grow up, Benny. Besides, I tried to tell you before you left for the funeral, but you didn't have a spare minute to talk."

"I was about to miss the damn plane Karmin!"

"Well, now the plane is back and now you know. Welcome back!" Karmin force fed Benny with her snide remarks.

"And you think that this is fair, telling me about it, instead of talking to me about it?"

"I think it's more than fair. I think it's considerate of me to make a sacrifice like this for you."

"What do you mean for me?"

"Because Benny, you've got three more years of school left and..."

"Two and half, I can go to summer school."

"Well, two and a half, but anyway how can you possibly be concerned with a child all that time and take care of everything you need to do? You said you wanted to pledge Omega and that's gonna take more time away from your studies, so how could you possibly juggle a baby with all of that?"

"It's been done before and I hope I won't have to do it alone. You talk like you're leaving for a tour in the Peace Corps or something."

"It's not all that cut and dry. What will our parents say about the baby? What will they say about our age difference? What will they say about us getting...well it's just not as easy as you make it out to be."

"You mean what will they say about us getting married? I think we both know it's way too early for us to think about that. But for now Karmin, I can't be a part of an abortion. Not under these circumstances."

"What's that supposed to mean?" Karmin asked. Benny walked away from her, rested himself and his emotions on her sofa. Quiet for a moment, he was momentarily haunted by the vision of Ryan carrying out the destruction of his daughter's life. He trembled for a moment and Karmin noticed his disturbing transition. "Benny what's wrong?" she asked, joining him on the sofa.

"Karmin... I... I just can't be part of another baby dying. This is different, I know, but you just can't imagine what it's like to watch someone kill a being that's so pure and innocent. I was just shocked. It took at least four hours before I could explain to the police and my pops how I had nothing to do with Ryan's drugs. You know I never really put it into perspective even after working the hotlines and even after reviewing some of the cases in the community, but these kids and especially the babies are in trouble."

"I know, Benny."

"But what are we supposed to do? Most of it is so deeply rooted."

"I know."

"I mean it's like these people that are hurting these kids have it in their blood. Their parents abused them, and their parents got abused, and so on. We're fighting a cancer that keeps on spreading and it's been spreading longer than we've been fighting. All we're doing is amputating limbs and patching on band-aids with our efforts. You know, I remember when Ryan and I were little, his daddy used to beat his tail, not like my pops did, but he used to beat Ryan with a vengeance. Ryan ended up almost killing his father one day, and I never thought about what would happen to Ryan, you know, long term. I never thought about how it would affect his life or how his life would affect others. And here it turns out our lives are just reflections from the mirrors of our past generations."

"What do we do? I've never thought about it that way," Karmin asked.

"We make sure we do everything we can to have the most positive and uplifting images in our mirrors. I don't think we'll be able to do that if we start breaking mirrors just because we aren't ready to look at our reflection, and by that I mean getting rid of the baby before we explore all of our other options. After being there that night and watching him hurt that baby, I can't be a part of what you're talking about. If you love me like you say, you won't be a part of anything that I feel so strongly about. If you love me, you're either for me or against me."

Chapter 32
Balm From The Beam

"Sheila, are you gonna get ready, baby?"

"I am ready, Ronald. What you talking about?"

"I was just wondering," Ronald answered, observing his wife's mangled mess of a hairdo resting upon her head like an inconvenience. "You gon' comb your hair or anything?"

"What's wrong with my hair," Sheila said in a voice that lacked enthusiasm and energy. "This is how I wore my hair yesterday."

"I know, but you didn't go anywhere yesterday and the day before that, and the week before that. Just because you started working part-time don't mean that you can let yourself go like you doin', baby."

"Ronald, I'm just so tired, honey. Can I just take a nap and then we can go?"

"Sheila!"

"Huh?"

"You just woke up a hour ago. It's one o'clock in the afternoon!"

"I went to bed late though."

"Late? You went to bed at eight o'clock last night, and this ain't the first time you slept like this either. Baby, you ain't been the same since William died and that was seven months ago. Don't you think it's time for you to start back workin' full time and doing some stuff around the house?"

"Ronald…" Sheila prepared to give one of her patented intellectual rebuttals that would send Ronald into a frenzy and which Ronald, quite frankly, would have appreciated. Instead, all she offered was, "I'm just tired."

This lackluster woman that lived here with him was anything but a welcomed sight. Her whole persona died with the passing of William and more recently, her Aunt Flappy.

People converged down to Hope for Aunt Flappy's last days. Everyone remarked during Aunt Flappy's funeral that Sheila needed a little sun or some time outdoors. *She needed more than sun*, Ronald thought. His wife needed a blazing fire of rejuvenation and he tried desperately for months to ignite her soul. Ronald felt that Benny's absence over the summer made matters worse, because Sheila had never been without her son for so long. For Benny to stay in school during the summer months may have given Sheila the impression that he was avoiding her. They still hadn't met Karmin and the baby's arrival was only a few months off.

Margie stopped by once after church at Ronald's request and she gave a you-look-pitiful assessment of her sister and suggested that Ronald take her to see a Christian Counselor she knew. Then she suggested that Ronald take her to the beauty salon. Margie suggested the beauty salon be the first item on the agenda, Sheila needed it.

"Baby, we got to be at the counselor's office in twenty minutes and it's on the other side of town."

"Why we got to go see this counselor anyway?"

"Sheila, you begged me a long time ago to get some counselin'. Now you sayin' you don't want to go?"

"That was along time ago. We're all right now aren't we?"

"No, we ain't. Now let's go before we late. I'll go upstairs and get you a hat."

"Ronald…I'm just so tired."

Sheila and Ronald arrived at the Beam of Hope Church ten minutes after their scheduled appointment. Ronald's mad dash to the church was halted by the pitter-patter of rain on his windshield that eventually became a thunderstorm. At least now Sheila had an excuse for her hat. Once inside the church, they asked someone for directions to the counseling office. The whole experience was a new adventure for Ronald. He was in a church, which was abnormal, and he was in church on a Saturday, which was unheard of. Lastly, the church was filled with people conducting different ministries. The church was managed like a well-organized business.

Eventually they found their way back to the counseling office and met Dr. Jackie Caruthers. *This can't be the counselor*, Ronald thought

"We looking for a lady named Jackie Caruthers," Ronald explained to the person standing near the desk.

She doesn't work here, but I'm Mr. Jackie Caruthers."

"Oh, okay I'm sorry. We was lookin' for a lady," Ronald said apologetically, while Sheila simply took a seat that she assumed was appropriate to sit in. Dr. Caruthers paid close attention to her body language as she sat down. He was making mental notes about her attitude and her demeanor, then he focused on Ronald again.

"That's quite alright because most people come in expecting to see a woman and guess what, surprise! Oh, I hope you're not disappointed. I assure you I'll be as professional and concerned as you had anticipated even though I'm a brother, a doctor Brother if you will," the light hearted and high spirited man proclaimed. He forgot to say doctor big brother. Even Ronald's height was no match for the large man standing before him.

Dr. Caruthers' low haircut with a long part on the left side peaked out at six feet six inches tall, and he weighed in at least two hundred and fifty pounds. The walls of his office were plastered with Grambling State University football paraphernalia, pictures of him and the famous football players posing together as well as the traditional framed degrees. There was a B.S. from Grambling, an M.S. from North Carolina A & T, and a Ph.D. from Indiana University. Ronald noticed and read each one of them. His first degree from Grambling was enough validation for Ronald. The fact that he was sitting behind a nameplate with the word doctor on the front of it was all Ronald needed. Even if Dr. Caruthers had possessed a magic wand that could bring his wife back, Ronald would have accepted that for credentials at this point.

"So Mr. and Mrs. Dempkins, how have you two been doing?"

"How did you know our names?" Ronald asked.

"I read them in my appointment book."

"Oh," Ronald replied, embarrassed from his trivial probing.

"Well...," Dr. Caruthers offered.

"Well what?"

"How have you been doing?" Dr. Caruthers offered again glancing at Sheila who seemed to be lost in thoughts of absolutely nothing.

"Okay I guess. As well as we can be for what's been happening."

"And what's been going on? If you don't mind me asking, that is," Dr. Caruthers said, easing his way into their lives.

Sheila slowly turned to look at Dr. Caruthers and Ronald after hearing the polite verbal inquisition.

"Tell you the truth, I ain't much for tellin' nobody my business even if it is in a church, you know. I'm just doin' this for my wife. We been havin' a lot of bad things in our family, well not really bad things, but stuff just been happenin', one thing after another."

"Okay, that's a start, but let's talk about something not quite so personal just yet, unless that's what you really want to talk about."

"Nawh, I just thought that we was supposed to come here and tell you our problems, then I thought you was supposed to tell us what we could do."

"Mr. Dempkins..."

"You can call us Ronald and Sheila," Ronald announced.

"Ronald, I wish some of my other clients were as willing and knowledgeable as you are, but never the less, I'd like to get to know both of you a little better. You a big football fan?"

"Not really, most of my Sundays are spent on the golf course."

"Is that right? Not many blacks play golf, do they?"

"That's what you think?" Ronald asked abrasively. "I've been playin' golf since the seventies and Black folks been playin' golf since the 1920's. Lee Elders played in the Masters in the seventies, that's why I started.

Dr. Caruthers could see himself getting to know Ronald very well, but Sheila was not participating in the question and answer session.

"Sheila, do you ever get out and play golf with Ronald?" She shook her head no and attempted to respond but was prohibited by a dry throat. Clearing her throat, she spoke again.

"No, Margie and I were always at church when Ronald and Margie's husband were out playing golf."

"Would this be William, who just recently passed."

"Wasn't all that recent doctor, it was about six or seven months ago."

"Seven months, two weeks, and three days," Sheila said. Dr. Caruthers noticed Sheila's attention to the detail of William's passing.

"So is it safe to assume that you don't attend church regularly as a family?"

"Nawh, not lately. My wife ain't been up to attendin' church for quite a while now."

"What about prior to William's passing? Did you attend then? As a family, I mean."

"That's when they played golf." Sheila replied for Ronald who didn't have the courage to confess his regretful obsession of many years.

"Were you, William, and Margie close at all?"

"Yeah, we did everything together," Ronald answered "We was almost like brothers and sisters even though we was in-laws. Kinda like whatever they did, we did, and whatever we did, they did. That's how we kept each other doing fun stuff."

"So you all went on trips together and what not?"

"Not really," Ronald said then thought more about the question. "Well yeah, we used to go down to Hope for the reunions."

"Hope…?"

"Hope, Arkansas."

"Clinton country, huh?"

"Hope was country long before Clinton was President."

"These were class reunions I presume."

"Nawh, family reunions."

"Oh, okay. When was the last time you traveled to Hope with William and Margie to visit a reunion?"

"We went to Hope about two months ago. Sheila's aunt passed. That's why I said things been happening one right after the other."

"I see. That's very unfortunate timing for such life-changing events. And that was two months ago?"

"Two months, a week, and six days," Sheila added. Dr. Caruthers needed to hear more from Sheila.

"So Sheila was this one of your favorite Aunts?"

"Everybody's favorite. Aunt Flappy was the cornerstone of our family. Her spirit was very powerful and very positive just like Margie's."

"How is the family doing, Sheila?" Dr. Caruthers said before Ronald could respond.

"We'll be okay. She was ill for awhile, so we all had time to prepare. My cousins are rebuilding her old house and we're gonna cancel the next family reunion until the house is done. It'll be a few years before we go back down there." Ronald was surprised at Sheila's willingness to communicate now. Lately, her conversation had been limited to her proclamation of fatigue.

"Everybody's gonna be so old by that time. All of the kids will be half-grown and some of them will probably be married."

"Mm-huh, and how long have you two been married?"

"Eighteen years," Ronald replied boasting of his knack for historical data about his marriage.

"Eighteen years huh, that's a testimony in today's time?"

"Eighteen years five months," Sheila squeaked out.

"Oh excuse me. We wouldn't want to forget about the five months," Dr. Caruthers offered. Ronald looked over at this wife. He was shocked because she had shown some life and because she kept such an accurate record of their time together.

"Do you have any children?" Dr. Caruthers began probing again. Sheila ran back into her shell while Ronald, like a uninformed peacock, unknowingly confessed Sheila's seldom told secret.

"We've got one boy. His name is Benjamin, but we call him Benny. He down at Tennessee State right now. Just finished his first year and he's staying for summer school."

"Really, that's great I've got a nephew up at Howard. How old is your son?"

"He's 19," Ronald said, as Sheila sunk down into her chair then quickly looking over at Dr. Caruthers. She wondered if all those degrees on his wall equipped him with fast math exposing her shame to a stranger for the first time in years.

"How do you feel about that?"

"About what?' Ronald asked, still not realizing that the numbers didn't morally match. The numbers weren't known by many, except for old family members that knew their secret.

"About having your son before you were married." Dr. Caruthers candid question dropped in Ronald's stomach like a sickening virus. He was slightly embarrassed, more so for Sheila than himself.

"Well...," Ronald began creating a reply. "It's best that we married and still together no matter how we did it I guess. Some folks got married five years before they had babies and they broke up when the kids wasn't even in high school. I know people at my job that ain't even got no kids and they divorced. I guess Benny coming first don't mean nothing."

"Sheila?" Dr. Caruthers said, looking for a second opinion.

"That's right," Sheila said, denying her feelings.

"Do you think that your son's presence had any bearing on your commitment all of these years."

"What you mean by that? Ronald asked.

"Don't think I'm being rude, Ronald, I'm just asking do you think that because Benny is in your lives, you wanted to stay together for such a long time?"

"Nawh, we been together because we married and people that's married supposed to stay married just like my mama and daddy," Ronald replied.

Sheila looked at her husband, amazed that his thinking was constructed in such a way that he could not see her recent years of discontent.

"Sheila, is that your perspective as well?"

She gave signs of involvement again and spoke, "There are enough kids that come from broken homes without us contributing to the disaster."

"Unlike your husband, you believe that Benny has had a significant part in the longevity of your marriage, is that correct?"

Sheila looked directly at Dr. Caruthers trying diligently to forget that Ronald was even in the room. She never wanted to hurt her husband and now was no different.

"...He's the only reason why we stayed together," she finally confessed after years of verbally neglecting the truth. Ronald sat in his chair and glanced over at his wife as though he were in the wrong room and had no clue who the two people sitting with him were. He was confused, and now, he was silent.

"You feel strongly about that?"

"Very. I love my husband with all my heart. But I love my husband because it's what's best for my family. I'm committed to him, but I'm committed to whatever I get involved with. I was committed to my son, until he started his own family." Dr. Caruthers looked over at Ronald then back at Sheila after the unveiling of more facts occurred. "Now he has to become committed to whatever happens with him and that slut. I haven't even met the little tramp." Sheila's fire tried to ignite with the fueled thought of another woman taking care of her son.

"Sheila, if you were in that young lady's situation, and knowing what you know now, would you make the same decision?"

Ronald gave his attention to Sheila and waited for Sheila's response. He waited as his wife hesitated and thought.

"I don't know. Times are different, people are different, I'm different, society is different. It's more convenient and widely accepted now to just give up on your commitments. If I were in her situation, I don't know what I'd do, but I know what Benny is gonna do. He's gonna stay with her because he's me and he's everything about me. It doesn't matter if it turns out to be the biggest mistake of his life."

Ronald couldn't believe the profession that Sheila was making. He hadn't heard her speak this much in months not since she requested that he call her job and inform them that she was taking some time off.

"Do you think it's a mistake?" Dr. Caruthers went for the jugular.

Sheila temporarily went into hiding, but not very far and not for long. Her eyes were waiting for the response that her emotions had already made for the rest of her body. She turned and attempted to respond. While looking at her husband, the bottom of her eyelids released a stream of tears. She looked away from Ronald and back again towards Dr. Caruthers who had the power to reveal what she had always wished she could for many years. As she quickly became a sobbing regret for her own history, she replied, "Yes… yes it was… I'm sorry, but it was a mistake."

Dr. Caruthers allowed Sheila's emotions to circumvent the room. He felt as though it was a much needed release, as well as a vital part of the Dempkin's healing process, if there was any healing that could be done.

"Sheila, let me get you some warm tea," Dr. Caruthers suggested as he reached for his phone. "Sister Waters, would you please come and escort Mrs. Dempkins to the lounge and see if there is any warm tea available?" A few seconds later, a young dark-skinned woman entered the door with a smile that seemed to intensify the light in the room. She gently reached down and touched Sheila's arm gesturing for her to stand and follow her. Ronald was following suit until Dr. Caruthers spoke.

"Ronald?"

"Huh?" Ronald mumbled.

"Sister Waters will take care of her. Let's talk for a while."

Ronald watched his crying wife exit the room propped up against the gentlewoman who had come to her emotional rescue.

"I wanted your wife to leave the room for a reason."

"What for?"

"Ronald, I'm very concerned about you wife's depression."

"Depression?"

"Yes. It's clear to me that the recent string of events has had a great impact on her mental stability. It seems that there's a very strong link between your marriage and that of William and Margie. Now that she's witnessed the unfortunate ending of their marriage, her subconscious mind is fearing the same detrimental event in your lives. Moreover, she probably realized how many quality and meaningful events that William and Margie will never have. Now more than ever, the meaningful experiences you may not have partaken in, have been highlighted."

"But that's what I been tryin' to do for the last five months! I been tryin' to do everything I can for her. But she always tired and she don't never feel like doing nothin' no more. I had to beg her to get ready so we could come and see you. One time, she was asking me every other day to go and get some counselin'."

"That's just it."

"What?"

"When she was stable and willing to make your marriage healthier, you may not have been perceptive to the idea."

"But wasn't nothin' wrong with us."

"How do you know that?"

"Because I know."

"So what's wrong with you now that has warranted the counseling session that your wife wanted so long ago?"

"Look at her. She don't hardly say nothin'. My wife used to talk all the time. In fact she used to talk too much if you ask me. She was always on the go, always workin', doin' somethin' at the church. Seem like after Benny left and William and her aunt died, she just don't hardly say nothin'; she just won't talk to me."

"When Sheila wanted to go to counseling, how much were you all communicating?"

"Like I told you, she used to talk all the time?"

"No, how much communicating did you do? I mean did you listen and did you give feedback, did you talk back with her?"

"Well…yeah, I guess so?"

"Did she ever nag you?"

"All the time. It was times when she kept trying to get me to talk about stuff when I didn't feel like talking, and times when, you know, she wanted me to go places when I just wanted to take timeout and just do nothin'."

"So what you're saying is that when she wanted you to talk, it wasn't necessarily the best time for you, is that right?"

"Yeah, that's right."

"Sort of like you're doing now?"

"I guess so," Ronald unwillingly admitted after having his inconsistency exposed. "But this is different."

"How so?" Dr. Caruthers asked.

Ronald began creating again, "We done had the funerals and stuff and Benny is gone, and you know stuff just been happenin'."

"I realize, that your marriage is going through a great adversity right now. But what I also need you to realize, is that those early attempts at healthy two-way communicating and early attempts at counseling are all contributions that may have made your marriage strong enough to survive troubles like the ones you're facing now. It seems, from what you're saying, Sheila had the foresight some time ago to makes strides towards what you're trying to accomplish now." Dr. Caruthers delivered the final words of his analysis and left Ronald enlightened about his own shortcomings that he'd never had the ability to discover. Dr.

Caruthers was finished for the moment and Ronald was silent for a moment longer.

"...So what can I do now about this depression. She just gon' be sad for the rest of her life?"

"No, there are plenty of methods for combating depression, more counseling, medication even."

"All that stuff ain't cheap, though."

"Unfortunately, you're absolutely right about that, but I'll be more than happy to work with you in any way that I can. I think you'll be pleasantly surprised at the economical measures that are available for patients of depression. In many cases, patients who have been depressed for years and years with no successful intervention have had one single event to lift their illness. The human mind is a marvelous, complicated, and mystifying organ. For the time being, however, I would encourage you to keep doing exactly what you've been doing, giving her more love than you ever have in your life. But keep it consistent and pay attention to the details of her everyday life and any request she makes."

"I can do that."

"Let me ask you one more personal question."

"Is it anymore left?"

"I need to know, and this is in complete and total confidence. Have there been any extra marital affairs on either side?"

"What you mean by that?"

"To be quite blunt, have you or your wife ever had an affair?"

"Hell no!"

"Ronald!"

"Oh excuse me, I'm sorry. I forgot I was in church, but that's one thing I don't believe in. I got one woman and that's all I need."

"And what about Sheila?"

"What about her?"

"Has she been involved in any affairs?"

"Nawh, not that I know of. That don't concern me cause I trust my wife."

"That's good to know."

"What, that I trust my wife or that I ain't had no affair?"

"Both. There's a lot of temptation out there."

"You ain't got to tell me," Ronald said with strong conviction.

"That sounds like you're speaking from experience."

"Not really," Ronald admitted."

"Not really?" Dr. Caruthers probed.

"Affair means you did somethin' with somebody right?"

"Whatsoever a man thinketh, he also doeth."

"I ain't did nothin' to that woman, she was the one actin' all funny."

"What woman?"

"A long time ago, some old horny white woman trapped me in the bathroom with her and wanted me to do somethin' with her."

"When did this happen?"

"This was back when William and me used to play golf all the time. He had to go to some old fancy golf course…"

"It happened at a golf course?"

"It was in the bathroom."

"And what happened?"

"She snuck up behind me and started puttin' her hands all over me. I started to smack her silly, but I didn't want her to have no bruises on her if she would have called the police. She started cussin' and callin' me all kind of names when I didn't give her what she wanted. I thought for sure that she was gon' come outta that bathroom talkin' about I raped her, but she never did. I ain't done nothin' with that woman."

"What did Sheila have to say about the incident?"

"When?"

"After you told her about the woman approaching you."

"She don't know," Ronald said in a nonchalant voice.

"You never told her?"

"Nawh, what for?"

"And you don't see anything wrong with that?"

"Yeah, it was something wrong. The woman had no business touchin' me like that."

"I'm referring to the fact that you didn't inform your wife that a strange woman made sexual advances toward you."

"Nawh. What's wrong with that? My wife don't need to know stuff like that. Besides, she might have thought that stuff like that happened all the time at the golf course. And at that time, she seemed like she was going around fishin' for somethin' that I was doin' wrong."

"Now when did this occur?"

"It was some years back."

"And your wife still doesn't know?"

"Nope. And she *ain't* gon' find out either, you hear me?"

"Like I told you before, this conversation is being held in total confidence and discretion. But I must also make you aware that secrets such as these are the very root of breakdowns in communication. You would be amazed by how many couples come in here and have years of turmoil all stemming back to one small misunderstanding that may have occurred five or ten years ago. Do you realize how much negative energy can be generated in a relationship in that amount of time? In all honesty, I've counseled families whose marriage ended in divorce because of misunderstandings that led to distrust, that led to suspicion, that led to revenge, that led to affairs, that led to children from different partners, and one that almost ended with murder. I cannot express enough the value of talking and listening to your wife. She has to do the same thing, talk and listen to you, but it's got to be a mutual act on both parts."

"I just ain't never been no talker, though. That's how my daddy is and most of my uncles."

"Does that make it right?"

"Nawh it don't make it right, but it makes it us?"

"We can all use self-improvements, all of us and everyday."

"So what you want me to do, tell her?"

"It's not what I want you to do, it's a matter of what you need to do. Your wife needs you now more than ever, and she needs to hear from you and hear about you."

"Well, what if I tell her and she gets even more depressed?"

"If you're willing to tell her, that's a risk you'll have to assume."

Ronald looked down at the carpeted floor and wished he could lie down, go to sleep, and wake from this ongoing nightmare that was now his life. But he wasn't asleep and it wasn't going away.

Sheila and Sister Waters entered the room just as Ronald raised his head to say one more thing to the doctor who was sitting before him like a blinding light, exposing every bit of subconscious darkness Ronald was ever consumed with. Instead of making his remark, Ronald jumped to his feet and relieved the kind woman of his wife. He picked up her purse, and held her hand tightly, the same way he did when they first fell in love. Securely, the same way he did in the beginning when he never wanted to let her go. Ronald escorted his wife towards the door of the office and turned his back to Dr. Caruthers and simply said, "I'm gonna take my wife home now and talk to her, I mean with her."

"Make sure you listen as well." Dr. Caruthers replied, closing the door, which ended his session and began the healing.

Chapter 33
Welcome To The World

During the fall of Benny's sophomore year, he waited for his life to shift into warp speed as he attempted to join a fraternity and anxiously await the arrival of his first child. All the while, he contemplated proposing to Karmin. He realized it wasn't the most rational decision, and he was persistent about not following up a mistake with another mistake.

His line brothers knew about the trials in his daily life and were very respectful, as were the current members of the fraternity. However, Benny didn't want any special treatment, and he didn't want his rite of passage into the fraternity to be any easier than the rest of his line brothers. The only provision he requested was that he be allowed to carry a pager at all times so that he would know immediately when Karmin went into labor.

Karmin landed a counselor's position in Memphis after graduating and that was as far away as Benny would allow. As soon has he got the code, Benny would be in for the fastest, yet longest, four-hour drive of his life. It was already discussed how the operation was going to be carried out. If they were in a session, Corey, his line brother with the fastest car, was going to leave the session with him immediately. However if they weren't in session, an all out manhunt was outlined to find Corey and get him to the Circle K gas station at the end of the block where he and Benny would meet. Although somewhat inefficient, this was the plan and they'd even practiced it a few times, albeit with very little success.

When Benny finally got the message on his pager, he was relieved that he and his line brothers were in a fraternity history session. While studying about Ernest E. Just, the Black Apollo of Science, Benny felt the long awaited vibration on his hip. The pager illuminated and conveyed the secret code, '1' for their first born child. The confirmation page soon followed—911. Benny showed the page to Corey and then to his Big Bothers.

"What the hell you showing me for? Y'all should have left twenty-eight seconds ago!" the dean of fraternity history shouted at the two eager fraternity candidates. The two bolted out of Nashville and arrived in Jackson in about one hour. Jackson was a blur, and they catapulted from Jackson to Memphis in an hour and a half, slowing well to within the speed limit once they reached the Memphis city limits. Benny told Corey that he couldn't watch his child's birth from a jail cell or from the side of the interstate while a graveyard shift patrolman ticketed them and gave them a five minute lecture about speeding.

Upon arrival at the Shelby County Hospital, Benny left Corey in the waiting room and darted towards the delivery room. A nurse helped him scrub and cover himself in the appropriate clothing. Finally, he made his way to the delivery table where Karmin was already in considerable pain. It was eased slightly by the welcome sight of her unconditional supporter who, by arriving, had passed another test of manhood. With one more jolt of pain, however, he wasn't so popular with Karmin.

"Why did you make me do this?" Karmin screamed to her former hero.

"It's gonna be okay, Karmin. Aren't you supposed to breath or something?"

"I can't breathe, fool! This baby is crushing my lungs trying to get out of me, you idiot!"

"Okay, you want some BC Powder or some ibuprofen?" Benny joked. The nurses looked at Benny, letting him know that *he* was about to become a headache with comments like that.

"If I wasn't having a baby, I'd jump up off this table and smack you, boy!"

"Okay Karmin. Let's get two more pushes and I think we'll be there," the doctor urged.

"Benny, hold my hand. I love you! Stay with me, don't leave me, don't leave us ever!" Sheila exclaimed thrusting below her waist.

"I'm right here, baby, I'm not going anywhere, never!"

"One more push, Karmin." The doctor said again.

"Aggghhhhh!!!!" Karmin gave their child her final contact of their nine-month relationship. The doctor pulled the fluid covered infant from Karmin. He watched the baby take her first breath. She attempted to cry, but couldn't. The infant took another breath, then struggled to take a third. Everyone became quiet—too quiet.

"Is she okay," Benny asked? The doctors were silent as they began procedures to restore life as they had done many times before.

"We're dropping blood pressure! A nurse yelled out. "I've lost the pulse here."

"Nurse begin CPR immediately. Let's move people!" the doctor shouted.

"No, please don't let her die!" Benny pleaded. "She can't come all this way and not make it! Doctor please give her life!"

"Sir, could you wait outside please?"

"We all need each other! Don't let her die doctor please give her life, give her my life!" Benny cried as he was escorted out of the delivery area and urged to stay in the waiting room.

Corey was glad to see Benny come out so soon, but became freighted after he saw the tears streaming from Benny's face.

"What happened, bruh?"

"They having problems with her breathing or something."

"What, is the baby okay?"

"I don't know, I don't know. Shit! Why, why?" Benny exclaimed out over the delivery ward. He dropped in a seat waiting for a doctor and then rushed back to the delivery room door trying to look through the window. He ran back to the waiting room and leaned up against the wall shaking, trembling, crying, shouting, waiting.

Minutes later the doctor came out and delivered the news that forced Benny to collapse on the waiting room floor. Corey and the doctor helped Benny to a chair where he transformed instantly into an emotionless statue.

"Can I go and talk to her?" Benny requested. The doctor starred strangely at Benny fearing that he might be delirious from the disturbing events.

"Son, she's not going to be able to understand you just yet," the doctor offered.

"I don't care! Let me go! She needs me. I told her I wasn't gonna leave 'em!" Benny rushed back to delivery room so that he could honor his promise.

Chapter 34
Rejuvenation At The Reunion

Renovation of Flappy's old house lasted much longer than anyone had anticipated. Aunt Flappy's handyman had probably caused more damage with his years of country construction techniques. Assessed by a professional contractor, the family found out that floor joists were missing, roof joists were made out of wood scraps and old pipes tied together by wire and rope. Every place in the house where the handyman constructed, or destructed, empty Wild Turkey whiskey bottles were found, which explained the psychedelic paint jobs in the bedrooms.

The project was well worth the three-year wait. At last the house had an identity, red brick now covered the entire house and stopped at the glass enclosed front porch. Realizing the popularity of front porch participants, a new porch was constructed to hold three times the number of people that had occupied the gathering spot in the past. Most of the family in Hope had never seen a bay window. Many of them thought it was a mistake the contractor made when they entered the island shaped kitchen and saw the huge window extending out in to the yard. New plumbing and central heat and air throughout the entire house was a pleasant surprise for all that visited. Carpet was an option the family voted against because there would still be plenty of children rummaging through the hallways, and most of them would have a popsicle stick, Kool-Aid or some type of gooey candy that would kill that carpet's appearance. Instead, they settled for a marbled styled linoleum tile throughout the house. Three years later and too many donations to mention, the project was finally complete.

Cynthia and her son moved to Hope and occupied the mini-mansion. Surprisingly, no one put up a fight when she showed up during the last days of construction with her bags and her little boy. Most of the other family members didn't feel right about sleeping in the dead woman's house anyway, and the others had accumulated so much junk that they couldn't even consider moving all of their belongings. That left Cynthia, unopposed, to assume the role of the new cornerstone, and she was off to a blazing start.

She organized and informed everyone of what she called the re-establishment of the family reunion. Included was a separate children's agenda with a magic show, face painting, and a trip to the water slide. All the skeptics weren't skeptics long after they converged upon the beautiful home and smelled the aromas wafting from the kitchen as they did when Flappy was alive. As more and more family members arrived, the home became even more beautiful. The kitchen was filled with food and Cynthia decorated a special table in front of the bay window with a sign that read:

PLACE ALL PEACH COBBLERS HERE

Granny Osee and Macon were older and slower, but they were as loving and supportive as ever. Even Uncle Sho Shack was able to make his way over to the house. Everyone was surprised to see him with matching suspenders. He'd taken it upon himself to design and have T-shirts made for the reunion. Perhaps his suspenders matched because he wanted the attention focused on the shirts. The Navy blue cotton garments had a picture of a huge oak tree with branches extending out down near the bottom of the shirt. Underneath the tree was a caption *Reaching back for our roots*. The shirts were a hit. Everyone ran to Sho Shack and the big boxes he pulled from the back of the truck that housed the symbolic apparel. The stampede towards Sho Shack halted to a slow tiptoe after Sho Shack's back faced everyone. It seemed as if two people had given two very different inputs on the family shirts. On the back of the shirt was probably the tackiest jingle, slogan, or phrase anyone had every seen. Sho Shack stood upright and everyone saw the words on the back of his shirt: *Flap On Flappy!! Chile we shol du miss you!!*

Some people stopped in their tracks and shook their heads while trying to understand what *shol* meant.

"Granny Osee, did you see what yo' crazy brother put on the back of those shirts?" Cynthia said.

"Nawh, what did he write on there honey?"

"Talking 'bout some Flap on Flappy? I ought to Flap his Flappy."

"That fool ain't been right ever since they fired him from that juke joint down in Washington. Is that what everybody ran down there to do? Get some of them ugly shirts?"

"Umm-huh and now they standing out there in that heat like some cow's waitin' for the grass to grow."

"Macon, go out there and tell dem chillin' to get in this house. It's hot as the devil out there."

"Lord let 'em sit out there an' melt. We need some mo' chocolate pudddin' in the icebox." Macon said, reluctant to go and retrieve anyone.

"Macon," Granny Osee said sternly.

"All right. Good Lord," Macon whined as he made his way to the glass screen of the front porch. "Hey! Hey, y'all get y'all little black tails in the house fo' y'all get any blacker!"

"Aww papaw, why we got to come in?" one of the energetic kids said.

"Cause it's hotter than five-five hundred pound fat women fightin' over frog legs at a Friday night revival in Florida, that's why! Now y'all do what I tell ya fo' I get one of dem dare switches from dat tree!" The one item that had remained untouched during the house's restoration, was the switch tree that was as old as the first whippin' in the family. The kids came back towards the house and the adults did as well. One couple that was not hovering around the shirts gave Sho Shack a tongue lashing for his idea, as they walked towards the screened in porch. It was Ronald and Sheila. Margie was with them.

"There go my baby girls!" Macon cheered when he saw the threesome.

"Hey daddy," Margie said hugging her father, then Granny Osee, once they were inside the porch. Sheila came in and sat down solemnly across from her mother and spoke.

"How ya'll been doing?" Sheila said.

Macon and Osee looked at Sheila and gave each other an it-ain't-getting-no-better look.

"It's good to see y'all again," Ronald said, hoping to divert the attention away from Sheila and back towards the festive reunion. "This is nice! I didn't know they was gon' do all of this."

"They did a fine job. Old drunk man must not have been around," Margie said with her normal spitfire attitude.

"Hey Aunt Margie, Aunt Sheila, Uncle Ronald," Cynthia said appearing in the doorway of the house with an apron on.

"Girl, look at you! I never thought you were gonna grow up, and look at you." Margie began. "Came down here, took Flappy's house, and became a woman, huh?" Margie commented.

"Looks like you doin' pretty good for yourself, Cynthia," Ronald said.

Sheila had nothing to contribute, as usual.

"Thank you," Cynthia replied politely. "I made a peach cobbler; it's in the back with the rest of 'em."

"Girl, you making peach cobblers now?" Margie asked.

The baking of peach cobbler was a symbol of maturity and responsibility in their family. To bake a peach cobbler for the family, was to take part and give your offering towards the family's rich heritage. And now there was another entrusted with the old tradition. "I wish you could sew cause somebody else need to make the shirts next year instead of lettin' Sho Shack make 'em. Ooh that's to' up and tacky," Margie said.

"Daddy can we stop and get some MacDonna?"

"No sweety, we're gonna get something to eat real soon okay?"

"Daaaddy, I want some MacDonna now!"

"Sweetheart, don't act ugly okay? We're going to see some very special people and I want you to act as pretty as you look, alright?"

"Then we goin' to get some MacDonna?"

"Maybe if you act good."

"Daddy, where we goin'?"

"To see all of your cousins, and aunts and uncles and a very special lady."

"Mommee!"

"No, I told you about your mommy. Do we need to talk about mommy before we get out of the car, because we can, I don't mind."

"No Daddy."

"Good, because here we are!"

"Yeaaaa we here! ...Where we at Daddy?"

"We're at the family reunion baby girl."

"Yea! Family runan! What's a family runan Daddy?"

"A place to play and have fun. Hold still while Daddy gets you out of the car seat."

"Yea! Play-fun, play-fun, play-fun!"

"Come on, let's go in the house and meet some people before you go out and play."

"Okay."

"Little Benny!" Cousin Sho Shack yelled out when he saw the grown man step from the car with a small hand clutching his own.

"What's up Uncle Sho Shack? How you been doin'?"

"Fine as red wine from the finest grapevine. I got these family reunion shirts for you. They got a tribute to Flappy on the back and everything," Sho Shack explained as he flipped the shirt over in grand fashion. Benny examined the words on the back and gave the same gesture as many others had, he tried to walk away. "This yo' little girl Benny?"

"Yep, this is my daughter. Say hi, baby."

"Hi, fine red wine," the observant little girl replied. Sho Shack was overcome with laughter. Benny left Sho Shack and began his long walk toward the strange but welcoming house.

Benny hadn't attended a reunion since the last time one occurred. Christmas was the only time he'd returned home and the visits were often quick and meaningless. Ashamed of the mistake of a child out of wedlock, he conveniently left his daughter with Karmin's parents each time he ventured home. Benny felt as though he was following the pattern of Cynthia's father, always dropping her off with the family while he went about his own agenda. Finally he convinced himself that his journey to manhood would never be complete without the closure and confirmation only his mother and father could give. This trip, Benny would leave his pride and shame in Tennessee and bring his daughter with him. After three and a half years of college, a child, and a tragic death—he was going home to see his family with his own family.

He and his daughter walked toward the busy porch. All of the children taking shelter from the heat were filling the porch with good times. Benny knocked on the door and captured everyone's attention.

"Hey everybody!" he humbly said with his dimpled smile.

"Benny!"

"Little Benny!" People responded as they did whenever someone arrived at the door and then went back to their activities. Benny looked over towards the corner of the porch and saw three people who could pass for strangers because he hadn't seen them in such a long time.

"Daddy, I want to go play-fun."

"In a minute, baby, there's somebody I want you to meet," Benny said approaching his Aunt Margie, his father, and his mother. Ronald stood up to greet his son and gave him the affectionate hug he had deprived him of as a child.

"Hey pops. I missed y'all."

"We missed you too, boy."

"Hey mama," Benny said kneeling down to clutch his mother as he did so many years ago. "I'm sorry," Benny offered for whatever an apology was needed, his absence, her illness, the disappointment. Sheila stared blankly into his eyes while Benny guided his daughter's hand, into his mother's hand. He was presenting Sheila with another generation.

"Mama, here's someone I'd like for you to meet. Mama, this is Elizabeth," Benny announced. Sheila trembled when she heard the name. "Elizabeth, this is your Grandmama."

"Hi Granny. Do you love me?" the sweet child inquired of her new friend.

Sheila reached for the little girl and squeezed her like she once did Benny. Her faced was washed by tears of relief, regret, sorrow, and then happiness. Holding her granddaughter, Sheila looked at Benny and spoke ever so softly,

"That was Aunt Flappy's real name."

"I know, mama."

"Well, Granny, do you?" the small child asked.

"Do I what, baby?" Sheila said, slowly bursting out of her years of emotional entrapment.

"Do you love me?"

"Oh yes, baby, very much. Yes, Elizabeth. Grandmama loves you very much."

"You my Daddy's mama?"

"Yes baby. I am," Sheila tried to say as clearly as her tears would allow her.

"My mama is in heaven with God."

"Oh baby, I know. She's up there with a lady named Elizabeth who is very nice and pretty just like you."

"Granny, will you take me to MacDonna?"

"Elizabeth!" Benny snapped.

"Hush boy, go sit down somewhere," Sheila said with the resilience Ronald had waited for so long to witness. "Leave this baby alone. Come on up here so Granny can fix your hair. I can tell your daddy did your hair because it looks like the way he cut and shampooed his Willie & Lester ventriloquist doll." Sheila placed the child on her lap and held her close. She didn't want her to run off and play before they caught up on the time they'd already missed with each other.

"Elizabeth, let me tell you about the time yo' daddy got his butt beat because he was begging for some Captain D's the same way you're asking him for some McDonald's now. We had a bunch of food just like we have in the house now, and your Daddy comes up there talkin' about, *Mama I want some Captain D's now.*